Dear Readers:

There are certain books in authors' careers that remain in
their hearts long after the title has faded into obscurity.
Perhaps it's the plot, more often the characters, that contin-
ues to linger in our memory. The characters' lives reaching
out from the pages to demand more of us. If we're lucky,
they become unforgettable to our readers as well.

*Desire and Surrender* is such a book.

With *Desire*'s 1986 publication, my career was launched.
Set against the backdrop of the Texas fight for independence, I wove a story of a family torn apart by loyalties
and love. Through the last many years, *Desire* has become
a much sought after classic, although it has not been available to my growing readership since 1990. Few characters
have had as great a following as Angelique and Alejandro—
so much so that I followed *Desire and Surrender* with two
more books, *Renegade Love* and *Jezebel*—all due to the
readers' desire to continue their relationship with this fas-
cinating and unforgettable family.

I'm thrilled that Jove is giving *Desire and Surrender* an
opportunity to reach my much broader audience—readers
who have become faithful fans through the years. I would
like to take this opportunity to thank each and every one
of you from the bottom of my heart for your continued
dedication and appreciation of my work. After all, you, the
readers, are the most important and cherished element in
an author's career.

Much love to you all,

Katherine Sutcliffe

# DESIRE
# AND
# SURRENDER

## KATHERINE SUTCLIFFE

JOVE BOOKS, NEW YORK

DESIRE AND SURRENDER

A Jove Book / published by arrangement with
the author

PRINTING HISTORY
Avon Books edition / June 1986
Jove edition / November 1998

All rights reserved.
Copyright © 1986 by Katherine Sutcliffe.
This book may not be reproduced in whole
or in part, by mimeograph or any other means,
without permission. For information address:
The Berkley Publishing Group,
a member of Penguin Putnam Inc.,
375 Hudson Street, New York, New York 10014.

The Penguin Putnam Inc. World Wide Web site address is
http://www.penguinputnam.com

ISBN: 0-515-12383-8

A JOVE BOOK®
Jove Books are published by The Berkley Publishing Group,
a member of Penguin Putnam Inc.,
375 Hudson Street, New York, New York 10014.
JOVE and the ''J'' design
are trademarks belonging to Jove Publications, Inc.

PRINTED IN THE UNITED STATES OF AMERICA

10  9  8  7  6  5  4  3  2  1

I dedicate *Desire and Surrender*

To my husband and children
for their love and endurance

To the North Texas Chapter of Romance Writers of America
for the friendship and support I found when I needed it most

And to Shelly Darmon
for her enthusiasm in my writing career, and mostly for her
special friendship

# PROLOGUE

Slamming the door behind her, Angelique DuHon rested her head against its intricately scrolled panel and closed her eyes. God, what was she to do now? Basil Windamere had given her until six o'clock this evening to make her decision. If she became his mistress, he would not foreclose on DuHon Fields. Otherwise . . .

Fire-gold hair spilled to her hips as she pulled her straw-brimmed hat from her head and threw it across the room where it floated to Bernice Jones's feet. Hands planted firmly on her hips, the Negress puckered her lips. "That was just about the quickest trip to and from New Orleans I ever seen."

Angelique slumped into a chair. "I got halfway to town and couldn't continue. I just couldn't face him, Bernice. What shall we do?"

"Not for me to say, Miss Angie. I should switch yore breeches for even thinkin' of talkin' to that man. Why, if yore mama found out she be sent right back into one a them spells!"

Angelique closed her eyes and tried to think clearly. DuHon Fields was the only home she had ever known. Eighteen years before she had been born within these very walls, had taken her first step on these heart-pine floors. She shuddered to think she would lose it all; that someone else would be enjoying the same elegance that she had always loved. Unless, of course ...

Carlota DuHon looked up as her daughter entered her room. "Have you done with mourning for your father so soon?" she asked, noticing the girl was without her black mourning garb.

"I am weary of weeping," came Angelique's vague response. She turned her oval face toward her mother. Her green eyes were tilted slightly, their color exaggerated by her jet-black lashes. "Are you well?"

Carlota nodded. The black of her dress and hair made her skin seem pale and ashen. "I'm stronger."

Carlota's heart swelled with pride as she watched Angelique. Creole women were renowned for their vivacious beauty and her daughter was no exception. She patted the bed beside her. "Come, daughter, and sit."

Angelique sat.

Carlota took her hand. "You are a young woman now and so deserve the truth. Angie, our time at DuHon Fields is finished."

"I know, Mama."

Brown eyes grew wide. "You know?"

"I've known for some time. What I don't know is why."

Gripping her daughter's hand, Carlota struggled for the courage to continue. Yes, her daughter deserved the truth, to some extent. But should she reveal everything? Would it not be kinder to wait? Perhaps. For now, it was best Angelique know only what was necessary. "The debts your father incurred were due to gambling, Angelique, not unfortunate business transactions as I once confessed."

Angelique was stunned. "Gambling? Papa?"

"*Sí*. I fear Reggie had a penchant for the games. He lost and won small fortunes with the turn of a card. Unfortunately the losses continued to mount, and the more he attempted to claw his way out, the more ground he lost. I'm not certain he would ever have rectified the mistakes he made.''

Anger flushed Angelique's cheeks. ''Of course he would have! Had he not been murdered Papa would have found some way to save DuHon Fields.''

The thought of her husband's death brought a bitter twist to Carlota DuHon's mouth. At thirty-five, she was a beautiful woman, although her grief over the past months had dulled her once-sparkling black eyes and made her slender frame gaunt and frail. ''Life is often unfair, my sweet. But I feel everything that happens happens for a reason.''

Angelique jumped to her feet. ''But you cannot believe that of Papa's death! It was unfair! He was a young man with many, many years of happiness before him. The animal who murdered him should be found and slaughtered like the pig he is. And why have the authorities not captured this man? I've a good mind to go down to the *cabildo* and—''

''No!'' Carlota's eyes were huge as she sat upright in her bed. Her face appeared even whiter as she began wringing her hands. ''Please, let it alone. I'm certain the authorities are doing what they can. After all, New Orleans is a big city, and when they have nothing to go on . . .'' Her head dropped as she covered her face with her hands. ''Oh, Angie, it is enough that we are losing our home! Please don't make me relive our tragic loss any more than necessary!''

Angelique skirted across the room and cradled Carlota's shaking shoulders in her arms. ''I'm sorry, Mama; please forgive me! I am an unfeeling wretch to make you so miserable.'' As her mother's weeping ceased, Angie offered hopefully, ''Take heart, Mama. Perhaps, by some miracle, we will see an end to our troubles. Perhaps Monsieur Windamere will yet find some solution to our quandary. Wouldn't that be wonderful?'' Carlota nodded, then allowed Angelique to rest her back on the pillows. ''Would you like tea? Yes? Then I shall fetch Bernice. Perhaps we'll have some of those fine pastries she concocted this morning. Would you like that? Good! I won't be but a moment.''

Angelique didn't allow the burden of dread to slump her shoulders until after she had glided gracefully from the room. Her mind grappled for some recourse to their problem, but as always, it came back to her only alternative. Basil Windamere!

She looked up to find Bernice glaring at her from the far end of the corridor. As she approached the staunch woman, Angelique attempted a smile. ''Mama would like tea.''

Bernice tapped her foot on the floor. ''Um hm. And what are you about to do?''

''I think I should tidy up a bit before Mr. Windamere arrives. Would you see to my bath?''

Black eyes narrowed. ''What you got on yore mind, gal?''

''Nothing,'' she murmured, then hurried down the hall.

The clock sounded the quarter hour as Angelique smoothed her hands over her taffeta skirt. All was quiet. She recalled a time when the house had literally teemed with activity. Now there was nothing. All the servants but Bernice had been sold, as had the surrounding acres of sugar cane. But for one horse, the stables were empty.

By Angelique's reasoning, they had enough money in savings to last them one month, unless her mother's dwindling health caused the doctor's visits to become more frequent. Then the fine adornments decorating the inside of the house would have to be sold, though they would bring precious little.

The sound of an approaching horse caused her stomach to churn.

Windamere dismounted before throwing his gaze up then down the length of the grand front porch. At forty, Basil was moderately successful. He had worked all his life, and would until he died. He owned no property, other than the mediocre town house just on the outskirts of New Orleans. But he was a shrewd businessman and recognized a good opportunity when one offered itself. There was one standing before him right now.

Her throat dry, her smile brittle, Angelique closed the door behind her. "Mr. Windamere." She curtsied before him.

"My dear, have you made your decision?"

Angelique swallowed her revulsion. She had thought, for a time, that she could tolerate this man's familiarity. But recalling Windamere's overly wet, fleshy mouth on hers last evening, she wondered if she could stoop to such depravity, even for her mother's sake!

Angelique bit her lower lip. She was loath to beg, but at the moment, she had little choice. "Monsieur, the money I promised you is still unavailable. I've not been able to raise it." When he didn't respond she raised her delicate yet determined chin and added, "If you will only allow me a little more time . . ."

"Nonsense, Miss DuHon. You will never raise that much money in two days or two years." His fleshy cheeks folded over the corners of his mouth as he smiled. "Angelique, need I remind you that you might never worry over such matters again?"

His breath smelled of sour tobacco as he pulled her against his protruding belly. Closing her eyes, Angelique DuHon attempted to block out the sight, sound, and smell of the obese beast pawing her arms and waist. His mouth closed over hers and his tongue probed until she thought she would faint.

His beady eyes glittered as he pulled away. "I see you *have* considered the alternatives. Think of it this way, my dear. Your poor, ill mother will never have to worry that her beloved home will be snatched from beneath her. After all, she did work *so* hard to build it into what it is today, as did your father, God rest his soul."

Again she forced her emotions under control. Looking back over her shoulder, she beseeched him in a lower voice, "Please, Mr. Windamere—"

"Basil."

"B-Basil . . . Of course I shouldn't want my dear mother

to know anything of this. She would be destroyed. You do understand?'' Angelique turned her great, verdant eyes upon him. She smiled tremulously.

Windamere's eyes widened in surprise. Already he was fantasizing about how her lovely, virginal body would feel pinned beneath his. ''Of course I understand,'' he finally managed. He then added, ''As long as you understand that your secret is good just as long as our arrangement is kept?''

Turning her head from his kiss, she reluctantly nodded. ''I—I understand, Basil.''

Windamere pressed his full lips to her forehead. ''We are going to enjoy one another, Miss DuHon. Of that you can be certain.''

Carlota DuHon stepped from the shadows, aimed the long-barreled rifle a fraction above Basil Windamere's head, and opened fire. He stumbled from Angelique as if her touch had somehow scalded him.

Angelique gasped as she twirled to face her enraged mother. ''Mama!''

Her tiny form still draped in black, Carlota advanced on the astonished man. ''*Bastardo! Madre de Dios*, you are a pig!''

His flabby jaw sagged. ''L—let me explain, Madame DuHon!''

''Explain! Ha! Your explanation belongs on the floor of my barn, senor! I saw you touching her! I heard your vile innuendos! You are a pig! A pig, I tell you, and not worthy to be trod upon by my Angelique's feet! Now get on your horse, *idiota*, and be gone from my eyes before I lower my sights and relieve you of the burden I see swollen in your breeches!''

Indignation stiffened his spine as Windamere moved back toward his skittish horse. ''You understand, ladies, that as of midnight this house no longer belongs to you?''

A cold smile crept over Carlota's face. ''*Sí*, senor. Whatever remains on these grounds at dawn will be turned over to you, but for now, it is mine! Now leave before I decide to kill you after all!''

The horse kicked up dust as he disappeared down the winding drive. As Angelique started to speak, Carlota raised one hand. The other supported the gun now dangling at her side. "I have been a pitiful parent to have been so blind. I should have realized you would not show interest in such a man for any other purpose. To think you would have sacrificed your cherished innocence to save..." Shoving the weapon into her daughter's hand, Carlota turned toward the barn.

"Where are you going? Mama, please! You're too ill—"

"Bah!" she responded over her shoulder. Carlota then tore the black lace from her shoulders and threw it into the dust. "I am done with mourning! I am done with pity! See that my brightest dress is laid out, and when I return, I return a different woman!"

"But where are you going?"

"Make ready to leave!" she cried, "DuHon Fields is finished!"

# ONE

**October 1835**
**Gonzales, Texas**

"You were fortunate to arrive when you did. Had you arrived two weeks ago you would have witnessed a most unfortunate set of circumstances. Can you believe that Colonel Ugartechia, the commander at San Antonio, had the gall to send Lieutenant Castaneda with one hundred men to retrieve the brass cannon set upon the square for protection?"

Angelique shifted her green eyes from her uncle to a watchful Bernice, then back toward her mother. "Will there be war?" she asked.

Julio Sanchez shrugged. "There is little doubt. Santa Anna is a determined man." Waving his hand before him, he laughed. "Let us not talk of unpleasant matters. You have just arrived and so deserve your rest." With a snap of his fingers, a young *doncella* appeared. "Maria, please see to it my sister, niece, and their servant are made comfortable."

Angelique was thankful to have her own room. It was sparsely furnished, but large and comfortable, nevertheless.

Maria hurried to open the French doors which led to a balcony overlooking the patio. "May I have a bath?" Angelique asked the dark-skinned girl.

A pleasant smile brightened Maria's face. "*Sí, senorita.*"

Angie's shoulders drooped as the girl closed the door behind her. What in God's name had her mother done? These last weeks had been a nightmare. It wasn't enough that savages plagued the countryside, but now there was talk of certain war with Mexico. Not only that, but there was no turning back! Her mother had seen to that. Angelique closed her brimming eyes as she recalled DuHon Fields going up in flames.

Angelique's spirits lightened as Maria returned with the water for her bath. It had been weeks since she had reclined in a proper tub. Discarding her dusty attire, she sank into the luxurious heat and bubbles with a sigh. The maid washed and rinsed her hair, then, at Angelique's request, left her to her privacy.

She had just laid her head back against the smooth rim when the door flew open with a bang. Even though she was completely covered in foam, she crossed her arms about her breasts and sank further into the water. "What is the meaning of this?" she demanded. "In Texas, do you not knock before entering a room?"

A brown-eyed girl stormed across the floor. She threw her head back haughtily, causing her coiffured black hair to twinkle with blue highlights. "This is my house! In *my* house I do what I please."

"Indeed? Then it is no wonder your Texas is on the verge of war, if all of you possess manners like this!"

Juanita's black eyes narrowed as she scrutinized Angelique. With as much scorn as she afforded the twittering help, Juanita huffed, "I see *mi padre* did not exaggerate. Your hair is like a dark fire. Your skin is like cream. Creoles! Bah!" She spat on the floor.

Angelique sucked in her breath. The dawning then settled in the pit of her stomach. It seemed this little she-cat was the cousin she had often heard so much about, the one only two years younger than she. Angelique had hoped they would become friends; obviously Juanita held no such desire. "And what might be wrong with Creoles?"

"Everything, of course." Pondering a moment, the chubby girl propped her hands on her hips. "Your mother ruined the Sanchez line by marrying that Frenchman. I'm surprised my father allows her in his house."

Angelique sank again in her bubbles. She soaped one shapely leg and smiled. "Your *father*," she emphasized, "made us feel quite welcome."

"I suppose he has no choice since you've dumped your-selves and your meager trunks on our threshold. Besides, Carlota *is* his only sister." When Angelique made no fur-ther comment, she added, "Just how long do you intend to stay?"

As Angie tilted her head, one twisted tendril of copper hair fell to her glossy shoulder. "I'm not certain, cousin. Does it matter?"

"I suppose not, as I will be married and gone in a matter of weeks."

Angelique held up the other leg while allowing the water to pour from her cloth onto her knee. "How very fortunate for you."

"*Sí*. I am *very* fortunate. I marry the handsomest man in all of Texas, Mexico, and Spain combined!"

Angie rolled her eyes.

"I suppose you'll be attending our engagement party?"

"Will it be here?"

"No. We will be traveling to his family's rancho just outside San Antonio."

"Wonderful. Just what I need . . . more dust!" The door slammed. Angelique smiled. "Adieu, cousin."

Angelique awoke to the smell of fresh brewed coffee which Marie had placed at her bedside. She stretched, refreshed and grateful for her undisturbed rest.

"*Buenos días.*"

Angelique's eyes flew to the figure of the woman across

the room, as she pulled the counterpane to her chin. "Good morning."

The rustle of taffeta skirts accompanied the stranger's approach. Her dark eyes were dancing as she stopped at the foot of Angelique's bed. "Oh dear. I fear my daughter did not exaggerate your beauty."

"Aunt Francesca?"

The slender woman curtsied as she dipped her head. "*Sí*. I have come to welcome you, and to apologize for not being on hand at your arrival." Hesitating, she added, "If I know my Juanita, you were not made to feel welcome."

A smile toyed with Angelique's lips. "I think that is an extreme understatement."

"I feared so. Please, let me apologize for her behavior. It's just . . ." Her heavily lashed eyes fell over her niece's exquisite face and the disarrayed mass of luxurious auburn tresses spilling over the pillows and sheets. "It's just that my daughter is very—"

"Spoiled."

Francesca winced. "For the lack of a better term, yes, spoiled. And jealous of your beauty." She poured Angelique a cup of the stout brew. "Let me assure you, such behavior will not continue as long as you are our guest. My husband is so very pleased that his sister has returned, and what makes him happy pleases me as well."

Angelique, preferring tea, attempted a grateful smile. "How is my mother this morning?"

"She is resting. As you know, the trip took a great deal out of her."

Angie shook her head. "I wish I knew what plagues her so. The doctor could find no reason for her dwindling health."

Francesca Sanchez pulled her chair next to the girl's bed, then sat. "Your mother is still grieving over her husband's death, *niña*."

As she met her aunt's concerned gaze, Angelique decided she liked Francesca very much. She showed compassion, a trait sorely lacking in her daughter, and understanding. Angelique had often read Francesca's words of comfort in the many letters Francesca had sent her mother after her father's demise. It was sad, Angie reasoned, that it took death to heal an old breach that even time had not managed to eradicate.

Attempting to lighten the mood, Angelique flashed her aunt a smile of white, even teeth. "I understand Juanita is to be married soon."

"Yes. It is an arranged marriage; arranged by my husband and my daughter's fiancé's family."

Noticing the look of concern that briefly clouded Francesca's face, Angelique asked, "Is there anything wrong?"

"Juanita is only sixteen."

"That's not so young," Angelique countered. "My mother was married at that age."

"The one she marries is thirty-two; a man of the world; though I realize it doesn't matter to my daughter. After all, he is such an attractive man."

Her lashes grew wider in surprise. "Then he *is* as handsome as she said?" Realizing what she'd implicated, Angelique blushed slightly.

Francesca smiled in understanding. "*Sí*, he is *very* handsome."

"I see." She then added, "He must be very wealthy."

The woman nodded her head. Almost regretfully, she finished, "Very."

The remainder of the morning was spent sorting through the trunks that had accompanied Angelique, Carlota, and Bernice from New Orleans. The mood was light despite the news that had reached the rancho only this morning. It seemed a small garrison of fifty Texans, directed by a Captain Collinsworth, had captured Goliad, gaining a great many arms and supplies left behind by General Cos, Santa Anna's brother-in-law. Word was that a volunteer army at Gonzales had elected Stephen F. Austin as commander-in-chief of their forces and even now they were making plans to move on San Antonio de Bexar, where General Cos was now held up in a dilapidated old mission known as San Antonio de Valero, or the Alamo. But the threat of battle seemed too far away to ruin Carlota and Angelique's excitement over their new home.

Throughout the day, Angelique did her best to stay out of her viperish cousin's way. Bernice, however, was not so fortunate. It seemed Juanita took great pleasure in scaring the already jittery woman out of her wits with tales of Indian raids and scorpions. More than once she sent the wide-eyed Negress from the room, wringing her hands and praying, "Lawd have mercy!"

It was late afternoon before Angelique decided to venture from the hacienda. Strolling some distance from the sprawling adobe structure, she paused beside the bougainvillea-draped stone wall surrounding the house. She was not surprised to find, upon turning, that her cousin was standing a short distance away.

Angie's smile was pleasant, but Juanita's was not. Raising her yellow skirts, the short girl stepped closer. "It is not wise to be out here alone."

Angelique arched one brow as she sat in the wrought-iron chair beneath the willow. The smile never left her lips as she returned, "Your tactics will not work on me, Juanita. I assure you, I don't scare as easily as dear Bernice."

Juanita's insolent eyes raked her cousin as she too wedged her skirts into a chair. "This country is wild, Senorita DuHon. Are you aware what lies just beyond those hills?"

"I'm certain you will tell me."

"I think it is only fair to inform you." Juanita tapped her foot while shielding her eyes against the sun on the horizon. "Do you see the gentleman yonder?" At Angelique's nod, she continued, "What stands out most about his appearance?"

Angelique squinted slightly. "He is tall . . . and bald."

Juanita sat back in her chair. "Three years ago he had a thick head of hair. Have you any idea how he lost it? No? Then let me tell you. It was cut from his head by the Comanche. Even now it is decorating one of those savages' shields."

Opening her ribbed fan, Angelique coaxed a cooler

breeze about her face. "Go on," she requested dispassion-
ately.

Juanita's black eyes widened for an instant, and the corners of her mouth turned down in slight disappointment.
"The vaquero was tending my father's herd. He was attacked by five Indians. They knocked him from his horse,
held him upon the ground, and sliced off the top of his
head with their knives."

"And it did not kill him?"

"It is a misconception that scalping will kill a man . . .
or woman. Normally they take the hair only from the
crown of the head unless, of course, it is an act of vengeance. Then they are likely to take the entire thing. Pablo
must have been lucky, as they were only intent on maiming
him . . ." She then added with cruelty, "I once heard of a
man who had his scalp lifted. He was found five days later
and his bloody head was a mass of squirming, feasting
maggots. They say it was the worms that killed him by
eating their way into his brain."

Angelique damned herself for allowing the shudder of
her shoulders to show. She closed her fan with a snap.
"Dear cousin, are you finished now?"

Juanita jealously regarded Angie's silken, red-gold curls.
"While we venture the seventy miles to San Antonio, may
I suggest you keep that ridiculously colored hair hidden
beneath a scarf? I understand the Comanche take great
pride in collecting odd-colored pelts."

Long, curling lashes fluttered coquettishly over Angelique's dazzling green eyes. "Is that why you still have
yours, Juanita . . . because yours is so—common?"

With a gasp of outrage Juanita jumped to her feet. Her
face twisted and her eyes glazed with tears. "Oooh! You
are a horrid girl and I shall tell your mama on you!" She
lumbered back toward the house as fast as her stocky legs
could carry her.

Angelique sat for several moments, doing her best to
quell her anger and shame. She had told herself to feel
only sympathy for her cousin. But Juanita had stormed into
her room the night before intent on hating her. But why?

They had never laid eyes upon one another until yesterday. The girl acted as she were some sort of . . . threat!

Drumming her fingers, she searched her mind. Juanita Sanchez was far better off than she. After all, her cousin could boast of a fine home, a family who loved her. . . . There was her upcoming wedding to that rich and handsome—

"Ah. So, dear cousin, you are worried I will take your man?" Poor Juanita. Was she so insecure with herself and her fiancé that she believed he could be lured away so easily? Angelique decided she must do her best to eradicate those fears from her cousin's heart. Standing and nodding in resolution, she started for the house. She would see to her mother, then she would apologize for her unfeeling remark.

Carlota DuHon offered her daughter an understanding smile. "My niece is a brat, dear. She deserved the remark. I fear Bernice has already taken to her bed, thanks to Juanita, and has declined Julio's invitation to travel with us to San Antonio."

"But we are her guests, Mama."

"Indeed, and she should be going to great lengths to make us feel welcome." Sighing, Carlota accepted the coffee her daughter offered. "Angelique, you are much too kind. There are times when you must stand up for your beliefs. You *must* not accept people's cruelty as a way of life."

Angelique moved to the window. Never before had she witnessed such a sunset. The sky was splotched with dashes of gold, pink, purple, and blue. The sun, appearing as a great melon-colored ball perched on the stark, undulating earth, caused the vague images of scrubby trees to seem as if they were but precisely cut shadows. Turning again toward her mother, she sat on the ledge of the wide windowsill before speaking. "Must we venture to San Antonio?"

Carlota eyed her daughter over her raised coffee cup. "Have Juanita's tales frightened you after all?"

"I don't feel right about it. No doubt we'll find ourselves as unwelcome there as we are here."

"Nonsense. Francesca has assured me we will be welcome. Already she has sent a rider to inform our hosts that we will be attending." She then added, "By the sound of it the entire town will be in attendance. What are two more guests?"

Angelique eased onto her mother's bed. "Are you certain you're up to such a journey?" The voyage to Galveston had been bad enough, but the hellish venture from Galveston to Gonzales was a nightmare! She had choked on the suffocating dust and with every bend of the road there had been the threat of Indians.

Carlota squeezed her daughter's hand. "Stop worrying over this old woman. Besides, it promises to be a grand fiesta."

Curious, Angie asked, "Have you missed your life in Spain?"

"A little yes, a little no. I miss the customs, my family."

"I'll wager you were a very pretty senorita!" She giggled.

Carlota's black eyes twinkled with her memories. "*Sí*. I won the hombres' hearts with my dancing and my colorful dresses." Showing more enthusiasm than she had in months, Carlota slipped to the floor, laughing at her daughter's surprise. Crossing one arm over her waist and curving the other over her head, she spun and tapped her heels on the floor. "Remember when you were but a child, Angelique, and I taught you the steps of the flamenco and the bolero?" At her daughter's excited nod, she motioned with her hands. "Show me, then. Show me the Castilian blood of your forefathers is still prevalent in your veins!"

Before Angelique could respond, Carlota began rhythmically to clap her hands. "Paseo!" she encouraged her daughter.

Caught up in the sudden surge of her mother's excitement, Angie jumped to her feet. As her fingers snapped to the rhythm Carlota had set, she paraded about the room.

Her feet began moving, rapidly rapping the hardwood floor.

*"Pas de basque!"*

Angelique swung her foot and as Carlota called out *"Pasada!"* she spun and crossed the floor, following with the fouetté in which she raised her leg, then lowered it in a wide, curving sweep, and glided into the fouetté tour, a complete turn she executed as she stretched her arms out to her side.

*"Bien parado, Angelique!"*

Her movement came to an abrupt stop. Her heart pounding, Angelique could have been a marble statue, so still had she become. Her head was thrown back, and her auburn hair spilled to her thighs. One arm crossed her chest, while the other arched over her head. She retained that motion for almost a minute before she lowered her eyes to her mother's.

Carlota stood rooted to the floor, her hands pressed to her mouth. She began to applaud as tears spilled from her eyes. *"Bien parado!"* she wept. "Well stopped!"

Angelique dropped her arms and relaxed. "I have not forgotten, Mama."

The women hugged one another heartily before the older pulled away. Carlota then hurried to the chest that had earlier been shoved against the wall. Angelique followed curiously. As Carlota opened the lid, her daughter fell to her knees beside her.

"Oh, Mama! You didn't burn them after all!"

"Did you think I could?" Pulling the fabulous dresses into her lap, Carlota searched her daughter's radiant face. "Will you do me the honor of wearing them?"

She caught her breath. "But they are yours. You must wear them!"

Sadly, Carlota shook her head. "I am an old, weary woman and could not do them justice." Forcing Angie's trembling fingers about them, she added, "Take them and wear them. Show these people that you *are* just as good as they! Do this for me, Angelique!"

Angelique smiled into Carlota's anticipating eyes. "Very well, Mama. I will do it!"

# TWO

The breeze was hot and did little to relieve the heat on Alejandro de Bastitas's back. He shifted in his saddle. It had been a long journey from Gonzales and he was tired. What awaited him behind those distant fortressed walls left him little peace of mind.

"You certain you want to do this, Bastitas?" asked his amused companion.

Alejandro threw his friend a resigned smile. He was never certain of anything where his grandfather was concerned, but the last weeks had given him time to overcome his anger at the old man's latest trick—luring Alex back to the ranch with false hints that his grandmother was desperately ill. Thinking of Isabella de Bastitas, he shrugged one broad shoulder. "I have little choice. I promised Grandmother I would do nothing to upset Carlos."

Noble "Kaintock" McGuire shook his head, and his shoulder-length, carrot-colored hair blew in the wind. "But we didn't reckon on Texas bein' in such a mess. Seems she don't care much for that Santa Anna scoundrel. How is that grandpappy of yours sidin'?"

"Carlos de Bastitas is a *Gachupine;* a Spanish-born servant of Spain—or was."

"What changed?"

"Greed. When trade between France and the United States was forbidden, he profited in illegal contraband. That wealth multiplied when Santa Anna became dictator. There are those who believe my grandfather secretly helped Anastasio Bustamante overthrow Vicente Guerrero, then helped Santa Anna engineer the revolution against Bustamante."

McGuire shook his head. "Sounds like a chameleon to me."

"Exactly. He is an old man caught between tradition and greed and will stop at nothing to have both."

Scratching his chin through a bushy red beard, Noble focused on Rancho de Bejar and grinned. "Well, I don't envy you any. Carlos ain't gonna like it that you rode out of here less than a month after you arrived."

His blue eyes narrowed as Alejandro considered his friend's words. "Carlos will live. He's too damn mean to do otherwise." Pulling his black sombrero down further over his eyes, he asked, "You will be joining us tonight?"

"Wouldn't miss this little occasion for all the women in Kentucky."

"Until later?" Alejandro extended his hand. His friend shook it. But as McGuire turned his horse toward San Antonio he stopped him by calling, "Kaintock!"

Noble turned and smiled. Few people could call him Kaintock and get away with it—except Alejandro. It was a disparaging term Westerners used to deride the somewhat wild Kentuckians who were considered the embodiment of coarseness and vulgarity. But Alejandro used it as an affectionate nickname, a teasing token of friendship, and McGuire accepted it as such.

Alejandro waved and shouted a simple adios. He didn't have time to thank Kaintock for being at his side over the last months, for never saying "I told you so" when the little vixen he'd married made a fool of him before the entire city of New Orleans. Kaintock had never even questioned his decision to sell his prosperous plantation in Louisiana and return to Texas, just simply offered a shoulder, an ear, and a hand when he thought Alex might stumble.

Removing his hat, Alejandro thrust his fingers through thick black hair and groaned to himself. His return to Rancho de Bejar and Carlos de Bastitas could be delayed no longer.

Tomas Eduardo de Bastitas offered his older brother a cigar. "Our grandfather has been chewing his cane in impatience."

"Perhaps he will choke on it."

"Shhh, he will hear you. The old coot has the ears of a blind man and the eyes of a hawk. He misses nothing."

"I gathered that." Throwing his saddlebags into the corner of the red-tiled foyer, Alejandro released his breath. "I suppose His Highness has demanded my presence?"

"As soon as possible."

"Is Grandmother with him?"

Tom nodded as his blue eyes fell over his brother's dusty attire. "You haven't forgotten the party? Guests have already begun to arrive."

"I haven't forgotten." He turned for the door. "Have Rosie lay out my clothes."

*"Buenas suerte."*

"Thanks. I'll need it."

Alejandro hesitated, watching as his younger brother moved down the hall and up the curving staircase. His interest then wandered to the distant people promenading about the ranch's meandering walks. He sincerely hoped they all enjoyed the show. He would be sure to give them plenty to talk about when they returned to their own homes.

He supposed there was no point in delaying the inevitable. His grandfather was not going to be pleased that he had ridden out of here only two weeks after his arrival. But he had spent the last five days reacquainting himself with this place he had once called his home. Rancho de Bejar sprawled across the valley just five miles out of San Antonio. It consisted of thirty thousand acres of prime grazing land; not as much as some, but boasting more than most others.

He'd been delayed further by his chance meeting with Stephen F. Austin just before Austin met his volunteer army outside Gonzales. Alejandro had learned a great many things from Austin . . . useful things. Sympathy for Texas was growing, but most of the families in the surrounding area still refused to take sides. How could they? If they opposed Santa Anna, and Mexico won this war, they risked the Mexican's vengeance. On the other hand, if they supported the power-hungry dictator, and he fell to the handful of Texas warriors, they might find themselves outcasts in their own country. As Alejandro stared momentarily at the ornate carving upon the door, his blue eyes narrowed. There was no doubt in his mind where his grandfather's patriotism lay. Squaring his shoulders, he stepped into the room.

Carlos Echeverria de Bastitas had once been a much larger man. Now, at the age of seventy-three, his broad shoulders were stooped and his frame appeared almost emaciated, lost within the gaudily decorated chair that could have passed as a throne of sorts. Still, those sunken blue eyes burned with anger. They literally bore into his grandson as Alejandro de Bastitas stepped into the room.

It was not the old man Alex looked to first. A tender smile replaced the bleak acceptance on his face as he strode catlike across the floor to the woman there, then bent to one knee. Accepting her cool hand in his, he kissed it reverently before looking into *la patrona*'s twinkling brown eyes. "Grandmother, you look ravishing this afternoon."

The aged woman chuckled. "Get up, get up. You are a silly boy."

"But truthfully, senora. I'm not certain I have ever met such a ravishing creature—"

"—of my age," she finished. "Now get from your knee before you hurt yourself. Quickly, quickly!"

In one fluid movement he had regained his feet. "Are you well, Grandmother?"

"As well as can be expected for a decrepit old woman.

I shan't die in my sleep tonight if that is what concerns you."

Their eyes met in understanding before he turned to face Carlos de Bastitas. The fact that he did not perform the ritual of meeting before his grandfather was a blatant, unspoken insult.

Tapping his cane on the floor, the old man grated, "Stand before me." When Alex had done so, he demanded, "Where the hell have you been?"

"About."

Carlos's gaunt face worked furiously with frustration. "You are an insolent bastard, Alejandro. Do you think me too old to demand and expect respect?"

"Respect is a reward and should be deserved."

Carlos de Bastitas bristled in anger. Supporting himself with his cane, he struggled from his chair and with all the strength he could muster drew back his hand and swung it across his grandson's face. "As long as you are within my walls, you will grant me respect! I raised you, fed you, clothed you. I saw that you were educated. What am I given in return? You turn your back on me and walk out the door! You refuse your heritage, preferring to spend your time with that maladorous Kentuckian, or that slut you called your wife!"

Alex met his grandfather's eyes. He was shaking from his contained anger and his mouth was bleeding, due to the extravagant gold ring Carlos wore on his finger. His teeth clenched, he drawled ominously, "Keep my marriage out of this."

The old man's laugh was cruel. "She was a whore. A *puta!* Ha! She cuckolded you, Alejandro. She opened her legs for that man more easily than she did for you. What about the child she carried when she died? Was it yours or his?" Sneering slightly, he chuckled. "You might very well lower your eyes. Not only have you dishonored your name by turning your back on me, but you married an American, a gringa, a woman of tainted blood. Your father and mother were no doubt thrashing in their graves when you took her to your bed. Thank God the brat within her belly died along with her.''

Isabella de Bastitas, her horrified eyes fixed on her grandson's pale face, moved between them. ''Enough, Carlos!''

Wrenching away the comforting hand she had placed on Alex's arm, Carlos de Bastitas shoved her back toward her chair. ''You are a meddling old woman. Stay out of this!''

''But—''

''*Basta ya!*''

Isabella fell defeatedly into her chair, then covered her face with her hands. *''Por Dios,''* she wept. *''Por Dios!''*

Pointing a gnarled finger in Alex's face, Carlos hissed, ''You want what you once scorned; you will have it. But on *my* terms. *Comprende?* My terms, or I will turn you out and let you rot on your unworthy father's grave.''

Hate pounded in his skull as Alex stepped back. Had it not been for his grandmother's presence . . . ''You are an old man, Carlos, and someday you will die. Rest easy in knowing I will spit on your grave.'' He left the room.

Alex sagged against his bedroom door. Anger had centered in his gut and it was all he could do to breathe.

''Was it that bad?'' Startled, Alex jerked his gaze to where his brother lounged on his bed. Tom smiled sympathetically as he shifted. ''I have often envisioned our revenge. One of us could hold him down, the other could cut out his tongue.''

Moving across the floor and passing the tub of steaming water, Alex bent over the washbowl and tenderly touched a cloth to his splintered lip. ''I often wonder how our grandmother has tolerated the old bastard for so many years.''

''Tradition, my brother, and we both know divorce is out of the question.''

Throwing the bloodied rag to the floor, Alex snapped, ''To hell with tradition.''

Tomas de Bastitas clasped his hands behind his head. ''What are you doing back here, Alejandro?''

"Your letter had a great deal to do with it. If you recall, you did imply that Grandmother was virtually on her deathbed."

"Yes, yes, I know. I'm truly sorry, but the old man was breathing over my shoulder. I'm sure you can appreciate that."

Alex withdrew the gunbelt from his hip, then draped it across the back of a chair. Sitting, he pulled off his boots, then tugged at the calico shirt now stained with dust and sweat. "*Sí* I can appreciate that. But tell me, young brother, why do you remain?"

"Tradition."

"To hell with tradition, Tomas. You're a coward."

Blue eyes, not unlike Alex's, dropped to the floor. "Yes, I am afraid of the old man. But are you any different? You had your freedom, but you're back. Right where he wants you. He is molding you. Using you. How can you allow it?"

Alex sank in the water. Tomas had a point. Why was he back, allowing the old man to dictate his life? True enough, he didn't have anything else at this point, having sold his home in Louisiana. Still, he could have traveled to another state and started over, just as he had those ten years ago when he first left Rancho de Bejar.

Tomas disturbed his thoughts. "You had hoped that age and time had mellowed him. We want to love him. We want to be loved by him. Why *doesn't* he love us, Alejandro? Why?"

Alejandro de Bastitas shook his head, and his blue-black hair spilled over his eyes. "I don't know."

A knock interrupted. The door opened and a dark face peered into the room. "Senor de Bastitas? I have brought you your Madeira." The woman crossed the room, her hips swaying provocatively.

"Ah, Consuela." After allowing her to slide the tray onto the table, Alex caught the maid's arm and pulled her to his side. "You haven't aged a day."

"Bah!" she teased. "I was nearly old enough to be your mother ten years ago. Have you caught up to me yet?"

"That remains to be seen."

Her full lips parted in a pleasant smile. "As a young man of only fifteen—"

"I was an eager pupil."

Consuela ruffled Alex's hair. "I assume you have continued your studies?"

Alex's eyes shifted toward his brother. "And I assume you have carried on the tradition?"

Throwing her head back, Consuela laughed. Rolling from the bed, his face flushed with chagrin, Tomas moved quietly across the room, then out the door. He sauntered with no great haste down the hall.


Isabella de Bastitas rocked in her chair, her frail hands clasped in her lap. "Someday—someday he will kill you. Why must you antagonize him so?"

"He is a Bastitas."

"That means nothing!" she argued in a hoarse voice. "We are no longer in Spain, Carlos. The traditions of that country mean nothing here."

"Bah! Our blood is pure, Isabella, and it will remain so as long as I'm living."

"You will only succeed in driving him away again, or else your cruelty will see him dead, as it has his father."

The old man's face grew tight. "Do not mention Ramon's name to me again. He was a spineless—"

"Stop it! Do not sully his memory to me again. He was my son and you killed him. I will never forgive you for that."

Carlos's blue eyes turned hesitantly to the portrait on the wall. It had been finished only one month before Ramon's death. "It was his own carelessness which caused his death. I trust Alejandro will take much greater care."

Isabella's silver head jerked up. "*Por Dios!* Carlos, you will not demand that he enter the ring!"

"Certainly I will. What kind of fiesta would it be without the running of the bulls?"

"You will see him dead, Carlos, just like Ramon!"

"Enough! He has a responsibility to his name, and to me. By God, I will see he fulfills it."

The door opened. Rosita curtsied. "Don Carlos, Senor and Senora Sanchez have arrived."

Carlos de Bastitas settled into his chair, as did his wife. He smiled as Francesca and Julio Sanchez stepped into the room, followed by Juanita and their two guests who had recently arrived in Texas. He opened his arms to his old friend. "Welcome! Has your journey been pleasant?"

Angelique stood back with her mother as her aunt, uncle, and cousin greeted their hosts. Francesca then turned to her. "Carlos, this is Julio's sister, Carlota DuHon, and her daughter, Angelique."

The old man's face hardened slightly as he acknowledged Angie. "Welcome. *Mi casa su casa.*"

"You are very gracious, senor," offered Carlota.

Isabella stood. Her eyes were kind as she addressed the DuHons. "I understand, Senora DuHon, that this trip might have been taxing to you. Would you care to see your room?"

Angelique let out a relieved breath as she turned with her mother. It most definitely *had* been a wearisome jaunt! The entire time she had been subjected to Juanita's unending barrage of meddlesome gossip. There had been times she had seriously considered throwing herself from the carriage and pleading with one of the many *vaqueros* who had accompanied them on their trip to let her ride on his horse.

Isabella de Bastitas guided them into the entranceway. At their right was the Room of the Blessed Virgin, so named because of the shrine, which was used as a place of family worship. They then passed the *salon de baile*, or ballroom. Already it was being prepared for the festival that evening.

So busy was she in studying her surroundings, Angelique didn't realize her mother and Senora de Bastitas had stopped. As a pair of strong hands suddenly appeared on her shoulders, halting her progression, her wide emerald eyes turned up in surprise. "Oh! I'm very sorry."

A very handsome man grinned down at her, his vibrant blue eyes twinkling. "There's no harm, I assure you."

Carlota and Isabella stepped up. The older woman smiled. "Angelique, let me introduce my grandson Tomas Eduardo de Bastitas."

He bent over her hand. "I'm charmed."

Sooty lashes covered Angie's admiring gaze. Her rosy lips turned up coquettishly.

"I was just about to show Angelique and her mother to the guest rooms, Tomas. Will you see that Consuela brings them each a pot of chocolate and perhaps some fruit?"

His smile widened. "I fear Consuela is occupied at the time, *Abuela*. However, I'm certain Delores wouldn't mind the effort." Again he touched his lips to Angelique's fingers. "Later, senorita?" Before she could respond he had disappeared through the nearest door.

Carlota was shown to her room first. Isabella then walked Angelique farther down the hall and to her quarters.

"I hope you'll be comfortable," she offered.

"I shall, thank you. You're very kind to open your home to strangers."

Isabella shrugged, then pulled her knitted shawl closer about her shoulders. "We will be family soon, I trust."

Thinking of the handsome young man she had just encountered, Angie experienced a slight twinge of jealousy. "Yes, I suppose so."

Isabella studied the girl, from her graceful limbs to the shiny, reddish-brown curls twisting lazily about her slender shoulders. "Once you've rested, feel free to wander as you please. There are guests already about. Most, however, won't arrive until dark." Turning for the door, she hesitated. "At that time, Senorita DuHon, I will introduce you to the rest of my family."

Surprised, Angelique looked up. "Have you other children?"

Without responding the woman closed the door between them.

Angelique was grateful for her time alone. Her entire body ached from the constant bouncing of the carriage. Her skin was sticky with dirt and sweat, and she wished for Bernice. She desperately needed an understanding ear.

Lying on the bed, she covered her eyes with her forearm. Silly girl! Why should she feel such envy over her cousin's future husband? Someday she too would meet a man just as dynamic and handsome as Tomas de Bastitas. Some- day . . .

It was not yet dusk, but the shadows within her room had deepened, and Angelique's maid hastened to light the lan- terns adorning the stark white plaster walls. Music filtered through her open window, along with the fresh breeze which carried the tantalizing aroma of food.

Fidgeting in her impatience, Angie nibbled at her lip. She was anxious to see her mother. She wondered what Carlota would think of her costume.

Finally, Delores laid down her brush. "Done, Senorita DuHon."

Jumping to her feet, Angelique twirled. "How do I look?"

The Mexican girl smiled. "*Muy bonita, senorita*. You will turn many of the caballeros' heads tonight."

Angelique frowned as she smoothed her hands over the snug fitting bodice of her red silk dress. "Are you certain it fits me properly?"

"Oooh, *sí*, senorita. It is perfect!" Delores then caught the coiled curls bobbling down Angelique's back and laid them across her shoulder. "Are you aware that if the gen- tleman throws the flower from his lapel at your feet, you are to dance with him?"

"Yes," she responded.

Slyly, the girl added, "I think your path will be covered with flowers." As Angelique moved for the door, she added, "Senorita. I almost forgot! You must save your favorite admirer's flower, and at the end of the evening return it to him. That way, he will know he is the chosen one!"

Angelique laughed happily. "I'll remember, Delores."

Stepping into the corridor, she glided to her mother's

room. After knocking and getting no reply, she peeked through the door to find Carlota still sleeping. Angie considered waking her, then thought better of it. Her mother needed all the rest she could get.

Angelique was breathless as she moved through the grand hacienda. The house was buzzing with activity. From every room lively chatter filtered through the air. She first looked for her aunt and uncle, but found neither. In a last desperate attempt, she sought her cousin. She was relieved her search was in vain.

Leaving the house, she discovered the manicured grounds were ablaze with gaiety. Tables laden with food and drink had been placed about the many pebble-paved paths. Now that dusk was brushing the gardens with shadow, lanterns had been positioned along the walks and among the trees, reminding her of some sparkling fairyland.

Tempted by the colorful display of delicacies, she sampled a tiny bit of each, wrinkling her nose at the more pungent ones, then returning again to the cheese-stuffed surprises. The Madeira, flowing as profusely as the *acequias* drenching the gardens with their fresh, clear water, was exactly what she needed to wash down the spicy concoctions.

Satisfied and more relaxed, she moved through the growing crowd, becoming entranced in her surroundings. Rancho de Bejar was much grander than her uncle's home in Gonzales. This adobe structure seemed to sprawl forever across the level plain. Cottonwood and willow flanked its white walls, as they did the great barriers surrounding the house. The rancho could have passed as a presidio of sorts. There was no doubt it had been built as well as, if not better than, the fortresses dotting the populated countryside.

Following the meandering paved walk, Angie didn't realize she had left the fiesta behind her. Nor did she notice that the shadows had deepened. Stepping through the arched *portale*, which was covered with wild mustang grape, Angelique stopped. The darkness was interrupted only by the flicker of one tiny candle. Its inconsistent halo danced upon the round water-lily fountain, then darted about the surrounding patio walls, decorated with the same vine that drooped about her head and shoulders. She might have been stirred by this, or by the haunting strain of the Spanish guitar being strummed in the distance. She didn't think so, for the candle's fickle flame had found another sight to entice the sudden quickening of her heart.

# THREE

The man was slouched in his chair. His suit was black, his coat short. His shirt was of red silk, the color of her dress, and frilled down the breast, as were the cuffs of his sleeves. His hair was black, as black as the encompassing darkness. He was staring into the bottle of mescal like a prophet researching his future—or was it his past?

As he looked up her first thought was to run.

"Wait."

Angelique froze. Her heart pounding, she turned slowly to face him again. He was standing. The dim candle glow did not quite reach his face now.

"Please," he slurred, "join me."

Cautiously she stepped from the shadows. "I'm sorry if I disturbed you."

"I'm not certain I can recall a more delightful disturbance."

His deep, slightly accented voice was jarring. Fitting her many petticoats and silk skirt into the chair, Angelique struggled for her breath as he caught her mantilla and draped it over one shoulder. His fingers brushed the back of her neck. Her skin tingled.

Reseating himself, he smiled. "I am Alejandro de Bastitas. And you are?"

She smiled tremulously as he captured her hand and raised it to his wide, mobile mouth. "Angelique," she barely managed before he pressed his kiss upon her fingers. He then sat back, but did not let go of her hand.

"Angelique," he repeated. "Angel. It suits you."

Afraid she was staring, she dropped her gaze to the candle. He picked up the flickering light and held it below her chin.

"Ah, I thought so. You're blushing. I like women who blush."

She covered her giggle with the tips of her fingers. The man was a rogue! A decidedly handsome rogue at that! Finding her voice unsteady, she asked, "Are you not enjoying the party?"

"Not particularly. I find the enchantment of solitude much more enticing."

"Do you live here?" she asked.

"I do . . . for the moment. And you?"

"I'm living with my aunt and uncle. We're guests of Senora de Bastitas."

His dark features were relieved by a pleasant smile. "How very convenient."

"I beg your pardon?"

"Then we'll have the pleasure of your company beyond tonight."

"Yes."

They fell silent. Angelique continued to stare uncomfortably into the gold flame of the candle, wishing the man would discontinue his gawking and say something. Finally, she looked up. He was smiling.

"You're blushing again," he teased. "Do you blush so becomingly for everyone?"

"You have embarrassed me, sir," was her meek response. The intensity of his gaze deepened as she looked up again. Her eyes grew wide as he removed the white flower from his lapel and lay it before her. With trembling fingers, she picked it up.

"You realize if you retrieve the flower you are obligated to dance with me?" She nodded. Alex stood, pushing his chair away with the back of one leg. He offered his hand. "Then I choose this dance."

"Here, senor?"

"There's music and ample room. Besides, I dislike crowds when I'm attempting to woo a beautiful young woman."

Angelique was surprised to find, upon standing, that her knees were wobbly. Suddenly, however, one of Alex's long arms had eased about her waist, coaxing her against his muscular frame. She wasn't certain this was a very proper way to dance. Men and women rarely, if ever, danced so closely in New Orleans. Perhaps things were different in Texas?

"Relax, *querida*. I fear you will shatter in my arms at any moment."

His arms closed ever tighter about her. Afraid now to meet his eyes, Angelique rested her head against his shoulder, allowing the melodious tone of the Spanish guitar to cast its spell upon them. They moved effortlessly, gliding with the refreshing night breeze that carried the faint scent of lilies.

But Angelique was soon aware of nothing except the man moving against her. His was a clean yet musky scent. His chest was hard. The silk of his shirt whispered within his satin-lined jacket, and the even drumming of his heart beneath her ear was as enchanting as the tune being strummed in the distance.

They had stopped dancing, and still he held her. Her heart leaped in her throat as Alex's hand slid beneath her chin and tilted her face to his. Her mouth opened to protest. . . . It was too late.

Angelique felt as if the entire earth had turned upside down. Never had she been kissed in such a way. In no way could it compare to the chaste little flirtations of her former admirers, or even the disgusting assault of Basil Windamere's lips. This was such a gentle fire, an ember that took flame in her toes, then her knees. It centered in her stomach, then surged with wicked heat into her breast. Its intensity caused her to swoon further into his embrace until her subtle curves were molded against his and the heat of their responding bodies was a blend of encroaching desire . . . and surrender.

As if sensing her sudden weakness, Alejandro moved away. His eyes, now dark with need, stroked her flushed, flawless face: the high cheekbones, the tiny nose, the shadow of her jet lashes on her creamy skin. The black mantilla framed her reddish hair like a dark halo, as soft as the deepening shadows about them.

"It is getting late," she stated nervously, "I—"

He was kissing her—this time not so gently. His tongue parted her lips and slipped into her mouth, but instead of being repulsed, as she had been by Windamere, Angelique found she quite enjoyed this gentle invasion. He tasted slightly of liquor and tobacco, and suddenly her senses were reeling again.

Her arms came up about his shoulders; her fingers wove into the thick hair on the back of his head and neck. They caressed the strong column of his throat, then teased his partially concealed ear until a low groan escaped his broad chest. His face dropped to the tender underside of her chin, where his mouth scalded her with the teasing tip of his tongue upon her rapidly beating pulse.

The wine Angelique had indulged in earlier could never have compared to the intoxicating sweetness of his gentle lovemaking and she grew tipsy with his heady touch, taste, and smell. She had never known longing, or desire, as she felt at that moment. The coquettish games she had played in the past seemed so innocent. She *wanted* this man to love her; she *needed* to hear those love songs he was crooning into her ear.

Alex pulled away. Her hair had fallen from its combs and spilled over her shoulder. "Come with me," he managed in a hoarse voice.

"Where, senor?" she whispered, although at the moment Angelique might have followed him to the ends of the earth.

"My room."

"You—your room?"

"I promise you we'll not be disturbed." Catching her wrist, he pivoted on his heel, never suspecting she would not follow.

Angelique pulled her hand away. "Sir, I fear you have misunderstood!"

His blue eyes narrowed as he turned to face her. "Misunderstood, *querida*?" He shook his head. "I don't think so. Did you not allow me to kiss you?"

The table at her back, she leaned further from his menacing form. "Yes, but—"

"And did you not kiss me back?"

"Yes, but senor—"

"Call me Alex."

Infuriated, Angelique snapped, "Oh, but you are an unmentionable scoundrel to think with one touch of your lips you could sway my virtue! I am a lady, sir, and would never consider—"

"Wouldn't you?"

A clearing of the throat brought both to an uncomfortable silence.

Isabella de Bastitas stepped from the *portale* onto the patio. Her eyes flickered in amusement over the petite girl who was leaning backward over the table. "My dear, your aunt and uncle are frantic over your whereabouts."

Angelique closed her eyes in humiliation. She then offered Alejandro de Bastitas a scathing look as she righted herself and floated to *la patrona*'s side. "My apologies, senora. I fear the gentleman—"

"I fully understand, my dear. I'm quite aware of my grandson's penchant for a lovely hand."

Angie caught her breath. "This is your grandson? Oooh, please forgive me!"

Isabella waved her hand as if it were of no consequence. "No need to apologize, Angelique. Now hurry before Francesca grows frightened. We will talk later."

Clenching her teeth, Angelique threw her furious glance

toward Alex once again, then disappeared through the darkness.

Isabella waited as her grandson dropped into his chair. Alex smiled in chagrin. "I lost my head. What can I say?"

"You will, of course, offer your apologies."

"Of course."

Isabella allowed her eyes to caress her grandson's face. Alejandro was a duplicate of his handsome father. But there was one difference. Ramon had not boasted of a lion's heart and pride.

The woman slipped into a chair. "You realize the uproar your behavior would have caused had anyone else found you?"

He nodded as he poured himself a drink.

Sitting erect, her eyes watchful, she remarked, "She is an enchanting young woman and you are beautiful together, but it is too late for that."

"Not necessarily."

Her hand covered his and Alex looked up. "I will not see you hurt," Isabella stated. "Leave this place now and never look back. Do not let him destroy you as he did Ramon and Tomas."

Propping his elbows on the table, Alex leaned slightly toward his grandmother. "I have nowhere to run, Grandmother. Besides, was this place not my father's dream too? The old man cheated him out of his life and inheritance. I am here to make certain Papa's dream is realized. Bastitas land will remain Bastitas land."

"You are beginning even to sound like Carlos." She chuckled as Alex's eyes narrowed in anger. "You have a cruel streak in you, Alejandro. You are full up to here with spite." She made a quick slicing motion across her throat. "It will eventually choke you."

"Are you finished?"

"No. I came to warn you. General Martin Cos and several of his officers have arrived."

Alert now, Alex sat straighter. "Are you saying my grandfather invited that bastard here to mingle with these people? Damn!'' He jumped up so suddenly, his chair flew backward to the ground.

"Alejandro, please! You will make no trouble while he is here! For me!''

The pleading look on his grandmother's face dammed the frightening flood of anger that had momentarily enveloped him. Alex shook his head. "No. No trouble, Grandmother.''

"Swear it.''

He strode into the darkness.

"Felipe. Here.'' Alex folded the paper several times, then tucked it into the young man's grimy hand. "Take this to Gonzales. See that James Fannin and only Fannin receives it.''

"*Sí*, Senor de Bastitas.'' The boy ducked out the door.

So his grandfather had the actual audacity to bring Santa Anna's brother-in-law into this house, knowing three quarters of the people here were opposed to the "Mexican Napoleon's'' takeover. A smile crept over his sun-browned face. Perhaps that wasn't so bad after all.

As Alejandro stepped from the quiet den, the music of guitars and fiddles filled the air with a vivacious tune. The gardens, as well as the house, were a great splash of color.

"Alejandro!'' came Juanita's excited greeting.

Alex groaned before merging into the raucous crowd. Accepting an offered glass of wine from a silver tray, he approached a group of men.

Martin Perfecto de Cos threw his host an arrogant smile. "*Sí*, Senor de Bastitas, we are making plans even now to stop Stephen Austin. He is a buffoon if he thinks that ragtag army of farmers can defeat Santa Anna. He had best stay in Gonzales where he is safe.''

Carlos looked up as Alex joined him. "Ah, General Cos, meet my oldest grandson. He has just returned from New Orleans.''

The men faced one another. Cos smiled congenially. "You have returned at a bad time, senor. Are you aware of the likelihood of war?''

"The rumor reached me. I understand a Texas garrison just captured Goliad."

The Mexican's face sobered. "That was unfortunate, but it will not happen again. Even now we have reinforcements on the way from Mexico."

"Indeed? Will they be joining you at the Alamo?"

The man's dark gaze shifted and he lowered his voice. "I was just telling your grandfather—word reached us that Austin is on his way to San Antonio. He has some asinine idea of taking this city. We will be ready."

Unfortunately, the conversation then wandered in a less fruitful direction. Alex, grown tired of the general's idle chatter, sauntered into the crowd, pondering this newest information. If Austin was indeed on his way, he had to be warned that Cos was aware of their approach. But how? He sure as hell couldn't leave here now, not without raising suspicions. He spotted Kaintock McGuire and walked over to share his dilemma with his friend.

McGuire accepted the goblet of wine Alex offered and they walked together, constantly scanning the room. "The man's got balls, Alex, I'll grant 'im that. So when do we ride?"

"I'm afraid I won't make this one, amigo. It's up to you. You can be sure, however, that when the time comes for the attack on Cos at the Alamo I'll be there."

"Heard tell Cos has around four hundred troops."

"And more on the way."

Kaintock shook his head. "Winter's comin' on. Ole Santa Anna don't care much for the cold, I hear. Reckon he might wait till late spring to pull his surprise."

"Possibly."

The roar of the crowd in the distance and the upbeat tempo of music caused Alejandro to raise his voice. "No offense to Austin, but I sure as hell wish Houston would get back."

Kaintock quaffed his Madeira, then shoved the cup into Alex's hand. "Ain't nobody gonna help unless we got an army. Perhaps some of your friends here would care to join up."

Alex scanned the parading guests. Most were the *gentes de razón*, the Spanish and Mexican ruling classes. Their fine, pure blood would never allow them to dirty their hands in warfare. That was left to the farmers, clerks, and newcomers who had little more than a plot of dirt to defend. But defend they would. Unfortunately their numbers were far too few. And there was no money to pay them.

After bidding his friend farewell, Alejandro milled through the crowd. He spoke briefly to Ramon Musquiz, deputy governor of San Antonio, but his mind was occupied on another matter: the little minx who had bewitched him with those enchanting eyes. Had his grandmother not chosen that inopportune moment to meddle, he might have enticed the little kitten to his lair. Alex had little doubt she was inexperienced, but he had also recognized the green fire in those tilted eyes.

Recalling the sweet taste of her mouth, he lengthened his stride. There was little time to waste.

Angelique stood at her aunt's side, clapping her hands at the young couple spinning before her. She tried to lose herself in the dance before her, tried to forget the humiliation of her encounter with the infuriating Alejandro de Bastitas. Her foot tapped to the rhythm of the increasing tempo. At any moment the duo would cast their flower to the ground, a signal that the fiesta had truly started.

The dark-haired girl twirled on one foot and stopped before Tomas de Bastitas. The crowd shouted its approval as they began to move. The woman, dressed in a full peasant skirt and long-sleeved white blouse, her shoulders draped in a red shawl, moved energetically about the man's erect stature. Angelique recognized the movements of the jota which had originated in Aragon, Spain.

The couple faced one another with their arms out to their sides, clicking the castanets in their hands. As Tomas circled the young woman she sank to the ground, spreading her skirt about her until it appeared as some great multi-colored fan. Angelique was enthralled as she watched his rapidly beating feet and the precise rhythm of the unceasing instruments in his fingers.

The crowd grew as the intensity of the dance escalated. Hands clapped and feet stomped. As Tomas fell and began bumping the ground with first his left then his right knee, the bystanders' roar became a crescendo of praise. Jumping back to his feet, he signaled the onlookers to join them.

Angelique was pleased when one handsome caballero tossed his flower at her feet. She joined the exuberant crowd without hesitation, thankful her mind would now be occupied by something other than the blue-eyed man who had so easily tempted her with his mellow, drawling voice.

It wasn't long before Tomas stood before her. "You did promise me a dance," he teased, then swooped her into his arms and virtually carried her to the middle of the floor.

Angelique realized that Tomas de Bastitas would have to be Alejandro's brother. The resemblance was strong. Each was handsome, but Tomas seemed somewhat kinder. He lacked that fire in his eyes and the sardonic twist to his lips. He was not as tall, his shoulders were not as broad— his frame was as slender, but not as muscular. Still, he was a handsome man. Juanita should consider herself very lucky!

The music momentarily done, Angelique was surprised as Tomas accompanied her off the floor. It certainly wouldn't do if her cousin saw them together. She threw a nervous glance about the crowd.

"Looking for someone?" Tomas asked with a broad smile. He had talked briefly with his grandmother and knew that his brother and Angelique had been found to-gether.

Catching sight of Juanita, Angelique stiffened. "No!" Her only thought was to get as far away from Tomas as possible. The guitar had begun to strum again, and she curtsied toward the bemused young man and strode back across the patio.

"I believe this is my dance," came a dulcet drawl from behind her.

She spun to face Alejandro. Her green eyes widened in surprise.

His smile was just as arrogant as she'd remembered as

he said, "I suppose the proper thing to do is to throw a flower at your feet. But seeing that I already have . . ."

Before Angelique could respond, Alex wrapped his arm about her waist and escorted her to the center of the floor. Frowning, she asked, "Really, sir, do you think it wise? Your grandmother—"

"—is an understanding soul. She thinks us quite beautiful together."

"You are a rogue, Senor de Bastitas, and would no doubt think yourself beautiful with any woman!"

"Ah, the kitten has claws."

"You embarrassed me. I am a guest of your grandmother and was caught by her in a very compromising position!"

"Your position, at the time, was far less compromising than it could have been given another . . . say . . . five minutes." He laughed as her face caught fire. "Ah, *niña*, just when I think you could not possibly be more beautiful, you surprise me again. It seems anger intensifies those outrageously green eyes. I wonder what desire would do?"

She turned to leave. "You are much too bold, Bastitas!"

He caught her again. "It seems we have an audience, Senorita. Shall we give them all something to twitter over in the morn?"

The music had escalated and, too late, Angelique realized she and the man at her side were the center of attention. Throwing her startled gaze about the surrounding crowd, her eyes fell on Juanita, who stood scowling at Tomas's side. She then looked helplessly toward her companion.

The challenge in his blue eyes snapping, Alejandro took one step back, then bowed formally at the waist. Reluctantly, Angelique curtsied. As the strains of the gypsy dance spun into the anticipating night air, Alex's long fingers began to snap, and slowly he began to circle her. The raised heels of his black boots tapped lightly on the tile at first, then grew louder and faster. His arms soared above his head, then fell as he spun and in one lithe movement caught Angelique at his side. They moved together, stomping, sliding, their energy blending. She matched his every movement, forgetting the spellbound men and women who watched.

Her eyes fell across his shoulders, down his *chaquetilla* to the red silk sash about his waist. His tight-fitting trousers greatly enhanced the lean, sinewy lines of his thighs, his slender hips, and as he offered his back, the firm outline of his buttocks. It was very easy to forget this was only a performance. The sensual, graceful movements of her hands and arms became a display of enticement. She lured, then quickly spun from his embrace. She teased him as she peered over her shoulder, allowing the light from the lanterns to catch fire in her eyes. They danced with promise.

Alejandro recognized the taunt in her gaze. The woman before him now was no timid innocent. She was an enchantress, a succubus who would worm her way into his dreams and tease him with the taste of her honeyed mouth. He experienced a surge of desire in his loins that he had not felt in months, then threw himself totally into the dance. His feet moved at an incredible rate, as did his hands and fingers. He accomplished the difficult *caída* with no hesitation, falling to the ground and, in the same movement, standing back on his feet. The crowd roared, ''Olé!'' He leaped and pirouetted in the air from a stooping position, and as he hit the floor she was there, as she should be, allowing him to wrap his arm about her waist, so that as she slipped backward, he caught her just before she hit the floor. And in that last beat, they froze.

For a long moment they seemed carved from marble. Angelique lay partially across Alex's bent knee and was supported by one of his arms. One leg was curled beneath her, the other outstretched on the floor. Her hair spilled like a silken fire to the floor. His tumbled like a dark shadow into his eyes. Sweat rolled from his temples, across his cheeks, and dripped onto her breast.

For a flicker of an instant, she thought he would kiss her.

''*Bien parado*! Olé!'' The crowd rushed forward, and in a moment they were suffocated by the moved spectators.

Angelique, embarrassed now, smiled shyly as the men and women clucked in appreciation over her performance. She threw a shy glance back over her shoulder. Alex was some distance away. He too was surrounded.

His brow knitted in frustration, he called, "Angelique! I have to speak with you!"

The young women, anxious to know this talented newcomer, ushered Angelique toward the house. "Where are we going?" she beseeched them.

"Angelique! Dammit, I—"

Angelique realized it would do little good to attempt escape now. She accompanied the twittering girls to the hacienda, then into the *sala* where the fireplaces at each end of the room were being stoked. At one hearth, her cousin was standing.

A short young woman giggled toward Juanita. "We have invited your cousin to join us in the burning of the logs!"

Juanita's black eyes narrowed in an unspoken threat. "Perhaps my cousin best be careful before she finds herself in the fire!"

Forcing her attention on her new friends, Angelique asked, "What is the burning of the logs?"

A girl who introduced herself as Carmen explained, "If you have a young man in mind for marriage, you stand the log on its end inside the fire. If the log burns only on both ends, he will make you a suitable husband. If it burns in the middle, he is no good!"

Laughing, Angelique responded, "But I have no one in mind for marriage."

"Surely there is someone you secretly admire?"

Her steadfast gaze faltered as Alejandro de Bastitas flashed before her mind's eye. For heaven's sake! she scolded herself, you've known the man for little more than an hour and already you dream of marriage! Still, as they piled the logs into the pit she could not help but place Alex's name among those thrown to the fire.

As flames snapped about their tinder, Francesca Sanchez

appeared at the door. "Juanita! Quickly, *querida*, the announcement is about to be made!"

Angelique stepped aside as her cousin darted toward her parent. The giggling girls followed. For several moments Angie remained before the hearth, watching. Sighing, she joined the others.

"Angelique! *Perdición!* I must speak with you!"

The girl turned to find her mother approaching, her drawn face marred by concern. "Hurry, Mama, Aunt Francesca is about to announce Juanita's—"

"Angelique, I saw you with that man! You must stay away from him!"

Angie worked her way through the crowd. Juanita, Francesca, and Julio stood in the middle of the floor, as did Isabella and Carlos de Bastitas, along with Alejandro and Tomas.

"Angelique, are you listening to me?"

"Please, Mama, not now!" Her sight was trained on the man who was scanning the crowd. His eyes captured hers and did not relinquish their hold.

Julio Sanchez stepped forward. "We are very proud to announce the upcoming marriage of our daughter, Juanita, to the grandson of Carlos de Bastitas . . . Alejandro de Bastitas!"

There was momentary silence before the applause exploded inside her brain. Then she watched as the tall, handsome man of her dreams—the same man who had wooed her barely an hour before—the same man who had virtually made love to her with his sensual dance—stepped up beside her cousin.

Blood roared in her ears. Humiliation churned deep within her bosom. She had assumed it had been Tomas . . . but that had been before she had stumbled onto Alex . . . and it just hadn't occurred to her . . .

Turning her back on the scene, she pushed through the onlookers. There was no way she would allow him to witness her pain!

"Angelique!"

Her eyes wide with fury, she spun to face him. "Have

you left your fiancée so soon, Senor de Bastitas? If this is any inclination of your fidelity—''

He caught her arm, propelling her into the shadows. ''Let me explain.''

''There is no explanation. You played me for a fool!''

''I did nothing of the sort.''

Angelique snatched her arm from his determined grip. ''I hope the two of you will be very happy.''

Alex snorted. ''Happy? Good God, you aren't serious? Angelique, this farce means nothing.''

''Nothing?'' Her eyes pleaded for an explanation. ''How can you think that marriage means nothing? Love and marriage mean everything!''

He threw a cautious glance over his shoulder before coaxing her further from the lantern's halo. So far, the crowd was too busy fussing over the bride-to-be to notice he had slipped away. Catching her trembling chin within his palm, he tipped her face to his. ''You're too young, *querida*, to have experienced either love or marriage. How could you know of these things?''

''My parents loved one another very much. My mother grieves still because of his death, as do I. I learned from their example, sir, and will settle for nothing less.''

A tender smile touched his mouth. ''Angel, I—''

''Angelique!'' Carlota grabbed her daughter's arm and shoved her aside.

''Mama!''

''Get into the house, Angelique, quickly! Never under any circumstances will I see you in this man's presence again!''

Never having seen her mother so angry, Angelique was stricken speechless.

''Bastitas!'' Carlota raged. ''If you *ever* touch my daughter again I will kill you! Do you understand me?''

Alex's eyes, cold as ice, took in the older woman's irate features. ''Carlota DuHon,'' he drawled with contempt. His gaze then flickered over the girl quaking in the darkness. ''She is *your* daughter?''

''*Sí!* And I will not have her sullied by your hand!''

Both women failed to notice the fists that clenched, then unclenched at his side. His jaw tightened. "My apologies. I didn't realize." Offering them a mocking bow, he stalked back into the crowd.

# FOUR

William Travis smiled at his friend. "It's been a long time, Alex. Why in God's name have you returned now?"

Alejandro de Bastitas slouched in his chair, ignoring his friend's query. His mind was on Angelique DuHon, on the way she'd made him feel. Dammit, why her? Of all the women in Louisiana and Texas, DuHon's daughter! Christ.

His lip twitched as Alex rolled his slightly drunken gaze toward his companion. "Tell me about married life, Travis." The good part. He was well-acquainted with the bad.

Travis ran his fingers through tousled red hair. "Good holy God, I am hardly the ambassador of marriage, you know, thanks to my dear Rosanna." Shifting, he added, "I was sorry to hear about Pamela."

"So was I." Alex stood. Thinking to change the subject to one less painful for both men, he asked, "What about this war, amigo? Where do we go from here?"

"I suppose that depends on Santa Anna. I feel we should meet His Excellency somewhere between here and there. Don't ever let him reach San Antonio. If he does . . ."

"When is Houston due?"

"Most likely after the first of the year. He's doing his

best to smooth those Cherokees' feathers. It won't pay to have the Indians attacking from one side while the Mexes get us from the other." He shook his head. "I wonder what it is about this godforsaken place that entices us so? It's crawling with Injuns, Mexicans, rattlesnakes, and scorpions. We fry in the summer and freeze our butts off in the winter." Lighting a slender cigar, he added, "I understand the Vasquez place was hit by Comanche two days ago."

"I hadn't heard."

"Shame. A real shame. By the time a search party could be rounded up the savages had made off to the hills with the youngest girl. They left the grandmother alive, but barely. Something's got to be done about these damn Indians . . . and the Mexicans. Christ."

"When is Austin due?"

"Anytime. I expect to see Bowie just any day."

Alex slammed his fist against the wall. "Goddammit, Travis, we need men! We need ammunition!"

"I know, my friend, but we also need patience. If we move irrationally the entire thing will blow up in our face. We must act like an army, or we will never succeed."

The quiet laughing in the distance faded. Gradually the guests of Rancho de Bejar were turning in to their beds. Alejandro faced his friend. "I'm glad you came. It's been a long time."

"You'll stop by the next time you're in San Felipe? Perhaps by that time Rebecca and I will be married."

"I'm afraid we'll be seeing one another long before that, my friend."

William Travis nodded. He offered his hand. "Until then?"

"My best to Miss Cummins."

Travis dissolved into the darkness.

Alone, Alex was seized with the hopelessness of the situation. Texas could claim a population of only a little more than thirty thousand people, half of them being women and children. How could so few hope to contend with the might of a nation boasting of seven million, with thousands waiting to swoop upon them from across the Rio

Grande? Word had arrived only that morning that Santa Anna was rallying troops in Satillo.

Alex guessed their only hope was the few volunteers who were arriving from the United States every day. The Texas army, in defeating Goliad, had managed to gain a great deal in ammunition and nearly ten thousand dollars in gold. Unfortunately, that wouldn't go too damnably far.

Now there was the other problem . . .

Hell, what was he doing here playing swain to that spoiled little brat his grandfather had chosen as his wife? And why had he agreed to go through with it? Sinking onto the settee, he laid his dark head back and stared at the ceiling. There was no one to blame but himself. He should've laughed in the old man's face. Perhaps Tomas was right. His Spanish blood boiled too overly thick in his veins. Whether he cared to admit it or not, he *wanted* to please the old man. He hoped someday to witness a flicker of approval in those dead blue eyes. Besides, after Pamela, he reasoned he would never bother again to marry for love. Any woman could bear him an heir. There were always beautiful women to fill that greater need.

As Alex pictured Carlota DuHon's face, anger surged once again. So Angelique was a DuHon. Of all the damn bad luck! He had thought at the time there was something strangely familiar in those emerald eyes. By God, but they were beautiful eyes. Even now he could recall how they tilted slightly at the corners. Her mouth had tasted faintly of wine, her skin was smooth as satin.

He shook free of the thought. How could he feel such a need for . . . "Damn you!" he growled in his chest. "Why are you here? I came here to forget and now . . ." Throwing open the French doors, he entered the quiet patio where Angelique had happened upon him earlier in the evening. His empty mescal bottle remained on the table. He dashed it to the ground.

For months he had visualized the many means of vindication, but there had been no way . . . until now. His eyes falling on the tiny flower he had offered Angelique, he stooped and picked it up. It was white, pure—no doubt like her. Of course she was pure, but he knew well enough "good" girls could be lured. Pamela had been a perfect example. Her virginity had stained their marriage bed, but in six months she was squirming against another man.

Opening his fingers, Alex looked upon the crumpled petals of the flower. Hate reared brutally in his chest. Yes, he had come home to wipe out all the memories, to start over. Texas and its problems would have offered him the means to forget . . . then she had shown up. Damn her! She would pay. They both would pay!

Dawn was reluctant. The sun, which had blessed them the day before, had now surrendered to a misty awakening.

Angelique awoke to the smell of rich chocolate. As Delores placed the tray beside her bed, she offered a pleasant smile and curstied. "May God give you a good day, Senorita DuHon."

Angelique allowed Delores to help her into her freshest frock, then brushed out her hair. Thinking of the night before, she frowned. "I assume *everyone* will be attending breakfast?"

*"Sí*, Senorita DuHon."

The door opened and Carlota strode in. She waited until the *doncella* had hurried from the room before she addressed her daughter. "Angelique, we must talk."

Carlota wrung her hands. "You must promise me you will stay away from Alejandro de Bastitas. He is a barracuda. Why, his wife was not cold in her crypt before he was seen with another woman. He uses women, Angelique. You see how he used you."

Angelique shook her head. "Mama, what purpose do you have in reminding me? I care little if the man is a gigolo. He is Juanita's intended and for that reason alone I will keep my distance. I realize Alexander is no saint—"

"Saint? *Por Dios!* He is a devil! A devil, I tell you. Had I known he was here I would have returned to Spain!"

Angelique narrowed her eyes in speculation. Why was her mother so upset about Alejandro de Bastitas? Of course, her mother was right. He was a rakehell! He thought nothing of seducing her, then announcing his intentions toward Juanita.

Carlota studied her daughter, recalling the shock and fleeting pain that had frozen her features when she learned of Alex's engagement.

She shuddered. *Dios*, but the man was handsome . . . too handsome. Enough to sweep the most innocent soul off her feet. And what was worse . . . he knew it!

As always, breakfast was a large meal. The long table was laden with enticing foods and placed outside the *cocina*. There was thick cereal made of dried ground wheat. Silver platters were heaped with fried eggs, pork, hominy, and thin batter cakes. There was fresh fruit for dessert.

Angelique noticed the sudden stilted silence that fell as she and her mother paused at the *zaguán*, then entered the room. They continued to the *lavabo* where they washed their hands.

Carlos rose from his chair at the head of the table. "*Buenas días*, Senora and Senorita DuHon. I trust you slept well?"

Carlota nodded, as did Angelique.

"Good! Now tell me, did you enjoy our fiesta last evening?"

Angelique had felt Alex's blue eyes impale her the very moment she stepped into the room. Still, she refused to acknowledge the cocky slant of his mouth. Forcing her gaze to the opposite end of the table, she found Tomas de Bastitas smiling at her.

Tomas regarded her flushed cheeks and the burnished hair caressing her shoulders. "Perhaps, Miss DuHon, you would allow me the honor of showing you about my grandfather's ranch later in the day?"

"I would enjoy that, sir," she responded quietly.

"Perhaps we will all join you," chimed in the old man. "The fresh air will do much to clear our minds. *Sí?*"

The group agreed.

Angelique could not force herself to sample the delicious

food. Instead, she centered her attention on the steaming cup of chocolate the *doncella* had placed before her.

Juanita, who had been eyeing Angelique since she entered the room, forced her mouthful of food down with a gulp of hot coffee. "Perhaps Angelique would prefer to remain indoors. I'm certain her pale skin would not tolerate the heat overly long."

All heads swiveled to the startled young woman. It didn't dawn on her until that moment that she was the only one at the table who was not of pure Spanish blood. Her face tinted further until she was certain the roots of her hair had been singed. "I shall wear a hat," she responded with a lift of her defiant little chin.

"A hat will not shield your pale shoulders and arms."

"Then perhaps I shall remain in your shadow, cousin. I'm certain no heat from the sun will ever touch me there."

The silence was deafening.

Carlos eyed his grandson for several moments, recognizing the twinkle of interest in Alejandro's eye as he watched the woman at the far end of the table. It was obvious the boy had no interest whatsoever in his fiancée, but until now he had attempted to feign some slight notice for the benefit of her family. "Alejandro, perhaps there is something you and Juanita would enjoy doing alone today."

"That's not necessary, Grandfather. I wouldn't think of robbing Senorita Sanchez's family and friends of her company on such an important occasion."

Carlos's brow creased. Why didn't the girl say something instead of staring at the boy with those uncomely cow eyes? It was a shame Sanchez's daughter was so lacking in looks. But Carlos could find no other unmarried woman of childbearing age who could boast of untainted Spanish blood. Most had married the damnable Americans, French, or—God forbid—those disgusting Indians! Recognizing his grandson's stubborn streak, Carlos spitefully said, "I suppose you will soon have more than enough time alone. After all you *will* be spending the rest of your lives together."

Juanita's mouth curled in a smug smile as she looked upon her fiancée. She cared not one iota that Alejandro de Bastitas didn't love her. She knew he married her for the old man's sake. Still, as his blue eyes looked not to her but to her green-eyed cousin, her round face grew rigid with jealousy.

There was an uncomfortable silence before one unfortunate guest, thinking to alleviate the tension, asked Alejandro innocently, "So, senor, what brought you back to Texas?"

Alex's gaze cut to Carlota DuHon, who avoided his accusatory glower by pretending interest in her meal. She had grown quite pale. Alex set his jaw, then calmly responded, "My wife killed herself."

Someone dropped a fork.

"She locked herself in a room at our town house in New Orleans, took one of our sharpest knives, and cut open her wrists. Needless to say there was little left for me there."

Angelique's heart stopped pumping for an infinitesimal moment as she sat back in her chair. Forgetting how Alex had shamed her the night before, she saw now only a man, a very troubled and lonely man sitting in solitude, the company of a dancing candle his only comfort.

How very coldly he spoke of his wife's demise! His voice had held no emotion whatsoever; no sorrow or remorse. Still, as her green eyes, wide in disbelief, studied his precise features, she thought she saw more. Alejandro de Bastitas had suffered many days and nights . . . now he was drained of pain. He was numb . . . and very bitter.

Without thinking, she stated aloud, "I'm very sorry for you, senor. You must have loved her very much."

He stared at her in surprise. A haunting look rolled in his unsheltered gaze, then it was gone.

"Perhaps," he responded.

Tomas threw the mortified guests an unnerved smile before facing Carlos. "Grandfather, what do you have planned for us this afternoon?"

A sudden smile beamed across the old man's face. "I

had thought to surprise you all, but . . . what would the fiesta be without the *corrida de toros?*"

There was a gasp of excitement from the guests. Tomas's face, however, was white. "Senor? You cannot mean to fight the bull on such short notice?"

"My bulls are ready."

"But I am not! Grandfather, it's been two years since I've seen the ring!"

He dismissed Tomas with a flick of his hand. "I was not referring to you, Tomas, but to Alejandro." Then addressing his guests, he added, "Please forgive my grandson's cowardice."

Tomas jumped to his feet, but his outrage was quelled as Alex raised his hand and stated calmly, "I'm certain it is not cowardice that plagues my brother, but common sense. As I recall, Tomas, were you not gored rather badly two years ago?"

"I have a scar in my side to prove it!" Tomas fumed.

"Ah! You see, once injured it is not so easy to prance again before the bull." Alex added with the lift of one black brow, "As I recall, Grandfather, you have some of the biggest and meanest bulls outside of Spain."

Embarrassed over Tomas's hesitation, Carlos directed his attention to Alex. "Then you, at least, will honor me?"

Alex rested against the back of his chair. Should he embarrass the old bastard a second time, there would be hell to pay. "Certainly. But will you allow me this?"

"Anything."

"Give me two days to reacquaint myself with the ring. It has been ten years, Grandfather, and we both know that even a slight mistake could cost us much."

Their eyes met; the old man's flinted with guilt, the young man's with condemnation.

"You have until day after tomorrow."

The guests were excused.

Angelique had looked forward to her outing with Tomas. She enjoyed his undemanding company. As they rode slightly behind the rest of the group, she smiled into his twinkling blue eyes. "Your grandfather's ranch is beautiful."

As he nodded, raven hair spilled across his forehead. "It will all belong to me and Alex someday, then hopefully Alex's children."

"What of your children?"

Reining his prancing horse, he laughed. "I will never marry, Senorita DuHon. I fear I am not cut out for that sort of life."

The thought crossed her mind that Tomas seemed more attuned to matrimony than his belligerent brother. Teasingly, she asked, "Is there no special young lady in your life?"

He shrugged, but the smile on his handsome mouth did not quite reach his eyes. "Perhaps. Anna is a sweet girl, but my grandfather would never approve. Besides, at twenty-eight I fear I'm too set in my ways." He added thoughtfully, "I suppose that's why my brother conceded so easily to this marriage. It is left up to him to continue the Bastitas line." His eye acknowledged the sudden stiffness of his companion's slender shoulders. Slyly he whispered, "Believe it or not, my brother has a mind of his own. If he suddenly finds the idea of marriage to Juanita distasteful, he won't go through with it."

"But that would cause certain scandal!" she gasped with a shake of her auburn curls.

"Scandal and Alejandro are synonymous, *querida*. Always expect the unexpected from my brother."

Recalling the night before, Angelique allowed a tiny frown to quirk one corner of her mouth. Alejandro de Bastitas certainly cared little for propriety. He had attempted to seduce her in privacy, then again before an entire audience. At breakfast he had openly regarded her numerous times. By the time the repast was done the entire room had been rolling in disconcertion! Thank God the man had decided at the last minute to remain at the house!

It was not until their return journey to the hacienda that the cantering group came upon a herd of fierce-looking beasts. Following Tomas's lead, Angelique reined her horse beside that of Carlos de Bastitas.

Carlos, sitting erect on his stallion, swept his arm before him. "Before you is the finest herd of bulls outside of Spain."

"They are magnificent," replied Julio Sanchez.

"There is not one animal here less than thirty *arrobas*."

"Which of the bulls will Alejandro fight?" Juanita asked.

He pointed to the coal-black beast standing alone in the distance. "There," he responded almost reverently to himself. "Before you is Peregrino. He is five years old, the largest and most noble of them all. I had prayed that someday he would face one of my sons in the ring."

Angelique was startled as Tomas jerked the reins of his horse and moved away. His intense anger was obvious.

Carlos watched him go before barking, "Tomas! Has my decision displeased you?"

As he faced his grandfather again, the young man's features were taut with fury. "Alejandro has not faced an animal in ten years, yet you challenge him to a killer!"

"Peregrino is no killer."

"He was sired by a killer!"

Carlos smiled coldly. "Perhaps you judge your brother's talent to be as unworthy as yours, Tomas. Unlike you and your father, Alejandro is unsurpassed in courage. It comes from here." He pounded his chest.

His shoulders back, Tomas drawled, "Courage has little to do with it."

"No? Then you will display your courage and escort Peregrino to the hacienda."

Angelique dropped her eyes as Tomas hesitated. It was obvious the old man was goading him. She decided she cared very little for her host. No wonder Alejandro had left the family those years before. Carlos de Bastitas was a cruel, vindictive man with a heart of stone!

Finally Tomas garnered his courage and offered the curious spectators a pleasant smile. "Very well, Grandfather. Will you allow Pedro to attend me?" The vaquero responded immediately by coaxing his horse from the back of the crowd. At Carlos's affirmative nod, the duo approached the watchful beast. The group turned their animals and rode back toward the ranch.

By late afternoon the sky had turned dark, and approaching November brought a dismal mist that left the countryside unbecomingly dreary. Alex paced his bedroom floor, feeling a strange sense of anticipation. His long legs, clad in knee-high Spanish leather boots, carried him once again to his window.

Word had arrived only this morning that an army led by Stephen F. Austin had halted at Mission Espada. Their move came as a surprise even for Alex, for he had not suspected that they would strike so quickly. He turned as his door closed behind him.

Tomas frowned into his brother's rigid features. "You've had word?"

"Austin is camped just eight miles from the Alamo."

The younger man sank into a chair. "Do you realize what our grandfather will do if he discovers you are fighting against Santa Anna?"

Alex's laughter was abrupt. "Of course. He'll kill me."

Tomas flicked at a grass burr on his breeches leg. He shook his head. "I envy you, Alejandro. You thumb your nose at death as easily as you seduce your women."

"The two have a great deal in common." His hands on his hips, Alex nodded his dark head toward the door. "You're welcome to join me. With luck, I'll be back by noon of tomorrow."

"Have you forgotten your performance with the bull? I promise you, Grandfather awaits you with a surprise."

A devilish gleam in his eyes, Alex laughed. "I assumed as much. No doubt he is as big and mean as all bulls in Spain."

"He was sired by Andaluz."

The smile fell from Alex's face as he gritted his teeth. Then noticing his brother's pale countenance, he mellowed. "It still bothers you."

"I awake at night hearing Papa's screams. I see the blood in my dreams."

Alex poured them each a drink, his hand shaking. Covering the floor with his long stride, he forced the glass into Tomas's fingers. "You must remember, Papa did the inexcusable. He entered the ring drunk. He had no *cuadrilla* to back him up, and you know no man enters the ring alone. It is suicide."

Tomas quaffed his drink before bitterly laughing. "I see you have forgiven the old man after all. Have you forgotten it was because of his constant prodding that Papa did it?"

"Papa was suffering over our mother's death. He was drunk and didn't know *what* he was doing . . . or possibly he did."

"Are you saying he purposefully got himself skewered on the animal's horn? What man would allow himself to be killed in such a way?"

Alex, now stretched out on his bed, crossed his ankles and laid his head back. Finally releasing his breath, he stated quietly, "Papa loved our mother very much."

"Is that enough to make a man commit suicide?"

"Possibly."

Tomas jumped to his feet. "You didn't when Pamela cut the life from *her* body!"

"I thought of it."

"But you didn't do it!"

"I decided living was hell enough."

His spurt of anger gone, Tomas relaxed. "What is all this talk of dying, anyway? You were always good in the ring. You will best *el toro* and fling his ear at Grandfather's feet!"

Rolling from the bed in one graceful move, Alex threw his brother a wry smile. "If I'm alive and home to do it."

"What do you mean? Surely you're not serious about joining Austin?" His jaw dropped as Alex pulled on his gun and began strapping it to his hip and thigh. "What do I tell Grandfather?"

"Tell him I'm . . . about. If I'm not home by noon, tell him I'm dead."

"*Madre de Dios*, Alejandro! Are you insane?"

Alex put on his black sombrero and tilted it over one arched brow. He shrugged. "*Quien sabe*, Tomas? Perhaps."

Angelique sat before her mirror, absently smoothing her red-gold hair with her brush. She was ashamed of her thoughts, but there appeared to be little she could do to stop them. It seemed Alejandro de Bastitas monopolized her every waking moment.

Her door opened, then quietly closed.

Thinking Teresa had returned with her chocolate, Angelique, not bothering to turn, directed, "Please put the service by my bed, Teresa."

The image that was reflected in the mirror was not Teresa's.

Angelique left her chair. Twirling, she looked up into Alejandro's dark, smiling face. "Sir, you might have knocked."

"I might have, but I didn't."

She threw a nervous glance toward the robe on her bed. Knowing the gossamer shift she had earlier donned for bed did little to hide her womanly attributes, she crossed her arms over her breasts and frowned.

Alex stepped closer. "Relax, Angel. I've only come to bid you a good night."

"Then good night to you. Now please leave." She made a dodge for the wrapper, but was stopped by a warm hand around her wrist. Alex spun her around to face him.

"Good night," he whispered. His breath was intoxicatingly sweet against her mouth, and Angelique weakened. For an infinitesimal moment her supple little body swayed against his, and in that instant he bound her to his rockhard form with the vise of one strong arm. "Just a kiss to see me through these next sleepless hours," he said softly.

Where was her strength? "Alejandro, please . . ."

"Please what? Please hold you? Ah, *querida*, but I am. Kiss you?" He caught her face with gentle fingers. His dark head lowered. "My very reason for being here."

As his open mouth molded against hers, all thought of denying him fled. His mere touch sent her senses reeling, toppled every argument against him. He belonged to her cousin. Her mother despised him. But she could only cling to him tighter.

The tender hands moving gently up and down her back made her shiver. The tongue sliding boldly across her lips made her whimper. But as the heat of his hand then hovered over her breast a sudden rap at the door caused them each to freeze.

"Senorita DuHon, I have brought your chocolate."

Angelique, her eyes wide with fright, jumped guiltily from his arms and spun toward the door.

Again the knock. "Senorita?"

"Alejandro, you must—" Spinning, Angelique directed her gaze to the open French doors.

The room was empty.

# FIVE

The troops huddled about their camp fires looked up briefly as the newcomer materialized through the darkness, passed their sentries, then slid from his horse and entered Stephen Austin's tent.

Austin looked up. "What took you?"

"Kaintock arrive?"

"He's with Colonel Bowie now." He offered Alex a cigar. "Thanks for the message about Cos. Unfortunately we were still too far from the city to make any moves. Had it not been for that . . ."

Alex inhaled, then forced the smoke out through his nose. "He knows you're coming."

"Yes, but does he know when?" Austin smiled patiently. "Good God, Alex, are you so damn anxious to fight?"

"I'm anxious to put this war behind us. I'm equally anxious to put Mexico behind us."

"Does your resentment stem from some lingering patriotism for Spain?"

"That is behind me. I don't consider myself Spanish. I would suppose that makes me a Texan."

Studying his companion, Austin asked, "Why did you leave Texas for so many years?"

Alex thought a moment, recalling the day he had walked out his grandfather's door. Staring at the tip of his glowing cigar, he shrugged. "I was an impertinent young bastard, and very bitter."

"And you've changed?"

"Not really."

Austin laughed pleasantly. "I understand you're about to be married."

His jaw flexed as Alex ground his cigar out with the heel of his boot. "I have no intention of being married, at least not to Juanita Sanchez."

"No? I heard—"

"Disregard what you've heard. My plans have changed."

"Does she know?"

Thinking of the haughty young woman, Alex nodded. "If she doesn't suspect, then she is as ignorant as I've given her credit for."

Settling back onto his cot, Austin grinned. "Is there someone else?"

"Possibly."

"Ah."

Alex turned from the man and studied the hastily drawn map strewn over the makeshift desk. It was a layout of Mission San Antonio de Valero and the surrounding grounds. The Alamo, founded by Franciscan friars in 1718, had been abandoned as a mission in 1793 after Spain's efforts to bring Christianity to the savages of these plains had failed. Like the few other missions sprinkling the area, it boasted of the usual Franciscan pattern. Its grounds covered approximately three acres, and it was surrounded by three-foot-thick walls that stood twelve feet high. Within these walls were adobe rooms. The center court was divided by a stockade. Within was the fort prison and the low barracks where the soldiers made their quarters. Toward the back was the chapel, which before Cos's arrival had been filled with the debris of its caved-in roof and walls.

Lifting his blue eyes to Austin, Alex asked, "Is it possible?"

"The mission? Of course."

"That's not what I mean."

Austin swung his feet to the floor, then ran his hands through his hair. His head dropped. "I don't know. As it is, with our meager troops—no. But there's help on the way. I understand the New Orleans Greys will be joining us just any day."

"They'll do us little good unless they get here in time."

Their eyes met before Austin replied, "They'll come."

It was just after midnight on the morning of October 28 when Alejandro de Bastitas greeted Kaintock McGuire. The mist was heavy. Its chill brought a shudder to the men's tense shoulders as they huddled together for warmth. Building a fire would prove too risky. It could be seen by Mexican troops.

Jim Bowie greeted Alex with a smile. "Thanks for comin'. Reckon we're gonna need all the help we can get if you're right about Cos."

Alex handed a young man the reins to his horse. "He knows you're coming. I'm just not certain that he knows you're here."

Bowie winked. "I'm countin' on that."

Alex had first met Jim Bowie on the Natchez Trace. He and Kaintock had traveled with Bowie briefly, and had witnessed the birth of the "Bowie knife" legend, when the man took on two aggressors near the Mississippi River. Bowie too had lost a wife only three years ago. Perhaps that had a great deal to do with his being in Texas now. It seemed the place to go to forget.

Pulling his heavy serape closer about his shoulders, Alex followed his friends to the base of a pecan tree crouched close to the San Antonio River. He then relayed the messages from Austin. The garrison remaining behind would join them by noon. All troops would be ready for attack, if the weather was right.

There was little sleep for the men. It was hours before Alex finally dozed. His mind had been too full of thoughts of Santa Anna, of his grandfather, and of the green-eyed minx who waited back at the ranch.

He had plans for her ... very intimate and confident plans. Rarely had he ever hunted and not been rewarded with a prize. And what a delectable little prize she would be. He licked his lips, recalling the sweetness of her mouth. Damn, but what he wouldn't give to have her here beneath him now!

Dawn crept secretly through the dissipating fog. Suddenly, as if the ninety-two men were of one body, they moved to their feet. A gun fired, and as the blanket of dense vapor began to dissolve, they realized their situation was dire. They were surrounded by General Cos's troops from the Alamo!

Richard Andrews was the first to raise his gun, and the first to die. The war cry of four hundred Mexicans filled the air, and momentarily the tiny garrison of Texans thought for certain they were doomed. But the long-barreled rifles of the Americanos were precise. Stationing themselves for battle, they met their foe head on.

Angelique tossed in bed. Opening her eyes, she listened intently to the muffled booms which rolled like retreating thunder across the horizon. Jumping to her feet, she flew to her window, threw back the latch, and pushed open the shutters. The sky was gray but for an occasional flash of light in the distance. She turned toward her door as excited voices penetrated through her stupor. Suddenly her mother was before her.

Carlota, her black hair falling to her hips in glossy waves, was wringing her hands with worry. As she swept toward her daughter, her robe flapped about her bare ankles. "Angelique, the war is upon us!"

"Mama, what are you saying?"

Tomas, who had been making his way down the corridor, stopped. He was buttoning his shirt and tucking it into his breeches. "*Sí*, it is the sound of cannon fire. The Texans have laid siege on the Alamo!"

Carlota's eyes were huge as she spun to face him. "Are you saying San Antonio is under fire?"

"*Patron!* Senor de Bastitas!"

The threesome hurried into the hall as a Mexican boy rushed from the front foyer. As Carlos threw open his bedroom door, the child pulled his sombrero from his head and fell to one knee. "*Senor*, General Cos has ambushed a troop of Texas rebels who were camped and making ready to attack the Alamo!"

Tomas stepped forward and grabbed the young man by his shoulders, jerking him to his feet. "What are you saying, Paco? Do you not mean the Texans have attacked the general?"

His eyes huge, the boy shook his head. "No! The general learned of the garrison's move, and during the night, under cover of fog, he surrounded them. The Texans are finished! There are four hundred Mexicans to their one hundred!"

Angelique gasped as Tomas turned his pale face toward her. His eyes looked frantically into hers as he appeared to search his mind.

Hobbling on his cane, Carlos shoved by the stunned spectators and pounded on a bedroom door only two down from Angelique's. "Alejandro! Alejandro, throw the wench from your bed and stand before me! Alejandro!" When there was no response, he entered the deserted room. "*Ay!* Tomas! Where is your brother?"

He gulped hard, recalling Alex's explicit orders. "H-he is . . . about."

"About? About! It is barely after dawn and he is about!"

Isabella, appearing quite frail wrapped in her woolen shawl, approached her irate husband. "Please, Carlos, remember—"

"Remember? I remember he turned his back on me for ten years! He shamed his heritage by marrying that gringa!

Now he shames me by supporting these rebellious—''

"You don't know that!" his wife wept.

The man turned his piercing eyes on his grandson, then leaped and wrapped his fingers in Tomas's shirt, hurling him back against the wall. "Tell me, you sniveling coward, where is he? And be certain if you lie I will lay open your back as I have in the past!"

"I . . . I don't know, Grandfather."

Carlos de Bastitas spun on his heel. "Bah! Paco, have my carriage made ready. By the time I arrive home I want every wagon loaded with spare ammunition and food!"

Julio Sanchez stepped forward. "What are you doing, Carlos?"

"I intend to help General Cos in whatever way I can. And if I have to kill my own flesh and blood to do it, I shall! I will harbor no traitors to Santa Anna's cause within my walls!" He disappeared through his bedroom door.

Angelique stood aside, helplessly watching the sudden flurry of activity. The excited babbling of the help, along with Juanita's less than believable weeping, caused a low throb to center behind her eyes. Her every muscle seemed frozen, as if she were waiting in anticipation. But for what? Then she realized. She was straining to catch the intermittent roar of a cannon.

Lifting her eyes to Tomas, she silently questioned, Is he there?

He nodded before turning away.

As the carriage jounced purposefully over the road into San Antonio, Carlos de Bastitas's eyes burned with revenge. He cared little that the bleak sky, so dark and forbidding from a distance, was now burning with the flash of fire.

The round-shouldered Mexican driving the fine coach shrank as the explosions caused the pair of bays to rear and whinny in terror. They refused to move farther into the din of fighting soldiers. Bastitas did not wait for his man on horseback to assist him. Instead he threw open the door and clumsily, with his weight resting on his cane, stepped onto the rutted road.

A delighted chuckle rumbled his chest. What chance did Stephen Austin's small garrison have against four hundred Mexican troops? At any time this idiotic skirmish would be finished, and if Alejandro was involved, and not killed outright, he would wish he had been!

Ahead the smoke cleared and the vision of the old presidio emerged. Its fortified pale gray walls were awash in smoke and crumbling from the many years of weather and neglect. For the time being, however, they remained steadfast, allowing the many Mexican soldiers to enter at breakneck speed.

The smile Carlos had so proudly boasted gradually declined as he began limping determinedly past the line of flat-roofed homes where wide-eyed children huddled behind their *mamacitas'* colorful skirts. As a uniformed Mexican soldier dashed from behind one such house, Carlos raised his cane and shook it in the boy's startled face. "You! Where are your arms? Why do you run when the Texans are there?"

The soldiers' eyes grew round at the man's audacity. "*Caramba!* You are a fool, old man! Run while you can before those *diablos* see your mirrors covered with the black veil!"

"What are you saying?" Carlos raged. "Have you killed them or not?"

"*Dios,* Cos is retreating! The Texans have quartered our cannon and have turned it against us! They are *loco!* Loco!"

In disbelief, Carlos de Bastitas watched as the Mexican troops escaped into the sanctuary of the old mission walls. Beyond them, the whoop and holler of voices belonged to no other than the Texas Volunteer Army.

The small garrison was jubilant as the Mexicans retreated. What had first been a desperate struggle for survival had twisted in their favor. Daring enough to have captured the army's cannon, the fighting Texans had turned the weapon on their attackers. Only Richard Andrews had been killed. Cos's army listed over one hundred casualties.

Suddenly this war was *very* real, and it was obvious even to Carlos that these Texans could not be taken lightly.

The door opened and closed silently, allowing Angelique to leave unnoticed. She had grown tired of Juanita's fretting, and for a time had wandered around the house, eventually joining the help in their lunch of beans, fried meat, chili, and tortillas. There was talk of the war. Angelique, however, got the distinct impression there were many of Bastitas's peons who did not share his loyalty to Santa Anna, although they had not said as much in her presence.

Angelique leaned against the door of the salon. It was siesta time, but she couldn't sleep. The silence entombing the hacienda rang with anticipation. Whatever war had been fought in San Antonio de Bexar was finished. No guns could be heard.

"If he finds him, he will kill him."

Angelique gasped as she turned to find Isabella de Bastitas eyeing her from across the *sala*. The woman sat upon her velvet wine-colored high-backed chair like a queen before her court. She lifted one hand. "Come."

Hesitantly Angelique approached the aged but beautiful woman. She passed the fireplace, its marble mantel adorned with a bouquet of wax flowers, its hearth empty of any warming embers. As her petticoats whispered against her ankles, her emerald-green dress was reflected briefly in the mirror resting atop a marble pedestal.

She offered the *patrona* a simple curtsy. "My apologies. I thought the room unoccupied." Angelique's eyes grew wide as a single tear slipped down her hostess's cheek, streaking her *cascarilla*.

Unembarrassed, Isabella swiped at the wet betrayer. She repeated, "He will kill Alejandro. I know this. Why does my grandson tempt his fate? Does he care nothing for his life?"

"Perhaps he has no reason to care," she offered. "Perhaps since his wife's death, he cares little if he lives or dies."

"Perhaps." A resigned sigh followed before Isabella

continued. "He blames Carlos for his father's death. Of this I am certain, though he has never mentioned it. It is not Alejandro's way to offer his feelings openly. Never once have I heard him offer the word *love*, though I know he feels it here." She touched her heart. "In that way he is much like his grandfather. In fifty years of marriage, never once has he . . ."

The woman paused, then with a shake of her head focused on the lovely young woman before her. "Why must man continually make war? What is it about us that will not allow us to simply be satisfied? This is a big country, yet we barter and bicker over boundaries, water, tradition . . . and women. We left Spain to put repression behind us, yet my husband supports this dictator."

"Perhaps he is afraid to do otherwise," Angelique suggested.

"Perhaps, but I think not. He is an old man and afraid of change, and so he rules this family as Santa Anna rules his country. You abide his word, or you cease to exist." As Isabella lifted her hand, the servant who had been standing in the shadows glided to the table where a service of silver rested. "Teresa will serve our *merienda*."

Obliging her hostess, Angelique accepted the chair at Isabella's right. Unconsciously she mimicked *la patrona*, sitting straight and tall. Isabella noticed and inwardly smiled, for it was custom for the wife of a don or *patron* to be regal. It was tradition and taught to all daughters who would someday reign about the hacienda.

Teresa poured the hot chocolate. She then offered the two women each a plate of individual cakes. Some were flavored with aniseed and filled with ground meat or dried apricots. Others resembled a tart with the meat of the piñon, or pine, mixed into the stuffing.

As she settled back in her chair, her cup poised at her mouth, Isabella's brown eyes studied her companion. "There must be some way to stop this marriage."

Angelique coughed, strangled more from her surprise than from the piece of dried fruit that had become entrapped in her throat. Gulping at the chocolate, which only succeeded in burning her tongue, she turned wide green eyes toward Isabella. "I beg your pardon?"

"This farce of a marriage. Forgive me, but I cannot help but notice your disconcertion when in my grandson's presence."

Color bloomed in a becoming way on her cheeks. "*Senora,* I fear you misinterpret my feelings. The man is—is—"

"An ass."

Angelique looked down at her cup and smiled. "For the lack of a better word . . . yes, I think so."

"He is like his grandfather, but perhaps not so cruel. Take care with him, my dear. My Alejandro reacts from his heart more so than his head. I believe he loves as devotedly as he hates."

Reddish curls fell over her shoulders as Angelique replaced her empty cup on the tray. "You should be having this conversation with Juanita. *She* is his intended."

"And that bothers you?"

"Certainly not."

Isabella fondly patted Angelique's hand. "I saw the way you danced together. I saw the way he held you when you were alone on the patio. There was something in his eyes . . . and yours. He has a passionate nature, as do you. The forces between you collide as resoundingly as the clash of swords."

Angelique's jaw sagged as she stared into the woman's amused eyes. This conversation was ludicrous! She had wandered into the room to rid herself of the thoughts that had been troubling her these past hours, and here her hostess was practically proclaiming her grandson as her future husband!

The doña stood. "Ease the terror from your face, my dear, and join me in my walk. Siesta time is finished and I must now see to my garden. . . . It is tradition, you know."

It was customary for a fiesta concerning the announcement of a wedding to drag on for an entire week. This was no exception. There was, however, one difference. Usually the wedding ceremony followed the announcement in a matter of two or three days. This occasion was different due mostly to the unrest plaguing the city and its inhabitants.

If anyone worried over the escalating war between Texas and Mexico, they didn't show it. The women dressed for their evening meal as flamboyantly as they would for any other special occasion. Embroidered jackets fit snugly above the wide flare of flowered silk, velvet, or taffeta skirts and tortoiseshell combs held red, white, or black mantillas. The gentlemen, always sporting well-fitting black velvet suits, wore bright-colored serapes or scarves swinging from their shoulders.

It was a dignified group who milled about the table. But the tension hovering about the room was palpable as everyone waited for Carlos Echeverria de Bastitas to make his entrance. And every eye flickered briefly toward the empty chair usually occupied by Alejandro de Bastitas.

At the stroke of ten the scraping of the old man's foot and the thump of his cane announced his arrival. Each guest stood behind his or her chair until *el patron* bade them sit.

Julio cleared his throat. "Carlos, we have all been terribly worried. What news do you bring of San Antonio?"

Angelique held her breath as Carlos hesitated. His lip curled as he looked toward his younger grandson. "I will give you one last chance to tell me the truth, Tomas. Was Alejandro in any way responsible for this brutal attack on the Alamo and General Cos?"

For a solitary moment, fire flinted in Tomas's eyes. "You call it brutal, but would it be so if the general had inflicted such great harm on the Texans?"

"Answer me and consider the ramifications of lying."

Someone cleared his throat as Tomas grappled with his conscience and courage. Where *was* Alejandro? Had he actually gotten himself killed in this useless war? Tomas could stall the old man no longer with his flimsy explanation.

He released a resigned and reluctant breath. "Grandfather, he is—"

"About."

All heads swiveled toward the figure standing arrogantly in the double door of the dining room. Angelique bit her lower lip as her green dewy eyes found Isabella's relieved brown ones. They shared a knowing smile.

Carlos pushed himself up from his chair. "Alejandro!"

Alex grinned past the slender cigar jutting from between his teeth. Approaching his grandmother, he fell to his knee and bowed his head. Isabella made the sign of the cross over his dark hair, then he kissed her hand.

Her voice was shaky. "Get up, get up. Your meal is growing cold."

"So it is." Standing, he threw his fiery blue gaze about the table until it rested on Angelique.

Juanita scowled. "Alejandro, where have you been? You left us with no word—"

"Nonsense. As my good brother mentioned, I was . . . about." He sauntered toward his place setting of silver.

Angelique tensed. Was it accident that the sleeve of his coat slightly brushed the back of her neck? She swallowed a sudden surge of anticipation.

Carlos fell into his chair. "*Ay!* About! What does that mean? Are you aware that San Antonio is under siege?"

"I am."

Francesca shook her head. "It was horrible. We heard the cannon fire even from here. Tell us what has happened!"

He raised one eyebrow as he handed his partially smoked cigar to the servant who appeared to pour his coffee. "I assumed my grandfather had accompanied the word from San Antonio." Looking at Carlos, he finished, "I understand you were in the city to offer your support."

"Why shouldn't I?"

"No reason, I suppose. I'm not surprised you would support a murderer."

There was a gasp from about the table. Carlos's face

grew red with rage. "Will you deny you were involved in this overthrow?"

"Overthrow?" Julio interrupted. "What are you saying, Carlos? Surely you cannot mean—"

Alex's amused drawl silenced the twittering crowd. "He means just that. Stephen Austin's volunteer army has caused Cos to turn tail and, like the coward he is, take refuge in the Alamo. Ladies and gentlemen, it is only a matter of days. His case is hopeless; with their food and ammunition sources cut off, his surrender is inevitable."

Carlos's hand cracked against the table. "I will not have it! Even now my wagons are loaded with food and guns for his men. No one would dare stop me from entering that mission!"

A grin curled one side of Alex's mouth as his eyes drifted toward Angelique DuHon. His voice was husky. "Dreadfully sorry, Grandfather, but I'm afraid someone *has* stopped you."

"What are you saying?"

His blue eyes narrowed as Alex appeared to memorize Angelique's delicate features, the curve of her slender neck, the flutter of her rapidly beating pulse. Her rose-pink lips were moist and parted in a wordless way that left him somehow winded. He answered Carlos absently, for in that instant the spell had been cast. "Quite simply, Grandfather, if you will look out the window to your back you will see that the light torching the darkness is not due to lanterns, but to fire. Your wagons, senor, are ablaze."

As of one mind, the many guests jumped to their feet and hurried to the windows. There were gasps of outrage, of incredulity, even of resignation. But it was a different fire that burned between the two who had remained in their chairs, a fire far more intense than that distant inferno . . . and far more dangerous.

# Six

Angelique spoke calmly as her mother paced back and forth across the floor. "Mama, Doña de Bastitas has asked me to attend the performance with her. As her guest, would it not be improper for me to decline?"

Carlota examined her daughter closely. "This woman seems to have taken a great deal of interest in you, my daughter. Even Julio and Francesca have noticed the attention *la patrona* has given you. Is there some reason for it?"

Angelique's chin tipped defiantly, but she answered truthfully, "I don't know."

The stiff crinoline of Carlota's petticoats rustled as she advanced toward her daughter, tapping the handpainted fan she carried in her right against the palm of her left. "Have you seen Alejandro de Bastitas since his arrival home?"

"No, Mama. Not since our meal last evening."

Carlota considered her answer. "You retired early, as did he."

"The man is engaged to my cousin, and for that reason alone I would avoid him."

"Francesca fears he is taken with you. He has not lain one of those damnable blue eyes on Juanita since our arrival. They are always on you. Need I remind you—''

Angry now and confused by the breathlessness her mother's observation had aroused, Angelique snatched her heaviest shawl from the bed. ''Mama, must we go into this again? I do not search out this man's attention, and can hardly avoid him while we stretch out this eternal visit! I wish we had never left New Orleans for this godforsaken, war-infested country!'' She swung her shawl about her shoulders, biting her lower lip. ''We are to meet Senora de Bastitas in the salon in five minutes. Will you be joining me?''

Carlota's face was white. ''No.''

They stared at one another for several uninterrupted moments. Angelique then moved for the door. ''I will tell them you are indisposed.''

''*Gracias.*''

Distressed and shaken, Angelique hastened down the hall.

The Plaza de Toros was not nearly so grand as one would find in the farther reaches of Mexico, or in the heart of Spain, but it was a fine example of Carlos de Bastitas's determination to hold on to Spanish custom. Everyone from the *gentes de razón* to the peons and mestizos had been invited. Their excited chatter filled the arena, but all fell quiet as Don and Doña de Bastitas, with guests at their side, entered the box and took their seats. No one spoke until Carlos stood and opened his arms in a gesture of welcome.

Angelique remained seated, ignoring her cousin's fiery glare. God, but she would be glad when this rigorous fiesta was finished. She longed to put the entire Bastitas family behind her!

She looked toward the frail figure of Isabella de Bastitas and relaxed slightly. She had grown very fond of the old *patrona*. Although Angelique knew little of the problems plaguing the Bastitas family, she sensed that if Isabella's gentle hand were allowed more freedom, perhaps the tension crackling about the walls of Ranco de Bejar would ease.

As Isabella smiled serenely, Carlos raised the kerchief in his hand. A roar from the crowd replied, and with the sound of the trumpet, the corrida began.

The *alguaciles*, dressed in sixteenth-century costumes of black velvet, had just mounted their horses when Carlota DuHon stepped up behind the matador, resplendent in his *traje de luces*. Her heart was pounding, and her voice was raspy as she spoke. "Alejandro."

His well-muscled arm, propped on the top rung of the *barrera*, tensed, and his face turned to stone. The silk cape draped across his shoulder flared slightly as he pivoted to face her.

Removing the cigarillo from his mouth, Alejandro flung it to the ground. A smile curled one side of his mouth. "Have you come to wish me good luck, Carlota?"

"I hope *el toro* plunders your soul."

"My, but we've a heart of gold, haven't we?"

"I hate you with all my being."

His laughter was abrupt. "I'm flattered."

"Stay away from my Angelique."

"I have rarely seen her since the night of the dance. I see little that should aggravate you so."

She ventured a step closer. "You have not touched her with your filthy hands, but she is defiled by your eyes and thoughts."

He slipped on his black hat, taking care not to disturb the artificial pigtail—the coleta—which had been added to his sable hair. He cocked the hat over one eye, then stepped closer to lightly trace her jawline with the tip of one brown, tapered finger. "I wonder why we hate one another so, Madam DuHon, when we've so much in common. Could it be, perhaps, that you are jealous?"

She spat in his face, and before he could recover from his shock, slapped him soundly across his cheek. "I will see you dead before you break her heart!"

Jaws flexing, Alex glowered down into Carlota's outraged face. "If this is a verbal demand for honor, madam, then you have it. Take heed, as you know, I'm quite adept with the sword and pistol. I'm equally adept with my tongue. The prize of a heart is as easily lost, as easily won. The winner takes *all!*''

Carlota's gasp was lost among the sudden roar of the crowd. Spitting at his feet, she twirled and hurried back to the house.

Angelique was more than aware of the growing tension. On her left, Isabella seemed oblivious to the clamoring of the spectators. Instead, her eyes were riveted on the far *arrastre*. To her right, Tomas bowed his head. His lips moved silently, then he made the sign of the cross.

As he raised his eyes to hers, he smiled. "I pray my brother completes his role with no injury."

Angelique turned again to watch the *alguaciles* doff their plumed hats to Carlos de Bastitas, then back their horses to the *arrastre*. Although she had listened many times to her mother's descriptions of the fights, never had she actually experienced one. She had often thought the sport barbaric. How could civilized men and women find enjoyment in the slaughter of a helpless animal?

The *arrastre* was opened again and as the paseo of men filed into the ring, the air was shattered by the reverence of the crowd. Angelique's breath caught as Alejandro, followed by the banderilleros, puntilleros, then picadors, moved into view. Although the day was cloudy, a reluctant sun reflected off the gold and silver embroidery of his black velvet jacket and knee-length silk pants. His calves were covered in the customary pink stockings, and his shirt was partially covered by a short-waisted jacket, the sleeves of which were left unsewn under the arms, allowing him more mobility. A wide red sash accentuated the slenderness of his waist and hips, and his feet were clothed in supple leather slippers.

Angelique feigned interest in the other caballeros who partook in the occasion. It would be foolish to add fuel to Juanita's scalding visual fire. Still, her attention was continually drawn back to the matador sauntering arrogantly about the ring.

The paseo parted, leaving Alex at the far side of the ring. He swung the cape of red silk from his shoulder and spread it over one bent knee. A hush fell over the crowd as all eyes turned to the opposite wall.

The *toril* swung open and back against the wall of the *barrera*. In that same moment Peregrino was before them. There was a gasp.

"Mother of God," Tomas whispered.

It was a moment before Angelique realized her hand was in the firm grasp of Isabella de Bastitas, for her eyes were captive to the fierce beast looming before them. Surely this could not be the same animal she had witnessed before! There, upon that open and sparse prairie, he had seemed so inconsequential. But here he was like some great black dragon, his nostrils flaring and snorting his hot breath, disturbing the earth at his feet.

"He weighs just short of two thousand pounds and stands five feet at his withers." Angelique forced her glazed green eyes toward Tomas. Her lips parted, but she was too winded to speak. He added, "His horns have been honed to a needle-sharp point and his hooves could cut a man to ribbons. He was sired by Andaluz. Alejandro and I watched as our father was skewered upon *that* bull's horn. We saw him dangle helplessly and scream in pain as the bastard animal lifted him from the ground and tossed him about as if he were nothing but air."

She blinked hard. Her mouth was dry. "Is he afraid?"

Tomas's mouth twisted. "Yes, but unlike me, he will not show it."

Alejandro faced his dragon grimly. He had prepared himself for this moment, yet as the beast lunged from his chiquero, a sudden weakening in his knees warned him that his bravery was not as unwavering as he believed. Tomas had pleaded with him to sneak a look at the animal *before* the fight. But that would have meant breaking the rules. The matador and the bull must never set eyes on one another before the game.

Funny that he had faced many men in his lifetime, men who had been intent on killing him, and he had never doubted his ability to survive. Men were predictable, and after the first few moments of contact, their weaknesses could be found. But a bull, a smart bull, would be wary. He would not be so easily tricked.

Damn his grandfather. Damn him to hell!

The veronica, the most beautiful of all movements, was performed with his cape. As the bull charged, Alejandro's tall frame tilted and the red silk billowed. One arm dropped against his side, and for a solitary moment, he appeared to defy gravity.

The heat of the animal's body was like a foul breath against his belly. The ground thundered beneath his feet.

"Olé!"

Angelique sank back against her chair, forcing her breath out between her teeth. As the man fell to his knees to perform the *larga cambrada*, she grabbed at the arms on either side of her, for just as the charging bull seemed intent on goring the matador to death, Alex vanished within the folds of the cape he swung up and over his side and head.

"Olé!"

On her feet, Angelique pressed her trembling fingers to her temple. She was embarrassed over her emotional state and looked apologetically toward her hostess. Isabella's smile was a mixture of relief and understanding. Together they sat down in their chairs. Turning then toward Tomas, Angelique quietly asked, "Is this foolishness done?"

"Done? Ha! I wish it were so. This folly, Senorita DuHon, has been only a game. They have become acquainted. From now on, each will be intent only on killing the other."

The picadors entered on their horses. The bright crimson *petos*, or paddings, strapped to their animals' sides immediately caught the bull's attention. He charged, but just before the man moved his horse out of danger, he drove his lance just forward of the bull's shoulder.

Angered now, Peregrino turned to face his main adver-

sary. Alex offered his back to the beast, and as he moved
to the barricade the animal followed, standing his ground
in the center of the ring. Alex, met by his banderilleros,
accepted the steel-pointed wooden sticks decorated with
the Bastitas color of royal blue. As he and the bull faced
one another again, they moved simultaneously. Alex
feinted to one side as the animal swerved. Stepping back,
Alex drove the sharp, single-barbed point into Peregrino's
shoulder, repeating the feat with each lance.

The picadors reentered and caped the animal to one side
as Alex strode to the burladero and relinquished his cape
to his sword handler. He rinsed his mouth with water, then
was handed his muleta, which he accepted with his left
hand. His sword was placed across it.

Tomas leaned close to Angelique's ear. "It is time for
the kill. Alejandro will also dedicate the bull either to the
entire audience, or to an individual." He sat back in his
chair and grinned as Angelique looked toward her cousin,
who was smiling smugly. Angelique frowned as he whispered against her ear. "Remember what I told you; expect
the unexpected from my brother."

Alejandro de Bastitas removed the black hat from his
head as he approached his grandfather. His face was emotionless as Carlos stood. "*Patron*, Don Carlos Echeverria
de Bastitas . . . do you grant me permission to kill this
bull?"

"*I do.*"

Alejandro turned to the women and stated in a voice
tinged with mockery, "In honor of this occasion, and in
utmost respect, I, Alejandro de Bastitas, dedicate this kill
to . . ." He raised one brow as he saw Juanita fumbling
with her skirts. He wished like hell that Carlota was present. ". . . Senorita Angelique DuHon."

There was silence until Juanita's outraged whimper
caused the onlookers to squirm uncomfortably in their
seats. Angelique closed her eyes. The blood left her face.
He had done it again! He had humiliated her in front of
an entire arena; not only that, but he'd verbally slapped
the Sanchez family across their mortified faces. Oh, but

she would never be able to face them again! Why? Why had he done this?

"Stand."

A hand was coaxing her up. Perplexed, she turned to Tomas. He was grinning from ear to ear.

"You must stand. My brother has dedicated this fight and his kill to you. If you refuse, you dishonor Alejandro as well as the entire Bastitas lineage."

Pressing her lips together in a firm line and tuning out Juanita's frantic babbling, Angelique bestowed upon the arrogant matador a look that might have scalded a lesser man. Slowly she stood with her shoulders erect and her chin tilted.

"You honor me," came his smooth voice. He then threw her his hat.

Angelique caught it easily, then nodded her head and sat down once again. Alejandro bowed, and with no apparent concern sauntered toward the center of the ring.

What would she say to her family? Julio and Francesca Sanchez had opened their hearts and home to her and she had caused them great humiliation. And her mother! Oh, *mon dieu*, but her mother would be furious!

She turned and shoved the hat into Tomas's lap. She didn't want to touch it, for her fingers had detected his body's heat, making her recall the warmth of his body against hers that night on the patio, then later as his dance had seduced an entire audience . . . and her as well.

Tomas gently placed the hat back in her hands. His smile was understanding, yet his voice held a scolding quality that brought two hot spots of color to her high cheekbones. "You have accepted his tribute. If he kills the bull successfully, you are to reward him with its return."

A sudden gasp from the spectators, followed by the crescendo of "Olé!" caused both her and Tomas to direct their attention to the man and beast.

Alejandro began with a series of passes with the muleta held in his right hand and spread out by his sword. He positioned it dangerously low, offering the animal the target of his own body as well as the stiff cape. All knew it was not the color of the cape which aroused the animal's attention, for *el toro* was color-blind. It was the movement—even a slight movement—which caused the beast to charge, for by now he was angered by pain and frustration.

The animal bellowed. His head was down, exposing the hump, or *morillo*, where the matador must thrust his sword precisely to be successful in his kill. Anything less than a clean thrust and the banderilleros would be called in to taunt the bull and make the sword move within. If the animal fell, and still did not die, the puntillero would administer the coupe de grace. Any of these actions would diminish the matador's skill in the spectators' eyes.

Alejandro was ready. Peregrino was stationed perfectly, just ten yards before him, his breath exploding against the earth in short, angry bursts. He pawed the ground and his raised tail signified the charge that would come at any moment. Alex blinked as sweat ran into his eyes, temporarily blinding him. This moment had brought his father's death, for of all the passes, this one offered the bull the best chance to gore the matador to death.

It was a moment before Angelique realized her anger had been forgotten. Her breath was caught deep in her breast. Tomas left his seat with a muttered oath. Isabella covered her hand with her own cool fingers. There was absolute silence. They waited.

Alejandro stood erect and tall. He offered the bull his left profile and held the muleta doubled over the end of the stick inside it, and across his body. He raised his sword to shoulder level and aimed. As if on cue they moved toward each other.

Angelique leaped to her feet as the entire audience stood. She longed to close her eyes but she was mesmerized by the performance.

Just when it appeared he and the bull would collide, Alejandro thrust the muleta down and to the right so at that last second before the horn found respite in his gut, the bull followed the lead of the cape. As Alex rose upon his toes and arched, he felt the wind and slight abrasion of the horn as it passed within a breath of his belly. His aim was sure as he drove the sword into the wither of the animal. The bull feinted, stumbled, and before Alejandro could finish his spin, the animal had fallen to the ground, dead.

*"Olé estoconazo!"*

Carlos de Bastitas was on his feet. As the crowd roared their appreciation, Angelique was stunned to find she was crying. Tomas appeared in the arena and met his brother halfway. The air was filled with paper flowers which covered the ground at Alejandro's feet as he approached Angelique DuHon. His eyes had not left hers since the moment he had turned to face her.

Her heart in her throat, Angelique leaned slightly forward to offer him his hat. Instead, she found her hand caught gently in his. Alex bowed, but instead of kissing her fingers, he turned her hand up and lightly traced his tongue from her wrist to the center of her palm. Her breath caught as he turned his face up to hers.

"Have you no gift to offer a hero?"

Recognizing the teasing lilt to his voice, Angelique attempted to retract her hand. It was impossible. Knowing she was offering him a grand display of her heaving decolletage, she bantered nervously, "Senor de Bastitas, you find me . . . unprepared. I have nothing—"

"Haven't you?" A flood of fire surged in the girl's face as she snatched her hand away. His blue eyes dropped to her cleavage and to the hand that was so inadequately attempting to shield her breasts. He then turned to his grandfather.

Carlos motioned for the puntillero. "Award my grandson the *oreja!*"

"That won't be necessary," came Alex's quiet drawl. His smile was suddenly cold as he continued, "Allow me to offer you this memento." The old man's face was the color of gray ash as Alex reached into the sash about his waist and pulled out his prize. He threw it against *el patron's* chest. "Receive this in honor of my father."

The tiny silver cross, dull with age and blood, fell at Carlos's feet. Alex turned and, as was customary, walked to the center of the arena.

The cheers continued.

# SEVEN

Carlota smiled nervously at her host, then watched as Teresa poured them each a steaming cup of chocolate. Carlos de Bastitas waited until the servant had slipped from the room before he settled his aged eye upon his guest. "I regret you were unable to attend the corrida, Senora DuHon. I understand it has been many years since you have attended such an affair."

"My apologies, Senor. I was not well."

He smiled and shrugged. "Your daughter enjoyed it."

"So I understand."

There was an uneasy quiet between them. Carlos shifted in his chair. "Your daughter is very . . . beautiful."

"But . . . ?"

"You must keep her away from my grandson."

Anger widened her eyes, but outwardly Carlota remained calm. "In due respect, senor, my Angelique has done everything imaginable to avoid contact with Alejandro. He continually taunts her, and me as well." Staring into the dark chocolate for several moments, she then faced him again. "I knew Alejandro while in New Orleans. His reputation is far from spotless. You cannot blame my daughter for your grandson's ill behavior." The china clattered slightly as Carlota placed her cup and saucer on the tray. "Angelique's virtue is beyond reproach."

He laughed. "I've no doubt of that, dear lady. It is not her beauty or reputation that I find unfavorable, but . . ."

"Yes?"

Carlos spread his hands between them. "Let us be realistic; she is not of proper lineage. Her father was French, so her blood is less than pure. A shame, but we both realize the hopelessness of the situation. If it were otherwise I would do my best to entice a relationship between your daughter and my youngest grandson. Unfortunately, a marriage between them is out of the question."

Feeling as if she had been slapped, Carlota forced herself to stand. "I did not venture here with any hope of finding a husband for my daughter. In truth, had I known who my niece's fiancé was, I would have returned to Galveston and sailed for Spain. I pity Juanita Sanchez, for she marries a godless bastard, senor. Your grandson is without morals or principles. He is a villain and not fit to be stepped on by my daughter's feet!" Spinning, she headed for the door. She stopped, however, at the sound of his laughter.

Carlos struggled to his feet, then rested his light weight on his cane. The blue of his eyes was no longer so cold. The creases in his face had deepened in mirth. "You must have known my grandson well, Senora DuHon. Tell me, was he an adequate lover?"

Her jaw sagged. With a gasp of outrage, she flew from the room.

Angelique gripped her shawl tighter about her shoulders. Although the day had not been overly warm, the chill of approaching winter was now more than evident in the air. She couldn't sleep. The room had grown stifling; she had tossed and turned for hours until she was driven from her bed to open the French doors. It was then she noticed Isabella sitting alone on the patio.

The old woman smiled as she looked up to find the girl standing in the shadows. "Come and sit. This may be our last chance to speak openly with one another." As Angelique approached, Isabella poured her a glass of mulled wine from an ornate silver pitcher. "It is a pleasant drink. Indulge quickly and soon you will forget this cold."

The wine warmed her. Angelique smiled. "Mama says we are to leave tomorrow. I fear it is my fault."

"Nonsense. Had my Alejandro behaved himself . . . I would suppose that is asking Santa Maria for the impossible."

The drink was sweet and Angelique drank deeply. "We will meet again at the wedding."

"There will be no wedding, at least between Juanita and my grandson."

Angelique was stunned. "I—I don't understand."

"My husband and I have discussed the matter with your aunt and uncle. Alejandro's insult was the last straw. They have withdrawn their permission to marry Juanita."

Angelique attempted to quell the sudden surge of anticipation in her breast. She finished her drink, then just as quickly found her glass refilled. She drank again.

"He would never have gone through with it. I only question why he agreed in the first place." Finishing her drink, Isabella chuckled. "I would guess it to be for just this reason. He finds great pleasure in displeasing the old codger."

Angelique covered her giggle with the tips of her fingers. She was feeling relaxed now. "Will you remain here with the war about you?"

"This has been my home for too many years. I won't be driven away."

"Do you support Santa Anna?"

Isabella thought a moment. "No."

"Then you support the Texans?"

The doña refilled her glass. "The Texans threaten our way of life. The foreigners bring plagues and discontent, but they are the lesser of two evils. Perhaps . . . yes, perhaps I *do* support Stephen Austin's army."

"Ah, Grandmother, you should leave such confessions for the priest." Both women looked up as Alex stepped through the heavily vined portal. Even in the dark, the white of his smile was unmistakable. "May I join you?"

Before either could answer Alex slipped into an accompanying chair. "Ladies, am I intruding?"

"You are," his grandmother responded.

He cocked one brow. "Grandmother, have you grown tipsy again on one of Teresa's concoctions?"

"That is none of your concern. Now, tell us why you are here."

"I thought of seducing Miss DuHon."

Angelique's green eyes blinked rapidly. Isabella clucked her tongue. "Alejandro, you are much too honest. Angelique is not accustomed to your wit. You should woo her. Entice her with flowers and whispers of devotion."

His finger caught a droplet of wine before it could surrender its grip on the pitcher's glittering spout. He touched it to his tongue. "Am I to tell her she is the loveliest young woman I have encountered in my lifetime? That the night we kissed on this very patio I found her lips far sweeter than the wine she now sips."

The glass at her lips, Angelique froze. She could hardly believe her ears. They dallied in conversation as if she were not there! She glared at Alex's profile, highlighted only by candlelight.

Isabella's eyes cut from one to the other. Though her grandson's face was calm, the girl's was vibrant with anticipation. "You are wasting your breath on me," she finished. "The senorita is leaving tomorrow."

He covered a yawn with the back of his hand, then offered a sleepy smile. "There is time, Grandmother. Afford me some common sense. After all, I've just been jilted by my fiancée."

Isabella pursed her lips. "I hope you are not *too* disappointed."

"I'll live."

They were quiet. Isabella de Bastitas finished yet another glass of wine. Angelique followed suit, dumbfounded as she waited for their next spurt of witticisms. Alex's eyes traced the balustrade of the upper balcony until they rested on the open doors of the bedroom. He rotated his head slightly, as if to relieve his tension. His chair scraped and suddenly he was towering above the women.

"The hour grows late and it's been a long day." He bowed and accepted his grandmother's hand. His kiss was a brush upon her fingers. He turned then to Angelique and laughed as she tucked her hand in the folds of her robe. "Good night, Angelique. Rest easy."

He disappeared into the shadows. Only then did Angelique release her breath. "He is arrogant."

"Yes he is."

"He has humiliated me in the face of my family, and has humiliated my family."

"Yes he has."

"He should be flogged."

"He will be."

Angelique frowned. "What do you mean?"

"He will know the back of his grandfather's hand. His back will feel the bite of Carlos's thong. But my husband will not wield his justice until the guests have departed." Isabella rose from her chair. "I will leave you alone to finish your wine. If you care for more, ring the bell. Teresa will assist you."

Like an apparition, the woman was gone. Angelique poured another glass of wine, then relaxed in her chair. She dreaded the dawn. There would be her mother to contend with, and if what Isabella said was true, undoubtedly the entire Sanchez family would be in a grand state of apoplexy! How could she face them? No one would believe she had offered the man nothing to reciprocate his advances. Why had he chosen her as his pawn? Had he been so against this marriage, he could have made any excuse at all to end the betrothal.

Angie rubbed her throbbing temple. Thank God they would be leaving tomorrow. She missed Bernice. She longed for New Orleans and most of all, she wanted to put as much distance as possible between herself and Alejandro. Sighing, she ran her fingers through the bronze coil of hair which slid like silk across her shoulder. Her lids were heavy and her head felt leaden. She yearned for sleep—an uneventful sleep, for her last few nights had been plagued with nothing but *his* face.

Standing, Angelique swayed as she pulled the satin tie of her robe tighter about her waist. *Dieu*, but she was tipsy! If her mother were to see her now the dear lady would be sent back to her bed with the vapors!

Moving to the stairs, Angelique studied each individual step as she scaled her mountain, tottering slightly as she finally reached her destination. The candle that had offered her light upon her earlier venture had been mysteriously snuffed below her, and she found it necessary to grip the balustrade as she made her way to her room.

She dropped her velvet robe in a heap on the floor before she slid between the satin sheets. With heavy lids she stared at the canopied top of her bed. . . . Something wasn't right. There was some difference and she sat upright in shock. *Her* bed had had no canopy! She was in the wrong room!

Angelique cast her covers aside and slipped to the floor. But even as she clumsily snatched up her robe, she was too late. The shadow-shrouded figure moved before the doors and stopped.

Clutching the wrapper to her breast, she stammered, "St—stand aside. I fear I've made a dreadful mistake. This is *not* my bedroom!"

Soft laughter was his only response.

She pressed her lips and retreated a step. Though the room was black, the night outside the door was not so oppressive and offered a more subtle darkness. His silhouette was intensified, but his face was lost in midnight's unyielding grip.

"Stand aside!" came her harsher demand. "You have tricked me and I will not stand for it!"

"Keep your voice down, *querida*. Think how humiliated your family would be were you found in my room now . . . dressed as you are."

Quelling her gasp of outrage, she spun and grabbed the bedroom doorknob. It wouldn't budge. Stomping her foot in frustration, Angelique turned to face him again. He was gone. But just as she sprinted for the French doors, thinking escape imaginable, he was against her, wrapping one long, hard arm about her waist and spinning her around to face him.

Her arms caught between them, she struggled futilely, for the harder she squirmed the more demanding was his hold. Realizing her thrashing was only intensifying her predicament, she reluctantly relaxed and waited for his next move. Angelique dared not look up into his smirking, arrogant face, for if she did she knew his battle would be won.

"Look at me."

"I won't!"

"Look at me, Angel."

"Don't call me that!"

How dearly she regretted the wine she'd sipped as her resolve waned beneath the crooning murmur of his voice. As he tenderly slipped his fingers into a stray bronze curl and tucked it behind her ear, his touch caused her heart to leap and her blood to roar in her ears. No matter how she tried, she could not subdue the flood of excitement surging through her body.

The arm about her waist tightened. Alex tilted her head until her face, highlighted by an awakening moon, was facing him fully. His gut tightened as he traced the outline of her cheek and jaw with his finger, for it seemed her beauty and innocence was exaggerated by the sooty shadow.

Angelique squirmed, though perhaps not so persistently. Her eyes traveled from the expanse of his chest, revealed by a gaping shirt, to the middle of his flat belly, upward again to the broad column of his neck and the precisely planed chin and jaw. Was it the wine that made her so weak? At any moment she was certain to melt in a tiny little puddle at his feet!

"Please, you must let me go," she managed more calmly than she felt.

"And let you fall? Ahhh, sweetheart, I think not."

"I have legs on which to stand," she countered, with shaky defiance.

"And I have arms with which to hold you . . . if you'll let me."

His palm cradled her cheek. He pulled her closer until she could feel the pounding of his heavy heart against her own. "I shan't let you. . . . You—you are a cad, a bold—"

"Am I?"

"My mother says—"

"To hell with your mother."

"You have humiliated my family—"

"How could I do otherwise after meeting you?"

Her eyes widened, and she met his gaze fully. She groaned, for the need to swoon was breathtakingly real. "Are you saying I am the reason you jilted my cousin?"

"I am a man of my word. Her father broke the engagement."

"Then you would have married her?"

"*Quien sabe*, my dear Miss DuHon. Perhaps . . . and perhaps not."

"Did you care nothing for her?"

His dark gaze stroked her features as he shrugged. "No more, no less than any other acquaintance." She stiffened. "I could have been satisfied with that," he finished, "until you appeared. How can I forget a green-eyed witch who seduces with her innocence as easily as with her kiss? Since that moment I saw you, I've yearned for no other."

As he pressed his lips against her temple, then her ear, and nuzzled the fluttering pulse in her throat, Angelique succumbed to her weakness and swooned in his arms. She was floating . . . until the pressure about her waist and legs was relieved by the downy softness of his bed against her back. Her eyes flew open, but as her lips parted to plead with him his mouth met hers in a firm embrace.

His weight felt faintly heavy as he stretched out against her, but it was not a burden. Instead, Angelique was warmed by his body's heat. Her senses soared with revived stirrings of desire she had never experienced. Gently at first, he teased the delicate contours of her lips. She felt

his teeth graze and his tongue probe, and as she opened
her mouth, he filled her moist cavity with his velvet-soft
thrust. Despite her need to resist him, she responded ar-
dently, for her blood had turned to wine, and the delicious
ferver of sensuality had eradicated her better judgment.

The sheer material of her gown was a slender barrier
and gave no resistance to his searching hands. His fingers
trailed their mercurial fire up the outside of her thigh, over
her smooth hips, then up her ribs until they settled on her
breast. He felt her jump, but he deepened his kiss while
stroking the tiny bud with his thumb until it grew hard and
erect. Only then did he move to take her nipple in his
mouth, to tenderly allow his tongue to fondle, his teeth to
nip until her hands, twisting into his thick hair, told him
she was ready for more.

As he shifted and pressed his mouth against the sensitive
white skin of her stomach, she moaned and grabbed for
his shirt, afraid of what might follow. The dark head tilted
as he looked into her face. "Beautiful. You were made for
a man, Angel. You were made for me."

As Alex eased her legs apart, Angelique's resistance
melted until she found the need to cover her mouth with
the tips of her fingers, or she might even then have cried
out. What had happened to her reason? Angelique bit her
lower lip as his fingers sought and found her, and she
gasped at the sudden, startling need, which shot like quicksilver between her thighs.

Alex pushed to his knees. In a single movement he
caught his shirt and lifted it over his head. As he crouched
there, his dark eyes visually embracing her, his own body
responded until he ached with the fullness that could find
release in only one way. Damn, but she was beautiful.
Even in her innocence she was unexcelled by any other.
Her alabaster breasts were high and full, their peaks straining now for his touch. Her hair, now loosened totally from
its coils, twisted across her shoulders and fell in leisured
auburn waves across his pillows. After dropping his shirt
to the floor, he picked up a handful of that silken fire and

draped it across her stomach. It blended with the fine copper hair at the apex of her thighs.

Angelique closed her eyes. Her world was spinning. A tiny voice deep in her consciousness whispered that what she was doing was wrong. So why didn't she care? Why had she thrown all thought of denial away the first moment Alejandro looked at her through those beguiling blue eyes? He was wicked and cruel. He had shamed her family and her mother despised him. Still, there were moments when she sensed that he was far different than he chose to appear.

Would it be folly to believe he needed her? That his indifference to life and love was a masquerade? Did Isabella sense it too? It was too much to hope for. She ached for the security, love, and companionship he could grant her. If she could only be certain he truly cared . . .

Angelique whimpered, for there was a straining, aching sensation growing inside her. Her lashes parted, and had the night's cloak not washed the green from her eyes, Alex might have watched them glow with an emerald fire. His belt was open, and as his long fingers deftly plucked the buttons down the front of his breeches, she sat up before him and wrapped her arms about his waist, then pressed her cheek against the musculature of his broad chest. As his hands came up to wrist in her hair, hers moved over the flexing ridges of his back, down his spine, then into the material draped about his hips.

Her innocence was as sweet as a siren's song, driving a low growl from deep in his chest. Its sound was frightening yet exciting, for Angelique was discovering that she too had the ability to seduce. As she lay back, her shoulders cushioned by cool, satin-draped pillows, she was vaguely aware of rocking her head back and forth, of softly uttering words of refusal. But she knew as well as he that there was no turning back.

His skin was hot and smooth and their shared heat bonded them together as their mouths met once again. As the sudden pressure between her legs caught her off-guard her fingers dug into the skin of his back until he was driven to turn his head and grit his teeth against the cruel inflictions. Still, he pressed against her.

Angelique thrashed slightly beneath him, and looking up into his hooded eyes, she gasped. What was it she'd seen there? Laughter? Scorn? Mockery? Something had been there—something cold and calculating, and though the rigidness of his face had now softened, and her virginity had surrendered to his gentle invasion, there was something so frightening about him, she could not help but whimper at his touch.

"You hurt me."

"I'm sorry."

Still, he kept moving, stroking that reluctant ember to a fickle flame. As he buried his face in the hair about her neck and shoulder, her fingers stroked his back. The movement of his hips caused her heart to swell until she thought for certain she would swoon. "Why have you done this?" she finally managed.

"Mmmm, because it is most enjoyable."

"But I never—"

"You were a virgin. *Querida*, had I thought otherwise I might not have been so gentle." His laughter was quiet in her ear. "Hush now, Angel, and let me take you."

Hesitantly, her legs pulled about his thighs, her arms slid around his back. "Where will you take me?"

"Heaven." His face was damp as he stayed poised above her.

"Heaven is forever," she softly chided.

His eyes narrowed. "Nothing is forever, *querida*."

Angelique sensed the underlying insinuation. Again she asked, "Why have you done this?"

"I wanted you. I want you. Now hush and let me love you."

Her heart skipped a beat. Her eyes searched his face. "Do you love me?"

Alex sank against her and muffled any further words with his kiss. He moved with extreme restraint, taking her gently toward that consummate peak. He kissed her leisurely, then passionately, then almost angrily, and with each intimate yet fiery assault his body both punished and pleasured. His loving was as mercurial as his mood, and it was an hour before he finally allowed himself to bring her to that abyss into which she plummeted, crying out as she fell from heaven's precipice down to reality. Only then did he allow himself that ultimate reward, only then did he allow that surging desire to surrender, and as he spilled hot and deep inside her, his cry of "Angel! God, Angelique!" was sweet music to her ear.

As he withdrew and sank beside her in the soft mattress, their eyes locked and held. There was a look of both incredulity and amazement on his face.

"Have I displeased you?" she shyly asked.

He touched the flush in her cheeks, then dropped a kiss on the tip of her nose. As he rolled to his back, she moved with him and nestled her head against his shoulder. "Quite the contrary," he managed in a husky voice.

Angelique studied his profile for several moments. "I leave tomorrow." There was no reply. Disappointed, she looked away. She had hoped that her mother's warnings about Alejandro would prove false. That he wasn't the womanizing rakehell she professed him to be.

Angelique closed her eyes. She could only imagine Carlota's reaction should she learn her daughter was now one of those unfortunate young women whose heart he had broken. Feeling the desperate need to understand what was between Alejandro and her mother, she asked bluntly, "Why do you and my mother dislike one another so? Were you well-acquainted in New Orleans?"

He stiffened, closed his eyes, then ran a hand through his hair. "Answer me this," came his deep, somehow angry response. "Why have you come to Texas?"

"We've no place else to go."

"Meaning?"

"Our home was lost."

He stared at her, unmoving. "What of the renowned DuHon Fields?"

Sighing, she responded, "After my father's death there were numerous debts to pay. We sold what we could, then there was nothing left but the house. Even that went in the end.''

"All due to your father's death?"

She nodded. Her voice became tremulous. "I've only just learned of his gambling habits. He had lost almost everything by the time of his murder."

Rolling, Alejandro sat up and reached for a cigar on the nightstand. He didn't like the feelings churning at his guts. Didn't like them at all.

Standing, he strode to the window. The night's chill made him shiver before he turned to face her again. She was but a shadow within the cavernous four posters of the bed. "I didn't realize your father was murdered," he stated quietly.

Angelique bunched her pillow beneath her and rested against it. "Yes," came her soft voice. "He was on his way home from a game when he was jumped by thieves and shot. They never found his killers. But I swear to you, Papa will never rest in peace until that man is found. Nor will I. My father's death brought about an end to everything I ever knew or loved. My home is gone and even now my mother is grieving herself to death, for they loved one another beyond comprehension. That murderer destroyed more than my father . . . much more."

There was quiet before the glow of the cigar surrendered its hold on the darkness. The bed creaked beneath his weight as Alex slid down beside her. He cradled her against his chest. "And tell me, sweet Angel, what would one so tiny and tender do to this man who murdered her father?"

"I—I would kill him."

"Indeed."

"I would see him dead. I shan't rest easy until I do." Alex turned and kissed her, and for a moment she forgot everything else but him. Closing her eyes, she repeated, hoping for an answer, "I leave tomorrow."

# EIGHT

"Angelique, wake up! We must hurry to finish packing.
Angelique!"

"Mmmm, in a moment. I won't be but a moment."

Carlota frowned at her daughter. "Angelique, quickly!
Julio and Francesca are even now saying their goodbyes
to Carlos and Isabella."

Goodbyes? What . . . her eyes flew open as she sat upright in bed. Her mother was scurrying from one trunk to
another. Angelique released her breath and smiled as she
recalled being roused just before dawn. Alejandro had carried her to her own bed, but before she had allowed him
to leave he had loved her again.

Carlota eyed her daughter suspiciously before stopping
at her bedside. Her fingers touched Angelique's flushed
cheeks. "Are you ill?"

"No, Mama."

"Your face is chafed. I have some cream which will
remedy that."

As she recalled the roughness of Alex's cheek against
hers, her heartbeat quickened.

There was a knock at the door. As Angelique pulled the
counterpane to her chin, Francesca Sanchez peered into the

room. "We are almost ready. The help will be in soon to collect your baggage."

Angie slipped from the bed. "Aunt Frances, I'm truly sorry for what's happened."

Francesca smiled gently. "Angelique, I was aware of Alejandro's shortcomings, as well as my own daughter's. It is just as well that this marriage is dissolved before it is begun. I assure you, none of us blame you for this. You cannot help what you are any more than Juanita can."

"I fear Juanita will not be so understanding."

"Juanita will be fine. Perhaps this will be a lesson for her."

Carlota shook her head. "You are much too forgiving, Francesca. Alejandro de Bastitas is a debaucher."

"Then perhaps we should count our blessings, my sister, that neither of our daughters' lives was ruined by such a man."

Angelique dressed quickly, barely taking the time to run her brush through her hair before tying it back with a blue ribbon that matched her dress. Luckily, her mother had allowed her to sleep through breakfast, so she wasn't faced with the distasteful task of fencing with Juanita. She would have enough of her cousin on the two-day journey back to Gonzales!

It had taken all of her self-restraint to keep from asking whether Alex had joined them for breakfast. Where was he at this moment? Was she in his thoughts, as he was in hers? He had made her every fantasy come true the night before. Never had she dreamed that lying with a man could be so . . . fulfilling. She touched her breast, for the ache within left her breathless.

The trunks were removed. As Angelique stepped from her room, she was met by Isabella de Bastitas. She curtsied. "Senora, it has been a most pleasant sojourn."

Isabella studied Angelique carefully. The girl seemed even more beautiful today. "Your company has been most pleasant . . . for us all."

"Angelique!"

Excitement knotted Angelique's stomach as she whirled

to face the newcomer. Her slight flicker of disappointment did not go unnoticed by Isabella. "Tomas, have you come to bid me goodbye as well?"

"*Sí*, though it is with a heavy heart that I do so. We shall miss you, *querida*."

Angelique followed Isabella and Tomas downstairs and to the main foyer of the hacienda. Her gaze drifted toward each door and her ear strained for the sound of Alex's voice. It was not until she turned to leave, however, that she heard him. She froze as he approached her.

The silence between them was charged with tension. He no longer appeared the aristocratic grandson of a don. Dressed in dusty attire, his jaw shadowed by a morning beard, he could easily have passed as one of the many vaqueros working the ranch.

Alejandro bowed slightly toward Isabella. "Grandmother, I understand I am to meet with your husband when these people are gone?"

*La patrona*'s eyes grew hard. "Where are your manners, Alejandro? Have you no word of goodbye for our guest?"

Alex pulled his blue gaze to the girl who stood dumbfounded in the doorway. Deep color crept up her neck, onto her face. Her jade eyes were wide and glazed. "Goodbye. Miss . . . ?"

"D—DuHon."

"Of course," he drawled insolently. "Carlota DuHon's daughter. You *will* give her my best. Won't you?"

A rancid taste crept up her throat as Angelique digested the implication of his words. She felt ill and unclean, for the indolent curve of his mouth lent a cruel slant to his words. He had used her.

Tomas cleared his throat as he protectively caught Angelique's arm and ushered her toward the waiting carriage. He had rarely felt such a surge of anger for his brother.

Upon settling beside her mother, Angelique forced a smile onto her ashen face. "Tomas, will you write?"

"But of course!" Looking eagerly toward Carlota, he continued, "Perhaps your mother will allow me the honor of calling on you when I am in the area."

"Nothing would please me more."

Tomas slammed the carriage door. As he stepped away, she could not contain the impulse to lift her sights toward the hacienda. Isabella waved. There was no sign of Alex.

"I see your satisfaction has soured in your belly. Were you a younger man I would thrash you myself."

Alex allowed the curtain to slide from his finger. "Grandmother, you've never lifted a hand to me yet."

Isabella stepped closer. "Never have you been so spiteful as to shed a virgin's blood on my sheets!" As she watched hot color rise into his face, she nodded. "My servants are trustworthy, Alejandro, so don't deny it. You young fool, do you not realize what your revenge has cost that child? She is in love with you. Yes! In love with you, whether she realizes it or not. So wipe the insolence from your face and consider your actions!" Offering her back, she finished, "You have a guest on the patio."

The woman disappeared through the nearest door, leaving a stunned Alex to reflect on her words. He grunted to himself as Tomas reentered the room and threw him a scathing glance. It seemed the beautiful Angelique had made conquests throughout the hacienda. He tried to arouse the sweet taste of revenge he had mulled over earlier. It was gone. As badly as he hated to admit it, letting her go had *not* been so easy after all.

Kaintock McGuire glanced up. His friend's look was dark. "By golly, Bastitas, you look like you seen Santy Anny peekin' over your john wall."

Alex dropped into a chair. "How's our General Cos?"

"Tucked up tight as a tick, I reckon. Them Mexes won't be goin' nowhere soon. We're just waitin' for him to sign on the dotted line."

"Winter will be settling in soon."

"No doubt about that," the redhead responded.

"Our troops will need respite from the weather."

Kaintock agreed. "There's already been talk between 'em of disbanding until spring. They don't much believe we got anything to worry about until then."

"They could be wrong."

McGuire pulled a cigar from his serape and threw it on the table. He offered a gap-toothed smile. "Try it. It'll do wonders for your soul, or I ain't from Kentucky." Alex accepted, even allowing his friend to light the cheroot. As he inhaled, his brows shot up.

"Ain't that enough to cockle yer innards, Spaniard? Got it from the prettiest little mestizo you ever seen. I reckon we can hand that out among the boys, then they won't even notice the cold."

Alex released his breath. "You hand this out and Santa Anna would float over the Alamo walls without their ever knowing."

They shared an appreciative laugh.

Kaintock relaxed. "Little lady's gone, I assume?"

"Good riddance."

"Now, Alex. You don't mean that. I keep rememberin' your face the night of the fiesta. I suspect you was green around the gills when Sanchez made that announcement. I ain't seen that look in your eyes since—"

"Enough."

"Since the time you fell for Pamela."

"I could use a drink."

"Take another pull of that root. Yep, I ain't even certain you looked that sick over Pam. Course, I reckon it might have a lot to do with who she is. You know, Angie's mammy ain't bad-lookin'. I was thinkin'—"

"Ah, hell."

"Where you goin'?"

"I've an appointment to keep with my grandfather." Alex swayed slightly as he stood.

"You gonna be sick?"

"Not half as sick as I'm going to be *after* I talk to Carlos."

"Want me to stick around?"

Alex couldn't remember if he responded or not as he turned back for the house.

•   •   •

Isabella's eyes narrowed as she acknowledged her grandson's condition. She then turned her attention toward her outraged husband.

"You have humiliated me in the eyes of this city, as well as my friends."

"I didn't renege on the marriage, she did."

"Shut up and listen to me. You will give Julio time to recover from this insult, then you will call on him and request his forgiveness. If you have to plead for his daughter's hand, then you will do it."

"No."

Carlos stopped. Using his cane, he caught his grandson's face and pulled it around toward his. "I fear I misunderstood."

"No."

"You know the ramifications should you disobey."

Alex nodded as he caught the cane against his cheek and shoved it away. "I'm not a child you can bully any longer, Grandfather. In case you have grown blind, as well as senile, I've grown up."

Carlos sucked in his breath. His frail body shook with anger. "Strip."

Alex lifted one black brow in disbelief. "Good God, do you really believe I will cower at your feet?" Flipping his hand toward the lash in Carlos's left hand, he taunted, "You'll need something more substantial than that to send me to my knees shrieking for forgiveness."

"Strip."

"Very well, if thrashing me will appease you . . ." He pulled his shirt up and over his head, then dropped it to the floor.

Bastitas slowly circled his grandson. Alex's shoulders, dark from the sun, were back and relaxed. Carlos ran his hand across them, as if he were mesmerized with their perfection. Then with no warning he planted his cane with all the force he could muster across the small of Alex's spine.

Pain splintered Alex's senses for a moment. Before he

could stop himself, his legs gave and he dropped to the floor.

"Damn you," he hissed as he attempted to regain his footing. He turned his face as the whip sliced the flesh of his arms, back, and neck, each connection leaving raised bloody welts. His body broke out in a sweat, which added to the excruciating sting of the inflictions.

"There, you young upstart, tell me now what a big man you are! Stand up and face me, hombre! Stand up and face an old man!"

Alex struggled to his feet. An unsteady smile lifted the corners of his mouth. "Perhaps next time you'll inform me before you attempt any more of your underhanded tricks." The muscles in his chest flinched from the bite of Carlos's crop. "Go ahead," he prodded, "you wield a far less menacing brand than you did twenty years ago."

Carlos continued until Alex's entire torso was striped in blood. Not once did the smirk leave his grandson's face.

Isabella could take no more. "Stop this! Stop this, Carlos, before you scar him for life! He will bleed to death before you force him to his knees!"

Breathing heavily, Carlos acquiesced for the moment. Isabella then stepped before her grandson. "Your belligerence will someday see my heart broken completely, Alejandro. Please, if you care anything for this old woman, do not force me to witness another moment of this cruelty."

The blue eyes that shifted to hers were glazed. His face was damp and spotted with blood. Alex touched her cheek and stilled the tear before it could spill onto her breast. Then turning, he fell to his knee before his grandfather. "In honor of the Bastitas name, I . . . beg your forgiveness for my misdeeds, and swear to all that is holy I will do my best to rectify the mistakes I have made."

"Leave me."

Without looking back, Alex stood and left the room.

Angelique stomped her feet, coaxing the circulation back into her legs. God, what an eternal vigil! It seemed they had been traveling for an entire day, when they were only just halfway to their overnight stop. She cast her sights about the gloomy day. Where was the sun? Where was the insufferable heat which had greeted their arrival in Texas? She longed for New Orleans. She longed for her childhood. But most of all, she longed to put the past few days behind her!

For the hundredth time since their departure from San Antonio, Angelique's thoughts drifted shamefully to Alejandro de Bastitas. Even the thought of the man caused her face to flush with anger and humiliation. How naive she'd been to believe his sly flirtations had been anything other than silent mockery. No doubt he was laughing at her this moment in his wickedly deceitful way. He had used her . . . used her! And she had allowed it. Oh, if she hadn't indulged so liberally in Isabella's wine. *Damn!*

Covertly, she glanced at her quiet companions. The tension had been so thick these last hours, no one had dared speak. She watched her mother walk beyond the far mesquite shrub. She would wait, then join her. This unsettled peace between them must end, Angelique reasoned, for she could not tolerate another moment of Carlota's silence.

"This is all your fault."

Angelique turned to face her cousin.

"I knew from the moment you arrived you would be trouble."

She took a nervous step backward. "Please, cousin, I did nothing intentionally—"

"Liar! I saw the way you looked at him, how you rolled those slanted green eyes his way each time he entered a room. You have made me a laughingstock!"

"There will be other men, Juanita. I honestly feel you should not concern yourself so—"

"Other men?" Juanita stepped closer. "Ha! What other man will compare with Alejandro de Bastitas? The simpering *idiotas* who used to come calling could not light a candle to him. All the girls in the area were envious over our bethrothal!"

"Juanita, I—"

"I hate you! Someday I will see that you pay for this, I swear!"

Angelique averted her eyes as her cousin spun and trudged back toward the carriage. Perhaps now was the time to join her mother.

A whistling noise followed by a sudden dismal thud made her turn. The vaquero who had been attending the skittish bays appeared to freeze, and as his stunned eyes met Angelique's, he toppled to the ground.

A crescendo of noise exploded around them as the surrounding hills trembled with the thunder of man and horse. Dumbly, Angelique watched as one by one their escorts twisted in pain before falling dead onto the ground.

Julio Sanchez was yelling while attempting to pry a gun from a dead man's hand. "Run, Angelique! Mother of God, it is the Comanche!"

Someone shoved her toward the carriage. Behind her a man was screaming. Shots were fired. Horses were everywhere, rearing and whinnying in terror. Horrified, she watched as a painted madman drew back on his bowstring. She opened her mouth, but before her warning could spill from her constricted throat she saw her uncle spin and clutch at the bloody arrow that jutted from his neck.

"Mama!" She had to find Carlota. She thought nothing of dying, only of saving her mother. A woman's shriek filled the air and she turned to see her aunt fall beneath a savage's weight.

Where was Juanita? Spinning, Angelique caught her cousin before she could move from the confines of the coach. She knew she was too late to shield her from the gruesome reality, but she knew she must not allow the girl to vent her hysteria upon the savage's back.

Juanita was weeping and babbling nonsensically as Angelique forced her back down onto the leather seat. She then covered her mouth with her hand. "Hush!" she pleaded to the incoherent girl. "You may care little for your life, Juanita, but I value mine, I assure you! Shut up! Please, for God's sake!"

The whooping continued until their guttural noises were

replaced by the maniacal laughter of conquest. Suddenly, the door was lurched open and both girls were looking into a flat face boasting of black war paint. Juanita went limp in her arms. Angelique prayed she too might find the respite of unconsciousness. It was not to be.

The Indian's eyes glittered with interest, and with no warning he buried his hand in Angelique's auburn hair and pulled her out into the crowd which was beginning to gather. She was shoved to the ground amid howls of laughter, then was kicked and poked until her sides were one immense bruise. Finally she retaliated with a lunge that sent one brave onto his back and the others jumping about in surprise. She kicked and gouged, but he easily overcame her. Twisting her hands again into her hair, he jerked her to her feet.

They were surrounded now. Angelique looked frantically at the men, hoping to find some compassion in their faces. Instead they shouted in harsh, guttural syllables. Several pointed to her hair, and as one reached forward with his knife and chopped a long strand from across her shoulders, her knees gave way beneath her and she sank to the ground.

How long they stood there about her, Angelique couldn't reckon. She lay stunned on the ground, barely breathing.

It was Juanita's hysterical weeping which brought an end to her momentary shock. Her cousin screamed and thrashed until a brave struck her viciously across the face. The Indian who had earlier struggled with her pulled Angelique to her feet. Both girls were dragged toward the Comanches' horses, past the bodies of Julio and Francesca Sanchez.

Like weightless dolls, they were thrown onto the ponies. There were several vaqueros who had been allowed to live, but were bound with their hands behind them. Although each girl rode with an Indian sitting behind her, the Spaniards were forced to ride on the horses' bare backs with only the leather straps which ran from one ankle, down under the animal's belly, and to the other ankle to help them keep their balance.

It was dusk before they stopped. The fog which had sparsely blotched the countryside had grown thicker. One of the ten Indians gathered the horses, while several more ushered the hostages into a group where they huddled together for support and warmth.

Juanita sank to her knees. "*Madre de Dios*, Mama, Papa, both dead!" She covered her face and wept.

Angelique thought of her own mother. Was it too much to hope she had escaped? She dropped to her knees and kindly wrapped her arm about her cousin's shaking shoulders. "Dear Juanita, my heart bleeds for you."

Hysterical eyes turned up to hers. "Bitch! You lie! You hate us all!"

"That's not true! Francesca and Julio were *very* kind to us. I have no reason to hate you, Juanita."

Her full lips pulled back in a sneer. "Had you not turned Alejandro's head we would still be at the ranch and my parents would still be alive. This is your fault!"

No! Angelique forced herself to stand. "You will not blame this on me!" she countered. "Do you forget my own mother is no doubt lying dead as well?"

"I hope she is!"

"Juanita!"

Their group was divided as the three men were shoved to one side of the clearing and Angelique and Juanita were forced to the other. A fire was started and a horse killed. The roasting meat filled the air with a pungent aroma.

Angelique suspected their tortures had only begun. Her stomach turned as she rolled her eyes to the Indians' shields that had been placed to one side. The hides were decorated with bear teeth, horse tails . . . and human scalps. She shuddered to think her own would most likely be adorning a shield in the next few hours . . . unless she were taken as a slave. Death might be the better alternative.

As the night progressed, the Spaniards staked on the ground began pleading for death. Juanita's nonstop weeping only added to the confusion. When the last victim fell silent, Angelique closed her eyes. She bit her lip as the cold blade of a knife was pressed against her ankle. The

strap was cut, freeing her legs. The band about her wrist
soon followed.

Juanita let out a shriek as they were both jerked to their
feet. Turning her wild eyes on the savages she screamed,
"Take her first! Please! I'll do anything, but kill her, not
me!" She then dropped to the ground, picked up a handful
of dirt, and threw it in Angelique's stunned face. "See? I
hate her! She is a *puta!* A whore!"

Angelique slapped her face.

The Indians laughed rauciously and shoved the girls together, as if goading them to a fight. Instead, Juanita threw
herself at one man's feet.

"Spare me!" she wept.

"Get up!" Angelique railed. "Get up, Juanita, and fight
them! You cannot think to allow them—"

"I will allow them anything they want!" she screamed.
"Anything if they will spare me!"

Replacing the horrified expression on her face with a
sultry look, Juanita began tearing her soiled blouse from
her shoulders. Her shoes followed, then her skirt, and finally her undergarments. The Indians continued laughing,
but now the sound took on a different note. Juanita pressed
herself against the man who during the day had appeared
to be their leader. His face tensed, and suddenly he
knocked her to the ground.

Hands closed about Angelique's arms and pulled her
away from the sickening scenario. Numb, she watched as
the Indian fell onto her cousin. "Fight them! *Mon Dieu*,
Juanita, you mustn't let them—" She was shoved to the
ground, and again her hands and feet were bound with
leather.

As Angelique watched in horror, they each took their
turn with Juanita, and when they were done they cut her
throat. Angelique refused to cry out, even when the dark
faces turned toward her. As one man approached, she
raised her defiant chin with as much courage as she could
muster. When he stopped and stooped before her, she spat
in his face.

The blow that followed made her ears ring. Falling back

from the force of it, Angelique prayed the nightmare would end now. But she felt the man's fist strike her face several more times before unconsciousness released her from her pain and fright. Gradually, she slipped into oblivion's firm, black grip.

# NINE

Angelique pretended to sleep, cursing her body's betrayal, for no matter how she willed it, it would not quit its spasmodic twitching. At any moment Angelique knew for certain her life would be ended. She would be raped. Her throat would be cut. Her hair would be raggedly sliced from her head and draped from a belt or hide shield.

A burst of laughter caused bile to surge in her throat and Angelique knew fear far more intense than she had yet experienced. She peeked through her lashes to see that all but one brave had settled onto blankets strewn about the ground. The remaining Indian was moving toward her.

He poked her with his foot. She didn't move. With any luck he might believe she was still unconscious. Sitting by her, he crossed his legs and continued to smoke the pipe he had earlier shared with his friends.

Angelique had grown stiff. Her every joint ached. To think the night before she had been safe and warm in Alejandro's arms. Her family had been alive and . . .

The Indian laid his pipe on the ground. As he removed the knife from the sheath on his hip, he turned to face her. Her whimper of terror could not be suppressed as he slid the blade in between her skin and dress. The material separated reluctantly over her breasts, but the chemise gave little trouble. He then lay down beside her.

God, let it be over quickly!

The man didn't move. Instead he stared into the darkness. Angelique strained for a sound, a movement. There was nothing; only the snort of a horse and the stomping of a hoof. The Indian studied her face, then shifted to his feet and dissolved into the shadows. Angelique squeezed her lids tightly together. Could she will herself dead? Perhaps if she prayed very, very hard . . .

The snap of a twig caused her stomach to knot in dread. She sensed his presence beside her. Then he was touching her. His large hand was suddenly pressing against her mouth; his knife was at her throat. He was lifting her to her feet and pulling her farther into the shadows. The faint glow of the camp fire dwindled to nothing and the black-gray shroud of fog was suddenly her only barrier against the savages asleep in the distance.

"Be very quiet, Angel, or the morning will see us *both* without our hair."

Oh, God! Suddenly the hard form against her seemed familiar. His arm about her waist was the only thing which kept her from sliding to the ground.

Alex removed the knife from her throat, which had succeeded in keeping Angelique quiet. Certain now that they were far enough from the Indians not to be heard, he allowed a moment to share his strength with the shaking girl. "Angelique, now is not the time to lose your senses. Can you walk?" She nodded, but barely. "Good, then you can run. May I suggest we get the hell out of here?"

Within minutes he had located his horse, and once again Angelique found herself the captive of a man's strong embrace. But this time the viselike band about her waist was firm, yet comforting. Her hips fit perfectly inside his thighs, and before Alex moved his animal from the copse of mesquite trees he tenderly coaxed her head back against his shoulder.

Her small frame was like a taut spring, giving him the impression that should he make the slightest questionable move, she would collapse completely. As his arm slid about her waist she bucked and her hands attempted to pull the ragged remains of her dress across her breasts.

"Steady," came his quiet voice in her ear. The words disturbed the hair about her temples and stroked her cheek.

Angelique closed her eyes, rocking slightly with the horse's movement. She sensed the warring inside Alex, for the thunderous pounding of his heart against her back was in direct contrast to the soothing cadence of his voice. If the Indians discovered their murdered companion within the next few minutes, escape would be impossible. Even if they made it until dawn the savages would undoubtedly do their best to avenge the brave's death. God, they needed time, or a miracle.

She opened her eyes. In that moment it began to rain.

The rain had been falling steadily for hours when Alejandro pulled Angelique from the horse's back. Cradling her in his arms, he kicked open the shack's door. The one room was deserted. He knew it would be. Five years before the family living here had been massacred by the same tribe of Comanche who had killed the Sanchez family. It was considered bad luck to occupy such a place.

Alex rested Angelique's stiff form on the tattered mattress, then gently stretched her legs out, rubbing them slightly to alleviate the cold and return their circulation. Her lashes fluttered.

"Angelique, I'm taking the horse to the barn, then I'll start a fire."

She rolled to her side and pulled her knees to her chin.

He unsaddled the bone-weary animal, then stooped and inspected the horse's front right hoof. It was cracked badly, had been for the last half of their journey. Searching about the dark confines of the deteriorated building, he located a rotting blanket and wire brush. He took a moment to brush the animal down, then finding a bucket of old oats, offered what he could in the way of food before throwing the tattered material onto the stallion's back.

There appeared to be no readily accessible firewood. Accepting the only alternative, Alex pulled several unsturdy boards from the barn walls. Throwing his saddlebags over one shoulder, tucking his bedroll under one arm, he hoisted what wood he could under the other and made for the house.

The tinder was so dry it took little effort on Alex's part to coax a roaring blaze in the stone hearth. For several long moments he stood before it, staring into the snapping flames and ignoring the fact that his body was shaking with cold. His mind kept seeing the Sanchezes' bloodied and ravaged bodies strewn like lifeless dolls across the ground.

Angelique groaned. In two strides Alex was with her.

"Angel, can you hear me? Angelique?" He brushed the hair from her face. It was past dawn now, and though the heavy clouds continued to shadow the countryside, enough light filtered through the window and cracks in the wall to allow him to finally see her face.

Behind the bruises and lacerations her skin was ashen. Hours ago blood had trickled from the ear and nose, but that had dried. Her hair was a mass of tangles. Pulling the flimsy remnants of her dress back, he counted an untold number of bruises across her ribs, breasts and hips. Leather thongs about her wrists and ankles had chafed the delicate skin.

She was still beautiful. Perhaps more than he had even realized. But he was beginning to realize a great deal, and had been since he'd seen her leave the ranch that morning before.

It was a moment before he realized she was watching him. Her eyes glazed, her lower lip trembling, she rasped something unintelligible to his ear. He lowered his head to hear her better.

"Mama," she repeated weakly.

Alex sat back. He touched her lips to hush her incoherent whimpers. "Your mother is alive, Angel."

She didn't appear to hear him. As her head thrashed from side to side, she cried, "You have to help her. Please. She is all I have left!"

"I swear to you, Carlota is safe."

Her restlessness eased, though Alex wasn't convinced she'd understood him. Tilting his head and stroking her hair, he asked, "Are you cold, Angel?"

The nod of her head was almost imperceptible.

Alex gently lifted Angelique in his arms and carried her to the fire. Making certain she was steady enough to stand on her own; he then pulled the mattress to the floor beside her. He coaxed her down. There was little he could offer her for warmth, other than a tin cup of whiskey. She accepted it with no hesitation, choking slightly as she swallowed.

Their clothes were wet. Alex removed his shirt and lay it before the fire. When it dried it would offer Angelique some comfort. But that would be hours in coming. So he laid her down beside him, pulled her close, so close their every curve molded and blended as one, then they slept.

A last ember within the ashes was winking and gasping for air when Angelique awoke. How long had she slept? It was dawn. The rain had stopped. Somewhere beyond the horizon the sun was nudging aside the clouds to make room for a warmer day. She became aware she was being held by a man . . . by Alejandro. Her head was resting on his outstretched arm and, staring at the hand before her, she watched as the pulse throbbed in his wrist and the slightly curled fingers twitched as if responding to some movement in his dreams.

His other arm was thrown casually about her waist. His legs were curved around her buttocks, pressing intimately at every angle. She was wearing his shirt; he was naked from the waist up.

Angelique moved and Alex rolled to his back. Easing away, she stared at him for several long moments. His black hair appeared shaggier than she remembered. It fell across his brow and spilled onto the floor from the back of his head. A coarse beard covered his jaw, at least three or four days' growth that matched the slightly wiry mat on his chest and belly. Angie frowned and more closely inspected the crisscrossed welts on his skin, then moved farther away.

It was a certainty she wasn't dead, unless Alejandro de Bastitas had died and gone to hell with her. That's it, she reasoned. They had both been doomed to spend the rest of eternity in one another's company. He would be her reminder of virtue gone awry, and she his reminder of what comes from seducing virgins!

He opened his eyes. His eyes . . . they jarred her. Never had she seen eyes so blue. Was their color enhanced by the thickest jet lashes she had ever encountered on a man? Or was it the deep bronze of his skin?

"Good morning."

Pulling the shirt tighter about her breasts, she asked him, "My mother?"

"Alive. She stayed hidden through the attack."

She closed her eyes. Dear God, she hadn't dreamed it.

"Kaintock and I were following and came upon Carlota an hour after the attack. She was attempting to return to the ranch."

"She wasn't hurt?"

"Just understandably upset. Kaintock returned her to Rancho de Bejar while I followed your trail."

Relieved, Angelique forced her eyes to the cabin's single window. "Where are we?"

"Someplace between here and there."

"Purgatory?"

Alex grinned. "That's out west I think." She didn't laugh. He tried to touch her, but she slipped away.

Angelique didn't trust her legs to stand. Instead, she crossed them beneath her and crouched as close to the fire as she could.

"Would you like to talk about it?" he asked quietly.

She shook her head, but in the same second whispered, "Why?"

Alex wasn't certain he understood. Why had he asked? Or why had this entire nightmare happened? Sensing she meant the latter, he answered, "Who the hell knows, Angie, but it's been happening since the white man began settling this land. It is the savages' way of life. Maybe they don't know any better.''

"Are you excusing them?"

"Of course not." He got up slowly. "Angel . . . I'm sorry about your aunt and uncle—"

"—and cousin."

"Yes."

Pulling her legs up, Angelique rested her chin on her knee. "They raped her, then cut her throat."

Alex frowned, then stooped before her, resting one knee on the floor. Using his finger, he tipped her face to his. "What do you feel, Angelique?"

"Nothing."

He touched her swollen jaw and broken lip. "There?" She shook her head. He then probed at her bruised ribs. "There?"

"Nothing."

"Would you like to cry?"

She looked away. "No, I . . . don't think so."

Shock. She was numb with it. He should have recognized the signs. She was so pale and her green eyes were dull. Her breathing was shallow, her skin clammy and cold.

"What do you remember?" he coaxed.

Angelique pointed to her throat. "My uncle had an arrow jutting from here, and"—she touched her hair and relief swept her face—"and they scalped my aunt. Is she dead? Juanita told me once that scalping doesn't always kill . . ."

Her voice died as her green eyes shifted about the tiny room. A blow to Alex's belly would have wounded him far less.

"Yes," he responded in a tight voice. "Francesca is dead."

"Juanita is dead, also."

"I know."

She met his eyes. "How do you know?"

"I was there, Angel." Angelique stared at him, uncomprehending, until he looked away. "I watched from the trees."

Musing over his last statement, she asked in a firm voice, "You watched, and did nothing to help?"

Standing and running a hand through his hair, Alex shook his head. "What was I to do, Angel? What could one man do against a dozen?"

"And what if it had been me instead of my cousin?"

His head jerked around. Her eyes were wide, not so dull now. A touch of color had returned to her lips. God, how could he answer that? Had the savages fallen on Angelique as they had Juanita, he would now be a dead man. He would have given his all, his body and soul to delay her torment for even a brief moment. But how could he confess that when she was clearly ready to condemn him for it?

Damn, but Juanita's murder would forever plague his dreams. He hadn't hated the girl, but neither had he . . . Meeting Angelique's direct gaze, he responded in a husky voice, "I had a choice to make . . . I made it."

Angelique pushed herself to her feet and slapped her open hand against his cheek. "God. That's what you have proclaimed yourself. You chose to let one die and—"

Snatching her wrist, Alex jerked her rigid little body against his. "May I remind you," he interrupted, "that had I not made that choice and had charged them with one meager gun, *you* would not have any choices whatsoever. *Querida*, that beautiful body of yours would be filling their dogs' bellies by now." He then flung her away.

Angelique stumbled slightly and might have fallen had Alex not reacted. Cursing his insensitivity, he jumped and caught both her shoulders with his hands.

Her lower lip was quivering when she at last turned her face up to his. "I—I'm dreadfully sorry." Burying her face in Alex's chest, her body wracked with sobs, she purged herself of all the horror and pain she had experienced the last few days.

Alex rocked her, thankful her stupor was crumbling, for he knew without grief's cleansing effort her wounds would never heal.

"Angelique, look at me." Catching her tear-streaked cheeks in his palms, he tilted her face up. He had the dis-

turbing need to talk to her about his dispute with Carlota.
"I'm very glad your mother survived."

"Liar," she surprised him by blurting. "You hate my
mother!"

"I never said I hated her. She's a thorn in my side . . .
hell, you *both* are, but I don't hate either one of you."
Catching the tail of his shirt, he lifted it to her nose.
"Blow." She did, then he nudged away her tears.

"Why were you following us, Alejandro?" she asked in
a shaky voice.

He thought of lying, but what good would it do? Re-
signedly, he admitted, "I was coming after you, Angel."

Angelique backed away. Could she trust such a confession? Could he be so deceiving? Pulling his shirt tighter
about her shoulders, she watched him watching her. His
face was set, his shoulders squared. The dark mat of hair
on his torso was like a shadow, and his leather breeches
appeared like a sleek outer skin, molded to every angle and
curve.

It was a certainty he could be so deceiving. He had
tricked her into his bedroom, taken advantage of her ine-
briated state, then scorned her for her weakness. He was a
soldier of fortune, proclaiming his own private war on his
grandfather, her mother, and now her. The fortune he
amassed was the pleasure he gleaned by each spiteful,
vengeful act!

To Angelique's bemusement Alex's mouth twitched and
a slow, lazy smile curled his lips. Tossing her disheveled
hair so it settled like a rusty mane about her shoulders,
Angie demanded stubbornly, "Why should I believe
you?"

"Why would I lie?" Thumbs hooked through his belt
loops, he waited. "Well?"

"Because . . . it would be the easiest way to calm a hysterical woman."

His smile grew. "Are you hysterical, Angel? Sorry, I
hadn't noticed." Angelique would have responded further,
but in an instant, Alex had stepped forward, gripped her
upper arms in his hands, and pulled her against him. Just

the feel of her barely clad curves sent havoc churning through his lower body. "You're absolutely right, sweetheart. I *do* have my ways of dealing with irrational, hysterical women. Lying, however, is not one of them. You'll find I am blatantly frank, often unfeeling, and occasionally rude, but I do *not* lie. It is a waste of effort."

Before Angelique could respond his mouth moved onto hers with a fierceness that drove the breath from her. "Brute," she forced between her teeth as he pulled away. Her eyes never leaving his moist, set mouth, she finished, "You care little that yesterday I was subjected to . . ."

He held his breath, and as her face blanched again with her memories, he caught her jaw and squeezed until her green eyes grew wide in apprehension. "What *were* you subjected to, Angel?"

"My family's murder," she forced herself to respond.

"And?" When she didn't reply, he shook her. "Did they rape you as well, Angelique?"

For a brief moment she considered lying. If she said she had been taken in that savage way, it would add to his guilt and that thought was perversely satisfying. But as she mustered her courage to speak the falsehood, his cold proclamation caused the statement to swell in her throat.

"Know that I would never hold that brutality against you, but should you confess that they hurt you in such a way, know that I will search them down and kill them. What I will do to them to avenge that act is beyond your comprehension, *querida*. But I swear to you, your honor will not suffer."

She was stunned. The man who had stolen her virginity as if she were nothing but a lark to occupy a moonlit night now heralded *his* right to vindicate *her* honor? Shoving against his granitelike chest, Angelique attempted to squirm from his hold. "Hypocrite! Are you any worthier than they?" She laughed bitterly. "You may not have forced me physically, but emotionally you raped me." Her words left him as winded as the earlier slap across his cheek. "You wooed me, wined me, and promised me—"

"I promised you nothing," he snapped.

"No, not with so many words, but your kisses implied a great deal. You took advantage of my needs and a weakened heart that would have responded with nothing short of love, and when I offered it, you twisted it from my bosom and flung it in my face! Oooh, you are the most insufferable pig I have ever encountered and I rue the day I ever laid eyes on you!"

Anger flooded his face until it radiated with heat and a fine film of perspiration. His jaw locked, he gritted as he shook her again, "You didn't answer my question."

"Does it matter?"

"Hell yes, it matters. You're mine, dammit, and I won't allow what is mine to be used by another man!"

The roar of his voice had escalated until his final words were shouted with the force of a full-scale storm, and as if to prove his point, he jerked her against him once more and silenced her outrage with his mouth. His tongue slipped between her lips, and though she clenched her teeth in refusal, he explored the soft outer recesses, stroking, dipping, drawing her lips between his until she was certain he would consume her completely.

Angelique longed to claw his face, for it was far too handsome. A man with such appeal should not be so shamelessly wicked. She yearned to beat his chest, for she was certain it would echo with emptiness. Whatever tragedy had shattered his heart must surely have replaced it with a rock, for the man was far too unfeeling to be human. And yet . . .

Neither Angelique nor Alex noticed the sudden swirling need that like a gust of turbulent wind lifted their anger and tossed it to the far corners of their memories. His head still lowered over hers, Alejandro pulled away from her long enough to murmur, "My God, Angel, don't force me to confess that the thought of you being used by another drove me out of my mind. Yes, I would go now and kill them, for my own sanity's sake. And if that would make amends . . ."

Was he about to apologize for his former behavior toward her? Was Alejandro de Bastitas actually capable of that? Angelique waited. She stared into his blue eyes, watching her own reflection, and she felt as if he were fencing with some inner turmoil that could wound him far more than any simple lance she could hurl.

The need to believe that he cared was too much to bear at that moment. Without thinking, knowing only that she needed some strength to keep her from melting to the floor, Angelique moved against Alex again. Wrapping her arms about his waist she buried her face against his chest and began weeping.

Alex tensed, knowing if he allowed her to she would crumble that wall of indifference he had built so stalwartly about his heart the last year. Dammit, he'd bared his soul once for a woman, but given the first opportunity she had turned to another. He would not let it happen again.

Angelique didn't notice that as she wept against Alex's chest, he did not bother to offer a comforting word, or the strength of his embracing arms. She was stunned as he suddenly shoved her away, his face dark and almost forbidding, and growled, "Just stay the hell away from me. Save your tears for your mother's bosom and leave my heart alone." He spun on his heel and left her crying like a child in the middle of the floor.

# TEN

It took the first blast of bracing wind against his naked skin to snap Alex from his anger. Shoving his hands in his pockets and hunkering his shoulders against the cold, he allowed his long stride to separate him from the quiet whimpering inside the house.

Perhaps he shouldn't have been so harsh, but he'd be damned if he'd let a woman manipulate him with her tears! His wife had taught him how craftily they could be used. She had sniveled and pouted him into a marriage proposal before he was absolutely certain it was what he wanted. It was certainly what *she* had wanted. It granted her respectability and the leverage to sneak in and out of her lover's bed whenever it pleased her most. Then the first time he had questioned her on her mysterious disappearances, Pamela had rolled those huge brown eyes at him, and as they spilled their crocodile tears he had melted into a pool of regret.

No more! By damn he would *not* be duped again!

Kicking open the barn door, Alex strode to the far side of the building where his horse waited skittishly in the shadows. But instead of soothing the nervous animal, he twirled and with all the force he could muster drove his fist into the wall. He was angry now, not because of Angelique's emotional outbreak, but because he realized he *had* been moved by her crying. And he was angry because he wanted nothing more than to return to that house, throw her to the mattress, and spend the next twenty-four hours making wild, passionate love to her. He longed to kiss away her tears, her bruises, and her horrifying memories of the last two days and replace them with the glorious release they had shared that blissful night before her departure.

Dammit, but there had been a time in those hours between midnight and dawn that he had forgotten that his seduction had been an act of revenge. He had forgotten Carlota DuHon and what she represented. Instead, his nostrils had been filled with Angelique's intoxicating scent. His mouth had tasted the sweetest lips and breasts he could ever call to mind, and his manhood had thrust into the softest, most agonizingly beautiful warmth he'd experienced since he sampled his first woman at an ignorant, innocent fifteen years of age.

Rubbing his knuckles, Alex sank against the wall and closed his eyes. He was toppling head over heels for Angelique DuHon and he was helpless to stop the fall. She was like quicksand. The harder he fought her the deeper he sank.

And that would never do. She represented everything he had hated. And without her knowing, she hated him as well. He couldn't count on Carlota to keep her mouth closed. The bitch would bide her time, and like a coiled snake strike when he least expected it. She wouldn't bother to rattle. She'd just hit where it hurt him the most.

"Alexander?"

Snapping alert, he pivoted toward the door. Her slender body was silhouetted against the pale shaft of morning light spilling onto the muddied floor. "What the hell are you doing out here?" he demanded.

Venturing farther into the stables, she responded, "I was afraid. Please don't leave me alone like that again."

Alex sensed, by the proud tilt of her chin, that her re-

quest had not been an easy one. Leaning again against the
rough support beam at his back, he allowed his eyes to
leisurely explore her scantily attired frame. His white shirt
fell to just above her knees. Its shoulders drooped well
down her arms, and should she have bent forward, the
slashing collar would easily have revealed her firm young
breasts. The sun reflected from her hair in shafts of red-
gold from the crown of her head to the twisted, tangled
curls flirting against her hips.

Testing her footing in the slippery muck, Angelique
blinked hard while her eyes became accustomed to the
darker interior. Trying to smile, she asked, "Are we leaving now?"

"No," came his terse reply.

"When?"

"When I'm good and ready."

"But my mother is no doubt frantic and—"

"I don't give one little damn about your mother." Using
his shoulder, he pushed himself upright. Feet braced apart
and hands on his hips, Alex smiled. "Perhaps I'll refuse
to take you back. I don't like your mother and would sure
as hell hate to see you turn out like her. I think I would
do you a great justice by putting as many miles as possible
between you."

Angelique covered her ears. "Stop it; I will not hear you
talk about my mother like that!" She turned, but then he
was beside her, forcing her into his arms. "Let me go!"

Alex raised his hand and caught her wrist before she
could slap him. "If you hit me again, you little *bruja*, I'll
find those damn Comanche and dump you in their laps."

"You're hurting me," she managed in a calmer voice.

"Am I? So sorry, love." His free hand plunging into
her hair, Alex jerked her head back until she whimpered.
Her eyes were wide, frightened, and their innocence was
like an aphrodisiac to the growing need gnawing at his gut.
"So sorry," he muttered again . . . just before his mouth
smothered hers.

Angelique was aghast at his behavior. Removing his fingers from her hair, he openly fondled her breasts with his

free hand. Even through his shirt the heat of his fingers and palm was like a brand against her damp, shivering skin.

Alex felt her shudder, and as she became almost pliable in his arms he released the excruciating grip on her wrist. He was mad with wanting her, and to his own amazement, he realized he wanted her to feel the same for him.

Pulling from her swollen mouth, he searched her face. "Kiss me, Angelique. I know you can. You have."

"I think I should die first." Stepping back, Angelique discounted the roiling emotion in her breast as anger, complete mortification over his heathenish behavior. "I—I think I would prefer a Comanche's disgusting assault to yours, Senor de Bastitas. At least he is honest in his intentions."

Alex stiffened. Face dark and his eyes cold as ice, he snarled softly, "Honesty? Is that what it will take to thaw your heart, *querida?* Then so be it."

Hands twisted into the linen material of the shirt, and in one quick motion, rent it in two. Angelique staggered backward, stumbling, sliding in the mud. Stunned and disbelieving, her voice quivering in alarm, she wavered, "Animal! You *are* no better than they. Now I demand that you stop this and return me to my mother this moment!"

"When I'm finished." He advanced. Long, brown fingers pulled at his belt. "You want honesty, then you shall have it. I want you, senorita. It is as simple as that. I want you and before we leave here I will have you, with or without your consent. How is *that* for honesty?"

Angelique glanced frantically about the gloomy room. "Stay away from me. I—I will kill you if you lay one hand—"

"I plan to lay more than a hand," he drawled.

Her breast heaving, Angelique took several steps backward. She was certain to faint at any moment. Alejandro de Bastitas was even worse than she had first believed. On top of being a debaucher, he was a madman!

His last stride was more of a lunge, and to Angelique's horror she found herself plucked from the ground, both her

arms pinned to her side as his enveloped her completely.
She kicked at his shins and knees. She wiggled and attempted to bite his ear, almost succeeding before he buried
his hands in her hair, dropped her to her feet, then flung
her to the far corner of the stable.

The impact stunned her and, struggling, she attempted
to regain her breath. She thought of surrendering meekly.
It would be far less painful, but that would give Alejandro
cause to gloat. No, she would fight him! He would not use
her heart and break it again. Ever!

Like a wildcat, she faced him. Alex's eyes narrowed
over her inflamed cheeks, the transparent shirt that was
hiked nearly to the tops of her thighs, the same thighs that
were separated and thrashing to find some hold in the mud.
If he had harbored any second thoughts on taking her, they
vanished the moment she slipped and sprawled completely
on her back. The shirt fell open as though she were purposely tempting him.

Angelique's eyes widened as he approached, and for a
brief moment, as his arms extended and plucked her from
the mud, she actually believed he had reconsidered his
plan. Too late, and to her horror, she realized that was not
the case as he dropped her unceremoniously onto a stack
of dry hay.

With no hesitation Alex fell upon her. His belt and buttons bit into her thighs, and responding to the discomfort
she opened them farther. He was bracing himself on outstretched arms, so she had little trouble in beating his chest
and shoulders with her fists. Then his weight dropped onto
her completely, and as he buried his face against her throat,
he thrust inside her with a fierce driving motion that caught
her off guard.

"Oh God!" she cried out. Her head thrashed back and
forth as she attempted to avoid his searching mouth. And
as he captured her, his tongue matching the sensual, rhythmic thrust of his body into hers, she bucked and whimpered. But to her horror, Angelique realized her vain
attempts to escape and scream were far from sincere. Instead she was matching each motion, lifting her legs

around his waist, wanting him deeper, exalting in his buried heat, the warm shaft of living flesh that was driving her out of her mind with need.

"God, yes," he repeated in a slurred voice, for he was intoxicated with her arousal. Nestling his mouth to her ear, he groaned, "Come with me, Angel, quickly! Ah, God, you're a witch. Too beautiful to be real and too hot to be human."

Angelique closed her eyes, allowing his deep, crooning voice to release that gate of quicksilver heat through her heart, mind, and body. Arching against him, she offered to his passioned mouth the tips of her aching breasts, and as he took them and pulled the engorged peaks with his lips and tongue that delicious fervor slid through her stomach to her legs and caught fire.

It was torment—a beautiful excruciating pain that suffused their entwined blended bodies in its molten embrace. Each meeting was the scaling of that mystical peak of completion, and for both that momentary death that would rock their world and send them spiraling through heaven's door.

They were close. Angelique could sense it. It was grating low and breathy in his chest. He was swelling inside her and his lean, hard frame was like granite on hers. Her nostrils were filled with his salty, musky scent that was like an erotic liquor to her senses. She touched her tongue to the moist skin behind his ear and heard him gasp.

"Don't," he hissed. "Don't unless you desire to end this now."

She turned her head further and met his mouth. Their faces were wet, slippery, and he filled her mouth with his tongue and she sucked it. Alex was suffocating, and for a moment he paused, pulled his head away and threw it back, shivering as her nails dug into the flesh of his buttocks, hips, and ribs. Angelique was moving against him now, abandonedly, unashamedly, giving her all to him.

The shared moment was a communion beyond limit. It lifted them both, brought them together in a storm of such shattering fulfillment they each cried out from the painful, wondrous magic. And with that final, exquisite release,

Alex cradled her in his arms and rolled to his back. Neither spoke, or needed to.

Angelique nestled against his shoulder, confused and troubled that Alejandro could so forcefully overcome her better judgment. Then she heard it. Her eyes wide, she scrambled to pull the remnants of Alex's shirt around her breasts. "Alexander, there is someone here!"

He heard it then: an approaching horse. "Damn!" Easing from the soft bed of hay to his feet, Alejandro righted his clothing. He met Tomas at the door.

The younger man looked from his brother to the cowering girl hidden within the gloomy shadows of the barn. Ignoring Alex completely, Tomas hurried to Angelique's side, pulled his slicker from his back and, stooping beside her shaking body, draped her shoulders with the heavy coat. By the look on both her and Alex's faces, he could only imagine what had gone on just moments before his arrival. And he wasn't certain she was overly pleased about it. "Has he hurt you?" he asked softly.

With a muttered oath, Alex grabbed Angelique's arm and jerked her to her feet. "Cry rape, sweetheart, and I will call you a liar. Do not forget there are several servants who can attest that you once climbed quite freely into my bed."

Tomas couldn't quite make out his brother's hoarsely whispered words, but he watched Angelique pale and her eyes grow wide with disbelief. She was biting her lip when she faced him.

"I'm not hurt," she lied. But she was. Alex was forcing her to admit that she had acted wantonly, that she had surrendered totally to his assault instead of fighting him. He was forcing her to admit to Tomas that she was his whore.

Tomas's blue eyes shifted reluctantly to his brother. "Juanita?"

"Dead."

Alex spun and, leaving Angelique to Tomas, strode to the door. As he stepped into the sunlight he was met by Kaintock McGuire.

The burly man's face brightened in relief. "Whoo-wee, am I glad to see you!" He clapped Alex on both shoulders, just as he spotted Tomas and Angelique. Stepping back, he regarded his friend's rigid frame. "If I's you, amigo, I'd face north. It might cool you down some 'fore grandpappy arrives, if you know what I mean . . . and I think you do."

In that moment a party of some fifteen men rounded the barn on their horses. Carlos de Bastitas was in the lead.

"Alejandro!"

Alex groaned.

Carlos slid from his mount. "Alejandro, you are safe!"

"Disappointed?"

Gray brows plunging between his eyes, the old man scoffed, "Fool, of course not. Where is Juanita?"

His stomach knotted because Carlos had not bothered to ask about Angelique's welfare. "Juanita is dead!" he fired angrily.

Lips thinning, Carlos raised an unsteady hand toward the girl supported by Tomas's arm. "And how do you explain her? How very conveniently you rid yourselves of a problem—"

McGuire leaped and locked his arms about Alex's chest before he could lunge toward his grandfather. "Calm down," he whispered into the Spaniard's ear. "Calm down, friend. We've seen enough murder the last few days to tide us over nicely, thank you."

Totally unperturbed by his grandson's intense anger, Carlos demanded, "Where is her body?"

"Eagle Pass."

Facing his companions, Carlos barked, "Decide between you who will retrieve the girl's remains. Alejandro, you will attend them."

There was an uncomfortable quiet before Tomas stated, "Grandfather, Alex has been days without food or rest."

"Silence unless you wish to go with him!" Bastitas chuckled. "I thought so. You are too much a coward to face the reality of death."

Weariness now pounding against his skull, Alex dropped his head between his shoulders. It would do no good to argue. This was his grandfather's punishment for surviving. Perhaps his own as well. "My horse is lame," was his tired response.

"Manuel!" The horseman flanked his mare and moved to Carlos's side. "Give my grandson your animal. You will ride double with one of the other vaqueros."

"*Sí*, senor." Manuel jumped from the saddle and handed Alex the reins.

"My undying gratitude," he stated blandly.

In disbelief and shock, Angelique watched as Alex threw his leg over the animal's back. Turning to Tomas she numbly said, "With no shirt he will catch his death of cold."

"You are right, senorita." Running to his saddlebags, he withdrew a dry flannel shirt, then tossed it to Alex. "The lady is worried about you," he explained quietly.

"Is she?" Sapphire eyes lifted to green, and as a young man offered him his retrieved gunbelt Alejandro smiled and draped it across his shoulder. "Give *the lady* my heartfelt gratitude."

"I will."

"And Tomas." Alex's brother pivoted to face him again. "Take care how you hold her."

The grin slid from Tomas's face. "My brother?"

"Her ribs. They're bruised."

Relaxing, Tomas nodded. "I'll remember."

Refusing to look again toward Angelique, Alejandro de Bastitas directed his horse south. He had a hell of a long ride back to Eagle Pass.

Before the search party began their grueling trip back to San Antonio, Tomas got coffee and food for Angelique. He was at her side constantly, fetching her meal, warming her coffee, offering friendship, a smile, and a shoulder to lean on, if she needed it. She might have accepted his offer to rest and sleep awhile longer, but she was anxious to return to San Antonio. Carlota would be out of her mind with worry, and Angelique knew her mother would be suffering greatly over her family's death.

It was nearly noon before they began their journey. Tomas eased Angelique gently onto his horse, then swung up behind her. His words were soft against her ear as he whispered, "My brother warned me to be gentle with you."

Her head turned slightly. "Did he?"

"*Sí*. He mentioned your ribs."

"Oh."

He sensed her disappointment. "Actually I believed him to be warning me, casually of course, to keep my hands to myself." His arm slid about her waist. "I will do my best, but it won't be easy."

Light laughter caused Angelique's ribs to ache. "Tomas, if I didn't know you loved Anna I'd think you were flirting with me."

He tipped his head, and the chuckle was more like a rumble inside his chest. "I could not hope to compete with Alejandro in affairs of the heart. He was always immensely popular with the senoritas about the area."

"And who is to say there is any reason for competition?"

Tomas's burst of laughter drew several quizzical glances from the surrounding vaqueros. "My dear Miss DuHon, remember that I grew up with my brother. I know him as well as, if not better than, he knows himself. From the moment I watched you dance together, I realized the heart in his breast was no longer his."

"He has a very odd way of displaying his affection," she murmured as she recalled the angry yet passionate mating of their bodies.

Tomas rested his cheek against her head. Her earlier mention of Anna brought a flicker of guilt to his heart. Since he'd first set eyes on Angelique, Anna had become less and less important to him. Odd that at one time he'd been so certain . . .

Forcing his mind to the problem at hand, he continued, "It was very gallant of you to lie for Alex. I know he hurt you earlier, perhaps not intentionally, but you must know, senorita, that my brother is hard. He's grown callous beneath my grandfather's authority and knows little of tenderness. But do not cower from him. It will take a stern and patient hand to bring him to heel, and he may bite on occasion. Know that it is not intentional, but instinctual. He will be wary of being hurt again.''

Relaxing against Tomas's lean frame, Angelique closed her eyes. She was weary. And she hurt. But she didn't want to cry, not on a stranger's shoulder. She must be strong for her mother's sake. She would show the world she could cope with her loss, her pain. Her mother had not cried when her husband was murdered. Certainly she had grieved—quietly and alone at DuHon Fields—but in the company of others she had held her chin up with poise and determination. Carlota had been strong while Angelique had wept in the sanctuary of her room.

Not this time.

As Angelique's weight grew heavy, and her head and shoulders drooped against his chest, Tomas realized she had finally surrendered to sleep. His arm tightened. His hand slipped. Even through the coarse material of his slicker he could detect the slow throbbing of her heart, and the swelling underside of her breast.

His loins aching with fullness, Tomas felt ashamed. Why couldn't Alejandro have been satisfied with poor simpering Juanita? Then maybe, just maybe he would have had a chance. No. No point in even thinking about it. From the moment Angelique laid eyes on Alex, her soul was his.

There was something women found tremendously desirable about Alejandro. Perhaps it was the fire or strength of character that he himself lacked. Someday he would find the courage to fight for a cause, a belief, or just for the hell of trying. But it wouldn't be over a woman. Not this woman.

She was already lost.

# ELEVEN

The leaves of the pecan and oak trees had begun to change, dotting the rolling hills with bright splashes of gold, orange, and yellow. The morning briskness was being warmed away by the hazy sun. It was a day for picnicking on Widow's Peak above the Mississippi River, just where DuHon Fields ended and the neighboring plantation, Willow Grove, began. It was a day for lounging under cypress trees, sipping lemonade, and fantasizing of marrying a tall, dark, handsome stranger.

It was not a day to recall death, or to weep for the dead. Unfortunately, Angelique DuHon had little choice.

The bells of the hacienda announced the weary group's arrival. Servants hustled to open the front gates. As Carlos stopped his horse before the front entrance, a dark-skinned mestizo ran to snatch up the animal's reins.

The door of the house flew open.

"Angelique!"

Tomas gently slid his passenger to the ground. She ran with open arms to her mother.

"*Madre de Dios*, you are alive. My baby is alive!" Carlota embraced her daughter with bearlike strength. As she rocked her, brown eyes searched the group for Juanita's face. "Angelique, your cousin?"

Angelique couldn't speak. She responded only by shaking her head.

"For the love of God, how did you escape?"

"Alexander," she managed to whisper.

Her mother tensed.

As Angelique lifted her head from Carlota's shoulder, she noticed Isabella standing in the doorway. Her fingers were knotted together with worry. Her face was pale. It seemed she had aged a decade in the last three days.

As Carlota opened her arms, Angelique surprised her mother by hurrying up the paved path to Isabella's side. There was a moment's hesitation before she melted against the older woman's bosom.

"My child," Isabella murmured in her ear. "I prayed for your safe return. I am glad God has ears for an old woman's pleas, and an eye for her tears. Tell me. Are you unharmed?" As Angelique nodded the woman caught her chin and tipped her face. A shaky hand brushed the hair across her shoulder. "It has not been easy. I see this and know you have suffered. Juanita is dead?"

"Yes."

"And . . . my grandson?"

"He was well when he left me. He has returned to Eagle Pass for my cousin's body."

"By my husband's command?"

"Yes."

Angelique felt a brief shudder pass through her friend's frail body. Her warm brown eyes turned hard. "Then we will continue to pray. The two of us."

"*Sí, señora*. The two of us."

As Carlota approached, Isabella smiled. "Come. We will see to your injuries, then you will rest. Know that from this moment on you are at home, and are welcome to stay as long as it pleases you."

Twirling toward her mother, Angelique asked, "What of Bernice?"

"*La patrona* has already sent men to escort Bernice to

San Antonio. She should arrive tomorrow night at the latest.''

Relieved, Angelique followed her mother and Isabella into the house.

Tomas de Bastitas refilled his glass with brandy, unaware that his grandmother had entered the room. She stood in the doorway, watching as he threw his head back and quaffed the potent drink. He then slammed the empty crystal to the table.

"You are angry."

"Yes," he said, not at all surprised by her presence.

"Why?"

"I think sometimes my grandfather wishes to see us all dead. Why would he send Alejandro back to fetch Juanita's body if that were not the case?"

Lifting her skirt slightly, she floated to the chair before the hearth. "It is his way of denying love, Tomas. I'm certain he was relieved to find your brother alive."

"You wouldn't know it. He actually accused Alex and Angelique of purposely leaving Juanita to the savages."

Ignoring the jab in her heart, Isabella studied her grandson's face. She got the distinct impression he was upset for reasons other than Carlos's cruelty toward Alejandro. "Is it the girl?" she asked bluntly.

"What?"

"Angelique. Are you taken with her?"

Tomas's laughter was a harsh, brittle sound. "I don't wish to see her hurt."

"Would Alejandro hurt her?"

He nodded. "I make his excuses, but I fear at times that he is too much like Carlos."

Eyes narrowed in speculation, Isabella pointed to the opposite chair. Tomas eased into it and closed his eyes. The liquor was sluggishly pounding behind his lids. His tongue felt suddenly lazy.

"Do you know something?" she asked him. "Has he done anything I might frown upon?"

"Perhaps," he said slowly, for it was an effort to speak.

"What?"

"I think he might have ... When I happened on them they ..." Eyes rolled as he frowned. He couldn't shake the picture of Angelique, her hair wild and twisted about her shoulders and breasts. Her face was hot with color, her lips moist, parted and swollen. "She seemed ... upset."

"He forced her?"

"I can't be certain."

The black mantilla stationed to Isabella's gray head with a jeweled comb fluttered slightly as she stood and began pacing. She had always taken pride in Alejandro, knew him as well as her own son, cherished him as closely. But the young widower who had returned from New Orleans was a mystery. In the beginning, his grief had been understandable. His wife, pregnant with another man's child, had killed herself when learning of her lover's death by her husband's hand. Alex had a right to be bitter, but why suddenly was he so intent on centering his anger on Angelique DuHon and her mother?

"She's in love with him, you know," came Tomas's slurred remark.

"I know."

"Can you imagine the old man's face should he learn that the two of them—"

"He will not learn. Not yet. But in time. And then he will have little choice but to accept it."

Soft laughter shook Tomas's shoulders as he stretched his legs and crossed them. "That, my dear grandmother, will be the day hell freezes over."

"Perhaps," she responded. "Perhaps."

By dusk the breezes had again shifted to the north. Rain clouds were gathering low against the horizon, ushering in a premature nightfall. Angelique sat by her window, staring toward the hills. Her fingers plucked at a black lace handkerchief, then smoothed the taffeta skirt of a matching color.

Black again. Mourning again. Death again. She yearned to scream with it all.

The door opened and closed behind her. "Why are you not resting?" Carlota asked quietly.

Angelique shrugged. "No reason, I suppose."

"Are you watching for him?"

Angelique turned to stare at her mother without really seeing.

"Angelique." Carlota tenderly traced the bruise across her daughter's cheek. "Put him out of your mind. Do you not realize that this is all his fault? Did I not tell you how deceitful and arrogant he was? The man hasn't an honest hair on his head and—"

"Stop." Angelique faced her mother squarely. "Alejandro saved my life. Can you not afford him a simple grateful word for doing so?"

"Yes, for that alone he has my gratitude. But I cannot forget that it is because of him that my family is dead. I hope by dawn the top of his head is residing with Francesca's and—"

Angelique covered her ears and, jumping to her feet, moved from her mother's cruel words. Don't say it! she inwardly pleaded. Don't think it! She was ill with the thought that possibly, just possibly, he might never return. She was aware of his own thoughts, indeed his own guilt over Juanita. It would be the simplest act in the world to purposely ride into an ambush. It would end his suffering, his memories.

Determinedly, she faced her mother. "I demand to know why you dislike Alexander so."

Startled, Carlota looked away. "I told you. In New Orleans his name was synonymous with gambling, drinking, and womanizing. He kept a dozen mistresses at a time and flaunted them every chance he got. Rumor has it that not one week after his marriage to that . . . to Pamela Reynolds he was seen with other women. Mamas would hide their daughters when he walked down the street. No doubt he notched his bedposts each time he stole their virginity. It is no wonder his wife—"

"He must have loved her. Why else would he have married her, especially if he was as immoral as you claim."

"Who knows, my pet," Carlota answered in a tight voice. "Who knows why men act the way they do? Perhaps it is because they harbor the soul of the devil in their hearts."

Her face sad, Angelique responded, "Not Papa."

"No, of course not. Not your papa."

Carlota swept from the room. Angelique remained where her mother had left her, staring at the door, caught someplace between heaven and hell and thrashing in indecision. How could she confess to her parent that she was in love with Alejandro de Bastitas? She wasn't even certain of it herself. There could be a dozen reasons why her heart leaped to her throat each time he entered a room. The man could be terrifying. One could never be certain what would slip between those lips. Oaths? Sarcasm? Love songs? She had experienced them all.

How could one man be so damnably inconsistent? How could he rail at her one moment, proclaiming that his heart was to be left alone, then the next virtually plead with her, in his own way, to love him? Could it be that Alejandro de Bastitas, the all-powerful and brave soldier of wars and women, was actually ... frightened ... of her?

Her mouth turned under, and with a flip of her skirt Angelique marched again to the window. How foolish! Alejandro de Bastitas was afraid of nothing. He had faced four hundred Mexican soldiers and escaped unscathed. He had rescued her from the Comanche when he might have returned to San Antonio for help. He certainly *wasn't* afraid of dying. But love? Ah, love was a completely different matter.

That thought gave her a start. In love indeed! Alejandro de Bastitas was in love with no one but himself. Forcing herself to recall the calculating way he had lured her into his room and ravished her, and acted the next morning as if he couldn't even recall her name, Angelique set her jaw and shook her head. No, her mother was right. Alexander was a man twisted up inside with hate, bitterness, and pain. She must learn from her mistakes, put him behind her, and begin again.

If she could.

As midnight came and went with no sign of Alex, she tossed and twisted in her bed, dreaming of death and torture. His face pirouetted before her mind's eye each time she drifted to sleep, and more than once she bolted upright, covering her ears against Juanita's echoing screams. Some time before dawn she realized it would do no good to fight it. The sights and sounds would never leave her, so she must accept them or they would drive her insane. That relieved her torment little, but at least she slept.

It was noon before she awoke. Forcing her swollen lids open, Angelique focused on the tray of food and chocolate, now grown cold at her bedside. She was stiff and sore, and ached between her thighs. Acknowledging that brought a hot flush to her cheeks.

Staring at the ceiling, she strained for any noise. There was nothing. Then, turning her head, she frowned toward the mirror. Some time during the morning her mother had entered and draped the glass in black, a sign of mourning. Every time she peered at her reflection she would be reminded of her family's death, and in turn Alejandro. As if she needed any reminder.

After slipping from the bed, Angelique splashed her face with water. It was cool, and despite the fact she had worn her heaviest flannel nightgown to bed, she shivered. Rummaging through her trunks and locating a gown of light blue wool, she stripped off her nightgown, sponged her arms and legs, pulled on her underclothes—chemise, stockings, and drawers—then her dress.

Her mother wouldn't be pleased. Carlota would expect her to garb herself in the black taffeta again. And she would later. But now she wanted no reminders of her nightmare. She wanted the wind in her face, hoping it would cleanse her, temporarily replace the dull ache she was feeling in her veins. She didn't *want* to grieve. She yearned to feel like an eighteen-year-old again. But most of all she wanted . . .

Pulling open the French doors, she stepped onto the balcony. The sun that had seemed so warm from the shelter of her room was disturbingly cold—hardly comforting. But catching her breath and pulling a heavy wool shawl trimmed with silk fringe closer about her shoulders, she ventured into the brisk day.

"He's not back."

She froze.

Tomas hesitated at the top of the stairs before approaching. His face was pinched, his mouth set. Leaning against the balustrade, he folded his arms across his chest. "My grandfather has sent out another search party. Word came this morning that a farm just miles from Eagle Pass was raided. Seems the Comanche are on one hell of a rampage. I fear they're taking advantage of the unrest with the Mexicans to do their worst."

The Mexicans. She had totally forgotten about them. "Is the Alamo still under siege?" she asked.

"No change there. Cos will wait until the bitter end to surrender."

"Then what?"

Tomas shrugged and looked off. "It won't be an end. Santa Anna is certain to retaliate."

"Which means?"

"Someone is certain to die."

She took a deep breath. "I miss my home. It was safe and warm. I was happy there."

Tomas studied her carefully. She looked so beautiful, so wistful. Her face was still slightly swollen, but nothing could disguise the porcelain quality of her skin.

Her hair had been washed the night before. It was soft and floated about her shoulders in luxurious natural curls and waves. The breeze lifted it occasionally, twisted it about her face, and feathered it about her breasts. Tomas found himself recalling how it had felt against his cheek that day before. He remembered her heartbeat beneath his palm, the easy rise and fall of her breathing . . .

Angelique was aware that Tomas was staring. He was wearing a look that made her think he was about to sweep her into his arms and kiss her. It was a mixture of fear and yearning, and for a brief moment she wondered what it would be like to kiss Tomas de Bastitas. She sensed he would be far less passionate than his brother. Not so forceful. Perhaps timid. Tomas didn't radiate that masculine confidence, and it occurred to her that had it been Alejandro who had approached her those moments ago, she would have already found the need to slap his face or scream for help.

He surprised her by asking, "Would you care to walk?"

Tomas caught her arm and hooked it through the crook of his elbow. She smiled, then they descended the stairs.

The patio was empty, save for a number of crisp dancing leaves. They scattered about the hem of her dress before clustering against a far adobe wall. Ducking beneath the branches of the overhanging grapevine, she and Tomas stepped onto the hacienda's manicured lawns. It seemed unnaturally quiet. Where were the men, women, and children who made up this bustling village?

"The people will remain inside for several days," Tomas responded to her unvoiced query. "It is out of respect for you and your mother that they do so."

"That is most kind of them."

"You have already received guests. Senor Musquiz and his wife dropped by this morning. They will call again."

Her face warmed as Angelique thought of facing these strangers. They would view her as a curiosity. Something to stare at and wonder about. Not many white women who were kidnapped by Indians lived to talk about it. No doubt the gossipmongers would be thirsting for every morsel of news she might provide them about her harrowing adventure.

Tomas squeezed her hand reassuringly. "I have already informed them that my brother saved you before anything too unseemly happened . . . I assume he did?"

"Yes."

"Good for him," he answered in a relieved voice.

They continued on silently, comfortably. Tomas's friendship was a godsend to Angelique. He took the burden of grief from her small shoulders, offered her the brace of a comforting arm and warm smile. If she wanted to cry, she could. He wasn't afraid of tears. Not like Alex. In that sense Tomas was much braver than his brother.

But Tomas had not been so deeply wounded by a woman.

Carlos de Bastitas stood at the window, his eyes focused on the couple walking arm and arm in the distance. "She will be trouble," he stated almost to himself.

Isabella looked up from her sewing. "Who do you mean, my husband?"

"That Creole wench yonder. She has both our grandsons sniffing about her skirts like mongrels around a bitch in heat."

She put her needlework aside. "Has it ever occurred to you that should you accept a minuscule portion of their lives they might respond by pleasing you?"

"What's that got to do with that woman?"

"Leave them alone, Carlos. Should you badger Alejandro he will do exactly what displeases you most."

Turning his back to the window, he shuffled to his chair. "Are you aware that Carlota DuHon and Alejandro were once lovers?"

Isabella leveled surprised brown eyes on her husband. "How do you know this?" she asked in a controlled voice.

Carlos flipped a hand. "I confronted her with it. Why else should there be such open hostility between them? He used her for a while, tired of her, then disposed of her. Now she is hurt and angry."

"Why should he be any different than his grandfather?" Carlos looked away as Isabella sat back in her chair. "Did she admit it?" she finally asked.

"She did not deny it."

"But did she admit it?"

"No."

"Then I must assume she found your query too asinine to even consider."

Carlos studied his cane, smoothed the tips of his well manicured fingers over the crooked brace of silver and gold. They had once been strong fingers, cruel on occasion, but they had been known to love with a gentle touch. But that had been many years ago.

"There is something," he whispered. "Something there between them. I wonder . . ."

For a while Angelique actually forgot she was in mourning. Tomas was quite the storyteller and entertained her with tales of his and Alex's childhood.

"Yes, Alex was always the troublemaker," he expounded. "He would sneak out of the house and tie bells on the bull's tail just before a corrida. By the time the blasted animal ran in the ring it was already so frothing mad the paseo could do nothing with it!"

Her head fell back in laughter. "You must stop this, Tomas. I am to be grieving and you are making me laugh harder than I have in years. You should be ashamed!"

"Once my grandfather gave this huge fiesta. All the *gentes de razón* in the area were invited—political figures, church officials, anyone who was anybody came. For weeks Carlos planned and preened. There were braziers placed about the grounds and cattle and sheep were slaughtered for the feast. The night before the party Alex sneaked from his bed and buried great amounts of dried cow dung beneath their kindling. I will leave it to your imagination what happened when the fires were stoked. On top of smelling to high heaven, can you imagine the flavor it gave to the meat?"

"Stop this!" she pleaded, for her sides were aching.

"Carlos ordered my father to punish Alex, but he couldn't bring himself to do it. Instead, he jerked Alex up and carried him behind the barn and *both* fell to the ground laughing."

"I don't believe you!" Angelique gasped between breaths.

Blue eyes wide and his face boasting a devilish smile, Tomas bantered, "But you must! Every word of it is true. Ask Carlos, or better yet, my grandmother. After the incident, and until Alex was grown, my grandfather would lock him in his room before a fiesta. And when he was released, it was only in the company of guards who kept him in sight at all times.''

"And did you never play the mischiefmaker?"

"Only once," he responded in a lower voice. Dipping his dark head to her ear, he added, "I once hid a tarantula in Carlos's covered chamberpot. When he removed the lid the spider jumped right in his face.''

"You're teasing!"

"No. Of course Alex was blamed. Which, if my grandfather had stopped to consider, was ridiculous. If there is anything my brother *is* afraid of, it's spiders. He would sleep with a snake, but should a spider wiggle a leg his direction he is certain to pass out completely.''

"And did your grandfather never learn the truth?"

Leaning against the broad base of a pecan tree, Tomas looked away. His face more solemn, he shook his head. "My brother never denied doing it. He knew it was I, but preferred that I didn't feel the bite of Carlos's anger. Alex was always very protective of me, in that sense.'' Tomas surprised Angelique by catching her hands in his and placing them against his chest. "I shall never forget the beating he took for my prank. I am ashamed to say that I watched from a distance, but never said a word. I often wonder if my grandfather suspected the truth, and knew that watching Alex receive the lashing was a far worse punishment for me than being whipped myself.''

Her green eyes narrowed in speculation as she asked, "Your grandfather uses a crop?"

"It has a horrible way of slicing the skin, leaving razor thin stripes wherever it cuts.'' Tomas shuddered. "It is quite uncomfortable.''

Angelique pictured the angry welts she'd seen across Alexander's torso the morning before, and Isabella's proclamation that he would be flogged as punishment for his behavior toward the Sanchezes. She looked up, and though Tomas's eyes were drowning in hers, she got the impression he wasn't seeing *her* at all.

Tomas squeezed her fingers. "God, Angelique, if anything happened . . . *Dios mio*, I hope he is not dead.''

''Perish the thought, little brother.''

Angelique and Tomas twirled to find Alejandro standing just off the path, hidden partially by a drooping willow. Alex pushed aside the curtain of green and moved toward them. Tomas dropped Angie's hands and strode for his brother.

''Alejandro, what a relief it is to see you!'' Tomas threw open his arms and closed them about Alex's shoulders.

Alex focused one unrelenting gaze on Angelique as he returned the embrace. ''Am I interrupting?'' he asked in a smooth voice.

The insinuation stung Angelique, but Tomas failed to notice. ''Of course not. We've been out of our minds with worry. Have you just returned?''

''Moments ago.''

''Let me look at you.'' Tomas moved to arms' length. ''You've had one hell of a time, Alex, and look it. Shall I have Delores see to a bath and food?''

''Please.''

Facing Angelique, Tomas bestowed upon her a grin that brought hot color to her face. ''Then I shall leave you two alone. I'm certain you have a great deal to discuss.'' He caught her hand and raised it to his lips. ''Until later, Angelique.'' Pivoting on his heel, he was gone.

# TWELVE

"A very touching scene, my dear."

A sudden gust of wind billowed Angelique's skirts and lifted her hair. She didn't notice; she was too busy confronting Alejandro's accusatory stare.

"Your meaning," she demanded in a stony voice.

"Meaning you're not out of my sight for twenty-four hours before you're attempting to seduce my brother. I might warn you, *querida*, I'm very protective where he is concerned. It would grieve me to think of your hurting him . . . in any way."

She thought of clawing his dark, bearded face. Instead, she snatched up her skirts and twirled to leave. He was beside her in a moment, wrapping hard fingers around her arm. Angelique stopped. She didn't wish to fight with him; she knew it would be useless. Already his touch was sending that ever-present surge of anticipation through her veins. She was growing quite heady with it all.

Still, she met his eyes with nothing short of boredom winking in hers. "Are you done, Senor de Bastitas?"

"Hardly. Stay away from Tomas. I'll warn you once. The next time I may not act so civilized."

"You? *Un*civilized?" Her eyes wide, Angelique released an incredulous laugh. "As you breathe and eat and subject the world to your tedious ill humor, I can hardly detect *anything* about you that is *not* uncivilized already."

She thought he might strike her. Instead a slow grin curled his mouth.

"I think if I weren't so tired, I would take up where we left off before my brother found us. Then you seemed quite unconcerned with my 'uncivilized' behavior, and unless my memory escapes me, showed a flair for the wicked yourself. Unless, of course, you wish me to believe it was an act, by which I would applaud your talent for make-believe and suggest you take up the trait as a business . . . in one form or another."

Without taking her eyes from his, Angelique reached for his hand. "Remove it," she demanded quietly. Her arm was throbbing due to the intense grip. When he refused, her palm closed over his. "Please," she added between her teeth.

He did so.

Angelique yearned with all her being to turn and run for the house. It seemed every time they met his sarcasm became sharper, his belligerence toward her more pronounced. She suddenly felt weary. She had not asked to be delivered to this godforsaken place, then dumped in Satan's arms. What had she done in her short existence to deserve this torment, to deserve Alejandro de Bastitas?

Forcing herself to face him, she asked stoically, "What of Juanita? Have you recovered her body?"

"No."

She blinked. "What?"

Alex sauntered to a chair below the willow and after dropping into it pulled a cigarillo from his shirt pocket and lit it. He drew a deep breath, then flung the match away. "They burned her body. There was nothing left to recover."

"I see."

He watched her color fade. She wavered before his eyes. "I'm sorry," he said.

"Are you?"

Detecting the bitterness in her voice, Alex looked away. He had no intention of arguing with her. He was too damn tired. He wanted sleep and food. The muscles down his neck and shoulders were bunched with tension. And he dreaded the meeting with his grandfather.

"I'll be leaving later," he said quietly. "I'll be staying in San Antonio for a few days. If you should need me—"

"I won't."

He stood and watched defiance grapple with fear in Angelique's features. "Should you need me . . . let Tomas know."

As he turned, Angelique stopped him by asking, "Who are you running from this time, senor? Your grandfather, my mother . . . or me?"

His dark head turned. His blue eyes were the color of a warm, velvet midnight. "That remains to be seen," came his thoughtful response.

He left her.

Carlota DuHon smiled toward the great hulk of a man who, moments before, had snatched his hat from his head as she entered the room. She offered him her hand and curtsied. "Senor McGuire, I'm so very pleased you completed your journey with no misfortune."

A flush crept up his face and blended with the crop of fiery hair. "My friends call me Kaintock, Madame DuHon. It would please me if you'd do the same."

With a frown, she shook her head. "But is that not insulting? I'm certain the good people of New Orleans had others in mind when bestowing that nickname."

Ducking his head to hide a smile, he answered sheepishly, "You know how Louisiana folks feel about Kentuckians. I reckon we *are* on the wild side a bit. Somewhat inclined to conjure up bad dreams and superstitions."

"Certainly not you, sir. Whoever labeled you with such a name?"

"That would be Alex, some ten years ago."

"That does not surprise me, but be certain I will refrain

from using such a title." Smiling warmly, she added, "Have you no respectable name to go by?"

He shrugged. "You might call me Noble. That's what my mamaw named me, God rest her soul."

Nodding her head, Carlota floated to one of the matching high-backed chairs. Sitting and spreading her black skirt about her feet, she motioned for him to join her. When he had done so, she finished, "Noble suits you. It is a strong name, and so deserving of your stature. Noble it shall be from this moment on."

McGuire sat back and crossed his legs. "I'm mighty sorry about your family, senora—"

"Carlota." She smiled as he acknowledged her firm command with a dip of his head. "I am thankful that before Julio died we were able to put our differences behind us."

"Were you close?"

"Not really. Julio was much older than I and left Spain years before I thought to. Eventually, when my parents died, he sent for me. He was living in New Orleans at the time."

"And that's where you met your husband?"

"Yes."

Kaintock looked away, centering his attention on a pair of gleaming silver candelabra across the room. He wanted to bite his tongue, for he hadn't meant to bring up Carlota's husband. Thinking it best to change the subject, he said, "Angelique certainly is a beautiful young lady. Course I can certainly see where she gets her good looks."

Her brown eyes widened briefly as Carlota acknowledged a flutter in her heartbeat. "You are most gracious, Noble. I thank you. Yes, my Angelique is beautiful. You must understand why I am so very careful, and do not wish to see her harmed in any way. Hearts are such fragile things, and once wounded, never repair completely."

He nodded. "But I reckon none of us can go through life unwilling to take that chance. If we do, we might miss out on love altogether."

The man surprised her. Noble "Kaintock" McGuire

might not turn a feminine head with his buckskin clothes, bushy hair, and wiry beard, but he spoke in a pleasing tone, and the gentleness in his demeanor was most disarming. She wondered briefly why he would associate with a man such as Alejandro de Bastitas.

Folding her hands in her lap, she fenced in a soft voice, "I feel love is an overstated and too often used euphemism for lust."

A forthright man, appreciative of frankness, McGuire burst out laughing, filling the entire lower level of the hacienda with its rich, deep sound. It caused Carlota to blush, and lowering her lashes, she covered a smile with her fingertips.

"By golly," he guffawed, slapping a rock-hard thigh, "if you ain't a woman after my own heart!"

"Senor?"

"Tell me something, Senora DuHon. Ain't it possible to lust after someone you love?"

"I—I would suppose—"

"Suppose nothin'! I figured if I's to fall in love with . . . say . . . well, you for instance, I'd sure as the devil has horns find ever' reason I could to lust a little . . . if you know what I mean."

"Oh!"

"Now don't tell me that husband of yours didn't lust after you just a little?"

After thinking a moment, Carlota smiled and responded, "*Very* little, senor."

He burst out laughing again.

Angelique stood in the doorway, watching in disbelief as her mother flirted with the Kentuckian. She cleared her throat.

Carlota covered her mouth with her kerchief as she turned to find her daughter in the door. As inconspicuously as possible, she dabbed the tears of mirth from her eyes before they could fall to her cheeks, which, by now, were glowing becomingly. "Oh, Angie, will you join us? I was only thanking No—Senor McGuire for his returning me to the safety of Rancho de Bejar."

"Indeed," Angelique said, arching one eyebrow skeptically.

Standing, Kaintock bowed gallantly toward Carlota's daughter. "Well, we hadn't actually gotten quite so far as that . . ."

Carlota rolled her eyes.

". . . but I reckon we'd have eventually got to it." Turning to Carlota, he grinned even wider and replaced his hat on his head. "I'd be right pleased if you'd allow me to call on you from time to time, Carlota."

She stood. "Are you leaving the ranch?"

"I'm goin' into San Antonio with Alex for a few days."

Frowning, she murmured, "My sympathies."

"Ah . . . er . . ." Stumbling for words, he spun toward Angelique. "If you ladies will excuse me?"

Angelique swept her skirts aside, allowing him to pass. She then fixed her green gaze on her mother. "Do you think it wise to become so well-acquainted with such a man?"

Carlota was stunned by Angelique's hard, bitter tone. "My dear, Mr. McGuire is a kind and trustworthy man. With some grooming I think Noble would make a most acceptable—"

"Acceptable what?"

The tension in Angelique's voice caused Carlota to waver in her defense of Noble McGuire. "He—he treated me with utmost respect on our journey home, and was kind enough to inquire on my well-being when he returned again. I see little that should disarm you so."

"Have you forgotten we are in mourning?"

Carlota lowered her eyes. Sadness filling her voice, she answered softly, "Of course not. I owe you my apologies. I cannot imagine what happened to my senses, Angelique. Can you forgive me?"

Crossing the room, Angelique settled in the chair before her mother. Taking Carlota's cool hand, she said, "You are so very vulnerable right now, Mama, and I must warn you, a man like McGuire would take advantage of your

sorrow. You can never trust a Kentuckian. You know what
Bernice says about them.''

Carlota frowned. ''But Noble is neither coarse nor crude.
He is a very gentle man.''

''Noble?''

''That is his real name. Noble McGuire.''

''My, we *are* on friendly terms, aren't we?''

Biting her lip and feeling not unlike a chastised child,
the older woman sat back in her chair. Then, noticing Angelique's attire, Carlota sat up abruptly. ''Angelique, where
are your mourning clothes?''

Taken off guard, Angelique gasped. She had totally forgotten to change before seeing Carlota. ''Oh, Mama, I
could not bear the burden of black again. Please don't ask
it of me.''

''Ask it? I demand it! Would you insult my family by
refusing to acknowledge their death?''

''Of course not, it's just—''

''It's that man, isn't it?'' Jumping to her feet, Carlota
paced angrily across the room before spinning to face her
daughter again. ''You've seen him already, haven't you?''

''Alexander had nothing to do with my choice of a dress,
Mama.''

''Answer me, Angelique.''

Standing, Angelique nodded. ''He happened upon Tomas and me as we were walking.''

''Happened?'' Carlota's laugh was more of a bark. ''No
doubt he slithered in on his belly. It is a good thing he has
left this hacienda or I would find the nearest gun and kill
him. I shall if he tries to see you again.''

Defensively, Angelique countered, ''You apparently
have no distaste for his best friend.''

''Noble McGuire is not guilty of—'' Carlota froze.

''Of what, Mama?''

Her face drained of color, Carlota nervously waved her
hand, as if the act would somehow dismiss her earlier blun-
der. ''Nothing. He simply is not guilty of attempting to
seduce my daughter.''

Angelique stared at her mother, sensing something more

was behind her dislike of Alejandro de Bastitas. But what could it be? she wondered. What?

San Antonio's streets were bustling with the volunteers who had heard of Austin's siege of the Alamo. There were Texas colonists, Americans—including several companies from New Orleans—and those typical adventurers who cared for nothing more than the excitement warfare could offer.

Along with these men were the original garrisons who had chased Cos's troops into the Alamo. They waited, but far less patiently than before. They were growing tired of guarding the holed-up Mexicans and were yearning to return to their families before the onset of winter.

James Fannin faced his companions: Jim Bowie, Stephen Austin, and James Grant. His face was red with anger. "You can't honestly expect us to sit here and do nothing? Gentlemen, it is obvious Santa Anna will strike by sea. No one in his right mind would subject his men to the grueling journey from Mexico to San Antonio during winter."

The men looked around as Alejandro and Kaintock stepped through the doors of the cantina.

Lifting a hand to his friends, Bowie rolled his eyes back toward Fannin. "You're dead wrong."

Shoulders back, Fannin snapped, "And you, sir, are drunk again."

A slow smile coaxed the irritation from Jim Bowie's face. "That may be, my good man, but it doesn't change the facts. If Santa Anna wagered a strike from the coast he would have to enlist the help of another country just to transport all his troops. Look at the facts. He's already summoning men to Satillo, which is proof he intends to move across land."

Fannin leaned across the table, bracing his weight with his hands. "And what would you have us do, Bowie? Sit on our backsides until he saunters across the river?"

Fingering the rim of his whiskey glass, Bowie shrugged. "I say we meet them head on. Surprise 'em when they least expect it."

"Impossible," chimed in Grant. "If you spread the men too thin you leave San Antonio and what we have gained open to attack from any side."

"We ain't gained nothin' yet," McGuire added as he scraped his chair across the floor. Straddling it back to front, he said, "I think we should get this whole cocka-mamy thing over with. Cos ain't doing nothing but twid-dlin' his thumbs and buyin' time." Facing Grant, a red-faced Scotsman with a candlewick temper, he finished, "I suppose you're wantin' to take Matamoros so's you can expand your silver mine investments."

Alex slid into a chair next to Stephen Austin. Tuning out the ensuing argument, he asked, "Where is Colonel Burleson?"

"With the troops. I'm turning over my command to him, as I've a convention to attend at Washington-on-the Brazos. I have a feeling I'll be traveling to the United States. Support must come from someplace. That's our likeliest bet." Lowering his voice further, Austin whis-pered, "The troops are restless, and if Fannin and Grant get their way, three-fourths of these men will storm off to Goliad and Matamoros. If they do, San Antonio will be in one hell of a mess. Ben Milam will probably be joining you any day, and *that*, my friend, will be like a spark to a powder keg. Damn, but that man loves to fight, and after his win at Goliad he'll be hungry for more."

"What is your view on the situation?"

He shrugged. "I've tried to organize an attack on Cos, but hell, none of the company commanders will support me. They believe such a move might drastically deplete our numbers."

A soft voice interrupted their conversation.

"Senor de Bastitas?"

Alex turned to face a pretty dark-skinned girl. Her black-brown hair was pulled from her face and secured about the back of her head in a thick braid. Smoothing her hands nervously over a red skirt, she asked in a slightly accented voice, "May I have a word with you?"

A smile twitching at his lips, Alejandro followed her to

the bar of the cantina. His eyes took in the gentle sway of her hips, the smooth curve of her shoulders and back. About her neck hung a dainty silver chain and on it a simple cross. It was that fixture that caught his eye as she faced him again.

She fidgeted with the ornament before she looked up to reveal eyes the color of polished onyx. Her smile was unsteady, for Alejandro de Bastitas was openly frowning. "It was your mother's," she offered, silencing his query.

"May I ask why you have it?"

"Tomas." Struggling for the courage to continue, she poured him a glass of whiskey, then set the bottle aside. "He presented it to me some months ago. As a gift. If you wish, you may have it back."

With a slow shake of his head, Alex raised the drink to his mouth. "That's not necessary. It was not mine to give, nor is it mine to take away." Swigging the drink only slightly, he prodded, "I must assume you know my brother very well."

"Very."

"May I ask your name?"

She hesitated, then responded, "Anna."

His voice without its usual bite, Alex asked, "What do you want of me, Anna?"

Anna looked over one shoulder, then the other before turning her heart-shaped face up completely. Her eyes were large, soft, like a doe's. Her lips were pink and quivering either in nervousness or anticipation. "It has been some time since Tomas last ventured into San Antonio. I was wondering . . . is he well?"

"He was this morning."

"I have heard he has taken up with a young lady."

One brow shot up in surprise. Alex appeared slightly disconcerted before setting his glass down for a refill. Dreading the response, he asked, "What young lady would that be?"

"I understand she is from New Orleans. And very beautiful."

Angelique. Damn, but that gave him one more reason to

wring her lovely neck! Recovering himself, Alex released his breath. "You may dismiss the rumor, my dear. The lady is spoken for."

Relief flooded Anna's face, giving Alex the fleeting idea that had he stated otherwise she might have fallen in a heap at his feet.

Pulling a note from her pocket, she timidly held it out to the towering man. "I had hoped to send this to Tomas by a friend. Would you be so kind . . ."

He took the letter. "I had not planned to return to the ranch for several days."

"It doesn't matter. Who knows, perhaps I will see him before then."

His mouth twisting into a smile, Alex turned his back to Anna and leaned against the bar. Conjuring up his grandfather's face, he burst out laughing. Imagine Carlos's temper when he learned that one grandson was courting a mestizo . . . and the other a saucy green-eyed Creole wench.

# THIRTEEN

Wringing her hands, Bernice glanced about the spacious room. One complete wall held shelves of leather-bound books with gilded pages. White walls boasted intricately carved masks; ceremonial pieces belonging to the Indians of Mexico's interior regions; woven rugs in black, browns, and reds, trimmed with wool fringe; gleaming crisscrossed sabers; and a portrait of Ramon de Bastitas. In each corner were shelves burgeoning with ancient artifacts, gods in tribal headdresses, an odd sort of pyramid, and pottery which, to an untrained eye, might have been sculpted upon these very premises. They were five hundred years old.

Her dark eyes shifted to the pair of chairs gracing the far wall. They were high backed and intricately carved. Their covering of red velvet was slightly worn. Bernice's jittery nerves were on edge. The last two days' travel had been a nightmare. Now it appeared she would be subjected to the company of some demigod for the purpose of . . . what?

Would she be forced from the house to live in some flat-roofed hut like the other servants? Would she be sold, now that her mistress appeared even more destitute than she had been on her arrival in Gonzales?

"Lawd, Lawd, whatever gonna become of me?" she whispered to herself.

She jumped as the door flew open. Carlota was running toward her, arms open, her face a mixture of concern and relief.

"Bernice!"

The Negress opened and closed her arms about Carlota's shoulders. "Shhh," she soothed the weeping woman. "Bernice is here, ma'am, and she gonna take good care of you. Hush now. It all gonna be fine."

Carlota pulled away, her face streaked with tears. "Oh, Bernice, it was horrible. They are all dead—killed by those savages!"

Swallowing hard, Bernice forced her next question through a constricted throat. "What about my baby? What about Angelique?"

Sniffling, Carlota answered with a shaky smile, "She was saved, Bernice. Our Angelique was recovered and returned to us yesterday."

The great woman's relief was too much, and with a stumble she dropped into one of the matching chairs. Covering her round face, she wept into her palms. "Lawd, I prayed mighty hard. Mighty hard! Where is she? Where is my baby?"

"Napping," Carlota said. Throwing a cautious glance toward the door, she began, "Bernice, I must speak with you on a matter of extreme importance. Do you recall the name Alejandro de Bastitas?"

Her brown face expressionless, Bernice searched her mind, then shook her head.

Carlota shook Bernice's shoulders, as if she could somehow dislodge the memory. "But you must," she insisted. "Think! He is the man who—"

"Who what?"

Carlota twirled toward the door. Bernice swiped at her tears as Carlos and Isabella de Bastitas entered the room.

A tight smile stretching his face, Carlos demanded. "Tell us, senora; just who *was* my grandson to you?"

"You have drawn your conclusions," she responded.

"Which you never denied or confirmed."

"Nor do I intend to."

He nodded his head, then looked toward Bernice. Carlos waited, but the woman never left the chair. "Are you comfortable?" he finally barked.

Bernice nodded.

As Isabella slipped into her chair, Carlota jumped forward and ushered Bernice away so Carlos could mount his throne. He bowed in a mocking manner before doing so.

*"Gracias,"* he offered in a heavy voice.

Carlota's spine stiffened, for in that instant the old man had appeared almost handsome, an aged version of his older grandson. It occurred to her that although Carlos Echeverria de Bastitas had once been a good-looking man, he had never been kind. The woman at his side, however, was his opposite. Her velvety face had an ageless grace that showed few creases, despite her seventy years. The brown eyes were compassionate and her mouth continually carried a wise smile. Carlota, despite herself, recognized a startling resemblance to Alejandro there as well.

Impossible!

Settled, Carlos tapped his cane on the floor. "Stand before me," he directed Bernice.

Her eyes widened, and at Carlota's insistent nudge, she stepped forward.

"In case you are unaware, my good woman, slavery within these regions is abhorrent. We do not abide it. It is forbidden, and from this moment on you shall consider yourself a freeman." Cutting his eyes to Carlota, he waited for her response. There was none. Continuing, he said, "You may come and go as you wish. If you choose to remain as servant to the senora you will be paid a salary and provided for adequately. You will not be mistreated in any way, and should you be, the offender will be responsible to me."

"I have *never* mistreated Bernice!" Carlota exclaimed.

With a lift of Carlos's hand, a *doncella* appeared. "You will see the good woman to a comfortable room. Bring her fruit and chocolate, then she is to rest. She has had a wearisome journey.''

"*Sí, patron.*''

Isabella smiled. There were moments—brief ones—when she could still feel some pride for her husband.

Angelique could hardly believe her eyes when she awoke from her nap. Bernice's broad, dark face was beaming into hers, her white smile broadcasting her pleasure and relief at finding her baby alive and well.

"Oooh, child, let me see that face!'' The woman clucked her tongue as, cradling Angelique's cheeks in her palms, she turned her head first to the right, then the left. "Bernice will fix a poultice for that swelling and you'll be right in no time.''

Angelique settled again onto her pillows, smiling as the woman scurried about the room. She was always amazed at Bernice's dexterity, considering she would tip the scales at close to two hundred pounds.

"Don't nobody deserve to die like them poor folks,'' Bernice continued. Plunking hands on her hips, she shook her head. "You just do yore best to forget what you seen out there you hear me? Ain't fittin' for no young lady like yourself.''

Lowering her lashes, Angelique said softly, "I shall never forget what I saw and heard. And if it were not for Alex . . .''

"Alex?''

"Alejandro de Bastitas.''

Brown lips pursed, Bernice turned away. "I reckon we should be thankful to him for savin' yore life, hon, but don't let gratitude get in the way of everything else.''

"Oh, Bernice, please! Not you too?''

Bernice looked into Angelique's wide, pleading eyes. Thanks to Carlota's hasty explanation, she was aware of most of the circumstances surrounding Angelique and Alejandro de Bastitas. Still, he was a man running from a tragedy, just like Carlota. It was a certainty, in her own mind, that if he was intent on revenge toward the DuHons, he wouldn't have bothered to risk his own life in rescuing Angelique. Would he?

It wasn't long before Bernice had matters well in hand. Delores was sent to fetch mustard, cayenne pepper, and chicken fat, which, blended together, was smoothed onto Angelique's cheeks.

"This is gonna take that swellin' and color right off yore face," the woman boasted.

Angelique rolled her eyes as the plaster began drawing.

"*Madre de Dios,* what is that smell?" Tomas stepped through the door. Upon seeing Angelique, her face a gooey mess and her eyes like two green saucers, he burst out laughing. "I thought for certain one of my grandfather's dead bulls had been dragged in here to season."

Wiping the concoction from her fingers, Bernice scolded, "Don't you talk, girl! Won't do no good if you crack it. Now," she directed to the newcomer, "are you Bastitas?"

Tomas pulled his eyes from the embarrassed girl. Flashing Bernice his most disarming smile, he lifted her fingers—hesitating over their smell—and touched them to his lips, then dropped them as quickly as possible. "*Sí, senora.* I am Tomas Eduardo de Bastitas." He clicked his heels. "At your service!"

Angelique and Bernice exchanged amused glances.

"Um hm, and am I supposed to be impressed by that?"

"Certainly," he answered emphatically. Swinging again to the bed, he stated while putting his hand over his heart, "My dear Miss DuHon, I'm not certain I have ever seen you look so . . . ravishing."

"You are most kind," she responded, barely moving her lips.

"Yes I am. Oh, by the way, have you seen Alejandro? He decided not to dally in San Antonio after all and—wait, I believe I hear him now."

Alexander?! Not like this! Oh! With a squeal Angelique dove under the covers. "A wet cloth, please, Bernice, and hurry!" came her muffled plea. Hearing Tomas's mischief-tinged snicker, followed by Bernice's chesty laughter, she realized she had been duped. Snatching the covers from her head, she glared at them both. "You shall each pay for your foolery, I promise you!"

"Promises, promises," Tomas sighed with a flick of his hand.

"What do you want, senor? Tell me quickly before I am subjected to another attack of the vapors."

Touching the tip of a tapered finger to her yellow nose, Tomas grimaced. "Isabella wishes to offer Bernice an invitation to join in her *merienda*."

Surprised, Bernice asked suspiciously, "What is that?"

Angelique answered. "A snack of sorts that's served after siesta. Like our afternoon tea. Go along, Bernice. You will enjoy the cakes as well as the company."

This was something new. Although she had been a part of the DuHon family since before Angelique was born, never had she taken the liberty of actually joining them in a repast, though both Carlota and Angelique had offered an invitation on several occasions. Now she was being summoned to do just that.

"Go along," Angelique coaxed again. "Enjoy yourself, Bernice. I shall be fine and promise I won't touch your poultice until you return."

Smiling, Tomas offered his arm.

Angelique waited until the two were out of sight, then jumping from the bed, snagged a damp cloth from the washstand and began scrubbing her face.

Bernice smiled appreciatively as she entered the grand bedroom. It faced west, allowing the afternoon sun to spill its warming rays through the windows and onto a highly polished hardwood floor. The walls were clean, but for a large framed portrait above the tester bed. She moved closer for a better look.

It was a painting of a handsome and happy family. In the center, surrounded by children, was a youthful woman with light-brown hair, an oval face, and startling blue eyes. She was a fragile thing, small-boned, with porcelain skin. On each side of her was a boy, one about fourteen years old, the other several years younger. The younger one she recognized as Tomas. So the other must be the infamous Alejandro. He stood with his hand resting almost possessively on the woman's shoulder. Her hand lay with a mother's gentle reassurance on Tomas's knee. At her feet was a child, a girl, with her mother's light hair and complexion. She could have been no older than four.

In the background stood a younger Isabella de Bastitas. Her hair was not so gray, but other than that, little was noticeably different. A man stood at her side, erect and tall. Like the boys, his hair was black. They shared the same eyes and smile. A hand rested on Alejandro's shoulder. His other, should one use his imagination, might have been slipped about Isabella's waist.

"They are all dead," came the weary voice. "All but Tomas and Alejandro. They and Carlos are all I have left."

Bernice, who had been waiting patiently for several minutes, threw a startled look about the room.

"Here."

Isabella raised her hand at the same moment Bernice spotted her in the chair before the window. Its tall back had completely hidden the frail woman from sight. Releasing a long breath, she approached her hostess.

"Sit, my dear. You must be tired from your journey."

The rocker creaked beneath Bernice's weight. Automatically she reached to attend the silver service of chocolate and cakes, but Isabella waved her aside. A door opened and Delores appeared, quickly poured them each the beverage, spread a linen over their laps, and, upon it, steadied plates of cakes.

Bernice sat back, a smile curving her full mouth. "Um hm, I could get used to this."

Isabella chuckled. "Indeed you shall. As long as you are a guest in my home, you will be treated as such. Now tell me. What do you think of my family?" One finger pointed to the portrait over Bernice's shoulder.

"They are mighty pretty."

"Yes they are. Ramon was my only child. He was gored to death by a bull."

Lifting a cake to her mouth, Bernice froze.

"Elizabeth, his wife, gave me three beautiful grandchildren. The child Maria died not long after the portrait was finished. She was playing and wandered from the house. Alejandro found her body in a nearby creek. Elizabeth died in childbirth the following spring, as did her babe."

Isabella's head rested against the back of her chair. Her eyes closed. "I am not one to dwell on the past," came her quiet but steady voice, "but choose to contemplate the future. The boys, now men, in that portrait *are* my future. They are headstrong, but I love them. They are the product of their upbringing and cannot be faulted for that."

Bernice wondered where this conversation was leading. She eyed her cake but didn't eat it.

"I want great-grandchildren," *la patrona* said more forcefully. "But most of all, I want my grandchildren happy. Which brings me to Angelique." Raising her head, Isabella met Bernice's wide, unblinking eyes. "She is in love with my grandson, and whether he realizes it or not, he is in love with her. I feel it would be in our best interest to see that they are married."

"Yore talkin' about Tomas, aren't you?"

"No, my dear."

"Um hm. I's afraid of that." Slipping the plate onto the tray, Bernice shook her head. "Won't be no way for that to happen. Um um. No, ma'am." Narrowing one eye, she asked, "How come you havin' this talk with me? I got no say in who Missus Carlota let marry her baby."

"I realize that. And I realize your loyalty does, and should, belong to Carlota. I have no idea what problem lingers between my grandson and the lady, but whatever it is, it should not take precedence over the happiness of those two young people. *We* must see to their happiness. It must not be left up to Carlota and my husband." Leaning forward, Isabella clasped one of Bernice's huge brown hands in both of hers. "I need your help, Bernice. *Will* you help me?"

•　　•　　•

Angelique was laying out her black attire when Bernice reentered the room. The woman didn't seem to notice that she had removed her smelly mask, but was lost in her own thoughts as she coaxed the girl into a chair and began brushing out her hair.

"Did you enjoy your *merienda?*" Angelique asked. When Bernice didn't respond, she probed, "Is something wrong?"

Bernice's hand hesitated over the crown of Angie's head. Their eyes meeting in the mirror, she asked, "What you got goin' with that Bastitas man?"

"I beg your pardon?"

"What you feelin' for 'im?"

"Have you spoken with my mother?"

"Has he been botherin' you?"

Alexander de Bastitas is a conceited, deceptive scoundrel with a heart of stone! Angelique yearned to rail, but her tongue declined to cooperate. Instead, the remembrance of his mouth's warm, sweet embrace, tasting faintly of brandy and tobacco, replaced that bite of condemnation.

What right did he have to intrude upon her heart? He had misused her in a most despicable way. Now his memory was *forcing* her to lie in behalf of *his* reputation!

Bernice knew Angelique too well. She might not have birthed the girl those eighteen years before, but she had suckled the babe at her breast and she had suffered and dealt with every pain the child had experienced through the years. She sensed the maelstrom going on inside Angelique, watched anger, pain, then something else roil within those opaque jade eyes.

Closing her hands upon Angie's shoulders, she queried quietly, "Is there something we need to talk about, child? You got anything you want to tell me?"

Had Bernice read her thoughts so easily? Angelique focused her vision on the window, the floor, the black veil obscuring most of the beveled mirror. Could she trust Bernice with the truth? Wouldn't sharing her secret lighten the burden of guilt bearing on her conscience? But what if Bernice were to tell Carlota?

The thought of her mother's reaction should she learn of her dalliance with Alejandro de Bastitas caused her face to pale.

"You can talk to me," came the quiet coercion.

"You won't like it."

Acknowledging the proud tilt of Angelique's chin, Bernice sucked in her breath. "Lawd, girl, you tellin' me that he done . . . that you done . . ."

Jumping to her feet, Angelique faced her friend. "Dear Bernice, you asked for the truth."

The woman rolled her eyes. "How did it happen?"

"I fear it was the wine."

And the night, the man, and the feelings that caused her heart to race like a frightened rabbit when he was near.

"You sayin' he took advantage of you?"

Angelique considered her answer. "Perhaps it was the circumstances. He is a very handsome man and—"

"Ain't no man that handsome, girl!" Bernice tapped her foot on the floor. "Did you refuse him at all?"

Had she refused? Angie couldn't remember. All she recalled was that first glance, the first touch of his mouth against hers. Finally, "I don't recall. I—I don't think so."

Bernice stared at her for several unending moments, then, wringing her hands, began pacing. Her posy-printed cotton skirts swayed back and forth in a slow, easy fashion, at odds with the conflicting emotions warring across the woman's features. Without facing Angelique, she asked, "Is there any possibility of you bein' with child?"

The question hit her like a stone. It hadn't even occurred . . . "I don't know. I would suppose . . ."

"How many times you been with him?"

Angelique longed to throw herself under the nearest fixture of furniture and hide. "Twice the night before we left the ranch . . . and once when he found me."

Bernice's big frame rotated toward Angelique. "You sure the act was completed?"

"What do you mean?"

Very few times had Angelique witnessed Bernice's anger, but now, as the great woman leaped at her, grabbed her shoulders, and began shaking her without compassion, she could not help but cry out in surprise and pain. "Stop!" she wept. "Why are you doing this?"

"Girl, girl, don't you know nothin'? I'm askin' you, did that man spill himself inside you?"

She gasped and covered her ears. "Please don't talk that way. It sounds so—so—"

"Filthy!"

"Yes! Yes it does and it wasn't like that, Bernice. It wasn't!"

Bernice shook her again. "Answer me, child!"

Grimacing from the pain, she nodded. "Yes, he did."

"Lawd, have mercy!" Hands covered her face as Bernice stepped away. "Girl, you harborin' the devil's seed in yore belly! We got to be rid of it now, before it takes root and grows."

Angelique stumbled away. "What are you saying? There is no child!"

Bernice's head snapped up. "You sure?" She counted her fingers. "By my reckonin' you should have been breedin' ready when he mounted you."

"That is the most disgusting thing I have ever heard you utter! How dare you speak to me in that offensive manner?"

"Just how do you think yore mamma gonna speak when she finds out Bastitas be ruttin' her daughter?"

"Surely you won't—you aren't—"

"Gonna tell her?"

Angelique nodded.

"You gonna have to cooperate, or I will."

"That is blackmail! No, I won't do it. I refuse!" As Bernice turned for the door, Angelique grew clammy with fear. "Where are you going?"

"To see yore mama."

She sprang at the Negress, her green eyes wide and pleading. "You mustn't! She has sworn to kill Alexander if he even comes near me. If she was to learn . . ."

Black eyes searched Angelique's terror-stricken face.

"You would plead for this man's life after what he done to you? Why, Angelique? Tell me, girl."

Angelique looked away. The words formed on her lips, but she couldn't say them. Would she not look the fool even more after such a confession? Miserably, she withdrew and shook her head. "My mother has borne enough these last months. I cannot expect her to bear any more."

"Then you got to trust me to do the right thing, to do what is best for you all." At Angelique's nod, Bernice turned for the door.

But not before the shadow outside the room disappeared around the nearest corner.

# FOURTEEN

The animal laboring beneath Tomas de Bastitas was lathered with foam, its sides heaving with exertion as it slid to a halt before the cantina. He wrapped the reins about the hitching post in a loose knot then leaping onto the wooden porch, marched with grim determination through the swinging doors.

The bar was crowded with drinkers standing shoulder to shoulder. Only an occasional tinkling of bottle against glass escaped the rowdy laughter of men as they quenched their thirst and boredom with free-flowing whiskey. Tomas nudged his way through the crowd, straining to see over the men's heads and shoulders as he searched for his brother. Damn Alejandro! He could be anywhere. San Antonio was a big town, boasting many cantinas.

He was about to turn and leave the establishment when a soft voice caught his attention. "Tomas! Tomas, wait!"

His blue gaze settled on the gentle features of Anna Gonzales. Catching her hand, he raised it to his mouth. "Anna!"

"It has been so long, Tomas. I thought you had forgotten me."

"Hardly," he replied with a laugh. "Tell me, Anna, have you seen my brother?"

Her face fell as she realized Tomas had not come to the cantina intent on finding her. Tucking her tray beneath her arm, she nodded. "Your brother is in back."

"I have to see him." His voice was tight with suppressed anger.

"I think it would not be wise—"

"I don't give a damn whether it is wise or not!" he exploded. "Now tell me where I can find my brother!"

Anna swallowed hard as she lowered her eyes. "He is in the third room from the rear."

Tomas shoved past her. He made his excuses as he plowed through the congestion, then ducked through the doorway, clattering its strings of glass beads. His long legs carried him down the dimly lit corridor, then, stopping, he glared at the door.

"Alejandro! Alejandro, it is Tomas. Throw the woman from your bed and open the door. It is imperative that I speak with you!" He banged twice on the door.

He heard a burst of laughter just before the door was jerked open.

Tomas stepped away, shrinking slightly beneath his brother's frown, and as his blue eyes slid from Alex's face to the table of gamblers in the smoke-filled room, he blushed in embarrassment. He'd thought for certain Alejandro had purchased himself a woman for the night.

Alex stepped forward, twisted his fingers in his brother's shirt, and shoved him against the wall. "Do you want to die now or later?"

Tomas gulped. "Later I think."

Alex released his hold. "Why the devil are you here?"

"Angelique."

Alex smiled slowly.

Tomas stepped back. "How could you fritter away your time with them when Angelique is waiting?"

"Is she?"

"She is there. That should be reason enough for you to remain at the ranch."

"It seems to be enough for you." Alex closed the door behind him. "Thanks to your untimely intervention I'm out pesos for little more than conversation. Now tell me what has happened."

"It is what is about to happen."

The brothers moved up the hall. After working their way out onto the cantina's front walk, Alex asked, "What has you so upset?"

Summoning his courage, Tomas replied, "Your robbing the senorita of her maidenhood is common knowledge among a few of us, but you might know she has confessed all to that mountain of a woman who arrived this afternoon. It seems she and this Bernice person are very close. After learning of you and your . . . intimacy with Angelique, the woman convinced her she should do everything possible to avoid having . . . your child."

The taller man stiffened. "I'm not certain I understand. There is no possible way Angelique could determine—"

"I'm saying the woman is taking no chances. I don't know what she intends to do, but she is going to great lengths to assure that Angelique rids herself of what she called 'the devil's seed.' "

Alejandro stared down the dusty street, his face revealing nothing. "Is this some sort of trick you and my grandmother have devised to bring me home? For if it is, I assure you, my brother, the consequences will be dire."

"No. Upon our mother's grave, Alejandro, I swear to you the woman is out to do something."

"And what are Angelique's feelings, or didn't you eavesdrop long enough to catch her response?"

"She was against it at first, but changed her mind after Bernice threatened to inform Carlota of your tryst. And if you must know, she agreed mostly for your benefit. She is afraid of what Carlota might do to you."

Surprise was obvious for a moment, though Alex continued to look off into the darkness. How long would it take him to reach Rancho de Bejar? An hour? Possibly less if he rode his horse into the ground. By that time it might all be over . . . that is if there *was* a child. There was that possibility. But the chances of that were slim . . . weren't they? Of course.

Damn, but he was a fool for even speculating. An even bigger fool for imagining what it would be like to share a child with that saucy little wench!

Alex, though he continually fought the memory, recalled the very instant he had realized that Pamela was expecting. She hadn't told him, but her illness had been confession enough. When confronted, she had reluctantly admitted it. He had thought at the time that luck was with him since Pamela had been a wife who tolerated him in her bed once a month, twice if he was lucky. He had dismissed her coldness as befitting a lady of her social breeding, little knowing she was just too damn busy expending her efforts on another man.

But there were no other men in Angelique DuHon's bed. If there was a child, it was *his* child.

Angelique sat on the edge of her bed, watching as Bernice hefted yet another bucket of steaming water into the room and dumped it into the tub. Condensation trickled down the windows and settled like fog across her dresser mirror, and to make certain no heat escaped, the woman drew the drapes and tucked linens along the bottom edge of the locked door.

"Missus Carlota be asleep for the night," came Bernice's breathless response to Angelique's curious gaze.

Fingers gripping the bed sheets, Angelique looked away. "I'm not certain I can do this, Bernice."

"Nonsense. If a child be there then best to end it now. If there ain't, won't do you no harm. Now stand up and let's get you out of them clothes and into that tub 'fore the water cool off."

She hesitantly slipped to her feet. Bernice worked the buttons down the bodice of her dress, then tugged the delicate straps of the camisole over her shoulders. Gentle hands coaxed her toward the bath.

As her tender feet touched the hot water, Angelique rebelled. "Please, I cannot do this. There is no child, Bernice, and—"

"Then what you afraid of, girl?"

She stared again into the tub. Biting her lip, she eased into the water. She felt ill with the intense heat. Steam and sweat collected about her hairline and temples, then poured down her face, neck, and shoulders. Her skin flushed an angry red. Closing her eyes, she felt her world begin spinning.

"Drink this, hon."

She gasped at the smell. Wrinkling her nose, she asked, "What is it?"

"Don't matter none. Just drink it."

With a shaky hand, Angelique held the glass to her mouth. It had a rotten stench, and she gagged.

"Go on."

Staring into the unappetizing concoction, she shook her head. "No. I cannot do it. Alex must be consulted and—" Bernice wrapped determined fingers about her arms as she attempted to stand. "What are you doing?" she demanded. "You cannot force me to continue with this. Let me go!"

"But what about yore mama? Lawd, whatever this gonna do to her?"

Angelique shook her head. "Enough! My decision is made, Bernice." Attempting to lessen the severity of her tone, she smiled, "Perhaps there is no child. Then all of this worry has been for nothing. Now help me from this water and get rid of that vile drink."

Oddly enough, relief swept the big woman's face. She reached to grip Angelique's arm as she stepped from the tub.

It was that sight which greeted Alejandro as he threw his weight against the door, sending it shattering back against the wall.

Bernice jumped and turned. The door was filled with leather-vested shoulders and long, braced legs. Raven hair, tousled from a harried ride, hung disheveled into fire-blue eyes. "Lawd, have mercy on my soul," she rasped deep in her throat. For it was a certainty this was the devil who had ruined Angelique's life.

"What the hell kind of voodoo is going on in here?" came the caustic demand. Eyes now accustomed to the dark steamy interior focused on the girl in the tub. With a muttered curse Alex grabbed Bernice and shoved her toward the door. "If you've done any damage—"

"Damage!" Bernice barked. Her bosom swelling in indignation, she propped her hands on her hips and countered, "Lawd, man, if there be any damage done here it was done by you. Um um. No, sir, I ain't goin' nowhere."

"Out."

Her eyes widened. "Get yore clothes on, gal, and be quick about it."

Alex stepped closer and repeated, "If you've done any damage, by God, you'll suffer hell at my hands." When she thought to deny him again, he snarled softly. "Your last warning, madam."

As Bernice stumbled backward from the room, Alex kicked the door closed with his foot. He then slowly turned to face Angelique.

Holding the damp linen to her breast, Angelique lifted her chin. His anger was most obvious, but she would be damned before she would quake at his feet like a timid sparrow.

"Well?" he thundered.

Her green eyes widened. "Sir, you are intruding." Water trickled down her throat and between her breasts.

"And you have not answered my question. What the hell kind of black magic has that woman inflicted on my child?"

"*Your* child?"

"Are you denying you were about to—"

"Yes!" Swallowing her outrage, Angelique stepped from the tub. "How dare you come barreling into my room like some bull in a china shop and scare poor Bernice out of her senses? Oooh, you are the most ill-mannered, insolent, hotheaded beast of a man I have ever known!"

Alex was stunned. For the last hour he had ridden his

horse into a froth, convincing himself Angelique loathed
him to such an extent she would stop at nothing to rid
herself of his child, should there be one. And upon entering
the room and finding her and the servant on the verge of
God knows what, he had just assumed that Angelique had
bent to the woman's will. Chagrined, he stepped back.

Angelique advanced, not in the least bothered by her
nudity. "It would serve you right if I plunked an ill-
conceived, illegitimate babe on your doorstep. I would love
to watch you explain *that* to your boorish grandfather!"

As her rigid index finger pounded one last time against
his breastbone, Alex caught her wrist and twisted until she
had no choice but to lean against him. His eyes slipped
over her damp hair, now kinking slightly from the humid-
ity, past her milky shoulders, to the soft outline of her
rounded hip. "That hurts," came his voice, feigning irritation.

A smile curving her petulant mouth, Angelique cooed,
"Not nearly as much as Carlos's whip across your back-
side should I drop your bambino on his lap."

"Is that a threat?" One dark brow drew up.

"Most assuredly."

He fumbled for the doorknob behind him. "Good night,
Angelique."

"Goodbye, Senor de Bastitas."

# FIFTEEN

"She is with that disgusting man again. Really, Bernice, you must attend me while I speak to my mother. I find it abhorrent that she would associate with such a man so soon after my father's death."

Bernice, in the process of folding Angelique's clean laundry, shook her head. "Yore daddy been dead well over a year now, hon. She got to start over sometime. Mr. McGuire is a real nice man, and seems to think a great deal of Missus Carlota."

"Oh, pooh!"

"Watch that tongue, missy!"

Hiding a smile, Angelique turned from the window. The poor dear woman would swoon if she knew what words floated between her lips upon occasion. Sighing, she moved toward the door. "I think I shall find Tomas. The day is warm and he offered earlier to take me for a ride on horseback."

"Um um. No, ma'am. You goin' no place without me and I ain't about to climb on top of one of them animals."

"Where is my riding habit? Have you cleaned it?"

Bernice moved between Angelique and the wardrobe. "It bein' yore time of the month you got no business even out of bed. You should be on yore back with yore feet up."

"It will do me little good!" Angelique argued. "It never did. Now let me pass. I wish to change and see Tomas."

Bernice wagged a finger in Angelique's face. "It ain't Tomas you wantin' to see."

She stopped. It seemed she could do nothing any longer without Bernice's suspicious eye following her every move. "Alexander is not on the premises, hasn't been in over two weeks. And I'm certain if you have anything to do with it I shall never see him again."

Bernice nodded decisively.

"Do you not believe he has a right to know that I'm not pregnant?"

"He got no rights at all where you are concerned."

Angelique opened her mouth once more to respond, but a knock at the door interrupted. Her skirt belled as she spun and snapped, "What is it?"

Isabella and Tomas floated into the room.

"Are we intruding?" *la patrona* asked, smiling.

Smiling herself, Angelique responded in a softer voice. "Certainly not." Directing her attention toward Tomas, she finished in a firmer tone, "I was just about to change and join you for a jaunt on horseback."

Behind her Bernice *humphed* and turned away.

Tomas caught Angelique's hand and lifted it to his mouth. "I'm delighted, but my grandmother has some exciting news which might take precedence over such an occasion. Grandmother?"

"Yes." Isabella nodded, and her eyes twinkled. "We have been invited to the Musquiz home in San Antonio."

Angelique's face brightened. She had not been out of the house in days, and the thought of actually venturing into San Antonio caused her to grow giddy with excitement. "But is it safe?" she asked.

"As long as we stay clear of the battalions," Tomas responded. "Cos and his troops are still barricaded in the Alamo, but—"

"Will we see the Alamo?"

"We should pass a little distance from it. Yes," he nodded, "we should be able to see it."

"How very exciting!"

"Excitin'?" Bernice exclaimed. "Nothin' excitin' about a gun bein' aimed at my head. No, ma'am. I ain't budgin' from this house."

His deep laughter filled the room before Tomas explained, "They have no war with us, senora. Their foes are the men holding them hostage. Besides, my grandfather's coach boasts not only our colors but Mexico's flag as well. If anything, you should worry over the Texans' and Americans' aimless fire."

Biting her lower lip, Angelique shook her head. "I cannot imagine my mother's allowing it. As you know, we are still in mourning."

"Your mother is joining us, Angelique," Isabella said. "Now hurry, as we will be leaving within the hour."

Bernice did not miss the wink Tomas offered Angelique as he closed the door between them.

The next hour was harried as the household prepared for this unexpected trip. Trunks were packed, for although they would be staying only three days, the women would change their attire several times each day. Bernice voiced her disapproval as Angelique drew her brightest mourning dress from the wardrobe. She didn't long to drape herself in black, but bending to Bernice's wishes, opted for a similar dress in gray instead of the emerald green.

Angelique yearned with all her being to include one, possibly two, of her mother's gay party dresses. But that would never do! Carlota would be furious, and though she wanted nothing more than to forget her aunt, uncle, and cousin had been murdered a mere three weeks before, she could not do it. Still, she couldn't suppress her sigh as she pushed the red dress aside for one of dark blue. She would wear her black.

Carlota's face was beaming as she met Angelique in the hall. Standing to one side, both waited as two laboring men hefted the trunks through the door and down the hall. The younger woman studied her mother's features as Carlota quietly instructed Pablo to place her daughter's baggage with hers.

It had been many months, possibly years, since Angelique could recall her mother looking so vibrant. Her face, which only weeks before had been pale and drawn, was flushed with anticipation. The creases about her mouth and eyes appeared less deep, and in her eyes, a twinkle had appeared that Angelique could *never* recall seeing before.

"Are you well, Mama?" she asked quietly.

Smoothing an errant hair from her face, Carlota smiled toward her daughter. "I have never felt better."

"You look feverish."

"Do I?" She lifted the back of her hand to her forehead. "Perhaps it is the excitement."

Both moved down the hall, followed by a scowling Bernice.

Angelique glanced covertly at Carlota's mouth. Her lips were rosy and settled into a discreet little smile. Angelique frowned. "I saw you with Mr. McGuire today."

Carlota hesitated in the corridor. "Have you placed spies about the hacienda?"

"Certainly not." What an absurd idea! "I saw you from my window."

Blushing from Carlota's inquisitive stare, Angelique finished, "I'm not certain I can recall your ever laughing that way with Papa."

Carlota lifted her chin. "I find Noble quite charming."

"Obviously."

Reaching the bottom of the stairs, Carlota faced her daughter again. "Just what do you find so distasteful about Noble?"

Angelique realized her worry did not stem from any dislike for Noble McGuire; after all, he was Alejandro's best friend. No, she was disturbed over the relationship he had begun with her mother. It was so difficult to image her loving *any* man other than her father. "A gentleman would not tempt a lady so soon after her husband's death," she responded halfheartedly.

"Oh, Angelique, your father has been dead over a year." With a flurry of petticoats and skirts, Carlota flounced toward the door. "If that is the only reason you can find to dislike the man, then be silent."

Angelique was stunned. "Mama, are you so smitten with this man?"

The question stopped Carlota in her tracks. "Certainly not!" With a second thought, she added smugly, "Certainly no more than you are with that vile Bastitas dog."

Vaguely aware that Bernice was now shaking her head furiously, Angelique stormed after her mother. "Do not mention Alexander de Bastitas to me in that tone of voice. Besides, I have not seen him in weeks."

"That is good. I will shoot him if he touches you again. He is arrogant, deceitful, and an insult to every virtuous woman's sensibilities."

Angelique opened, then closed her mouth. Her mother was absolutely right.

Angelique and Carlota bid Bernice goodbye, then joined Isabella and Tomas in their coach. Carlos had left Rancho de Bejar much earlier and would join them when they arrived at the Musquiz home. It was a pleasant time. All thoughts of Noble McGuire and Alejandro de Bastitas were put aside as the doña and her grandson entertained them with stories about their breathtaking surroundings.

San Antonio de Bexar had once been the provincial capital of Spain, but after Mexico achieved her independence, and without Spanish rule, its bustling streets and adobe businesses had fallen into decay. Most of the population had left, for the threat of Indians was great. It had been only in the last few years that the area had begun to repopulate.

The bridge rumbled as they crossed the San Antonio River. Although the chill was evident in the air, children splashed in its sparkling waters while *mamacitas* labored over laundry, many calling out hurriedly if a child ventured too far from shore. And though it was not quite dusk, fires were being lit in every yard, where families would congregate with friends to pass the hours before bedtime. From some doorway guitar music drifted through the air and settled pleasantly on their ear.

It caused Angelique to daydream of dancing. And of Alejandro.

"There," came Tomas's quiet voice, interrupting her thoughts. "There is the Alamo."

She caught a glimpse of gray walls and timber barricades in the distance. A red, white, and green flag snapped in the breeze from atop the crumbling enclosure. They did not dally, and Tomas explained why. To their right was the La Villita, a group of ramshackle huts and shacks that during the days of Spanish rule had harbored soldiers and their common-law wives. It was rumored that many of Cos's troops who had not managed to escape into the Alamo were holed up there.

As the Bastitas coach entered the town and rolled down its narrow streets, children darted from between squat little houses and begged for pesos. Some had the dark faces of Indians. Still others were fair offspring of the *norteamericanos* or Spaniards; all appeared gleefully happy.

The entourage of brightly dressed vaqueros, reining their prancing bays, made room for the coach as the driver wove through the busy central square, Military Plaza, where Mexicans spent idle time in conversation. All spectators hushed and turned to watch, many removing their broad-brimmed sombreros and bowing in homage.

Isabella tipped her head and raised her hand in their honor, as did Tomas. Many senoritas waved handkerchiefs in his direction, or batted long lashes over intricately decorated fans. At his smile, they blushed and giggled.

Passing the San Fernando Church and entering Main Plaza, they stopped before Musquiz's grand home. Its walls were graced with bougainvillea vines, and though they were barren now, Angelique could imagine their harvest of crimson blossoms in summer.

The front door of the house was flung open and several servants dashed to open the coach doors and lower the steps. Tomas descended first, then helped his grandmother, Carlota, and Angelique to the ground.

"Welcome, my friends," came Ramon Musquiz's booming voice.

Isabella made quick introductions. "Senor Musquiz is the *jefe politico* of Bexar," she explained to Carlota and Angelique.

Both smiled at the deputy governor and his wife.

Mrs. Musquiz stepped forward, accepting Carlota's hand. "My sympathies are with you, senora. I knew your brother and Francesca well."

Tomas fell in beside Angelique as they moved up the cobblestone walk. Bending low to her ear, he asked quietly, "Might I convince you to wear something other than black during our stay here? I'm sorry to say the color does not flatter you as did the red silk dress you wore during our fiesta."

"I hardly think we have come here to dance," she whispered with a tilt of her head. Thinking a moment, she asked, "Why exactly *have* we been brought here?"

Flashing white even teeth, he shrugged. "*Querida*, we Spaniards hardly need a cause for celebration. Besides, Musquiz and my grandfather are friends. They will talk about these barbaric Americanos and what must be done to stop them. Isabella and Senora Musquiz will prattle about needlepoint. *Abuela* will nod off, or pretend to, while she strains her keen ear on her husband's conversation, which, in the end, always turns to bulls. At that point she will awaken and suggest having chocolate in the courtyard."

Her laughter was light. "You know her well."

"I have lived twenty-eight years under her gentle reign. There is little the lady could do to surprise me."

They were shown to rooms very similar to those at Rancho de Bejar. Floors were bare. Only a large carved cross hung on one of the room's walls, over the bed. There was no fireplace to heat the chill from the air, but a brazier containing hot coals had been placed near the foot of her bed.

Shortly after Angelique had been shown to her room, servants appeared with trays laden with a silver chocolate service, as well as bowls of fruit. Clean linens were laid out, so Angelique might be able to freshen up before joining her host and hostess.

It was a jovial party that met in the *sala grande* an hour later. Isabella was in a glorious frame of mind, and on several occasions was heard laughing uproariously at some secret comment made by her friend Senora Musquiz. Other guests arrived—a gentleman called Yturri, who was a nearby neighbor; Ambrosio Rodriguez; then a middle-aged man and his young wife: Almeron and Susannah Dickinson, with their baby, Angelina.

Angelique took an immediate liking to Susannah. She had a quiet disposition and appeared to dote on her husband, a blacksmith formerly from Tennessee. They exchanged stories about their homes, Angelique holding everyone's attention as she expounded on New Orleans and its gaiety.

"Yes, it is a nice place," Tomas surprised her by admitting.

"Have you been there?" she asked.

His eyes widened briefly as chagrin swept his features. "Once," he responded in a lower voice. Changing the subject, he called out, "Anyone for a game of faro?"

Angelique wasn't about to let the matter alone. "You never mentioned you had visited New Orleans."

"Didn't I?" Then again, "Faro, anyone?"

"*When* did you visit New Orleans?"

"I suppose that would be a couple of years ago. I really can't recall."

"Why?"

"My memory plays hell with me. Sorry."

"I mean why did you visit there, Tomas?"

With a resigned sigh, he rolled his eyes toward the ceiling and answered in a hushed voice, "I attended my brother's wedding."

Oh. That's not what she had expected to hear. Nor wanted to hear. An odd sensation uncoiled in her breast. She had conveniently continued to forget that Alejandro had been married before. Now, as she acknowledged that the thought disturbed her, she wondered why it should.

Because he had loved a woman devotedly enough to marry her, because they had shared a wedding night—those quiet, intimate whispers of devotion and secrets only husbands and wives could know?

"Shall we stroll?"

She looked up.

Tomas grinned. "I see I've dampened your mood. A walk might help."

Conversation had drifted to the subject of war, so their departure was hardly noticed by anyone other than Isabella. Her gray brows lifted as her grandson hooked his arm through Angelique's, and both started for the door.

Doors left open about the house allowed for a cooling current through the wide hallways. As they paused just outside the patio, Angelique rested against the wall and crossed her arms.

Shoving hands in his pockets, Tomas stared at his boots before beginning. "I was best man at Alejandro's marriage to Pamela Reynolds."

Turning away, Angelique stepped into the courtyard. Moonlight reflected from polished flagstone and coated great pottery urns in subtle light. Lacy grillwork cast twisted shadows over the center fountain, which was highlighted by the flicker of a single candle. She was reminded of Rancho de Bejar and the first moment she saw Alejandro.

"Well?" Tomas demanded quietly. "Let us not play games, *querida*. You want to know about her. Admit it."

"Why should I?" She was finding it extremely difficult to breathe.

"It is natural to want to know about former loves."

Angelique's laughter sounded forced to her own ear. "Tomas, you really assume too much."

His eyes had not left her the entire time as she glided almost nervously around the pool. "Do you deny you are in love with Alejandro?" She stopped. The moon spilled over her face like cream, and Tomas cursed his body's response.

The width of the courtyard separating them, Angelique strained to better make out Tomas's features. How very much like Alexander he appeared now. There was a huskiness to his voice that mimicked his brother's irritation and arrogance.

Clearing her throat, she replied, "I might."

Slowly, very slowly, he moved toward her. A smile twisted his mouth as Angelique stepped away, hesitated, then moved away again, obviously uncertain of his motives. Hands still in his pockets, he drawled in a low voice, "If I am to believe you make a habit of sleeping with men you care nothing for, I might try to seduce you myself."

Her first instinct was to strike. The crack of her palm against Tomas's left cheek was instantaneous and sharp.

Sucking in his breath, he stumbled backward. "*Dios!*" he hissed between his teeth.

"How could you speak to me in such a manner?" she demanded in a hurt tone. "Tomas, I believed you to be my friend, my confidant, and you are calling me a whore!"

With hand planted against his face, he snapped, "I did no such thing. I was attempting to pay you a compliment."

"Compliment? By suggesting I could be so easily seduced by you or any other man?"

His cheek still stinging, Tomas lowered his eyes. "I only meant for you to admit that you care for my brother."

Rushing forward, Angelique caught his hands in hers. "Dear, sweet Tomas. You must know I care very deeply for Alexander. I have since the first moment I saw him. It would grieve me to think you thought so little of me that you could believe I would ever consider sharing myself in such a way with one whom I cared nothing for."

"But I never considered it for a moment!" Startling her, he lifted his hands and cradled her face. "Ah, Angelique, had I not believed you to be pure as virgin snow before my brother touched you I would have wasted no time in attempting seduction."

Her jade eyes twinkling with moonlight grew wide in surprise. "Tomas!"

"I'm sorry, but are you so ignorant of my feelings? You are the most beautiful woman I have ever put eyes on, and if I were not so devoted to Alejandro I might draw you in my arms now and kiss you with all the passion I am feeling throughout my body."

"But you mustn't!"

His intense face was relieved by a smile. "No? Who would know?"

"We would know," Angelique stressed. Her heart pounding, she grabbed his wrists. "Please don't do this, Tomas. I have grown to trust you, to love you like a dear brother and—"

"Brother!" His deep laughter was dry as he pulled her closer. "If I claim you as a sister I have committed the most degenerate sin of all, for every night I dream of nothing but holding you in my arms, of loving you, kissing you."

She thought she would swoon there—at his feet—in a mortified little puddle.

He tipped her face to his. "If you are not certain of your deepest feelings for Alex—"

"Oh, but I am!" she protested breathlessly. "I am in love with Alexander and could not think . . ." She was stunned silent as a broad grin swept his enlightened face.

"*Are* you in love with him?"

"B—but of course. Have I not said so before?"

Arms dropped to his sides, he shook his head. "No. You said merely that you cared for him. I care for Anna and Consuela, but I do not love them."

Confused, Angelique staggered backward until the fountain caught the backs of her thighs. "God, what have I done?"

"You have just admitted to his family that you are in love with Alejandro. That is all we needed to know." Turning toward the door, he called back over his shoulder, "And in case you are wondering, Pamela Reynolds was pretty . . . but not nearly so pretty as you. And she didn't love my brother."

# SIXTEEN

"These Anglo-Americans may be a foolish lot," Ambrosio Rodriguez stated, "but they are determined. It is not the desire to see Santa Anna honor the Mexican Constitution of 1824 that possesses them now; it is their desire for complete independence. I was speaking with William Travis recently—"

"Travis?!" Carlos de Bastitas barked, causing the placid Rodriguez to cower slightly. "William Travis is a snot-nosed young hothead."

Musquiz and Rodriguez exchanged glances. Although both were supporters of Mexico's government, both had made friendships with many of the North Americans and newly settled Texans.

Carlos continued, "They are ruining our land, I tell you. Do you realize that seventy-five percent of our population is made up of these Americans?"

Realizing Carlos de Bastitas was glowering at him, Ambrosio shifted nervously. "No, senor," he admitted falsely.

"They disregard our stand against slavery and refuse to pay their taxes; less than two thousand pesos were collected in the past two years." He waved two fingers beneath his friend's nose. "Now they ignore the sacrament of our religion. *Ay*, but they *all* should be lined before a firing squad and shot!''

"But there are many good men among them," Musquiz argued. "Take Jim Bowie for instance."

"Bowie! Ha! Had he not married Juan Veramendi's daughter he would have been nothing but an intruder as well. Just because he was granted Mexican citizenship and turned Roman Catholic does not make him of our blood or heritage."

Centering his attention on some point above Carlos's head, Musquiz counted backward until his irritation was no longer out of control. He realized Carlos's anger toward the now-deceased Veramendi stemmed from the strings he had pulled in the government that allowed Bowie to attain options to titles totaling nearly a million acres of Texas land. All knew a limit of fifty thousand acres of land had been set on all Mexican citizens. Carlos himself had tried numerous times to attain more land.

"Speaking of land," Rodriguez interrupted, "how are your bulls, Carlos?"

"My what?"

"Your bulls, senor."

Isabella lifted her chin from her chest and smiled sleepily toward her conversing hostess. "Shall we have chocolate?"

It was early when Angelique awoke. The clatter of horses and wagons outside her window was proof that although the hour was early, dawn was well under way. Listening intently, she concentrated on the muffled movements in the room next to hers. It wasn't like her mother to be up and about so early. Then her mother had been acting very queer of late, humming to distraction and daydreaming.

Hair spilling to her hips in glorious disarray, Angelique bounced to her knees and, grinning, pressed her ear to the wall. There! Her mother was at it again. She was warbling like a canary and . . . shuffling? Dancing!

Rolling from the bed and pulling her cotton gown over her head, Angelique tugged open the wardrobe, grabbing the dark-blue morning dress. She wouldn't wait for the maid Senora Musquiz had been so kind to furnish her with. There wasn't time. First she must see Tomas and apologize for her behavior the night before. It wouldn't do to lose him as a friend and, of course, she must rectify any misunderstandings about his despicable brother.

Certainly she didn't *love* Alexander de Bastitas. Good heavens. Infatuation was the more appropriate term. Yes, Tomas had tricked her into that ridiculous confession, for whatever purpose. No doubt Alexander himself had put the poor dear up to it.

After struggling with the buttons on her dress, she proceeded to pull on her shoes and tie them. She was just beginning to brush out her hair when she heard her mother's door open and close quietly. Angelique waited, expecting a soft rap on her door. Instead, Carlota's footsteps grew faint before disappearing completely.

In a flash she was at the door, peering down the hall. Nothing. On tiptoe she hurried down the corridor, out into the foyer. Her mother wasn't there. She jerked open the front door, rushed down the path leading to the street and out the wrought-iron gates. Shielding her eyes against a morning sun, Angelique searched one way, then the other.

There! No, she was mistaken. That wasn't her mother dressed in bright yellow, her hair spilling freely over her shoulders in glossy black waves.

Angelique began walking. Dodging occasionally around ox-driven carts, street peddlers, and pedestrians, she trained her eyes on the woman who seemed so intent on following penned instructions in her hand. A map, perhaps? Closing the widening gap, she stopped dead.

It was her mother! She gasped as Carlota disappeared into the rooming house. There had to be some explanation. Darting across the dusty street, Angelique hesitated, then entered the quiet quarters. A round-faced Indian looked up and smiled. "I am looking for a senora in a yellow dress," she explained.

He nodded and thumbed toward the stairs.

Indeed? Swallowing her trepidation and hiking her skirts

to the tops of her shoes, she mounted the stairs slowly, her ears attuned for her mother's voice. Reaching the upper level of the building, she paused again. Now what? She had no way of knowing which room her mother was in. Gradually she moved down the dimly lit hall, offering her ear for any sound that might hint of Carlota's whereabouts.

Carlota's soft laughter hit her like a blow.

Staring at the door, then the knob, she backed away with fingers twisting nervously into the unruly hair falling over her breasts.

"Looking for me?"

Jumping, Angelique twirled to stare up into Alejandro's unshaven, smiling face. Stunned speechless, she backed away, shaking her head.

"You needn't have troubled yourself, love. I had every intention of seeing you today." With the tip of his finger, he caught her sagging chin and shut her mouth. "Miss me?"

Angelique looked around for something that might offer her wobbly legs support. There was nothing but the wall. She sagged against it.

Alex hated to admit to himself that he was not only surprised to find her here, but also delighted. He had hoped, at some point, Angelique would contact him. But he hadn't expected this. Moving past her, he reached for the door. "We'll find more privacy in my room."

"No!"

His head turned.

"I—I didn't come here to see you."

Bracing a forearm against the doorframe, he laughed silently. His blue eyes, however, held no humor. "Then just who the hell *are* you here to see?"

Biting her lip, she responded softly, "My mother."

"Your mother." Lifting a handful of burnished hair from her shoulder, Alex slowly shook his head. "I don't think so, *querida*. By the looks of this tousled silk, you've just tumbled in . . . or out of bed. I prefer to think it the latter."

A defiant spark in her green eyes, Angelique slapped his

hand away and spun to leave. Hard fingers closed about one arm and jerked her back around. "Take your filthy hands from me this moment!" she hissed. "You have the most grossly inflated self-perception of any man I have ever known to think I would want to see you again, much less sneak to this disgusting hovel to do it!"

Angelique struggled to withdraw her arm. She had attempted to put the memory of this man's touch out of her mind the last two weeks, but suddenly here he was again, the warmth of his hand splintering her senses no less than they had that midnight so many sleepless nights before. Choking back her anger at her own weakness, she lurched backward and might have fallen had Alejandro not dropped the saddlebags he carried in his left hand and grabbed her with both arms.

"Easy, Angel," he soothed. "*Dios*, but I had forgotten what a little firebrand you are." Pulling her closer, so the softness of her breasts pressed against his chest, he groaned deep in his throat. He was falling again. With a flash of those outrageously wide green eyes, she could twist his guts and not think twice of her havoc. "Tell me the truth. Were you here to find me?"

Eyes riveted to his mouth, she whimpered, "No—no." The tip of his tongue moistened his lips; hers parted. He noticed and grinned. Alex might have kissed her in that moment, and she would have allowed it. The idea that he realized it caused two bright spots of color to center high on her cheeks. Again, she tried to escape.

His hold tightening, Alex frowned. "You're going nowhere until you tell me why you're here. So unless you intend to spend the rest of the day in this hall, I suggest you begin talking now."

"I told you. My mother is in that room."

His eyes narrowed. "That is Kaintock's room."

Her futile thrashing ceased abruptly. Angelique's head fell back as she stared into the dark face above hers. "You are a liar, senor. My mother would *never* stoop so low as that."

Alex pulled his gaze from her eyes, to her mouth, to the

mussed hair entangling about his fingers. One hand slipped from her arm to her waist, and he pulled her closer. "I warned you once, *querida*; I do not lie."

His insolent smile faltered for a flicker of a second as he studied her pale, stunned face. Obviously, she was not going to accept that her mother was a grown woman and capable of leading her own life. Pulling himself from his thoughts, he stated in a quiet, deep voice, "Go home, Angel, and wait for your mother there."

She shook her head.

"Go home, unless you'd like to join me in my room. I would enjoy holding you for a while with your hair wild and free and your face kissed by roses. Um, *querida*, but I can only imagine what it would be like to have you again."

Frantically admitting to herself that his proclamation was weakening her resolve, she fought to put as much distance as possible between them. Knees shaking, Angelique wedged her arms between them and shoved against his chest. "You are a wretch to do this to me," she whispered as much to herself as to Alejandro.

"And just what *am* I doing?"

"I think you know."

Carlota's soft laughter broke the spell.

"Angel." Alex attempted to touch her as she backed away.

"Stay away from me," she hissed. Twirling, she ran back down the hall, aware that Alex was following. She escaped the boardinghouse in a flurry of blue taffeta and silk.

"Angelique!" Christ! Alejandro jumped to the side of the street before the wagon could run him over. An irate Mexican shook a fist in the air as his horses whinnied and lunged at their reins. "You too," Alex grunted as they clattered by. "Angelique!"

Angelique heard his voice, but didn't dare hesitate. Lifting her skirts and squaring her shoulders, she dodged her way down Soledad Street, back to Main Plaza. *Dios*, this was all an incredibly horrible dream!

As the Musquiz home materialized through her tears,

Angelique heaved a sigh of relief. She longed to lock herself in her room, bury her face in a pillow, and cry her heart out. Oh, why hadn't she insisted that Bernice come along? Why! Running up the hacienda's walk, she faltered as Tomas stepped from the house.

"Angelique, I searched everywhere for you. Where—"

His jaw sagged as she shoved him aside and bolted toward the door. "I cannot speak of it!" she cried.

"Speak of what?"

"Angelique!"

Surprised, Tomas looked around to find his brother barreling up the walk. His face dark with anger as well as several days' growth of beard, Alex cursed toward the sky as Angelique slammed the door between them.

"*Buenos dias*, Alex," Tomas greeted him reluctantly.

Blue eyes smoldering in frustration, Alex faced his younger brother before thundering, "It is *not* a good day!" He then stormed back down the walk.

With lifted brows, Tomas released a long, low whistle.

Her black hair was like a deep blue shadow against her creamy skin as Carlota DuHon pulled the bodice of her dress from her shoulders to her waist, and with a sway of her hips sent it to the floor. She stood before Noble McGuire, her hands crossed modestly over her breasts, which were covered with the sheerest soft, ivory lace. She could not bring herself to look at him.

"Come 'ere," came his gentle command.

As he sat on the bed, Carlota moved between his legs. His large, powerful hands wrapped about her waist. Closing her eyes, she bit her lip.

"Look at me, darlin'." She did and he smiled. "By golly, you're about the prettiest little thing I've seen in my lifetime."

Color crept up her neck and settled across her face. "Please," she beseeched in a shaky voice, "do not say those things unless you mean them."

Noble's clean-shaven face broke into a grin, and a gleam appeared in his hazel eyes. "Sweetheart, I'm a man of few words when it comes to women, 'specially pretty ones. I don't say things I don't mean.'' Catching her hands, he eased them to her side.

Where was her breath? Her courage? She had ventured here with such wonderful fantasies, but now . . . now she could not face him. She could do nothing but stand here before him and tremble like a frightened virgin on her wedding night.

"Am I that scary lookin'?" he teased gently.

"Oh, no!" She cradled his big head in her hands. "You are wonderful, Noble McGuire."

And he was. Without his beard, with his hair combed and trimmed, he appeared far more the gentleman than the wild Kentuckian. Shyness washing over her again, Carlota would have backed away, but he caught her. Her next confession brought a tightness to his throat that was difficult to hide.

"I—I have never known any man but my husband."

"And I'm reckonin' he didn't do you much justice, did he?"

"Please." The touch of her finger to his lips was light. "I do not wish to speak of that time. Ever. It is done and buried."

"But you're not," he stressed in a husky voice. "And I aim to show you just how alive you can feel."

His arms were around her then. Burying his face in her neck, he covered it with kisses, and his hand came up to tenderly enclose her breast. God, but she was soaring. Her heart raced. As his fingers slid the strap of her camisole over one shoulder, then down to expose a taut nipple, she might have screamed had she not bit her lip. His hand lifted the breast to his mouth so gently she could barely feel his touch until the tip of his tongue caressed the engorged peak, making her dizzy with a sudden desire.

Locking her arms around his neck, she swooned closer, allowing her body to quiver at each tender nip of his teeth. And when she could stand it no longer, she caught his face and turned it up to hers. Their mouths met gently, hesitantly, then fused together in a fierceness that made them lose their breath. Twisting, he laid her back onto the bed and lowered his body partially across hers. His mouth was everywhere, brushing her eyes, her nose, her temples. His tongue dipped into her ear, then down her neck again to her breasts.

"Sweetheart," he whispered, "I'm gonna make you forget there ever was a man before me."

Angelique sat in the window, staring at the bustling street and the boardinghouse in the far distance. One hour passed, then two, and with each tick of the tall case clock in the hall she attempted to convince herself that she had only imagined hearing her mother's laughter from McGuire's room.

Then the image in yellow appeared, her arm locked fondly through Noble "Kaintock" McGuire's as he escorted her back to the Musquiz home. It was true. Angelique couldn't deny it any longer.

Carlota laughed pleasantly as Kaintock wrapped his arm about her waist, refusing to let her go. "Noble, please," she teased him. "Someone may be watching."

"Good. Let 'em watch. Now kiss me, woman, before I shout to this whole damn town that—"

"Hush!" Blushing, she offered him a peck on the cheek.

He shook his head. "Is that gonna have to last me until tonight?"

"I'm afraid so."

He lifted her fingers to his mouth. "I'm in love with you, woman. Don't forget that."

Carlota swallowed the lump in her throat and resisted the urge to throw herself into the burly man's embrace. "We'll tell Angelique together?"

A shadow of doubt crossed Noble's face, but he nodded and smiled. He waited until Carlota had entered the Musquiz house before turning back up the street.

The house was bustling with activity, so no one appeared to notice Carlota's arrival. Servants rushed here and there as they prepared for the party to be given later in the evening. They would finish their responsibilities as early as possible, as there was afternoon Mass to attend.

Entering her bedroom and closing the door, she wrapped her arms about her waist and twirled, sending her yellow satin skirts flying about her legs. Imagine Noble McGuire being in love with her! Imagine his asking her to—

"Mama."

Carlota gasped and stumbled to a halt. Her dark eyes wide in surprise, she spun to face her daughter. "Angelique! What are you doing here?"

"That is obvious, isn't it? I was waiting for you."

"I—I see." Nervously, Carlota dropped her reticule onto the bed.

Her smooth face set, Angelique left her chair. "I've been waiting for some two hours now."

"I was . . . Mr. McGuire was . . . showing me about the city."

Angelique stopped. "That is a lie, Mama."

"Oh, Angelique, please let me explain. I—"

"I followed you this morning. I know you were with him. I heard you in his room."

"You had no right!" Carlota exploded.

"I have every right when my mother is making a fool of herself."

"How dare you, Angelique? My affairs are *my* business! Besides, I happen to be in love with Noble."

"Love!" Snatching up her skirts, Angelique stormed across the room until she was face-to-face with her mother. "How can you even think of loving another man so soon after Papa's death?"

"Reggie has been dead over a year, Angelique. Noble is good to me and would never think of . . ." Biting her lip and contemplating her words, Carlota took a deep breath and confessed, "He is in love with me. He has asked me to marry him."

Angelique's heart stopped.

Meeting her daughter's stunned eyes, Carlota finished, "I have accepted."

Curling her fingers into tight little fists, Angelique stated hoarsely, "You can't."

"I will." Catching her daughter's face in her hands, Carlota forced back her own tears long enough to attempt one last plea for understanding. "You cannot possibly know what it's like to need and be needed. Mr. McGuire wants *me* to spend the rest of my life with him. He thinks I am beautiful, Angelique!"

Wrapping her hands about her mothers' wrists, Angelique pulled the hands from her face and, spinning, left the room.

Noble McGuire met Alejandro de Bastitas just as he was leaving the boardinghouse. The men eyed one another thoroughly. Hazel eyes twinkling, Kaintock acknowledged his friend's trim-fitting suit coat and trousers. "By golly, Alex, ain't you all spiffed up. What's the occasion?"

"Church."

"Church!" McGuire guffawed loud enough to startle the horses tethered to a nearby hitching post.

Alex allowed himself a sleepy grin. "Thought I might ask absolution for a few of my more venial sins."

"Good God, the priest ain't got all day."

"Very funny, McGuire." Withdrawing a thin black cigar from his jacket pocket, Alex considered his friend's appearance. "I'm not certain I have ever seen you looking so civilized, Kaintock." Leaning slightly closer, he sniffed and nodded his head. "Your perfume is nice. Ask Carlota where she purchased it and maybe I can buy some for Angelique."

Noble stiffened. "Now don't you go and get nasty—"

"Wouldn't think of it." Alex interrupted. "But I might suggest you make your meetings a bit more clandestine. Next time I might not be around to head Angelique off."

Chagrin crept up Noble's face until its color blended with the fiery crop of hair smoothed back from his forehead.

Alex went on to explain, "She followed Carlota from the house."

"To the hotel?"

"To the room."

Noble closed his eyes.

"It would do me little good to try and dissuade you from this relationship, I suppose?" Alex looked off down the street.

"Absolutely."

"You know how I feel about the woman."

"Yep, and I'm aware about her feelings for you. Damn near puts me between a rock and a hard place, don't it ... 'specially since I plan on marrying her."

Alex's head snapped around. The cigar slipped from his fingers.

Meeting his friend's stunned blue eyes, Noble caught Alex's arm and turned him toward the nearest cantina.

# SEVENTEEN

The bells of San Fernando Church pealed their message across the flat-roofed adobe houses and up the city's few packed-earth streets. Children squealed and were hushed by their mamas. The line of worshippers filed into the doors and took their places about the roughly hewn pews and waited for the appearance of their parish priest, Don Refugio de la Garza.

Carlota DuHon glanced anxiously toward her daughter. Angelique sat stiffly at Isabella's side, ignoring her completely. She touched her daughter's hand. There was no response. But as she thought of again asking for Angelique's understanding, a quiet, taunting voice at her ear caused the words to swell in her throat.

"Have you some confession for the priest, Carlota? I'm certain he would forgive you, but absolution from Angelique might take greater effort, and much, much longer."

Carlota closed her eyes, willing her anger under control.

Alex, leaning forward and bracing his elbows on his knees, spoke so softly his words were but a breath on the back of Carlota's neck. "I spoke with McGuire earlier." There was nothing more. Leaning back, he folded his arms over his chest and watched her slender shoulders tense.

Hearing her mother's soft gasp, Angelique turned her head and met Alex's stare for a long, long moment. Then forcing herself to break the contact, she faced the front.

The church had mostly emptied before Alejandro slipped behind the black drape of the confessional. Sitting down on the wobbly stool, he bowed his head and whispered, "Forgive me, Father, for I have sinned."

"I've no doubts of that, senor, but if you are looking for absolution from me you have a very long while to wait."

A smile twitching at his mouth, Alex forced himself to frown. "My friend, what news do you have of Santa Anna?"

After a heavy silence, the voice lowered further. "It is not good. Word has reached him of his brother-in-law's incarceration. From my understanding he is planning a move from Mexico City to San Luis Potosí. As you know there is already some troop organization in Satillo." After another moment he added, "Why do you people continue to remain here, Senor de Bastitas? You cannot win this war with Mexico. Send these farmers and blacksmiths home to their families before it is too late for us all."

"You worry overly much, amigo."

"Do I? Perhaps. I sometimes believe His Excellency gives you less credit than you deserve. Should this volunteer army persevere, it will be by courage, and less by strength."

Alex stared at his clasped hands but didn't respond.

"I spoke with your grandfather last evening."

"Lucky you."

A soft chuckle caused Alex to grin. Then the voice added, "I fear for you should he learn you are in league with Stephen Austin and William Travis."

"Unnecessary."

"We will meet again?"

"In time. Travis will eventually contact you himself."

"Is there anything else you want from me now?"

Alejandro stared at the drape, his eyes becoming distant.

"Were you a priest, I might ask absolution."

"I cannot give it."

Standing, he turned to leave.

"*Vaya con Dios*, my young friend."

Stepping from the church and squinting from the sun's assault on his eyes, Alex pulled a cheroot from his jacket pocket, lit it, then waited. In moments Ambrosio Rodriguez left the institution and hurried to his home on Potrero Street, the last house before the bridge over the San Antonio River.

Angelique waited patiently before her mirror, watching as the maid plaited her hair, weaving pearl-gray ribbon through each coil, then stationing it to the back of her head with a tortoiseshell comb. She had hoped the sleek coiffure would give her a somber look and, to her own eyes, perhaps it did. But it also did much to accentuate the feminine contours of her face. Black-fringed emerald eyes appeared wider, tilting slightly over pronounced cheekbones and perfectly shaped lips of dusty rose. Her chin jutted defiantly, and the starched bertha of gray lace about her neck only enhanced the swanlike beauty of her pale throat.

She refused the strand of gray pearls, choosing instead a pale blue brooch centered with an ivory cameo. Once it was in place, she stood and accepted the gray gloves of sheer lace. Her dress was of the deepest blue-gray silk. Its upper sleeves were puffed slightly, then tapered to a snug fit below her elbows to a point beyond her wrist where the gloves began. The bodice fit her perfectly, molding to her breasts to emphasize rather than detract, and her waist, made even tinier by cinching, was accentuated by the flaring of the skirt.

Although she had dusted her face liberally with the pearly white *cascarilla* supplied by Isabella, there was no disguising the vibrant blush on her cheeks. The green of her eyes was startling, exaggerated by the anger she was feeling. She had recently been informed that Noble McGuire had been included in the Musquizes' invitation for dinner. No doubt at her mother's request.

"Will that be all, Senorita DuHon?"

"Yes, thank you. You've done an excellent job, Agnes. I shall speak favorably of you to Senora Musquiz."

Dark eyes brightened and a beaming smile broke across the rotund woman's face. "Oh, you are most gracious, senorita. *Gracias*!"

"You are very welcome." After a breath's hesitation, Angelique asked, "Has my mother joined the gathering?"

The woman's head bobbed in response.

"Then that will be all."

Guests were milling about the *casa grande*, speaking pleasantly and avoiding all talk of war, though it was uppermost in their minds. Angelique, however, was far busier keeping her eye on Noble McGuire and her mother.

So intent was she on her target, she did not realize she was in turn being scrutinized by Alejandro.

He had watched her for some time from the arched *portale*. He could not seem to look away. Angelique DuHon was a big complication in his life that he did not need. Still, she *was* here, and whether or not he cared to admit it, he *was* involved. But what of Carlota?

Looking to the far corner of the room where she stood smiling up into his friend's face, he clenched his teeth. Damn the woman! Not only did she stand in the way of any happiness he might hope to find with Angelique, but now she had wormed her way into Kaintock's life.

Alejandro shook his head. He should never have accepted the invitation to attend this party. He would much prefer the comfort of a bed beneath his back. The last few nights spent with the dwindling garrisons guarding the Mexicans had taxed his patience and cost him hours of sleep while the fools drank themselves to oblivion and continually fought among themselves. Only a few days before a man called Conway had lost his head and killed Sherod Dover of Captain Coleman's company. For his efforts, the men had hanged him from the nearest pecan tree.

There appeared to be no reasoning with them now. They were eager to get on with the war. Fannin and Grant, now that Austin had left for Washington-on-the-Brazos, were after Burleson to make a move on the Alamo so they could get on with their Matamoros venture, still believing Santa Anna would make a coastal attack. Bowie and Travis had done their best to sway the commanders' decision to leave Bexar, but it had done little good. And now that Ben Milam had arrived from Goliad, the ranks were even more anxious. It was all going to go up like a powder keg soon.

Alex briefly closed his eyes, savoring the sangria he sipped. It wasn't the explosion he dreaded most, but the aftermath. What would happen then?

As Angelique moved to the food- and drink-laden table, she was joined by Isabella de Bastitas. "Is there some problem with your mother?" the woman asked her bluntly. "You have avoided one another throughout the day."

Just as frankly, Angelique responded, "I don't approve of that man."

"And you think your disapproval will affect her feelings for him?"

"It should."

"Any more than her disapproval should affect your feelings for my grandson?" Isabella pondered over her choice of barbecued goat and braised chicken. "I find it all quite amusing. She ridicules Alejandro, and in a breath, you scorn Mr. McGuire. You will accomplish nothing, my dear, for the two men involved are as headstrong as you. They will not give up easily."

"Did I hear my name mentioned?" Alex stepped between the women just as Angelique lifted a heavy silver plate from a stack of many. "Allow me," came his dulcet offer. "May I suggest the goat? It is sweet. And tender. Not unlike a particular young lady I know."

"Certainly." Refusing to look up into his swarthy face, she speared the chicken in an exaggerated motion.

He waited until Isabella moved away. Bending closer to Angelique's ear, he whispered, "I prefer your hair as it was this morning. When it is down it reflects the sun's fire in my eyes."

Her head lifted. Although the heart in her breast was racing, the smile on her lips was steady. There was no way she would give him the satisfaction of knowing that his nearness was again having its unsettling affect on her.

"Will you excuse me?" Angelique asked in a droll voice.

He shifted, allowing her to move between him and the table, but no further. "I would have thought you too old for masquerade, *querida*. If you are attempting to paint yourself homely with my grandmother's face powder, you have sadly failed. Since you walked into this room, every *caballero*'s eye has been trained on you. And only you."

"I hadn't noticed." She wished now that she hadn't chosen this dress. The room was growing warm, terribly warm.

"*I* noticed," Alex muttered under his breath. "I've been contemplating this entire day on when we might see one another privately again."

Her green eyes automatically flew to Carlota. Her mother was staring, her eyes riveted on Alejandro de Bastitas. A calculated smile curled Angelique's mouth as she slowly turned to face him. "I've been pondering on that very matter myself," she responded in a sultry voice. "I've missed you, Alexander."

His eyes narrowed and a muscle twitched in his jaw before his mouth twisted into a smile. "I think this calls for a bit of privacy, love. Besides, as you may or may not recall, I detest crowds when attempting to seduce a beautiful young woman."

"If my memory serves me, the word you used at your grandfather's fiesta was woo, not seduce."

He laughed quietly. "We won't quibble over their meanings, Angel. They are one and the same."

Sliding the plate from her fingers, Alex placed it on the table, then catching her arm, gently escorted her toward the flagstone courtyard beyond the far corridor. Angelique was immediately grateful for the much cooler breeze and, releasing her breath, sat down on the wide ledge of the fountain. Watching from the door, Alex waited, and when she was settled approached in his swaggering, unhurried style.

"Better?" he asked, stopping mere inches before her.

She nodded but refused to look up. She was having second thoughts about venturing into the dark with this rogue.

"Good. Very good." Angelique gasped as Alex suddenly caught her jaw between his fingers, snapping her head back, her face up. Both hands clutched at his as he shook her. "The next time you purr at me, sweetheart, you sure as hell better mean it."

Her eyes watering from the pain, Angelique could only whimper as he pulled a kerchief from his coat pocket and began smearing the *cascarilla* from her face. When he finished, he jerked her to her feet and released his grip. She made a futile swing for his cheek, but no sooner had she swung her hand than his had wrapped about her wrist so cruelly she cried out in shock.

Twisting her arm behind her back, Alejandro drew her against his rigid frame, then with his free hand grabbed the comb from her hair, allowing the heavy braid to fall to the small of her spine. "That little display for your mother was most amusing, but I will warn you now . . . I was used by a woman once, but never again. Do you understand me, sweetheart? If you think I intend to allow you to play hell with my heart, you are badly mistaken." Grabbing a handful of her hair so she had no choice but to face him, he grinned wickedly. "Now I think it's just about time that you *show* me how much you've missed me."

Before she could respond, her mouth was crushed beneath his with such brutal force she thought for certain she would swoon. Her lips parted from the slanting, demanding pressure, and he filled her mouth with the thrust of his tongue until she could no longer breathe. Her free arm thrashed and pummeled helplessly against his shoulder, and with each connection the kiss intensified until his breathing was ragged and angry.

Gripped helplessly between the need to claw his face and to respond to his kiss, Angelique struggled against her body's betrayal as much as Alejandro's cruelty. Still, as the severity of his assault lessened and a flicker of tenderness replaced his need to hurt, her heart took over, and bringing her hands up, she closed her arms about his neck and swayed against him.

The spicy scent of his cologne, the steely hardness of his chest against her breasts drove all thoughts of denial from Angelique's mind, and Alex could sense the change in an instant. The mouth beneath his became subtle, responsive, molding to his every movement with an eagerness that surprised him. And when she timidly touched the tip of her tongue to his, it was like a jolt of lightning had shattered the anger over her earlier coy display and sent it to the far corners of the courtyard. All he wanted now was to hold her, to bury his face in her hair and breathe in its fresh perfume, to forget Carlota DuHon, New Orleans, and this war-infested country and sweep Angelique into his arms, into the nearest bed, and spend the rest of his life loving her.

It was impossible. Neither the woman, nor the city, nor the brewing war with Mexico could be so easily forgotten. Each could explode in his face at any moment.

Angelique was spinning as he pulled his mouth from hers. Had he not slid his large hands about her waist, she might have fallen, for the strength had left her legs and centered in the heart hammering so rapidly in her bosom. Her head back, she forced open her eyes to find him caressing her flushed features. Still, the bitter slant of his mouth hinted that all was not well.

"Why do you hate me so, Alexander?" she asked in a hurt voice. Angelique wanted desperately to understand this man who had stolen her heart for his own and took such pleasure in submitting it to pain.

"Hate you? Ah, Angel, is that what you think?"

Watching bemusement replace the anger across his face, she nodded. "Don't you? You appear to go out of your way to hurt me." She touched her face, still throbbing from the pressure of his fingers.

Alex frowned, and with a gentle hand cupped her cheeks in his palms. "It is not hate that causes me to want to touch you in such a way. Nor is it my desire to hurt you. Angel, I want nothing more than to absorb you, to feel you with every fiber of my being. I am a reckless man, but it is not my way to cause a woman pain, not intentionally."

"Are you saying your seducing me at Rancho de Bejar was not a ploy to hurt me?"

He drew her closer. Lowering his head to just above hers, he answered huskily, "Perhaps in the beginning. But the victory was not mine, and had I listened to my own heart earlier, I would have known it. When on the night of the fiesta I looked up to find you standing in the shadows watching me, I was a lost man."

Did she dare believe him? Was this just another one of his tricks that in the end would be used to humiliate her again? Smoothing her hands over the breast of his black velvet jacket, she might have turned away to collect her thoughts, but he caught her wrists, refusing to let her escape.

"You don't believe me."

Unable to pull her eyes from the lips hovering so closely over hers, she shook her head. "I—I don't know what to believe," came her breathy reply.

"Believe that I want you." Fingers now biting into her shoulders, he growled, "Never has a woman made me ill with the need to possess, as you have. Damn you for doing this to me, Angelique. Damn you to hell."

Suddenly his fingers released their pressure and his arms were about her, holding her to him with a gentle but demanding force. There was no hint of his former cruelty as he caught her chin and tipped her face, brushing the tender corners of her lips with his mouth. "God, you're sweet," he whispered against her temples, disturbing the fine wisps of hair there. "Let us leave this place, Angel. I've a need that—"

"Ahem."

They stepped apart, Angelique ducking her head while pretending to smooth hair from her face, Alex spinning to glower at the embarrassed courier.

Obviously distressed, the young servant cleared his throat. "My pardon, but are you Senor Alejandro de Bastitas?"

"I am."

The boy raised the note. "I was asked to deliver this to you, senor, as quickly as possible."

Accepting the missive, Alex dismissed the carrier with a flick of his hand.

"Is it important?" Angelique asked.

Alex studied the flowing script, uneasy yet curious over the brief message. Pulling his eyes to Angelique's face, he shrugged. "I'm not certain."

"Who is it from?"

Frowning, he refolded the note and tapped it absently against his palm. "It wasn't signed."

"How very mysterious!"

Turning his dark head, he smiled, amused she should find such excitement over a simple, unexpected message. But then that was one of the reasons he . . . *cared* so much for her. "Will you wait?"

"No promises." Tilting her head, she smiled, yet inside, her heart was screaming, *Yes!*

His eyes never leaving hers, Alex tucked the message in his coat pocket. "There are things we should talk about."

"Such as?"

"Children, for one."

She swallowed. What was his meaning? "I—I am not pregnant."

Caught off-guard, Alex's expression appeared stunned, relieved, then almost . . . disappointed. "You're certain?"

"Since yesterday."

He turned and moved toward the door.

"I assume you are relieved?" came the soft query.

Alex stopped. Pivoting on his heel, he demanded gently, "Aren't you?"

"Of course."

He said nothing but departed the courtyard.

Angelique waited for several moments, allowing the cool air to extinguish the fire Alex's touch had kindled in her veins. She wanted with all her heart to believe what he had said, but he had said as much before, and in the next moment had ridiculed her to the point of tears.

She touched her brooch with shaking fingers, for even

now her nostrils could detect his scent; her tongue tasted the lingering flavor of tobacco from his mouth, and she was shocked at the affect those blended memories could have upon her. Closing her eyes, Angelique sank to the fountain ledge.

Was love this unkind? Did it wrench your every breath and leave you too winded to speak? Did it twist your heart in two until you felt like weeping from the pain? Were you left feeling so incomplete in his absence that, like a lost soul, you floundered helplessly without him?

And did these feelings ever stop?

Somehow, she knew they wouldn't, not with Alexander. His presence was stimulation in itself. Even without his touch, with one caress of those blue eyes he could make her soar. One curl of that mobile mouth caused her heart to swell, and with a simple spoken word her every fiber vibrated with a *need* for that touch.

And she ached when she could not have it.

"Angelique?"

The deep voice, gentle yet jarring, startled her from her fantasy. Looking up, she caught her breath.

Noble McGuire took a cautious step toward her. "I don't mean to be disturbin' you, or nothin'."

Almost frantically she jumped to her feet. She searched for an escape but at the moment there was only one accessible way out, and that was beyond the hulk of man standing between her and the open door.

"I was lookin' for your mama."

"I have not seen her." Gathering her skirts, she swept them to one side so as to make her departure unencumbered. "Now you will excuse me, I hope."

He shifted, blocking her path. "I'm in love with her," Noble stated in a firm voice.

Green eyes flashing, Angelique offered him a cold smile. "My sincerest regrets."

"Why? 'Cause I ain't your daddy?"

"Exactly. And you never will be."

"Don't you think she deserves somethin' of her own?"

"And what can you give her?"

He offered her a kind smile. "Anything she wants."

"You will never take my father's place in her heart."

"Was he so special?"

Angelique nodded, her eyes filling with tears.

"Then you hold on to that, darlin', if it matters so much to you. But your mama's memories won't keep the chill off her at night like I can. I ain't out to take nobody's place. Just remember that, and maybe, just maybe, you and me can be friends."

She lifted her chin. "Friends. With you?"

"Exactly. I ain't out to be your papa, Angelique. Just your friend, if you need one."

There was silence between them.

Noble shifted, then threw a quick look about the courtyard. "You seen Alex?"

"Moments ago. He received a urgent message and had to leave."

"Where to?"

"Not far, I assume, as he asked me to wait."

Pressing his lips, McGuire shook his head. He didn't like the sound of that.

"Is something wrong?" she asked him.

"I'm not certain I like the idea of Carlota and Alex missin' at the same time."

Their eyes met in understanding. Surprising Noble as well as herself, Angelique grabbed his arm and choked, "You don't think—"

They spun together and entered the house.

The folded message dangling between long fingers, Alejandro moved down the hall, toward the far end of the house. Stopping before the closed door, he cast a cautious glance back the way he had come to see if he had been followed. He knocked quietly on the door.

No response.

The knob turned easily in his hand, and very slowly he entered the room, stopping just inside the threshold.

"Close the door, if you please," came the feminine voice.

Doing so, Alex searched out each corner of the study, its interior illuminated by the flame of several candles. There appeared to be no one . . .

Until the chair behind the desk swiveled to reveal the woman.

"Carlota DuHon. I might have known."

A pleasant smile lifted the corners of her red mouth. "I saw you with Angelique earlier . . . saw you kissing her."

Reaching into his pocket, Alejandro withdrew a cheroot. "Should I consider myself chastised?"

"What have you told her?"

"Nothing. Yet."

"And do you intend to tell her?"

"At the appropriate time and place."

"I cannot allow that," she returned in a silky voice. "I warned you, you know. I warned you to keep your filthy hands off my daughter."

A laugh rumbling in his chest, Alex slid the cigar between his teeth, then inhaled. "There hasn't been a woman yet who's managed to make me cower in my shoes, Carlota."

"Not even your wife?" Laughing throatily, Carlota shook her head. "It was my understanding you wept like a baby at her funeral. The great, rugged man among men actually fell to his knees and sobbed over that *slut!*"

"Shut up, or—"

"Is it true she bled to death in your arms? How very apropos."

He looked about for an ashtray. The cigar was making him sick.

Carlota stood. "I warned you to stay away from my daughter."

His mouth tightening, Alex dropped the cheroot into a vase of flowers. "Get to the point," he snapped.

"This is the point, senor."

Looking down the barrel of one of Ramon Musquiz's dueling pistols, Alex released a harsh laugh. "Point taken, madame. But it will take more than an impotent threat of a wavering gun to keep me from seeing Angelique, should I choose to.''

''But this is not an impotent threat. I intend to kill you.''

''Indeed?'' He moved toward her slowly. As he crossed the room, the smile on his face broadened as her black eyes grew wider. By the time he stopped before her, the weapon was shaking so badly Carlota found the need to grip it with both hands.

As he closed his fingers about the barrel of the gun, she believed he would attempt to take it. He didn't. Instead he moved ever closer, then pressed it against his heart.

''Go ahead. Kill me if it will appease you.''

The words catching in her throat, she demanded, ''Do you not believe I will?''

''You haven't yet.''

He was actually daring her to fire the gun! ''Only a devil would welcome death,'' she hissed.

He shrugged. ''Or a man who has been dead inside so long the sleep would be no more than an end to an eternal hell.''

''I hate you.''

''Then do it, because I warn you now, I will have her. One way or another, Angelique will be mine.''

In that moment, the door flew open. The next, Carlota DuHon pulled the trigger of the gun.

# EIGHTEEN

Angelique and Noble stumbled into the room just as the hammer slammed into the empty chamber of the gun.

"*Jesus!*" Alex groaned.

Angelique blinked in horror. "Mama!"

Carlota stared up into Alejandro's bleached face. "I'm dreadfully sorry, senor. I thought the gun loaded."

Noble McGuire jumped past a stunned Angelique and hurried to Carlota's side. Slipping his hand over the gun, he removed it from Alex's chest. It was that movement which snapped her from her trance, and looking about she spied the matching pistol.

"No you don't." McGuire caught Carlota's wrist as she made a grab for the gun, then turning to look into his friend's taut face, suggested, "You look like you could use a drink, amigo."

Alex stepped away, obviously shaken. Christ, he had known of Carlota's hatred, but had never taken her threats as anything more than the rantings of a jealous, hysterical woman. Blocking out the heated words being exchanged between Kaintock and Carlota, he raised his eyes toward the door. Angelique was there. Her eyes wide with shock

and her face void of all color, she shifted her attention from her mother to him.

Attempting a less than believable smile, he moved up beside her. "I see your mother is a woman of her word."

"She would have killed you." Wanting to understand, Angelique laid a gentle hand on his sleeve. "Why, Alexander? Why does my mother hate you so?"

"Ask her."

"I have." Lowering her voice she beseeched him, "Please! If I am to understand, I must know what there is between you."

"*Would* you understand?" He lifted his hand to touch her face, but didn't. "I'm not certain I'm ready to take that chance. Not yet." Moving away and throwing one last glance over his shoulder, he started up the hall.

Isabella turned from Ramon Musquiz as her elder grandson entered the salon. She knew immediately by the set of his shoulders and the look on his face that something was wrong. Excusing herself from her host, she glided to Alejandro's side. "Something has happened."

A half-smile on his lips, Alex dropped his eyes onto *la patrona*'s upturned face. "You know me too well, Grandmother."

"Not well enough, I fear."

"Carlota DuHon just tried to kill me."

"I see." She glanced about the room. "I could use a drink. Would you mind, dear?"

Lifting his hand, Alex motioned to the waiter, then retrieved a full glass of wine from the tray and placed it in Isabella's trembling fingers. "Don't let it upset you," he reassured her with a smile. "As you can see, I am without injury and have learned a lesson I won't forget shortly."

"Which is?"

"To think twice before voluntarily crawling into a pit with a rattlesnake." Shoving hands into his pockets, he looked about the room. "Where is Tomas?"

"He declined our invitation tonight and mentioned a young lady he was to see."

"Anna." Alex turned and, accepting Isabella's hand,

touched it to his lips. "My regards to the host and hostess, but I suddenly recall a previous appointment. You'll offer my apologies?"

Her fingers closing about his, she placed them against her heart. Their eyes met.

"I'm fine," he whispered, "Shaken, but unhurt."

"Will you continue to pursue her?"

"I have little choice."

"Why, Alejandro?"

He placed her hand against his heart.

Understanding, Isabella nodded. She turned back to the crowd, refusing to watch as he left the house.

The cantina was unusually quiet. Alejandro, upon stepping into the less than crowded room, had no trouble locating his brother. Tomas looked up as he approached, as did Anna Gonzales.

"Am I intruding?" Alex asked.

Withdrawing his arm from the girl's shoulder, Tomas sank back against his chair. "Hardly."

"You're missing one hell of a party."

"That explains why you are here and not there." Tomas grinned.

Flashing Anna a smile, Alex waited as she filled an extra glass with whiskey and shoved it before him. "I thought you had perhaps joined our garrisons," he said to Tomas.

"No thank you."

"We need all the help we can get."

"So I gathered." Tomas lifted his drink but paused, the glass pressed to his lower lip. "James Bowie was in earlier. Seems he and Travis are at one another's throats again. I can hardly imagine joining in a war with rebels who cannot avoid arguing among themselves."

Alex's blue eyes dropped to the girl at Tomas's shoulder. Her young face was tilted to his, a look of adoration twinkling in her dark eyes. Anna Gonzales was in love with Tomas. She hung on his every word, anticipated each movement before he made it. And when in a drunken move he dribbled liquor down his chin, she brushed it away with a tender sweep of her thumb.

Something turned over in Alex's chest. Good God, it had felt almost like . . . envy. He refilled his glass, with great reluctance acknowledging the uncomfortable ache as just that.

Raising his glass in a toast, Alex stated in a tight voice, "To a very lucky man." One brow shot up as Tomas looked over one shoulder, then the other. "I am speaking to you, my brother."

"Me?" Hesitantly, Tomas lifted his glass. "What the hell for?"

"The lady seems quite fond of you."

Anna lowered her eyes and blushed. Tomas, on the other hand, did not take his gaze from Alex. "I might offer you the same," he finished in a deep voice.

"I can't image why."

"To the *luckiest* man in the world. And should you open your eyes, you might realize it."

Sitting back in his chair, Alex shook his head. "I don't understand."

"In a word: Angelique."

Anna's chair scraped across the floor. Her smile was far less steady as she looked back and forth between the men. "I fear I have forgotten my duties. If you desire more whiskey, let me know."

Tomas watched her walk away. Frowning then, he rolled his eyes toward Alex. His brother was staring. That unblinking gaze was swallowing him whole and for a moment he thought he might be thrashed by the fists lying clenched upon the table. But his meaning had been clear. Although Tomas had not actually stated he had feelings, very deep feelings, for Angelique, the insinuation had left little doubt in anyone's mind. And it hadn't been intentional. Just a slip of the tongue.

Nothing more.

Clearing his throat, Tomas reached for the bottle. "You've nothing to fear from me. I've no chance with her. I was informed of that last night." He took another swallow. "But you have. Unless, of course, you intend to continue your role as an ass. Then I might challenge you to a friendly duel of hearts."

"When I duel, my brother, it is to the death."

Their eyes met. Still, there was no hostility reflected in their matching glances.

Alex stood. Emptying the remaining whiskey into Tomas's glass, he offered, "Anna is a lovely girl. She loves you, and at one time you must have cared for her or you wouldn't have gifted her with our mother's necklace."

Tomas's head snapped up.

"Between me and Carlos, there are enough fools in San Antonio. Take what you have and treasure it. A woman's love is hard to come by and worth far more than an infatuation over a gorgeous face." Alex flashed a genuine smile on his brother. "Adios."

"Is it?"

"For now. When the battle is over, I'll come home."

"Which battle? The one out there?" Tomas pressed an unsteady finger to his own heart. "Or the one in here?"

"Adios."

"Yes, yes. Goodbye." Goodbye and good riddance. He had no time for fools.


As Rancho de Bejar materialized through the rain, all occupants within the coach released a great sigh of relief. This had been one of the most disquieting journeys Angelique had ever experienced. Isabella had upon occasion offered Carlota a tolerant smile and inquisitive eye. Tomas, slumped in his seat, grimaced with each bump in the road. And of course there was little said between Angelique and her mother. She had no intention of accepting the relationship between Carlota and Noble McGuire. And Carlota . . .

Carlota had made her feelings toward Alejandro de Bastitas quite clear.

Carlota tugged her wool shawl tighter about her shoulders before squinting toward the hacienda. Gathering her courage and facing *la patrona,* she suddenly blurted, "Angelique and I are most grateful for your kindness during

the past weeks, Senora de Bastitas, but I feel we have out-
stayed our welcome.''

"Nonsense.''

Tomas peered at Carlota through the slit of one eye.

Carlota continued. "There is business to attend in Gonzales. My brother's estate must be seen to—''

"I will have my grandson see to it.'' As the carriage
halted, Isabella lifted her hand, quieting any further argument from Carlota. "With the Mexican and Indian problems as they are, I fear we must keep our vaqueros at the
ranch. For safety's sake. You do understand?''

"Yes. Of course.''

A smile lifting one corner of her mouth, Isabella pulled
the hood of her cloak up over her head before stepping
into the rain. She did not speak again until she and Tomas
were alone in the study behind them.

"Something must be done soon,'' she stated, sweeping
the wet garment from her shoulders.

Rubbing the back of his neck, Tomas wearily stated, "I
don't know what more we can do, Grandmother. We cannot force Alejandro home any more than we can force Carlota to remain here indefinitely.''

Angrier than Tomas had seen her in a long time, Isabella
lifted her fist into the air and gave it a shake. "*Ay*, but
were it not for this damnable war Alejandro would be at
home where he belongs!''

"Perhaps if you write Stephen Austin and Santa Anna
a very pleasant letter they will postpone any further ag-
gression until your grandson is married.'' He winced beneath her icy stare. "Sorry.''

Sinking onto the wine-colored chair, she pursed her lips.
"Something must be done. And soon.''

"Yes, but it will take cooperation on Alex's and Angelique's part and from what I've witnessed, that may take
some doing.''

"Not necessarily. Come sit beside me.''

Tomas slipped into the matching chair. "There is a
crafty glint in your eye, *Abuela*. Do I detect a conspiracy
clattering about that brain of yours?''

A velvety cheek folding with her smile, she faced him. "Carlos will not like it."

"My thoughts exactly."

"But faced with honor . . . he has been known—upon occasion—to do the honorable thing. Hasn't he?" She waited for Tomas's reply. When there was none, she waved him away with a flick of her hand. "Never you mind. There is always a first time. And if I have anything to say about it . . ."

She reasoned there were many details to be seen to before her grandson came home. And everything must be perfect.

The days ticked monotonously by. Skirmishes between Cos's troops and the Texas Volunteer Army kept the streets of San Antonio vacant. On the outskirts of town, however, trouble with the troops was growing.

"I'm tired of waiting!" William McDowell announced to his companions. "I didn't come all the way to Texas from Pennsylvania to sit and twiddle my thumbs. Hell, I say let's go get Cos! Run his butt out of San Antonio!"

Alejandro stood outside his tent, shoulders hunched beneath a multicolored serape and a cigar jutting from between his teeth. A dark-skinned mestizo walked past him for the second time, her hips swaying and her large breasts bouncing provocatively with each step she took.

"You interested?" she asked, flashing him a smile.

"Nope."

"You go crazy without woman for so long."

"Yep."

"You already crazy."

"Um hm."

"You fight, you die. With me you go smiling."

Unable to refrain, he burst out laughing, then looked up as two riders approached. Sam Maverick dismounted first. "Where the hell is Burleson?" he bellowed.

"Who wants to know?" someone replied.

"I got news from town!" Holding a sheaf of papers in

the air, he finished, "I'm ready to fight boys, and I got the means to do it!"

Alex bypassed the pouting soldadera and with a quick stride approached the newcomers. By now the crowd was growing excited, anxious to hear Maverick's news. The past weeks had been hell on their patience. Burleson had refused to take aggressive action, afraid the casualties would prove too great. The Mexicans had much greater knowledge of the city, and it was a known fact that many of the troops were hidden among the loyal Mexican families throughout the town, as well as in the old mission.

John W. Smith raised his voice as he too slid from his horse. "Them sapsuckers are starvin' to death, men. They're out of ammunition and cranky as hell. We say hit 'em now!"

Burleson stepped into the circle of men. "What's going on here, Bastitas?"

Slowly removing the cigar from his mouth, Alex pointed toward the men. "Seems Maverick and Smith have decided it's time to fight, General."

"Is that right?"

"That's right," Maverick thundered. Waving the papers beneath the officer's nose, he added, "I got maps of every house, hovel, and shanty that's harboring those sons of bitches. Now you got no reason to keep us from 'em . . . sir."

The air crackled with tension. Quiet now, the men surrounding the commander waited in anticipation.

Burleson shifted from one foot to another. "Very well. Come to my tent and show me your plan, Mr. Maverick. *Then* I will make my decision."

The crowd dispersed, satisfied for the moment that something was finally being done. Alejandro stood his ground, staring at the tip of his cigar and cursing his decision to ever return to Texas.

"Seems like this is it."

Alex turned. "Maybe," was his only response. Throwing the cheroot to the damp earth, he moved back toward his tent.

Kaintock fell in beside his friend. "Reckon we haven't talked in a while."

"Nothing much to say."

"I rode out to the ranch yesterday. Isabella's more'n a little tiffed cause you haven't been out."

"And Carlos? Frothing at the mouth, I assume."

"Reckon I pacified him. I just explained you're keepin' company with some of your friends."

"My undying gratitude."

McGuire hesitated as Alex reached the canvas shelter. Normally he would have thought nothing of joining his friend without the benefit of a casual invitation. Now he wasn't certain.

Alex dropped the tent's flap in place. Hunkered over, as the roof was not nearly tall enough to accommodate his height, he rummaged through the few soggy blankets strewn about the muddy floor. "Want a drink?" he asked without turning.

"You talkin' to me?" came the voice.

Alejandro made a face as he tilted the bottle to his mouth. "Unless I've begun talking to myself." Dropping to the makeshift bed, he took another drink.

Again, they waited. After two days and still no decision on Burleson's part, the men were drunk, angry, and not looking forward to another night huddled against the cold in inadequate shelters. Their bellies rumbled from lack of food. Many were sick, and many more had returned to their families in the surrounding area.

It was obvious General Edward Burleson could come to no decision regarding his troops. Jim Bowie had done his best to rally the men's sagging spirits, but even he had taken to his tent, more often than not ending up passed out on his bunk. William Travis had thrown up his hands in exasperation and left San Antonio for San Felipe, hoping he could accomplish more by helping set up the Provisional Government of Texas.

It was dusk on December 4th, and the men hunkered about the fire were a dispirited lot. For the first time since he had made his decision to join in this fight, Alejandro was considering returning to Rancho de Bejar. It made no sense to starve to death and die of pneumonia when his home was less than a hour's ride away. He was out of cigars and whiskey. His head hurt and he hadn't had a decent night's sleep in three weeks.

He missed Angelique.

The *soldadera* had been right those two days before. He was going crazy without a woman. But he had learned not long after arriving at this pig pit that a common whore couldn't appease the hunger he felt for Angelique. He had failed miserably, apologized for his drunken state, paid the *puta* for her services, and sent her on her way.

But the ache was growing.

Odd the way he could remember how Angelique blushed when she smiled. How her lashes lowered like a shadow against her cheek, then flew wide to reveal the most dazzling green eyes he could ever recall. And her hair. God, but her hair. Like silk it poured through his fingers and entrapped him like a finely braided cord when he buried his hands in it. It smelled of violets. Like the violets he once rested in as a young boy. And her lips were the color of the bougainvillea that draped their home in Spain, vibrant crimson when damp, scarlet when bruised.

And she tasted of honey.

Shaking his head, Alex peered from beneath his black broad-brimmed sombrero at Burleson's tent. He knew what the general was facing, the decision that must be made. He would not relish ordering men to a possible slaughter. But he had to take a stand if this war was to be won. No battle had yet been fought without casualties, sacrifices.

The flap of Burleson's tent was thrown back and a long-legged plainsman in buckskin stepped before the waiting men. His dark eyes darted among them, then lifting his rifle in the air, he called out, "Boys, who will come with old Ben Milam into San Antonio?"

Two hundred forty voices shattered the air with a roar and as many men jumped to their feet. But it would be dawn of December 5th before they attacked the unsuspecting Mexicans.

The volunteers of the Texas army had not expected the skirmish to be an easy one. But neither did they expect the siege to go on for days. Little by little they worked their way through the houses and streets of the city, killing, capturing Cos's weakening forces, and each day coming one step closer to the old mission where Santa Anna's brother had retreated those weeks before.

Ben Milam was killed soon after the fighting began. Stepping from the Veramendi house, he was shot through the heart by a sniper and died in Sam Maverick's arms. But with each Mexican who threw his weapon to the ground and surrendered, or died, the men's courage was bolstered. The Navarro house was taken; the priest's house and Zambrano row followed. Finally there was little left but La Villita and the Alamo.

It was just before midnight on the evening of December 8th when Alejandro moved through the shadows and up to the window of the flat-roofed hovel. The sky had cleared, allowing a crescent moon to reflect from the San Antonio River. He had just crossed the water. His clothes were wet and he was shivering with cold.

Peering through a slit in the barricaded window, Alex focused on the uniformed soldier slumped in a chair before the fire, a pistol resting on his lap. Head down, his eyes closed, he appeared to be sleeping.

Slipping around the corner of the house, Alex tried the door and found it locked. Taking two steps backward, he shifted, and with one quick lunge sent the meager panel flying from its hinges. Throwing himself to the floor, he rolled, and before the Mexican soldier could clumsily leave his chair to shoot his firearm, Alex was up on his knee, aiming and pulling the trigger of his weapon.

A woman's scream pierced the air as the explosion lifted the soldier from his feet and sent him back against the wall. In an instinctive reaction, Alejandro dropped his rifle and withdrew the pistol from his waistband, and as he spun, aimed its sights on the tiny cowering frame in the doorway.

The girl dropped to her knees, her hands clutched at her

bosom. "Oh, please, senor, do not kill me! I beg you, he was not of my doing, but my father's. Please, please do not kill me!"

Not without reluctance, he lowered the gun. "Get to your feet," he demanded. He then caught his breath as she lifted her face. "Anna!"

Her eyes wide with fright, she shuffled back to the wall. "I do not know you, senor."

Alex lowered the gun to his side. "I am Alejandro de Bastitas."

"No! It is not possible!" Gradually, she began to relax.

Shoving the gun back into his pants, he laughed. It had been weeks since he had last bathed or shaved. It was no wonder the girl did not recognize him. "Get up," he said more gently. "To harm you would be to harm my brother, and I have no intention of doing that." Offering his hand, he helped her to stand.

Anna melted against him, her face buried into his chest. She was weeping again. Her slender shoulders were shaking and he could not help but fold his arms about her in a comforting manner. When she had calmed down sufficiently to speak, he asked, "Why are you harboring this man in your home, Anna? I thought you believed in the volunteers' cause."

Sniffing, she turned away. "It is not me, but him." She motioned toward the partially closed bedroom door.

Cautiously, Alex pushed the door open with his foot. The dim light from the main room spilled across the obese man's sleeping face. Clothes were twisted about his protruding belly. His mouth was open, and the entire room reeked of sour whiskey.

"Your father?" Alex asked as he turned to face Anna.

"*Sí.* Though I am embarrassed to admit it." Wringing her hands, she looked away. "The soldier was paying my father for protection."

"We'll have to remove him," he said, pointing to the dead man. With Anna's help, he pulled the soldier from the house to the alley beyond, and there covered his body with debris from several crumbling shanties.

"You will spend the night here," Anna offered as they reentered the house. She knew the troops' circumstances, realized it had been many days since Alejandro had slept comfortably or had eaten a full meal. "Sit before the fire," she directed him. "Soon your clothes will dry and you will be warmer. I will make you coffee, and there are tortillas and chili left over from our dinner."

Alex did his best to prop the door upon its hinges, finally opting to drag the only other chair in the room against it for support. He would take the time to fix it properly tomorrow. By the looks of the place the drunk in the bedroom did little in the way of upkeep. He understood now why a woman with Anna's looks would be working in some filthy cantina. No doubt she was the only one in this household to bring in any money. And it was more than obvious why Tomas was so reluctant to acknowledge his relationship with the girl, at least to his family. Associating with a mestizo was one thing, but Carlos would *never* approve of a woman of Anna's meager circumstances.

Sinking into the chair, Alejandro stretched long legs out before him and crossed his ankles. Then Anna was there, a bowl of chili in one hand, a plate of tortillas in the other. Folding the flat cornmeal pancake in half, he scooped the spicy melange into his mouth. The pepper burned his tongue but did little to mask the flavor of the meat.

Dog. He had been hungry enough only once in his life to eat dog, but he would never forget its flavor or consistency. He returned Anna's smile, then accepted her offered coffee. "It's very good. Thank you."

"There is more, if you like."

"No." He waited as she sat down on the floor, her back to the fire. He then asked, "Have you seen my brother?"

"Not since I saw you both at the cantina."

Alex sipped at his coffee. "I'll be returning to the ranch as soon as this skirmish is over. I can take him a letter again."

Lashes lowering over her eyes, Anna shook her head. "There is no point. But I thank you." Noticing his empty cup, she jumped to her feet. ''There is more coffee. I will get it.''

Alex watched, smiling as she walked away. He covered a yawn with the back of his hand. In a moment, he was asleep.

# NINETEEN

"Quickly!" Isabella called. "The procession is ready, Angelique, and we are waiting for you!"

With skirts flapping about her ankles, Angelique burst from her room, excitement reflected like candlelight in her eyes.

"The Virgin Mary you are not," Isabella chuckled under her breath. Exchanging amused glances with Bernice, she stated more loudly, "My dear, this is to be a somber occasion."

Winded, Angelique giggled into her friend's amused face. "But isn't it exciting?"

"Celebratin' the birth of Christ is always excitin'," admonished Bernice.

"Oh, that's not what I meant!" Blushing at Isabella's and Bernice's uplifted brows, she rescinded, "The war is over. General Cos surrendered and even now is retreating for Mexico and—"

"Yes, but my grandson's eventual return should not take precedence over this occasion, my dear."

Eyes flashing like green fire, Angelique lifted her chin. "No one mentioned your scoundrel grandson, senora. I *do* wish you would refrain from mentioning his name to me a dozen times a day.''

"My apologies. Now hurry before Joseph leaves for Bethlehem without you.'' When Angelique thought to dash out the door, Isabella stopped her again. ''Aren't we forgetting something?''

Biting her lip, Angelique smiled and accepted the pillow. Offering her back, she swept up the flowing skirt of her dress and tucked it beneath the band about her waist. She patted her stomach. ''It is somewhat lumpy.''

"Pregnancy got a lumpy feel to it,'' Bernice proclaimed. ''Now, you best hurry. Everybody's waitin'.''

Hesitating in the doorway, Isabella watched as Angelique glided toward the group gathered just outside the gates. It was just after sundown, and this was the first night of *las posadas*. Each night of the nine days preceding Christmas the ceremony of Mary and Joseph traveling to Bethlehem would be reenacted. In a *casa grande* such as theirs, it was customary for the most well-liked young man and woman to be chosen by the peons to begin the tradition.

They had elected Angelique and Tomas.

With watering eyes, Isabella lifted her hand and returned Angelique's wave. Over these many weeks she had grown to love the girl. Angelique was the daughter, the granddaughter she would never have. They giggled together, talked of knitting, gossiped about the help and shared those secrets only friends—women friends—could discuss.

Tomas waved to Isabella and Bernice, then lifted Angelique to his burro's back. ''Now sit there and try to look . . . virginal.''

"Try?'' Squaring her shoulders, Angelique kicked Tomas in the rib. ''I look far more believable than a man with goat hair stuck to his face.''

Surrounded by children with candles, the couple traveled slowly through the gardens and paths, weaving through the peons' communities. It was quite dark before they again reached the hacienda, and as Tomas slid Angelique from the animal's back, the children burst out with squeals of delight.

"Piñata! Piñata!" they chanted in unison and raced for the patio.

"I suppose that is as close as I'll ever come to being worshipped," Angelique laughed. Removing her scarf, she folded it, then tucked it beneath her arm.

Staring at the top of her head, Tomas smiled. He was in total disagreement.

Angelique looked up. "Is there anything wrong?"

"Do you like piñatas?"

"I'm not certain."

"Ah, then let me be the first to introduce you the thrill of foraging for treats. Delores makes some of the best caramel chews this side of the Rio Grande. Guaranteed to either pull out your teeth or send your stomach into a knot of ecstasy." He offered his arm. "Shall we go?"

The children were darting here and there by the time they arrived. Standing to one side, Angelique and Tomas laughed as a small blindfolded girl made her first swing at the clay fish dangling overhead. As the stick made contact, toys and candy rained down upon her.

"It is Senorita DuHon's turn now!" called out Tomas.

Startled, Angelique waved her hands in refusal. "No!"

"Yes!" the children cried.

Grabbing the offered blindfold, Tomas draped it across her eyes, tying it comfortably tight. "The trick is to keep your bearings," he finished as he spun her around. "You get three chances and that is all."

Dizzy, Angelique stumbled in a circle, laughing so much she could hardly breathe. "Am I close?" she yelled.

"Yes!" came the children's excited response.

She swung. Nothing.

"To your left!" Tomas called. "No, your right. Good God, Angelique, do you not know your right from your left?"

Plunking hands on her hips, Angelique tapped her foot. "You might find this most gratifying, Bastitas, but I assure you it is frustrating as—"

"To your right."

The voice seemed different now. Closer: Disquietingly familiar. Surely it wasn't . . .

Arms out before her, Angelique shuffled to the right. "Here?"

"More," he said.

Her heart was pounding. There was something. Something. "Here?"

He was smiling now. She could hear it in his voice. "Hmmm. A little more."

Tomas exchanged grins with his brother, then joined the children as they secretly hurried out of the patio.

Her own voice less steady, Angelique demanded, "Tomas? Why has it suddenly grown so quiet? If this is some sort of trick . . ."

"No trick. I assure you," was Alex's response.

The stick dropped. Grabbing the blindfold, she tugged it from her head. Angelique had fantasized this moment. Lying in bed at night she had envisaged the very instant she would see him again.

But she hadn't expected to grow weak. The ground wasn't suppose to shake, to tip and sway and threaten to open up and swallow her in blackness. For she had decided that Alejandro de Bastitas was just like any other man, human, with more faults than most. His shoulders could not really blot out the sun and moon and stars from the sky. Those eyes had *not* been like blue ice, burning her, then freezing her with a slant of those wicked black brows. He was just a man.

A man.

"Alexander." Had she whispered it? Screamed it?

"Miss me?"

Her eyes fixed on his mouth, she shook her head. "No— no." Stepping away, she added, "I am pleased, however, that you were not injured in that dreadful skirmish."

"That's generous of you." He wanted to touch her. Wanted to wrap himself around her, inside her, and make her scream with wanting him. Like he wanted her. It was all he could do not to grab her. But he wouldn't do that again. She believed it was hate that made him react in such a way. How little she knew of desire.

Eyes falling to her stomach, Alex laughed. It was a deep, throaty sound, and it caused Angelique to blush in disconcertion. "Have you something to tell me?" he asked.

Punching the pillow from its band, Angelique wiggled, making it fall to her feet. She then kicked it aside. "Certainly not. I told you at the Musquiz party that I wasn't pregnant."

His quiet response surprised her. "Calm down, *querida*. I wasn't complaining."

"Oh?"

"You make a beautiful expectant mother. But much too angelic." He stepped closer. "Perhaps I should do something to remedy that."

"You have done quite enough regarding my virtue," Angelique snapped. Eyes flashing, she finished, "Now if you will excuse me, I'll—"

"I won't."

She was caught. The fingers biting into her arm were cruel, then gentle.

His voice husky now, Alex confessed, "I've missed you, Angel."

She wanted to run. Alejandro de Bastitas gloried in frightening her out of her senses. And he had . . . at one time. Back when she was a naive child who yearned with all her heart and soul to belong to someone. He repeated, "I missed you," and her wall of defiance was crumbling.

"Alejandro!"

He turned to face Isabella. As she offered her hand, he knelt on one knee and bowed his head. "Grandmother. As always it is an honor to—"

"Get up and stop that drivel," she interrupted. "You may save it for your grandfather. It does little for me, but for him . . ." As he stood, she placed a gentle hand against his cheek. "Your face is thin. Are you ill?"

"Tired. Nothing more."

"Then you must rest. I'll have Delores prepare your bath. Have you eaten?"

Alex nodded. "But I wouldn't turn down a glass of that mulled wine Teresa is so famous for."

A warm glint settled in Isabella's eye. Turning, she motioned for Angelique. "My dear, will you speak to Teresa for me? Bring the beverage to the study, please."

"*Sí, senora.*"

Isabella smiled into her grandson's face.

Angelique waited patiently as Teresa prepared the pitcher of wine. She also included a plate of aniseed cakes, pointing out they were Alejandro's favorite. This small chore was nothing new to Angelique. She had often prepared such treats for Isabella.

Still, as Angelique lifted the heavy silver service and found it rattling beneath her unsteady hand, she was reminded of what waited beyond that intricately carved door. It was just as well her mother and Bernice had retired early. She could only imagine their reaction to the news that Alejandro de Bastitas had returned.

The fireplace illuminated the study in a subtle glow. Shadows danced across the ceremonial masks upon the wall, making them appear almost alive. Alejandro was slouched in a chair before the hearth. He appeared to be sleeping.

He had bathed. Angelique stood in the doorway, watching as blue light reflected from his damp hair. There was a hint of soap in the air. The white shirt he boasted was clean—and open, revealing the gently curling mat on his chest.

As quietly as possible, she tiptoed across the floor and placed the tray on the table. She poured the steaming drink into a deep silver cup, ridiculing the tremor in her hands.

"Thank you."

She looked over at him. He was smiling and for a moment she forgot her chore and filled the chalice to its brim. "I'm terribly sorry."

He shifted. The peace was disturbed by a slight creak of leather boots and the rustle of linen against velvet, a quiet whispering that lent his very presence a masculine appeal. With long fingers, he gracefully lifted the cup to his mouth.

When she thought to move away, his eyes captured hers and held. And when he finally spoke, Angelique was certain the very walls vibrated with the resonant sound. "Stay." When she was seated, he poured her a drink. "You *do* realize what she's doing?"

She smiled and accepted the container. "No."

"She is courting us."

Her eyes widened as Angelique tipped the drink to her mouth.

"She has properly trained you to serve me my *merienda*. You have been introduced to our customs, and no doubt know her day-by-day duties as well as she." Alex leaned forward, resting his elbows on his knees. "Look at you. You sit before me as beautiful and proud as Isabella was fifty years ago."

Another deep drink, and Angelique relaxed in her chair. "You are imagining things."

"Am I?" His eyes never blinked, and the grooves in his face deepened as he smiled. "I think you would make a suitable doña, wife and mistress of a hacienda."

She drank again and, finding her cup drained, refilled it. "Fatigue is playing havoc with your thinking, senor." Laughing then, she dismissed his raised brow with a wave of her hand. "Isabella and I are friends. Nothing more."

God, she was beautiful. Alex forced himself to look away, afraid the blush upon her cheeks, contrasting with the green of her eyes, would sway his pledge of patience. But he wanted her. He ached to press his body against hers, into hers.

He refilled his goblet.

Angelique lowered her eyes to the fingers folded about the slender stem of silver. They were sun-bronzed, sprinkled with fine black hair, and strong. Very strong. Hypnotized, she followed them to his mouth, feeling warmer as he moistened his lips with the drink. A tiny drop of wine beaded there, and with his tongue he swept it away.

The fire spoke in soft hissing whispers, popping occasionally as green kindling expanded. Neither noticed as shadows deepened, leaving them haloed in a puddle of hazy light. There was an odd peace between them. They drank the warm wine and drifted in contentment.

Though Angelique tried desperately to keep her eyes open, the struggle was brief and she dozed. Vaguely, she felt the cup slip from her fingers. Hands stroked her hair.

"Angel."

It was a whisper of a sound, a gentle disturbance of air about her ear. Forcing her eyes open, she looked into his tender smile. "Sorry," was all she could respond.

"May I watch you sleep?"

The words were deep. Then she was lifted, and when she thought he would set her on her feet, he sank back in his chair and nestled her in his lap. God, but he was warm. She hadn't realized how cold she had grown in her chair. But suddenly she was safe and secure. His scent filled her nostrils and, with the wine, coursed through her bloodstream to suffuse her senses with a lulling intoxication.

Her hand opened and she slipped it inside his shirt, pressing it against his heart. Arms closed about her, and though she could not breathe, she knew it had nothing to do with the fierceness with which he held her.

"Angel. Look at me."

She tried.

"My sweet, sweet Angelique." Pushing the hair across her shoulders, Alex caught her chin and tipped her face. He opened his mouth on hers, and his tongue traced the satin insides of her lips, then dipped to entwine with hers.

"Come away with me."

"Where?" She smiled.

"Heaven."

A low chuckle escaped her throat. "*Your* heaven is shamefully sinful."

"Nothing I do with you is sinful."

"Why?"

"You care for me. . . . Don't you?"

Angelique released a heavy sigh. "I'm not certain."

He looked in her face, studied the way her closed lashes

curled against her cheeks. His finger traced the delicate shell of one ear before burrowing into her hair. The thought that he meant nothing to her was far more disturbing than he would have once believed.

Angelique opened her eyes, caught her breath. Blue fire engulfed her. She surprised him by touching his face. Like a blind man she traced a light finger over the noble brow, through the hair at his temple, to his cheek.

She was driven to respond. It was only natural to lift her face, to open her mouth and press it against his. Suddenly she was spinning, and reacting to the fall she clutched at his hair, his neck, pulling him closer, then nearer still until their hearts were pressed and each hammering was an echo of the other.

"God, oh God," Alex rasped. He was suffocating with heat and need. Plunging his hand beneath the hem of her skirt, he found the smooth outside of her thigh, the lacy underthings which exaggerated the picture of her femininity he carried in his mind. And then he traveled farther, to that warm, moist center that promised and fulfilled his wildest fantasy.

It was impossible for Angelique to rationalize beyond the feel of his mouth, his hands. Their tenderness was far more intoxicating than the wine that had compelled her to drop those dreary inhibitions that held her from him. She wanted Alejandro de Bastitas. And though she was shaken by the thought, she wasn't surprised. She had stopped denying it long ago.

They were sliding. The chair was slipping away and neither stopped it. Instead, they met the floor and hardly noticed. Their arms and legs were entwined, their mouths moved together, slanting, feeding off each other's need.

Suspended, each uncertain of the other, they listened to the crackling of fire. Angelique touched the hair falling over his brow. It was thick, slightly coarse, and as black as the midnight beyond this room. He, in turn, smoothed his palm over her glossy mantle of auburn hair which spilled like a silk fan across the rug.

He was a fool to believe he could ever hold Angelique

DuHon and not take her. And although he inwardly cursed his own lack of self-restraint, he knew this time would be different, for she was giving herself willingly. There was no deception or anger. And for a brief moment he wished he could turn the clock back to that midnight so many weeks before, when he might have worshipped her virginity as it deserved to be. He had ruined that for her. But not again. This time he had something to prove—that the act could be done with emotion and gentleness. It *could* be beautiful.

That's what he wanted for her.

They rolled. Suddenly Angelique was looking down in his face, and when she would have caught her hair to push it away, he refused her, preferring the flowing strands to fall where they may, between them, against him, twisting and entwining about his neck and shoulders. His hands moved gently up her ribs to her back, and there plucked at the row of tiny buttons along the bodice of her dress. And when it was done, when the material fell loose over her shoulders, he pressed his palms against her spine and massaged in gentle, circular motions.

Angelique shuddered. The motion, the heat of his hands was like a licking flame against her skin. His palms were hard, yet gentle, the fingers strong, but tender. And when he buried them in her hair and pressed her mouth to his again, the fire from the hearth leaped in a startled fashion, as if responding to the feel of his tongue as it slipped between her lips. Her body responded as well. An odd sort of heat suffused her. It centered in her heart and surged through her belly, coiling and coiling until she thought the pressure would give at any moment.

Needing air, she levered herself on outstretched arms. He sat her up and with the tip of his fingers tugged the dress down across her breasts to her waist. "Take it off," came his quiet command.

Shakily, Angelique moved to her knees. The material drifted by her hips. She stood and it floated to her ankles.

His long frame stretched across the floor, Alex extended a hand. "I'll do the rest." As she sank beside him, he wrapped his fingers about her throat, causing the pulse to jump beneath his palm. "My God, you are beautiful. I ache with wanting you, Angelique."

She felt the heat of his eyes as they dropped from her face to her shoulders, then to her breasts. The dusty pink spheres were barely covered by the filmy lace of her camisole. They thrust against the ivory silk, clearly definable to his admiring eye. With his thumb, he nudged aside the lace and stroked one blossoming bud, watching as it grew even fuller, darker. And when he moved to take it in his mouth, she quivered and arched against him, reveling in the feel of the velvety tongue twisting and pulling, suckling gently as his nostrils drank in her perfumed skin.

With great effort, he pulled away. And as he stood above her, hands slowly tugging the shirt from his breeches, she could have swooned with the leap of need that exploded through her lower body. She felt alive. Gloriously alive. Every nerve tingled and she grew dizzy with the sensation of breathlessness. His fingers plucked at the buttons on his pants, slowly revealing where the dark line of hair on his stomach blended with the soft black curling nest that revealed the proud shaft of his manhood.

She couldn't move. She didn't want to. Her eyes drank in each splendid detail, the boldness, the beauty. For he was beautiful beyond anything she could imagine. Perfect sinew and bone. Long, sleek muscles that flexed and shone in the firelight.

Angelique opened her arms. He moved against her, pressing the length of his body on hers, absorbing hers, tasting hers. He covered her face, throat, and shoulders in kisses. Then her breasts. Cupping each in his palm he lifted them to his mouth, once, then twice before moving further, peeling the gossamer material over her ribs, abdomen, then beyond the softly rounded hips.

Then he was there, his fingers parting flesh, probing gently, deeply, causing her to tremble and her skin to become hot and damp. She was floating, soaring as his hands slipped beneath her hips and lifted her legs about his shoulders.

How daring. Forbidding. Beautiful. Don't stop. Don't stop.

Her stomach tightened. Thighs quivered and inside the pressure was growing, straining, unraveling like razor-sharp springs. She thrashed, lifted, clutched for some harbor that might keep her from losing all control. And still he continued until the cry in her throat could no longer be sustained. At its sound he was sliding against her. Face damp and body tuned for its final orchestrated pleasure he accepted her sheath and plunged, filling, swelling, throbbing with the wonderful pain.

She embraced him, all of him; the heat of their bodies fused hair and skin, limbs twisting and holding. Yet his eyes never left hers. With each parting, meeting, they held, closing only as they kissed. She felt like weeping. Though she tried, she could not stop the tears that gathered then trailed to her temples. There was so much she wanted to say. But dare she?

It was there, on her lips, and she couldn't stop it. "I love you."

He stopped.

She turned her head, embarrassed and wanting to hide. He caught her face in his palm, forcing it back toward him. And this time when he kissed her it was more intense, as if the act could convey what his tongue couldn't. It was completion beyond anything they could ever have imagined. The ecstasy climbed, the sensual, rhythmic mating of mind and body a wondrous scaling of that glorious pinnacle.

"Angelique." A name spoken in a long, painful whisper, but as sweet as all music to her enraptured ear. "Angelique."

It was stunning, the blissful stretching and filling of his body in hers. He carried her up and over that threshold, and she cried out as her world exploded, her song matched by the shuddering of his long low growl of release as he spent himself entirely.

There was a gentle fall, like feathers spiraling on a warm, timid breath of air. Drifting. Drifting until each settled in a contented peace in the other's arms. He rocked her. She clung, enthralled by the deep, emotional tie of fulfillment.

Alejandro rolled and for several long moments stared at the ceiling, smoothed her silken hair with his fingers. Angelique was shivering now, as much from the wonderment as from the cold, and he reached for his shirt, slipping it onto her arms and then her shoulders. Leaving her, he pulled on his breeches, but as she reached to gather her own belongings, he dropped on his heels and caught her hands.

"Look at me," came his hoarse demand.

It was the hardest thing Angelique had ever done.

His voice tinged in disbelief and hope, he beseeched her, "Again."

"I love you," she whispered.

He closed his eyes. "Angel, I—"

The door opened.

Carlos de Bastitas stepped into the room, his features blanched and twisted. Behind him Tomas averted his face. And beyond them . . . Isabella.

A sick feeling centered in Alex's gut. An angry, defiled sense of disgust that filled his body with such savage brutality his entire frame turned to stone. "Bastard," was all he could manage. "Bastard."

# TWENTY

Whore. Yes, that was it. Carlos de Bastitas had called her whore. *Puta*. Slut. Angelique closed her eyes, recalling Alex's futile attempt to shield her from his grandfather's eyes, to deflect his ugly words before they could reach her. It had done little good. She would never forget the ugliness of his ridicule, the slamming of the door as Tomas left the room, or the brief look of guilt in Isabella's eyes before she turned away.

Why had she done this? Angelique wondered. Why had Isabella brought her husband to that room, knowing she and Alejandro would be there together?

"You ready?"

She met Bernice's eyes. No, she wasn't ready. How could she walk into that room and face those people? They had turned something magical into an ugly, disgusting memory and now they demanded to see her again. For what? To berate her even more?

Bernice wrapped a shawl about Angelique's shoulders. "I just don't know what come over you, sugah. Whatever is this gonna do to yore mama?"

Angelique swallowed hard. "Perhaps I can convince Senor Bastitas not to mention this to my mother. If I promise to stay completely away from Alexander . . .''

"Humph. You made me the same promise and you see what good it done.''

"Then what shall I do?''

Bernice looked into Angelique's face. Her own softened, and cradling the girl's pallid cheeks in her palms, she shook her head. "Hon, you got to face up to yore mistake.''

"But it wasn't a mistake. Don't you see that? I *care* for Alexander!''

"Do you? Are you truly in love with this man? 'Cause if you are, I'll see you through this, Angelique. All I ever wanted, child, was for you to be happy.''

A tear shimmied down Angelique's cheek as she nodded. "I-I do love him, Bernice. You must make my mother understand that.''

"She ain't ever gonna understand nothin' where that man is concerned.''

Bernice's words brought a shudder to Angelique's shoulders. Pulling her wrap tighter, she turned for the door.

It was the longest walk of her life. Each step that brought her closer to the *sala* found her knees weaker and her resolution waning. No sounds could be heard now, though throughout the night both Carlos's and Alexander's raised voices had shattered the quiet. At some time just before dawn Isabella had come to her room. Angelique had pretended sleep. Tomas had tapped on her door just after daybreak, but she had refused to respond.

She had heard nothing from Alejandro.

Teresa was waiting, and upon seeing Angelique jumped from her chair and moved for the door. "I will tell Don Carlos that you are here to see him,'' she said in a light voice.

Angelique tried to thank the girl. It was impossible.

Much too soon, Teresa was back. "You may come in.''

It was a sunny day. The drapes had been pulled and windows opened, allowing a light breeze to freshen the room. Tomas stood with his back to the wall. Hands in pockets, he guiltily focused his eyes on the floor. It had not been his idea to participate in his grandmother's little plan. But he realized it had been necessary. One could never be too careful where Carlos and Alexander were concerned. Especially over a matter such as this.

Isabella sat at Carlos's side, appearing almost regal in a royal-blue velvet gown. Alejandro de Bastitas sat on the edge of his grandfather's desk, one leg propped against the floor, the other swinging slightly. He hadn't changed clothes since the night before. Hair hung shaggily to his eyes and the dark shadow across his jaw was again evident.

"Angelique, what is happening here?" Carlota asked.

The breath rushed from her lungs as Angelique spun. "Mama!"

Jumping from her chair, Carlota made a move to join her daughter, but was stopped as Carlos barked, "Sit down!" With his cane, he tapped the floor at his feet and demanded of Angelique, "Stand before me."

Head up and shoulders back, she refused to move.

"I suggest you do it," came Alex's quiet voice.

Still, she refused to budge.

Isabella lifted one hand. "He will not strike you, my dear. Come and stand beside me."

Detecting no hostility from Isabella, Angelique reluctantly submitted to Carlos's demand.

His cold blue eyes appraised her, then with a thundering voice he announced to Carlota, "Last night your daughter was found in a compromising situation with my grandson."

Carlota blinked hard. "I beg your pardon, senor, I do not understand."

"*Ay!* She does not understand! Will you understand when in nine months the girl is bouncing your grandson on her knee?"

"*Madre de Dios!*" Carlota swayed. Tomas moved to her side, offering support. "Angelique, tell me there is some mistake."

Isabella's cool fingers wrapped about Angelique's hand, bolstering her courage. "No mistake, Mama," she finally answered.

Outraged, Carlota turned toward Alejandro. "*Bastardo!* I will kill you for this." She flew toward him, her fingers hooked like talons. "You have ruined her! Ruined my baby! I will see you in hell for what you have done to me!"

Alex slid to both feet, catching her outstretched arms before she could sink her nails into his face. In a low voice he stated, "Calm down, Carlota. If you will give me the chance, I will make up to you—"

"What? How dare you believe you can make anything up to me! You destroyed me, and now you have ruined my daughter. You are a devil and I vow I will see you dead before you touch us again!"

Alex tightened his grip. "Perhaps you will wait until *after* the wedding? Unless, of course, you wish to take the chance of Angelique birthing you a bastard grandchild."

She gasped. "Wedding? No. I refuse to allow it!"

*Wedding?* The word struck with a force that left her winded, and slowly Angelique looked into Isabella's face. She understood now why the woman had sacrificed both her and Alejandro to Carlos's and Carlota's anger. Neither would have approved or accepted a marriage between them. This way, they had little choice.

Tomas hurried to his brother's aid. Closing his hands about Carlota's arms, he pulled her away. "Please, we must discuss this problem in a rational manner, Senora DuHon."

"There will be no talk of weddings. I refuse to allow this vile dog to touch my daughter!"

"You have little choice," came Isabella's quiet command. "I fear my grandson has already 'touched' her. Quite thoroughly, I might add."

Gasping, Carlota spun toward Angelique. "How could you cheapen yourself for this man? My own daughter, a *puta!*" She spat on the floor.

"Mama!"

"You have disgraced me, disgraced your father's name."

Isabella lifted one hand. In a hard voice, she said, "This

is enough. What is done is done and cannot be rectified. My grandson is an ignorant fool, but at least he chose to ruin a child whom I will be proud to call my granddaughter-in-law.''

"There will be *no* marriage!" Carlota reemphasized.

"Will you risk the chance of pregnancy?" Isabella asked.

"Yes!"

"And if she is?"

Carlota ignored the question. "If she is not there *is* no problem."

"I must disagree, my dear." Again closing her hand onto Angelique's, she squeezed reassuringly. "As you stated yourself, Alejandro has ruined her. What man of any social postion will accept her now?"

"She deserves no such man!" Carlos bellowed.

"Enough." The command came like quiet thunder, threatening in its absoluteness. Alejandro eased back down onto the desk. "I have listened to this constant ridiculing of Miss DuHon long enough." His eyes met hers. "While my grandmother offers my name to absolve her of shame, her mother forbids it. Angelique is a grown woman and capable of making up her own mind." Lifting his hand to Angelique, he smiled. "Come here."

At Isabella's insistent nudge, Angelique took the longest ten steps of her life. Her knees were shaking, and her face was pale, her eyes were dull and glazed. It was the hardest feat of her life to stand before Alejandro and not burst into tears.

"Angel." Brushing her cheek with a knuckle, he smiled. "What have you to say on the matter?"

She searched desperately for something that might absolve them both of guilt. There was nothing. There were three witnesses to attest to the fact that she had succumbed quite willingly to Alexander de Bastitas, so all she could do was stare into the bluest eyes she had ever encountered and hope she did not melt at his feet.

Slipping one hand about her waist, he coaxed her closer. "My grandmother suggests marriage. Your mother forbids.

What do *you* want?'' He waited. After several moments and no response, he quietly added, ''You said you love me . . .''

''But Mama—''

Catching her small jaw in one hand, he gritted, ''*Forget your mother*. Will you marry me or not?''

The floor shifted. She was certain of it, for suddenly the room was tilting all about her. Her knees were knocking and a flush was staining her fair complexion like deep fire. Was Alejandro de Bastitas actually proposing to her? Actually standing before these people asking for her trembling hand in marriage?

Closing her eyes, she nodded. ''I . . . yes, I would be most honored, senor.''

''No!'' Carlota cried.

''It is done.'' Isabella relaxed in her chair. ''The wedding will be the day after Christmas.''

Angelique had little time to reflect on the unseemly instance that had caused her situation. She was being prepared for her role as the future *patrona* of Rancho de Bejar.

The very same day Angelique agreed to marry Alejandro, Isabella surprised her with the traditional gift of a wedding gown. She was stunned as Delores and Teresa spread its multiple flowing skirts out before her.

The gown was a rich ivory. An apron of seed pearls encrusted both the front and back skirts, as well as the yoke of the high-collared bodice and the cuffs of the sleeves. Teresa pointed with a great flourish to the fine lace mantilla which would sweep all the way to the floor. ''You will be *magnífica*, Senorita Angelique!''

''Oh, it is beautiful!'' she exclaimed, trying to hide the tremor in her voice.

Isabella nodded. ''It was Elizabeth's. She was somewhat taller than you, but a fitting will rectify that.''

Angelique's voice was shaky. ''I don't know what to say, how to thank you.''

''There is no need for thanks. By agreeing to marry my grandson, you have honored me. But do this for me, my

dear. Love him. Honor him. Whether he is willing to admit
it or not, he needs you. Replace his hell with your heaven
and he will cherish you always. In that way, he is not
unlike his father. . . . Now, you will follow me.''

She did. Traveling down the long corridor, they made a
right, back to a part of the hacienda Angelique had never
seen. She got the impression that the rooms now being
freshened had not been opened in a long while; there was
a mustiness about the air. Servants were scrubbing the
walls and floors. Sheets that had been draped across the
furniture were being removed.

At the far end of the hallway was a pair of intricately
carved double doors, not unlike the ones leading to the
study downstairs. Swinging them open, Isabella entered the
room. ''These will be your quarters until Carlos and I are
no longer living. Then, of course, you may move into
ours.''

Angelique didn't respond. She couldn't. Her eyes were
trained on the portrait across the room, propped against the
wall.

Isabella snapped her fingers at the nearest servant.
''Take the portrait from here, *por favor*. See it is destroyed.''

Angelique stopped him with a lift of her hand. ''No.''

Isabella looked into her wide eyes. ''You mustn't let it
distress you. I had forgotten the picture even existed and—''

''It doesn't matter.'' Angelique slowly crossed the room,
then stood before the gold-framed portrait. ''Pamela was
very beautiful.'' Odd, but she could hardly take her eyes
from Alexander's smiling face. ''He seems so very happy.
It is understandable now that I have seen her.''

Isabella moved up behind her. ''It was done shortly before they were married. When Tomas returned from New
Orleans he brought it with him.''

Pulling her gaze from the stunning brown eyes and coiffured blond hair, Angelique stood. ''Does Alexander know
it is here?''

''I suspect he has forgotten about it.''

''May I suggest you return it to him?''

"Are you certain, my dear?"

No she wasn't. Her breast ached with the thought of Alejandro looking on Pamela's face again, but it was his past, and should be destroyed by no other. "Yes, I'm certain."

Placing a gentle hand on Angelique's face, Isabella smiled. "You are a compassionate and wise woman."

Fool was the more appropriate term, Angelique reasoned.

"Paco, will you see the picture to my grandson's room?" The brown-faced young man jumped to attend *la patrona*'s request. She then said to Angelique, "The room on each side of this one will be your sleeping quarters. Alejandro's there." She pointed to the far door. "And yours here." Angelique followed Isabella through the nearest door, then stopped. "Of course you are free to refurnish it."

"I wouldn't dream of it. It is perfectly beautiful the way it is."

"Yes, it is." A distant look in her eyes, Isabella recalled, "The bed came with us from Spain. At one time it was mine. My son was born in it, as were each of my grandchildren."

"Even Alexander," Angelique stated in a hushed voice.

"Yes. And now his children." Feeling light-headed, Isabella sank into the nearest chair, dismissing her companion's concern with a flick of a hand. "It is nothing, my dear, but age. I am an old woman, and thoughts of great-grandchildren tug at my heart."

Sitting on the floor, Angelique spread her skirts about her. She then asked, "Do you think he will want many?"

"Of course. Alejandro has a tender place in his heart for children. Even as a boy he found delight in those younger. He carried Tomas about on his hip, and was never without Maria on his shoulders."

"Maria?"

"He was ten when she was born. It was a difficult birth for Elizabeth, and I believe she never fully recovered. After the child drowned, it was her greatest desire to have another. In doing so, she died.''

There was quiet between them. Angelique looked out across the grand room, visualizing what it must have been like when Elizabeth and Ramon de Bastitas were alive. She could almost hear the laughing of young children as they bounced on the bed with their mother. Perhaps Alexander had lain before that very fireplace with book or toy in hand. Tomas may have hid beneath the raised mattress while Maria searched frantically for her missing brother.

At night the moon would shine through that very window. The door would creak and he would join her in a pool of pale light. They would become entwined in sheets and . . .

Angelique shook her head. It was obscene how her mind continually drifted to shared moments with Alexander. Perhaps her mother was right. She was becoming depraved!

She had looked forward to dinner, anxious to see Alexander. Choosing her most demure gray gown, Angelique allowed Bernice to help her dress, but as the woman made a move toward her hair, she refused by saying, ''Alexander prefers it down, thank you.''

''Oh he do, do he?'' Bernice clucked her tongue. ''That's a maiden's way of wearin' it.''

With a violent flash of green in her eyes, Angelique spun to face her companion. ''Would you have me brand an *H* on my forehead for harlot?''

''Yore lucky Carlos and yore mama don't do just that. Just 'cause that man's willin' to marry you, don't change what you did.''

Anger closing her throat, Angelique snatched the brush from Bernice's hand. ''That will be all. I will see to my own hair, thank you.'' Waiting until the woman had stormed from the room, she sank onto the bed. Lord, she would be relieved when this wedding was finished. At least she could hold her head up with some semblance of pride.

''Am I intruding?'' came Tomas's quiet voice from the door.

She looked up. "Of course not!"

"May I be so noble as to see my future sister down to dinner?"

Bouncing from the bed, Angelique beamed at the smiling man. "I'm glad you are still speaking to me."

"I might say the same. I've wanted to apologize to you." Tomas offered his arm. "I hope you can understand why I assisted my grandmother in her little scheme. We weren't certain how my brother would react. Alejandro and Carlos have been known to come to fisticuffs during certain confrontations. At least when they were both younger men."

"They actually fought?"

"The last time was when Alejandro decided to leave Texas. At that time Carlos threatened to kill my brother if he ever returned. Once he cooled off, he rescinded, of course."

They continued to the dining room, stopping at the *lavabo* before taking their usual seats. Everyone looked up at their entrance. Everyone, that is, except Alejandro. Slouched slightly in his chair, he was staring into the glass of wine he had situated in the center of his plate.

Tomas flashed his brother a bright smile. "I have seen the lady to your company, senor."

"So I noticed." His blue eyes lifted slowly. "It seems you take great pleasure in escorting the *lady* about. Just make certain you do not do it too often."

Isabella looked up. It was unusual to hear a disgruntled word pass between the brothers, and it startled her.

The servants hurried to dish out the *arroz con pollo*. As the woman offered the chicken to Alejandro, he shook his head. Enchiladas topped with spicy green and red peppers were also passed, as were frijoles and tortillas. These too he refused.

Angelique noticed her mother was conspicuously absent. Recognizing her concern, Isabella answered, "Your mother has traveled to San Antonio with her friend Mr. McGuire. She is staying with Senora Musquiz."

It was a relief, Angelique realized after a moment. Her

mother's disapproval would only have added to the burden
of disquiet as they prepared for the wedding. Clearing her
throat, Angelique asked softly, "Where will the marriage
ceremony take place?"

"San Fernando Church."

"Bah!" Carlos erupted, causing everyone to jump. "It
is a sacrilege, I tell you. It should be held in my barn and—"

The vibration of Alex's palm against the table sent the
dishes dancing with a clatter. "Enough!" he roared. Coming out of his seat, lips pulled back across his teeth, he
drawled, "If you as so much as flip your nose Angelique's
way I will take great care to rearrange it in a less likely
place. Do you understand me?"

Isabella jumped to her feet. "Alejandro, that will be all.
You have obviously imbibed too much wine and would be
best suited to your own quarters. Excuse yourself."

"I beg your pardon?" he demanded with a lifted brow.

"Get out."

Spinning and snatching the bottle of wine from the servant's hand, Alejandro stalked toward the door.

Isabella watched him go, then directed Tomas, "See to
your brother, my dear."

Excusing himself, Tomas left the room.


"Imbibed indeed." Alex left the hacienda and strolled
down the pebble-paved path, past the scattering of adobe
huts, community well, and storehouses. It was dark but for
the dim glow of candlelight in the windows. He heard the
sound of his name as Tomas ran to catch up with his long
stride, but he didn't stop. His brother caught his arm, spinning him around.

"What is the matter with you?" Tomas demanded.

"Do you know what I found in my room this afternoon?"

"No."

"The portrait of Pamela." Pulling his arm from Tomas's
grip, he continued down the path.

"So?"

Stopping again, Alex shook his head. "You don't understand. It was a reminder of why I cannot marry Angelique DuHon.''

''Are you still so in love with Pamela?''

''Love? Hell no, I don't love her. Maybe I never did.''

''Then what has this to do with Angelique?''

''Carlota DuHon.'' Her name rolled from his tongue, tasting vile and bitter.

''You are in love with Carlota DuHon?''

Alex's dark head fell back in sharp laughter. Raising the wine bottle between them, he wrapped long fingers about its neck and squeezed. ''Keep Carlota DuHon away from me, or I swear to the Virgin Mary I will strangle her.'' Pivoting on his heel, he continued on his trek.

''Where are you going?'' Thomas called after him.

''I don't know.''

# TWENTY-ONE

Two days gone. In one week she would be Angelique de Bastitas. Bastitas. Smiling, Angelique rolled the word on her tongue several times. It had a strong sound, suited to the man who would be her husband. Closing her eyes, she thought of her father. "Papa would like him," she stated aloud.

She spun as the door opened behind her. Delores offered her a smile and curtsied. "Senora de Bastitas is not well this morning. She asks that you see to her duties until this afternoon."

"Is she seriously ill?"

"No, senorita. But she prefers to rest."

Angelique released the maid with a quick nod. No sooner had Delores disappeared than another door opened and Carlos entered the room. "What are you doing here?" he growled.

Raising her chin defiantly, she answered steadily, "I was to meet your wife, but she is ill."

Carlos stopped. Raising one bushy gray brow he released a loud guffaw. "Isabella ill? Bah! My wife has not been ill in fifty years."

"If you would care to confirm my story with Delores, please feel free to do so."

Limping across the floor, Carlos dropped into his chair. "Now who the hell will serve me my coffee?"

Angelique turned to call Teresa, then stopped. A smirk of a smile on her face, she slowly approached the man herself. "I will pour your coffee, senor."

"You?" Blue eyes narrowed suspiciously. "You will get the hell away from me."

She ignored him. Surprising Carlos even further, Angelique sat in Isabella's chair. "Do you take it black, don?" When he refused to respond, she liberally added two heaping teaspoons of brown sugar to his cup.

His mouth tightened before he demanded, "How do know that I drink it sweetened?"

"Because Tomas and Alexander drink it with sugar. And since both do their best to please you, it stands to reason they would mimic you in such a way." She offered him the china cup and saucer.

He grudgingly took it.

Angelique poured her own, adding a tiny bit of sugar and a touch of milk. She didn't care much for the potent brew, preferring chocolate or tea. But she was experiencing a rebellious streak at the moment and wanted to prove to Carlos de Bastitas that she was just as stalwart as he. Sitting back in the chair, she smiled. "Isabella has asked me to see to her duties this morning."

His head came up.

"I assume that means attending you about the grounds?" Before he could respond, she added, "Of course there will be the peons to see. Did you know that Raoul's wife is expecting her baby at any time?"

"Who the hell is Raoul?"

"Your saddle maker."

Blue eyes twitched from side to side, then, grumbling, Carlos sank farther in his chair. "I knew that," he finally snapped.

"Of course you did."

All was quiet as the man stared into his coffee. When

he looked up, his face was emotionless. "I would not put too much stock in my grandson's eagerness to marry you. Juanita, of course, was his first choice."

Angelique should not have been surprised at his cruelty, but she was. As steadily as possible, she refilled his cup. "More sugar?" she asked.

Carlos leaned forward. "Did you not hear me?"

"Certainly. But it was my understanding that Alexander cared little for my cousin. He was marrying her only because you arranged it."

"Ha! Is that what he told you?" Coffee sloshed over the rim of the cup and onto the saucer as he snatched it from Angelique's hand. "I suppose you also think he was coming after you when he found your mother suffering from the Comanche attack."

Steam lifted from the cup at Angelique's mouth and settled against her eyes. Blinking away the moisture, she forced herself to smile. It wasn't an easy task, for the old man's insinuation was painfully apparent.

Carlos continued. "Alejandro thinks he is such a big man—*mucho hombre*—ha! I brought him to his knees until he was begging for my forgiveness. He left here with the intention of catching up to Julio, to plead for Juanita's hand. He followed those savages *only* to save Juanita's life, not yours."

Don't listen to him! her heart implored. Her mind, however, could hardly block out his cruel meaning. It made sense now—the lashings he took, the reasons for his being there. Had she been so naive to believe Alejandro came after her? Fool. Romantic little fool! He would not even be marrying her now had they not been caught in such a compromising situation. Alexander was doing this for Isabella, and to spite Carlos. It was as simple as that.

Angelique stood. With shoulders back and head high she faced Carlos and asked, "Are you ready for your rounds, Don Carlos?"

Bastitas glared into Angelique's flushed face and bright eyes. She was just like Isabella—proud, stubborn . . . and beautiful. Worthy of the Bastitas name.

Bah! He was growing senile, and soft as well.

By afternoon Isabella was better and she and Angelique continued with the wedding plans. The ceremony would be attended only by the Bastitases' closest friends. Invitations were addressed and sent out by courier. A reception would be held at the ranch.

At no time was Angelique left alone with Alejandro. Always Isabella or Bernice remained in the room, the latter with her meaty arms folded across her chest and one eye narrowed suspiciously. He courted her properly. They held brief polite conversation, though the glances he paid her on occasion were far from gentlemanly and said far more than the chaste kisses he pressed against her fingertips, when given the chance.

Still, there were times when Alex grew moody. He paced his floor at night, was found arguing with himself on more than one occasion, and became belligerent even to his grandmother. "Prewedding jitters," Tomas had called it. But was it? Angelique tried numerous times to coax the reason for his distress from him but it did little good. He would lock that handsome jaw so tightly his teeth popped then, with a muffled expletive, storm from the room.

By Christmas, the eve of her wedding, Angelique was beside herself with excitement. She dressed early and, tiptoeing from her room, tapped lightly on Alex's door, determined to have a moment or two of privacy with her future husband.

At the sound, Alex placed his razor in the bowl of tepid water and, crossing the room, jerked open the door. His eyes lit as he looked into Angelique's smiling, upturned face, and he grabbed her arm and pulled her into the room before Bernice could come barreling down the hall to intrude.

Before she could speak, his arms were about her. "God, how I have missed you," he groaned in her ear.

"And I you." Lifting her face, she met his mouth, responding as passionately as their brief time would allow. Pulling away, Angelique searched Alex's face. "It is

Christmas, and our wedding day tomorrow.''

"And our wedding *night*," he reminded her in a growl.
"Do you think Bernice will allow us our privacy for that?"

Angelique laughed. "I'm not certain. She doesn't approve of you, you know."

"Then remind me to supply Tomas with adequate rope
and gag. If I have to bind the woman, tomorrow night will
be our own."

The thought made her tremble. Struggling, she pushed
him further away. "I-I have something for you."

Alex watched as she pulled the tissue-wrapped gift from
her pocket, then he demanded, "Wait." Turning, he
crossed to his dresser, tugged open the drawer, and withdrew a velvet pouch. "I've something for you as well. I
thought to give it to you tonight, but this seems a more
appropriate time." Smiling, he tucked it into her palm.
"You first."

Angelique stared a moment at the royal-blue material
before pulling it open. A shining silver chain and cross fell
into her palm. "Oh, Alexander, it is beautiful!"

He placed it around her throat. "It is tradition for a
Bastitas to present his future wife with such a necklace."
Fingers slid up the back of her neck and entwined in her
hair. Alejandro pulled her closer, crushing the lace of her
dress against his chest. "Someday I will buy you the finest
emeralds to match your eyes, diamonds to dress your ears.
You will never regret marrying me, Angelique. Never!"

He would have kissed her again, but Angelique stopped
him with a hand against his shoulder. As he stepped away,
she pressed her gift into his palm. "I hope you like it."
Biting her lip, she waited as he fumbled with the wrapping.

Long, brown fingers lifted the gold chain and watch into
the air. Alejandro was stunned. "Good God, Angel.
Wherever did you get this? It's beautiful."

Angelique released her breath, laughing as she did so.
"You do like it! I was certain you would. It was my father's, and all that he left me. As a child I would sit on
his knee and play with it. He promised it would be mine

and I would someday hand it down to my children. I would rather you have it.''

His eyes fixed on the round gold timepiece, swinging like a pendulum between them. Then dropping it back into the paper, Alex shook his head. ''I cannot accept it.''

The smile drifted from Angelique's face. Alejandro looked almost . . . frightened. ''But I thought you liked it,'' she demanded in a hurt tone.

Alex lifted her right hand and dropped the watch into it. ''It was a very thoughtful gesture, love, but I'm certain your father did not have me in mind when he bequeathed it to you.''

''But I want you to have it. Please!''

*Ah, hell.* Alex closed his eyes, then almost angrily his hands came up to capture her shoulders. ''Very well. If accepting your father's watch will please you, then so be it. Just get those damn tears out of your eyes and kiss me.''

His head came down, and opening her mouth against his, Angelique slid her arms about his neck. It was almost a primitive need that brought them together. The deep, easy thrust of his tongue caused her to melt against him, to rise on her toes so she could match the pressure of his lips. His hands slid up her back, then down beyond the swell of her buttocks, and once there cupped and lifted her against the musculature of his thighs. The rise there was hot and hard, pressing indecently against Angelique's stomach, reminding them both what lay in store only one night away.

Disengaging his arms, she stepped unsteadily away. ''Sir, I think it is not in our best interest to continue as we are. Bernice would surely suffer a state of apoplexy should we be discovered again.''

''No doubt.''

''Will I see you at breakfast?''

Alex shook his head. ''I go to San Antonio and will wait for you there.''

Leaving the room, she closed the door behind her. Bernice was waiting, arms crossed and her foot tapping against the floor.

•   •   •

Dawn was forever in coming. Christmas Day was a blur, but nighttime had been eternal. By the time she arose, Bernice and Delores had packed the few belongings she would need and loaded them onto the carriage. It was a blustery day. Clouds were building on the west horizon, darkening the sky with impending rain. By the time they reached the Musquiz house, a light drizzle had begun to fall.

Senora Musquiz greeted both Angelique and Isabella with outstretched arms. "Welcome! Oh, my dear, you look radiant!" She beamed at Angelique. "But you must hurry. It is my understanding that the bridegroom has pounded on our door twice already, checking on your arrival."

They were ushered inside as their hostess ordered servants to deliver a bath to Angelique's room. A light lunch was requested, as well as chocolate to warm the chill from her bones. As Angelique and Bernice entered the salon, Carlota stood up to greet them.

"Angelique."

"Mama. Are you well?"

"No I am not. Angelique, I must speak with you privately."

Sensing the tension between the young bride-to-be and her mother, Senora Musquiz offered them their privacy. Bernice crossed her arms and refused to budge.

Carlota frowned before continuing. "Angelique, I will plead with you one last time to forget that vile dog and call off this wedding before it is too late."

"His name is Alejandro de Bastitas, Mama, and no I will not call off this wedding. I understand your concern for my welfare, but I assure you, whatever blackened Alex's reputation in New Orleans is dead and buried."

"Dear God, I wish it were so." Sinking into the nearest chair, Carlota released a long, unsteady breath. "Were I certain the dead would stay buried, then possibly I could live with your decision. Though I wouldn't like it. I will always dislike Alejandro de Bastitas with every fiber of my being, but short of murder there is little I can do to stop him without hurting you as well."

Hope flinting in her breast, Angelique glided to her mother's side. "Will you see me married, Mama?"

Carlota touched her daughter's flushed cheek. "You are the flesh of my flesh. How could I do otherwise?"

Her bath was scented with lavender. Sinking to her shoulders in the silken water, Angelique laid her head back and dreamed of the next few hours. Imagine marrying the most handsome man in all of Texas! Imagine awakening each morning in his arms, bearing his children, watching as they grew and gifted her with children of their own.

Bernice and Delores hurried in, carrying the freshly pressed wedding gown between them. After stepping from the bath, Angelique was quickly dried then dusted with pearl-white powder and sprinkled with cologne. Once dressed in her filmy underthings, she was plunked down before a mirror, and both women began brushing out her waist-length hair, parting here and braiding there. By the time they were done it lay in twin plaits, hooped around each ear and held in place by pearl-encrusted combs. Over this was placed a netting of fine lace. On top of that, the mantilla would eventually be secured.

Angelique could hardly breathe as she stepped into the magnificent dress. When the two dozen buttons had been fastened up the back, she moved before the mirror. "I may cry," she managed in a tight voice.

"I don't blame you." Bernice shook her head and smiled teasingly. "I'd cry too if I's about to marry that man."

Delores giggled, but Angelique only smiled.

Senora Musquiz's face brightened as Angelique entered the foyer. Carlota's eyes grew wide, just before she burst into tears.

"Oh my," came Angelique's concerned gasp.

Senora Musquiz hurried to her side. "Forgive her, my dear. It is a mother's right to weep when her only daughter is about to be wed."

Blinking back her own tears, Bernice flung open the door and stared toward the church. The rain had stopped, but the streets were muddy. She stumbled back as the entranceway was suddenly filled with wide shoulders and red hair.

Noble McGuire offered a toothsome smile to the stunned women. "I'm reckonin' you'll be needin' the services of a strong-backed escort. Well, he's at your service." Before she could protest, Angelique was swept from the floor.

"Sir, whatever do you think you are doing?"

McGuire cocked a bushy brow. "There's one helluva nervous bridegroom over yonder who ain't gonna cotton to the idea of you waitin' until this street dries. I'm the best you got unless you have some idea of sproutin' wings and flyin' over this mud puddle."

Angelique's eyes grew misty as she stared into the giant's face. "You don't have to, you know."

"Dang right I don't." He smiled again. "But it's the least I can do for a friend."

Isabella quietly closed the door behind her. Alejandro spun to face her, his black velvet coat fitting snugly across his shoulders. "You had expected Carlos," she stated in a hushed voice.

"Yes."

"He will not come. I'm sorry."

Alex looked away. "It doesn't surprise me."

"Still, you had hoped." Isabella watched as her grandson walked to the window. Stained glass cast a blue glow across his features, adding to the sapphire intensity of his eyes. "I wish your father could see you. But he can't, so I will speak to you as he would have. Sit down."

He sat. Alejandro wasn't surprised at his grandmother's tone of voice, but he was caught off-guard as she cradled his face in her palms.

"Put it behind you," she stressed. "Begin again. Learn from your mistakes with Pamela and never repeat them."

"I am what I am, Isabella. I can be nothing else."

"Which is?"

"A man."

"Where is it written that a man can feel nothing here?"

She touched her heart. "Carlos is a man, but do you wish to be like him?"

"I am nothing like my grandfather!"

With all the strength she could muster, Isabella pulled Alex from his chair and shoved him before the tiny mirror on the wall. "Tell me you are nothing like him!" she hissed. "You are his very likeness, my young don."

He closed his eyes. "What is the point of this?"

In a tight voice, the regal woman asked, "Did you love Pamela?"

"I don't know."

"Were you forced to marry her?"

"No."

"Then you must have *believed* you loved her."

"I suppose . . ."

"Did you ever tell her? Once, in the eight months you were married, did you never say, 'I love you'?"

He searched his mind.

"I thought not." Pushing him closer to the wall, Isabella rasped, "Look at Carlos's image and tell me you are not like him. Never, in the fifty years of our marriage, has he mentioned his love. Do you understand how I have ached to hear it? Even once would have soothed me. But never. Never!"

He lowered his eyes to the aged hands gripping his jacket. Covering them with his own, he whispered, "*I* love you."

The statement stunned her. But when the need to cry overwhelmed her, she squared her frail shoulders and met his steadfast gaze. "Was it so difficult to say?"

"No," he said.

"Then tell Angelique. Never let her doubt it for a moment."

The door swung open. Tomas smiled and announced, "The bride is here."

Alone in the tiny cloister, Angelique stared at the Bible in her hands. She opened the cover and glanced at the many

rows of signatures from all the former generations who had
carried the book during their ceremonies.

"Are you ready?"

Snapping the book closed, she whirled to face Isabella.
Unable to speak, she simply nodded.

"He is waiting." Isabella linked her arm through Angelique's. "I may be the oldest matron of honor in history."

"But no less beautiful."

The woman laughed. "You honor me, my child, as you
honor my grandson. . . . Shall we go?"

Their eyes met the very moment she stepped into the
room. Met and locked. Alejandro hadn't expected such a
vision. Angelique had the face of an angel, the heart of
one as well. He ached with the knowledge that she would
be his in name and soul, that together they would share a
lifetime.

Angelique was oblivious to the witnesses who turned to
admire her. All she could see was the tall, dark man with
intense blue eyes. He was smiling. His hand was outstretched and enfolded hers as she stepped up beside him.
How grand he suddenly seemed! A head taller than she,
he was a tower of black velvet and white linen. And yet
as he lowered his head and pressed a kiss onto her forehead
he was as vulnerable as she. His guard was gone and he
was laying his heart in the very vestibule of God, for her
and her alone. Forever.

"My God, you are beautiful," came the quiet flutter of
words against her temple.

The priest's words were solemn, hardly matching the
roar of blood in Angelique's ears. With great determination
she attempted to focus on his mouth, but her eyes were
continually drawn back to the man beside her.

". . . Alejandro, will you love her, honor her . . ."

"I will."

". . . Do you take this man, Alejandro Felipe Antonio
de Bastitas . . ."

Angelique's eyes widened as Alexander's full name
rolled from the man's tongue. "I do."

"... I now pronounce you man and wife." The priest smiled. "Senor de Bastitas, you may kiss your bride."

He tipped her face. "Angelique. My life. My love ... my wife."

It was done.

# TWENTY-TWO

Tomas was the first to greet Angelique. Stepping from his place on the altar, he caught her hand and lifted it to his mouth. "May I welcome you to this family, senora?" At her nod, he caught her shoulders. "Do I also get to kiss the bride?"

Before she could reply Angelique was lifted from her feet and up against Tomas's chest. His mouth moved onto hers with a fierceness that was startling.

"Enough," came the quiet warning. The smile never leaving his face, Alejandro laid a firm hand on his brother's shoulder. "One would think *you* to be the bridegroom."

Tomas was drunk. The overpowering taste of brandy on his mouth made Angelique shudder, as did the almost leering look in his eye. Alejandro turned her away to greet the approaching well-wishers. Still, she could not help but throw one last confused glance back across her shoulder.

"The two of you might try acting a little happier," Isabella teased the newlyweds.

Alex peered out the carriage windows toward the hacienda in the distance. Grinning, he turned to face his wife. "I have my suspicions that privacy during the next few hours may be hard to attain. Will you excuse us, *Abuela?*''

Angelique laughed as her husband hugged her close. ''Really, Alexander, must we make a spectacle of ourselves before dear Isabella?''

''Absolutely.''

She was lifted across his lap, and before any further protest could be managed Alejandro was kissing her. It was a deep, lingering kiss, full of all the need and passion he felt for his young wife. Her head against his shoulder, Angelique closed her eyes. As always his touch sent her senses reeling, caused that mellow fire in her heart to surge with greater heat down into her stomach . . . and beyond.

It was the jolt of the carriage door being opened that brought their shared ardor to an abrupt halt. Isabella was fanning herself as she slid from her seat, but before accepting the manservant's offered hand, she replied casually across her shoulder, ''If you wish for me to make your excuses to the guests, I will do so. If not, I feel it to be in *our* best interest that you keep a respectable distance between you until this party is over.''

Alejandro laughed. Angelique only blushed.

Distance there was not. At no time did they leave each other's side. He was always with her, gripping her arm with gentle fingers, lifting cake or champagne to her lips, and was occasionally seen brushing her mouth with his in a light caress. The women sighed, for Bastitas's affection for his bride was most obvious. Never once did he stop smiling, touching. Their eyes would meet and the world about them blurred into dim nothingness.

It was very late when, drawn by the quiet strain of a guitar, Alejandro coaxed his wife through double French doors and onto the patio. It was cold here and dark. Angelique shivered. Alex wrapped his arms about her waist and pulled her closer.

''Happy?'' he asked.

''I think I have never been so happy.''

''I intend to make you happier.''

''Oh?'' Tilting her face to his, she whispered against his mouth, ''I cannot imagine how.''

"I have my ways. Many ways. All of them different."
He wiggled his dark brows as he chuckled.

She nuzzled his throat, touching her tongue to its throbbing pulse. He tensed and she giggled. "Must we wait for much longer, good husband? Do you think these guests will ever turn in for the night?"

"We are free to leave any time we choose."

Her eyes were bright with excitement as they reflected the candles' glow. "Then why have you chosen to wait?"

The smile on his face less eager, Alex smoothed one knuckle over Angelique's flawless cheek. God, she was lovely. The loveliest woman ever granted to him, and he cherished her. He gave her one last penetrating look before moving away. "We need to talk," came his husky tone.

"About what?"

"My past mostly."

Angelique touched her husband's sleeve. "I don't care about your past."

"Your mother does."

Stepping closer, she wrapped the fingers of both hands in his lapels. Her voice was light as she bantered, "We'll have no more trouble from my mother. She has accepted our marriage."

Alejandro smiled tautly. "I doubt that."

"But it's true! I spoke to her just before the ceremony and she agreed there is nothing she can do but tolerate you."

His deep, rich laughter filled the courtyard. "Angel, nothing would make me happier, but those are words I will have to hear for myself."

Eagerly, Angelique wrapped her arms around Alex's neck. How she craved to be at peace with her mother again, and how wonderful it would be if she and Alejandro could put all their unpleasantness behind them. "Then go to her! Speak with her now and put all this ugliness behind us forever. It would be the greatest wedding gift you could give me."

"Now?" The question was threaded with reluctance, if not disappointment.

"While you speak with her I will . . . prepare myself for your return."

How could he refuse her? Alex knew in that instant he was a doomed man. "Very well. Shall we bid our guests a good-night?"

Amid hearty cheers and toasts to their future, Angelique and Alejandro left their guests. Carlota had already departed for her room, so Alex would have the privacy he needed for their final confrontation.

He kissed her. There in the threshold of their newly refurbished wing, Alejandro drank in the sweetness of Angelique's wine-flavored mouth. He dreaded seeing Carlota, but knew it to be for the best. Perhaps Carlota was willing to put their pasts behind them. God, he hoped so, for Angelique's sake. For their happiness as well as their future, the memories he shared with Carlota DuHon must be buried.

Teresa was all smiles as she helped Angelique from her dress. "Oooh, senora, you were the most beautiful bride in all of San Antonio. I will be pleased to be your personal maid from now on."

"My own?"

"*Sí, senora.* Doña Isabella chose me, as I am close to your own age."

"That was very kind of her." Stepping from the cloud of silk and satin, Angelique smiled at her attendant. "But you must promise me one thing."

"Anything, Senora de Bastitas."

"You must refer to me as Angelique."

"*Sí,* I will do that." Teresa hurried to hang up the gown, then retrieved the box that had been placed on top of the bed. "A gift for you from Senor Alejandro."

Surprised, Angelique accepted the gift then settled in a chair. With trembling hands, she tugged at the blue satin ribbon until it lay in a coil at her feet, then opened the box. Her eyes grew wide at the sight of the sapphire and diamond necklace spread across a black velvet background.

"The Bastitas jewels!" came Teresa's hushed exclamation. "They have belonged to the family for generations."

They were exquisite. Angelique could hardly bring herself to touch them. Very lightly, she traced the great, teardrop stones with her fingers. The sapphires were the deepest blue, almost black, each surrounded by the brightest diamonds she had ever seen. Nestled in the center were earrings to match, and beside them a ring, an oval sapphire placed within a bed of tiny diamonds.

"Put them on!" Teresa coaxed her.

Pulling her eyes from the stones, Angelique closed the box and shook her head. "No. I will leave that honor for my husband."

"Ah, I see. Then you must hurry to be ready when he arrives. The honeymoon should be delayed no longer than necessary. *Sí?*"

Angelique's face tinted more from anticipation than shyness. "Yes, Teresa. No longer than necessary."

But it seemed she had little choice. A delicate peignoir of white lace drifting from her shoulders to the floor, Angelique paced about her room. Why was Alexander taking so long? A half hour had seemed like an eternity, but an hour was sheer torture!

Lifting the hairbrush to her temple for the third time in as many minutes, she stared toward the door. She kept visualizing that moment at the Musquizes' hacienda when Carlota had placed the gun at Alex's chest and pulled the trigger. God, did her mother hate him so much? If so, could she be expected to lay her ambivalence aside, just because her daughter had married him? Perhaps this was some sort of trick to lure Alejandro into a trap.

Green eyes wide with fear, Angelique tossed the brush toward the bed and dashed from the door. What had she done? Of course her mother hated Alexander enough to trick him. Carlota had vowed only one week ago that she would see him dead before he touched her daughter again. On bare feet she fled down the corridor, past the closed doors that would someday house the children she would give Alejandro de Bastitas to the wing of the house she had called home these last months.

Eyes trained on Carlota's door and ears straining for any discordant message, Angelique quietly approached the room.

Alejandro, with fists clenched, stepped by a watchful Bernice and glared down into Carlota's face. "Madam, I have married your daughter. Let us bury the past between us and get on with our lives."

"I can hardly bury it again. Each time I look at you with my Angelique I will remember who and what you are."

His jaw tensed and he snarled softly, "Then marry McGuire and get the hell away from us."

Carlota jumped to her feet. "Oh, you would like that, wouldn't you? Then *you* would have no reminders of New Orleans and the crime you committed."

"I committed no crime!" Checking his anger, Alex backed away. "I knew it would do little good to try and discuss this problem with you rationally."

"Then why did you?"

"I promised Angelique. She was under some misguided assumption that you were willing to accept our marriage."

Her lips turned under as Carlota sank back into the chair. "Angelique. My beautiful, ignorant daughter. She is in love with you, and that cannot be changed without hurting her further."

"Perhaps if you had been truthful with her in the first—"

"Do not preach to me of honor!" she interrupted hotly. "Oh, damn! Whatever am I going to do?"

Alex stepped closer. His voice was far less angry as he pleaded, "Accept it, Carlota. We will forget and begin again. It's what we both wanted when we left New Orleans."

Her head came up. "Forget? How can I accept and forgive the man who murdered my husband?"

There was a soft gasp, a strangled sob of pain and disbelief. Bernice stumbled around, her jaw dropping and a hand pressing against her bosom. Alejandro whipped about. Carlota jumped to her feet. Angelique stood in the door, cloudy jade eyes the only color on her face. Her lips formed silent words, but as Alex made a step toward her she screamed.

"No!" She spun and ran, oblivious to the servants who stopped to gape at her.

"Angelique!" Alejandro broke into a run as he followed his bride down the corridor. The salon door slammed before him, but she had no time to lock it. As he entered the room her bedroom door slammed, and in three steps he was against it. It gave with little insistence and, entering, he faced his wife. Her face was as white as her negligee, her hair loose and full as it tumbled past her heaving shoulders to her hips.

Her heart breaking, she beseeched him, "Tell me it isn't true! Tell me, Alexander, that she is lying and I will believe you!"

"Angel—"

She covered her ears with her hands. "Did you murder my father?"

Bile rose in his throat as he leaned back against the door and closed his eyes. "I won't discuss it with you now. There are things you should know and—"

Alex groaned as the impact against his temple sent him stumbling to the floor. He looked up as Angelique lifted the poker above her head and swung it again.

"Bastard! Filthy, deceiving son of a dog who killed my father! You have defiled me! Used me! You destroyed my mother and now me! I hate you, I hate you, I hate you!"

With each proclamation the weapon thudded against Alex's shoulder, ribs and upraised arm. Suddenly there was a commotion beyond them and hands closed about the poker before it could strike again.

"*Madre de Dios!*" Tomas choked. "What is happening here?" Wrenching the iron bar from Angelique's grip, he tossed it across the room.

Noble McGuire wrapped his arms about Alex's waist and helped him to his feet. Beyond them Isabella, Carlos, and Carlota, supported by Bernice, stood in the main suite, Carlota wringing her hands and weeping.

Blood trickling down over one eye, Alex stared at his wife. "Will you not allow me to explain?" he asked in a flat voice.

She spat at his feet.

"Get me out of here," he directed his friend. But as they stepped from the room and he saw Carlota, his blood-ied face twisted into a mask of rage. Lunging at the woman, he caught her throat in his fingers and sent them both tumbling to the floor.

"Lawd!" Bernice wailed. Turning, she ran for Ange-lique's room.

It took Tomas and McGuire to pull Alejandro from Car-lota. As she scrambled to her feet she ran to the room where Bernice was cradling her daughter.

Isabella ordered, "Take my grandson to the other wing. I will join you momentarily." She waited until they had disappeared through the door before moving into the ad-joining room, Carlos at her side.

Her head in Bernice's lap, Angelique gasped between sobs, "Why did you not tell me in the beginning, Mama? How could you allow me to marry the man who murdered my father?"

Isabella swayed, but was steadied by her husband's hand. Neither spoke.

"I tried to warn you, Angie. I pleaded with you to stay away from him."

"But you did not tell me why!"

"I-I was afraid. Afraid of him. Yes! He threatened to destroy us both if I revealed the truth."

Listening intently to Carlota's excuse, Isabella frowned. Carlota was lying. Of *that*, she was certain.

Gulping for air, Angelique demanded, "If you knew who killed Papa, why was he never arrested and hanged?"

Nervously, Carlota brushed the clinging hair from her daughter's tear-dampened face. "I lied about the circum-stances, Angelique. Alejandro de Bastitas fought a duel with your father; he wasn't jumped and murdered. Your father caught him cheating at cards, and after he announced it, Alejandro called him out. He shot him through the heart before I could stop him.''

Carlota lifted her eyes to Isabella. With a shaky voice, she said, "My daughter and her father were very close. Reggie loved Angelique above all else. . . . Your grandson knows this."

Stepping into the hall and closing the door behind her, Isabella shook her head. In a resolute voice she said to her husband, "The woman is lying. I feel it here." She touched her heart.

Carlos agreed. "Alejandro may be a great many things, but cheater at cards and murderer he is *not!*"

Seated in a chair with a damp cloth against his forehead, Alex looked up as his grandparents entered the room. Isabella stopped before him. Face white with worry, she demanded in a quivering whisper, "Did you kill her father?"

"Yes."

Isabella did something she had never done before. She slapped him. Not once, but twice, then again. When after the final blow Alex's head remained down, she twisted her fingers in his black hair and pressed his face into her bosom, caring little that the blood from his torn skin stained the front of her dress. "Why?" she wept. "Why have you done this to Angelique?"

"I wanted her. I want her. I . . ."

"You what?"

". . . love her."

*Dear God.* "Carlota says you cheated her husband in cards; that he called you out and you shot him."

He said nothing.

"Is that true?" she asked, shaking him angrily.

"I killed him."

There was no further response.

It was much past midnight. Angelique lay in her bed, staring at the canopy overhead. Her wedding night. A time when she should be nestled in her beloved's arms. For a while, in her dreams, she had been. But as she rolled to press her lips to his, his face was a demon's face, with fire for eyes and blood spilling like tears down his cheeks.

But his voice had been gentle, that deep, quiet drawl that both hypnotized and enthralled her. His tender hands had soothed her and though he was ugly—terribly ugly— she had almost been tempted to surrender to his trickery. To believe that he truly cared and he wasn't a monster after all.

She wouldn't sleep again. Ever.

"Angel."

She sat up in bed. Her heart racing, she stared through the shadows toward the door. Had she imagined the voice?

"Ang'lique! Are you sleepin'?"

It *was* he! Sliding from the bed, she tiptoed across the room, her eyes riveted to the brass doorknob. It quietly turned, freezing her in her tracks. The lock held.

"Ang'lique!" The slurred voice was louder.

"Go away! I never want to see you again!"

A heavy sigh followed. Then, "Jus' for a moment."

"No. Never."

"Will you le' me esplain?"

"You killed my father. There is nothing beyond that."

"There's us."

"You used me."

"No! No."

The door creaked. Angelique sensed he was leaning against it.

"Ang'lique . . . you hurt my head."

Was he laughing? No. No, he wasn't. Her eyes fell to the dark stain on the rug and a sudden rush of tears welled behind her lids. Cursing, she wiped them away. "Go away," she shouted, her voice breaking. "I will hurt you again if you come near me."

"Did you find th' box?"

"I don't want the jewels, do you hear me? Give them back to Isabella!"

"Em'ralds will suit you better. If I buy you some em'ralds will you talk t'me?"

"No!" Stepping closer, she waited for his response.

It finally came. "As' Carlota. She's lyin'. Swear t'God."

Closer. "Did you, or did you not, kill my father?"

"I . . . love you."

"What?"

"See . . . tha's not so hard. I love you."

Angelique pressed her cheek to the door. Her hands lightly touched the point where his voice was deepest. Why was her heart pounding and swelling so painfully within her chest? Why was the temptation to release that lock so strong she had to fight with all her will to resist it? This man—*her husband*—murdered her father, the gentlest, dearest man who ever lived, and *she* was struggling to keep him from her bed!

Stepping away, she shook her head. "Go away. I hate you, now leave me alone."

"I never tol' Pam'la that. I never tol' nobody that 'cept Is'bella, and tha' was only t'day. See wha' good it did me."

"You are drunk, senor. Go to bed."

"Very well. Le' me in an' I'll do it."

"I told you. I never want to see you. If you do not leave this house tomorrow, I shall. I will return to New Orleans!"

"That's not a very nice thing t'do."

"I mean it!"

"Awright, awright, hell. Goo'night, Angel."

Don't call me that. Please, please don't call me that *ever* again!

"I love you," he mumbled, and then there was silence.

Dawn sent a freezing drizzle that pelted the windows with each blast of wintry wind. The fireplace in the corner of her room snapped and hissed, but did little to relieve the misery Angelique was feeling at that moment. Her head ached. Her eyes were swollen and the rawness in her throat made swallowing almost impossible.

Staring through the crystals of ice collecting about the panes of glass, she thought to return to her bed. She didn't.

Instead, her eyes focused on the tall figure emerging from the barn. He was hidden mostly beneath a dingy sort of serape. *Calzones* hugged long legs, and his head was down so the black sombrero he wore shielded his face from the falling sleet.

He was leading his horse.

"Alexander."

Teresa, who had just entered the room with Angelique's breakfast, stopped and looked up. "Senora?"

"My husband. What is he doing out in this dreadful weather?"

The servant sadly shook her head. "He is leaving, senora."

A pain uncoiled in Angelique's chest as she watched Alejandro mount his horse. "Leaving . . . why?"

"So you won't."

Angelique watched rain drip from the broad brim of the hat, onto his shoulders. Then, as if he had sensed her presence, he turned his face up to the window and found her there. She could see little in that bleak moment, for the rain was heavier and the shadow from the sombrero obliterated most of his face in its dark grip. But his mouth was visible. It curled in that irrepressible way of his, that slanting, infuriating way that caused her heart to flutter and her knees to grow weak with need.

His hand came up and touched the brim of his hat in a gesture of farewell. He spoke, his lips slowly forming words her ears strained to catch. "Goodbye, Angel."

The fingers of both hands splayed against the frigid glass, Angelique watched as he disappeared through the growing darkness.

Teresa paused before leaving the room. "May God give you a good day, Senora Angelique."

Angelique closed her eyes and wept.

# TWENTY-THREE

Alejandro hardly recognized the old fort. Walls had been rebuilt since he left three weeks before. Stockades filled in the gaps that had fallen beneath cannon fire and time. He raised his hand to the sentries and rode through the massive porte cochere, the main entrance of the mission, and what he found was startling.

Their numbers were slightly fewer than a hundred and fifty men. An assorted lot, some were dressed in the finer apparel of gentlemen, others in buckskin, and those who had remained in San Antonio since Cos had surrendered still boasted the tattered volunteer uniforms of casual and mismatched shirts and breeches.

There appeared to be a celebration going on, but he couldn't reckon why. The news he carried wasn't good. Santa Anna's General Ramirez y Sesma was camped at the Rio Grande with an estimated fifteen hundred men. Rumor was another six thousand would be joining him at any time.

The Mexican troops wanted for nothing. Quite a contrast to the Alamo's supplies and cannons. Due to the inadequate pay, many men had left in December and refused to return until late spring and Alex couldn't blame them. Only seven dollars in pay for four months' fighting hardly amounted to enough to survive on, especially if the men had families to support.

Kaintock McGuire was the first to greet him. "Well, if it ain't the Alamo's most distinguished scout, I ain't from Kentucky! Come on. I got someone I want you to meet."

Alex laughed, stepping away from his friend's whiskey-potent breath. "I've got news for Colonels Neill and Bowie."

McGuire's face sobered. "Jim's not well. Got some sort of infection in his lungs. Dr. Pollard don't right know what to make of it." With that, he was seized with a coughing fit himself.

That didn't surprise Alex, but neither did it please him. It had been an uncommonly grueling winter for this part of the country. Pneumonia, an assortment of fevers, even measles had sent many men home for treatment.

William Travis stood just outside the church walls, hands in his pockets and his handsome brow furrowed in concern. He looked up briefly as Alex and McGuire approached. "Look at them," he said pointing to the revelers. "You would think it the fourth of July instead of dooms-day."

Alex stopped beside his friend. "Why the celebration?"

"David Crockett and his men arrived three days ago."

"How many?"

"Not enough. There are one hundred forty-two men here now, and you are about to tell me that Santa Anna is wading the Rio Grande with three thousand."

"Think again. Rumor is there are over six thousand now."

Travis shook his head. "Perhaps we should have followed Sam Houston's orders in January and blown this mission up. Retreated to Gonzales and San Felipe where protection was more readily available."

"What about Fannin?"

"He's still holed up at Goliad. I have pleaded with him to come back, but there he sits with hundreds of our own men and I am helpless to force him."

"Where is Jim?"

William nodded toward the roughhousers. "There. Sick and drunk, and growing drunker by the day. Colonel Neill is taking leave tomorrow, something about an illness in the family, and he is leaving me in charge. Bowie won't like it. Neither will his loyal followers. There is apt to be trouble."

Alejandro followed McGuire to the group of men congregated outside the low barrack walls. A tall, slightly paunchy man in fringed buckskin turned to greet them.

"David Crockett." McGuire let a whoop of laughter. "Best-shooting congressman Tennessee ever had."

"What brings you here?" Alex asked in amusement.

Crockett spread his arms. "Andrew Jackson got too big for his breeches. I told them if he didn't keep his nose out of my business I'd show 'im what for. Well, he didn't, so I told 'em all to go to hell—I was going to Texas. And here I am!"

Alex listened intently to the big man's tirade about President Jackson then, excusing himself, wandered back toward the church. It had been a long, hard ride from Laredo. Every bone in his body hurt. His belly was empty and that nagging, dull ache had reentered his breast the moment San Antonio came into view.

Time and distance had managed to assuage Alejandro's frustration and anger. Six weeks had passed since he rode out of Angelique's life with no intention of ever returning. Why should he? She loathed him. It was as simple as that. Like a fool he'd laid his heart at her dainty little feet and she had spat upon it. He wouldn't give her the opportunity to do it again.

It was only moments before McGuire joined him. The burly redhead cleared his throat as they strode through the church, past the baptistry and into the tiny chapel. "Rode out to see Carlota yesterday."

"Lucky man."

"Seems she and Angie have been touched with a sickness."

Alex stopped. "Angelique's been ill? How badly?"

Kaintock hunched one shoulder. "Been lingering. Stomach flu, Isabella reckons."

Waiting until McGuire stopped coughing, Alex stated, "Seems you're not doing so well yourself."

"I'm dyin', dammit. No doubt in my mind about it."

"Have you seen a doctor?" At his friend's nod, Alex motioned back over his shoulder. "There's another bottle of whiskey in my saddlebags. You're welcome to it."

Though the room was dim, lit only by torches jutting from the crude stone walls, there was enough light so that Alex could search out the nearest pallet of blankets. "Think I'll get some rest. In the meantime I think you should see Dr. Pollard again. You won't do Carlota much good if you're six feet under."

Wheezing slightly, Kaintock pulled his coat tighter about his chest. "Speakin' of Carlota—"

"Please don't."

"I'm goin' back out to the ranch tomorrow. You reckon on comin'?"

Alex dropped onto the pallet. "I'll sleep on it."

Kaintock shook his head and, turning, rejoined the troops.

Teresa plumped the huge goose-down pillows at Angelique's back, then with concerned eyes shook her head. "Senora does not look well. May I bring you more broth?"

"I'm not hungry."

"But you must build up your strength. Perhaps some pan dulce?"

Angelique's mouth watered at the thought of the sweet treat. "Perhaps a touch. And some chocolate as well?"

"Sí, senora!"

Sighing, she relaxed against the pillow. "Is the doctor with my mother?"

"He joined her moments ago."

Angelique waited until Teresa had scuttled from the room before closing her eyes. A baby. She was having a baby. At this very moment a child was thriving in her womb and in slightly less than eight months she would be cradling it in her arms. A son or daughter.

Fathered by Alejandro de Bastitas.

Dear God, how would her mother react? Surely she could not hold it against the child? It wasn't the baby's fault he had been sired by a—a murderer. After all, at the time she hadn't realized what Alexander was. There had been nothing but total, wonderful bliss between them, a complete union of heart and spirit.

Her nausea subsided and Angelique felt stronger. Braving her unsteady legs, she slid from the bed and walked carefully to the chair before the fire. She decided she would tell no one of her condition . . . yet. Isabella and Bernice would be pleased, but Carlos would not. There was Tomas, of course, though over the last weeks he had withdrawn, spending most of his time in San Antonio with Anna.

Pulling her shawl tighter about her shoulders, Angelique lay her head back and stared into the hearth. She refused to cry. It was silly, really, and served no purpose. And though she constantly tried, she could not figure out *why* she continually did it. It must be her condition. After all, what did she have to be unhappy about? Yes, she had made a mistake in marrying Alexander, but it was obvious he had taken her at her word. He had ridden away from Rancho de Bejar six weeks before and never looked back. Tomas heard he had returned to New Orleans. Still someone else mentioned Mexico. Regardless, he had sauntered out of her life as easily as he had sauntered in. He was gone.

Dear Lord, she was going to cry again!

The door opened quietly and closed. Blowing her nose, Angelique dabbed at the tears forming in her eyes. "Please put the tray on the bed, Teresa. And will you help me from my chair? I'm feeling dreadfully dizzy again."

"Hello, Angel."

She stiffened. Her slender back snapped erect before she twisted to stare in disbelief at the huge brown hand he offered. The floor buckled, and with flailing arms Angelique made a grab for the nearest haven that might support her weight.

That happened to be her husband.

Alex caught his wife's tiny frame, easily lifting her in his arms. "You've grown too thin," was his simple admonishment.

The heart in her breast was constricting. Bracing her hands against his chest, she shook her head. "Put me down this moment."

He looked into the frightened, unfamiliar face. It was thin, too thin, and void of any color. Purple shadows smudged the translucent skin about her eyes and her lips were almost blue. Even her hair had lost its luxuriant gloss.

Alex gently laid her on the bed, then stepped back. "I'm not certain whom I should chastise, myself or my family for letting you sink into such a state. Should I hope it's because you've missed me?"

"Don't be absurd." She plucked nervously at the edge of her quilted counterpane.

"Very well, then let us assume you are not being adequately seen to. Has a doctor been called?"

Angelique nodded. "He only just left. He and Bernice are attending my mother now."

Noticing the chill in the room, Alejandro moved to stoke the fire. It was in that instant that Noble "Kaintock" McGuire made his unexpected entrance, bursting through the door with a whoop that caused Angelique to jump and Alex to drop the wood in his arms. It was just as well, for as he spun to face his friend, he found McGuire's arms wrapped about his waist, and he was lifted several inches from the floor.

"We're gonna have a baby!" the Kentuckian bellowed.

Angelique gasped and sat up. "Mr. McGuire, please! I haven't—"

"Me and Carlota is gonna have a baby!"

"Oh, Angelique!" Carlota DuHon ran through the bedroom door, wringing her hands. "I'm sorry, dear, but once I told Noble he could not contain himself." She stopped abruptly at finding Alejandro de Bastitas hovering above the floor in Noble's bearlike grip.

A sarcastic grin across his face, Alex commanded softly, "Put me down, Papa."

Clearing his throat, McGuire did just that. He was then against Carlota, his arm wrapped protectively about her waist. "There's not but one thing to do. That's get married right away."

Carlota could not take her eyes from Angelique. She thought her daughter would burst into a fit of tears at any moment, but was stunned as Angelique broke out in sudden, hysterical laughter.

"*You* are pregnant?" Angelique gasped between breaths. Her mother nodded. Angelique directed wide eyes toward McGuire, then her husband. For a moment the bitter memories fled and as their glances locked, both burst out laughing again.

Carlota and Noble stood to one side, feeling somehow sheepish as the younger couple found hilarity in their predicament. "I really don't find it at all humorous," the woman finally stated.

"You're absolutely right," Angelique agreed. "It's ridiculous."

Both Carlota and Noble stiffened.

Leaning against the carved bedpost, Alex folded arms across his chest. "You are old enough to be knitting booties for grandchildren, madam."

Carlota ignored him. "The babe will be born in September."

Angelique's eyes widened again. "How very interesting." Lying back on the bed, she finished, "I might encourage you to waste little time in being married."

"Then you approve of our marrying?" her mother asked.

"I do not. I detest this grizzly man." Why had those words sounded less and less believable the last few weeks? She lifted her fingers to her mouth, hiding a reluctant smile.

McGuire shifted beneath Angelique's fiery green gaze. "I suspect we can be married within a day or two."

Alex turned toward the fire. "Ah, marriage. The end of a perfect relationship. May I offer my condolences?"

"You may go to hell," Carlota snapped.

Sensing his future wife and his best friend had tolerated one another's presence long enough, Noble caught Carlota's arm and ushered her toward the door. Angelique waited until they were gone before lifting her eyes toward her husband. He was staring into the fire, his back to her. She wondered how he would react if given the news that he too would soon be a father. Would his face sparkle with pride? Would he show the concern and gentleness McGuire did?

Certainly not. He had married her only to spite her mother. Besides, should she announce her pregnancy he might *never* let her return to New Orleans!

"You may go as well," she invited.

He didn't respond.

"You made a mistake in returning here," she continued. "Your absence these many weeks has changed nothing. You killed my father and I loathe you for that." His silence was infuriating. She wanted him to turn and face her, to speak. She needed the deep caress of his drawl to wrap about her heart and warm her. But why? Why?

Raking fingers through his hair, Alex turned. There was slight color on her cheeks, he noticed, and her eyes were somehow brighter than they had been on his arrival. "Isabella has asked me to travel to Gonzales. There are some problems to deal with concerning your uncle's estate. When I return we'll talk. Perhaps by that time you'll feel stronger."

"But no different."

That familiar curl to his lips, Alex approached the bed, his smile broadening as Angelique clutched the blanket to her bosom. Bending, he placed a lingering kiss upon her forehead. "Perhaps, my love, the war will end the problem for us both." Her eyes flew to his and, pivoting on his boot heel, he strode from the room.

What had he meant by: "Perhaps the war will end the problem for us both"? What war? The war was over. The Texas Volunteer Army had ousted Cos from the Alamo

and sent him fleeing back to Mexico with a signed statement promising he would leave Texas and not interfere in
any way with the Constitution of 1824. Had they been
naive to believe Santa Anna would honor his brother-in-
law's promise? Should that detestable war reach San Antonio again, would Alexander take up arms and risk being
killed with those soldiers who still inhabited the city?

Angelique twisted in bed, unable to calm her restless
thoughts—of Carlota and Noble McGuire, and of her husband.

Sliding from the bed, she draped her shoulders in a
woolen shawl and tiptoed to her husband's room, remem-
bering only *after* pressing her ear to the door that Teresa
had mentioned Alejandro was taking his old quarters in the
far wing. Almost against her will, she took to the dark
corridor, her knees growing weaker the closer to his room
she got.

Angelique stopped, then ducking behind a corner, she
watched as Consuela moved up to Alexander's door, a silver tray and bottle of wine balanced on her upturned palm.
The servant rapped softly, and at his murmured recourse,
entered the room, closing the door behind her.

She couldn't breathe. Cold fury caused her to shake and
clutching at her shawl, she gritted, "So that's it. You move
away from *me* so that your *puta* can visit at your beck and
call. Well, my good husband, we shall see about *that!*"

Angelique sent the door back against the wall with a
bang. Alex, in bathwater up to his armpits, looked up in
surprise. Consuela nearly dropped the decanter she had
poised over a silver goblet.

"Am I intruding?" Angelique asked in a strangely high
voice. Her chin was up and tilted, her eyes were watering
treacherously, and her auburn hair was tumbling in disarray
to her hips.

Alejandro sank again against the back of the tub. Replacing the cigar between his teeth, he raked his eyes over
his wife's slender frame. "Yes," was his simple answer.

"May I ask *what* is going on here?"

"I am having a bath." Grinning past the cheroot, he patted the top of the water.

"At this hour of night?"

"It is only half past ten."

Startled, she glanced at the clock.

"Would you care to join me?"

"I beg your pardon?"

"In a drink, love."

She shook her head and stressed, "I am here on business."

Consuela slipped the cup into Alex's moist fingers, then spreading her hands over her skirt, stated, "I was asked in to help, senora, as many of the servants are ill."

A likely story. "Will you excuse us?"

Consuela nodded and, hips swaying, casually left the room, closing the door behind her.

Angelique stared at her husband. Steam from the water rose about his glossy torso, causing his face to flush and his hair to fall limply across his forehead. He was watching her, the thin stream of smoke from his cigar rising to hang suspended just below the ceiling.

"Well?" came his resounding demand.

She jumped, startled from her trance. Caught in a lie she could scarcely explain herself, she plucked the first thing she could think of from her mind. "I-I want a—a divorce."

The silence was impenetrable.

"What?"

Was she mistaken or had the room grown warmer? The nightgown was sticking to her skin and moisture was trickling from her scalp and running down her neck. "I want a—"

"I heard you!" Alex rolled the cigar between his lips, then stated flatly, "Not possible."

"An annulment then."

Alex dropped his cheroot into the water, killing its fire. Slowly then, he stood up before his wife. "An annulment."

"Yes. An annulment," she said, struggling not to look at him.

"On what grounds?"

"I can think of several," she reflected in a tight voice. As he moved from the tub, she retreated several steps. "Lying, for one. Nonconsummation of marriage, for another."

"I never lied to you. Had you ever *asked* me if I had killed your father, I might have admitted it. In the other case . . ." Lifting a towel, he wrapped it about his lean hips. "Verifying nonconsummation may prove difficult."

"There are witnesses. This entire house knows we have not spent one night together as husband and wife."

"Do I detect some hidden bitterness, my sweet?" Retrieving the glass of wine from the tabletop, he lifted it to his mouth. "If so, we can rectify the problem easily enough."

It was time to leave. Backing to the door, Angelique attempted a weak smile. "Perhaps by the time you return from Gonzales I will have spoken to the priest. Perhaps even returned to New Orleans." Before closing the door, she added, "Oh, and do be assured that if you attempt to follow me there, I will see that you hang for my father's murder. *Buenas noches, senor.*"

Angelique released her breath. Let the man stew over *that* for a while! she applauded herself. Let him fester in worry as *she* had the last six weeks. Her pace slowed with that thought. What a horrible realization. She had actually *worried* over that detestable man returning to her.

"Oh, Papa, forgive me!" she whispered, then crossed herself.

There was a click. Her step faltered. Slowing, she looked back over her shoulder. Alejandro was there. Standing in his doorway, he was dressed loosely in a red silk robe. The sash about his waist hung nearly to his knees and the collar of the coat gaped to the middle of his furred belly.

He was staring at her.

Angelique was paralyzed. It was only after he had closed the space between them by half that she finally forced herself to move. Escape was impossible, and in three long strides he had caught her.

Gripping her arm, Alejandro whipped her around. "I don't think we're finished yet, Angel."

"I beg to differ, sir. I've not one more word to say. You are free to go back to your *puta* if you like."

"Is that an invitation, love?"

She thought to strike him, but had no more lifted her arm than he closed his hand about her wrist. Alejandro then plucked her from the floor. "Put me down this moment," came her strangled demand.

He ignored her. Moving down the corridor, Alex found Consuela just descending the stairs. *"Por favor, senora!"*

*"Si*, Senor de Bastitas?"

"Bring the wine to Angelique's quarters."

Angelique struggled. "I don't want wine. I don't want you. I hate you! *Comprende*, Spaniard?"

"So you said, and I might have believed you until you came prancing into my room. You didn't much like seeing me with another woman, did you?"

"That wine has addled your brain!"

"Thankfully nothing else." He kicked the bedroom door closed then, and striding across the floor, he dumped her on the bed.

Pressing a hand to her temple, Angelique shook her head. The plaguing nausea of her condition caused her to break out in a clammy sweat. "Please, I've no stomach now to fight with you, Alexander. I'm not—"

"My feelings exactly. It seems we've done nothing but argue since we met, and quite frankly I'm tired of it." He tugged at his belt. The silk slid in a whisper off his shoulders and onto the floor.

Angelique averted her eyes. The bed gave slightly beneath his weight, but before she could turn away he was across her, pressing her down into the mattress. Long brown fingers bothered the buttons down the front of her gown.

"What are you doing?" she asked in an incredulous voice.

"Doing what I should have done six weeks ago. A husband has his rights. I am demanding mine." Pulling open the yoke of the shift, he pressed his mouth against her throat.

"Don't. Please, don't." She was feeling sick. Her skin was hot, then cold. "You don't understand."

"I understand," he snapped in a ravaged voice. Closing a palm over her breast, he squeezed, causing her to whimper. "You hate me. I need no reminders of that. Like a fool I stood outside that door and said I loved you, the first time ever in my life I said that, and you threw it back in my face."

Pinioning her to the bed with his forearm across her chest, he reached for the skirt of her gown, hiking it to her hips. When her legs moved together, he wedged his knee between them and shoved open her thighs.

The warmth of his hand as it touched that moist apex sent her betraying body into a quandary. How was it possible to feel such longing for the man who had killed her father? Surely it was a sin, a delicious evil that would send her hurrying to the priest for forgiveness. She groaned.

Alex laughed as he continued to stroke her. "Perhaps I should have kept you as a mistress instead. From my experience wives don't enjoy this much. Of course that depends on whose wife it is . . . and whose husband she's with." He was over her then, and when he would have kissed her, she turned her face away.

He thrust. In one swift move he filled her.

The warmth encompassing him was enough to extinguish that flame of anger and in its place ignite the tender passion he always felt when inside her. "Ah, Angel, I have missed you."

Fingers twisting into the sheets, Angelique closed her eyes and clenched her teeth. This wasn't right, yet it was undeniable. She *was* moved by his touch and words. Her heart soared with the sound of his voice and she was helpless to stop her body's response.

He continued moving, yet nothing he did seemed to wrench her from her state of refusal. He tasted her breasts, nibbled her ears, and covered her face with kisses. Nothing. His frustration mounted. For a fleeting moment he was reminded of Pamela, how she lay beneath him like a limp rag doll and closed her eyes, no doubt dreaming of that *other* man.

Angelique sensed the sudden change in her husband. He was tense. His movements became somehow cruel. The nausea she had managed to subside surged into her throat. "Please, you must stop this and let me go!"

With all the strength she could muster, Angelique shoved against Alejandro's shoulders, then twisted, sending him rolling to his side. There was a groan behind her as she jumped from the bed and fled behind her privacy screen.

Alex shuddered and at the sound of Angelique quietly retching, his head came up. His anger intensifying the humiliation he had just experienced, he rolled to his feet, and in one lunge sent the silk screen clattering across the floor.

"Do I disgust you that much?" he roared.

Pressing a damp cloth to her mouth, Angelique looked up. Alex's face was black with rage. "I'm sorry. I've been ill and—"

He heard none of that. Jerking his wife to her feet, he shoved her toward the bed. "Even Pamela had the good grace to hide her revulsion until I left the room."

"You've misunderstood! Please, Alejandro, let me explain. I'm—"

"Lousy two-timing little slut that she was, at least she let me love her. Of course, she let every other man too, I understand."

Her heart stopped. Backing onto the bed, she pulled the sheet up to her neck. Never had she witnessed such unleashed pain and anger from a man.

Alex snatched his robe from the floor before facing Angelique again. Pointing one finger, he thrust it into her face. "I've had enough. *Comprende?* I'm finished. I tried with her and now you, and it hasn't worked."

"Alexander!"

The door slammed.

"Alexander?"

Alexander . . .

It was a small, somber group that met in the Room of the Blessed Virgin at noon of the next day. Father de la Garza stood before Carlota and Noble McGuire, his hands clasped and his face bright with anticipation. "How very wonderful," he proclaimed to the few witnesses who had gathered behind them. "Only weeks ago we joined these two young people in holy matrimony." He pointed to a trembling Angelique, who stood at her mother's side, then to a rigid Alejandro, who attended McGuire. "Now her mother is marrying her husband's best friend. What a happy family this will be."

Noble's laughter turned into a bout of chesty coughing.

"Lawd, have mercy," Bernice whispered to herself.

Tomas and Isabella exchanged doleful glances.

With a bellow of "Bah!" Carlos retreated to his library and slammed the door behind him.

The priest cleared his throat before addressing the soon-to-be-married couple. "Are we ready?" he asked concernedly. They each nodded. "Then let us begin."

Angelique watched her mother's face closely, as well as McGuire's. They *were* happy, as happy as she had been. . . . Her eyes lifted slowly to her husband. Alejandro was staring at some point over her head, ignoring her completely. And as the father spoke of loving and cherishing, that mocking curl to Alex's lips proclaimed *his* thoughts on the matter.

He had vowed last evening that he was finished with her, but wasn't that what she wanted? Why did the thought of his hating her trouble her so? She should be thankful to be rid of him forever. Yet, acknowledging the pain in her heart, she realized that she wasn't pleased with the prospect of living without Alejandro.

It is only because you are carrying his baby! she reasoned to herself.

That thought jolted Angelique from her musings, and her eyes bolted to his again. They met this time. He looked away, slightly flustered and his face tinting from his discomforture. What had she seen in that instant? Anger? Frustration? . . . Pain.

She had to talk with someone. Father de la Garza, perhaps?

The vows over, Noble scooped his wife in his arms and kissed her passionately, causing the witnesses to laugh and Carlota to blush. She touched his cheek and noticed it was warm, very warm, but before she could mention it he caught her hand and turned toward Alejandro. She stiffened and her chin came up.

"Well now, Alex, there is someone here I want you to meet." McGuire caught his friend's rigid arm and pulled him closer. "My wife. Mrs. McGuire."

Alejandro and Carlota stared at one another for a long moment. Her eyes widened as he caught her hand gently in his. "Madam McGuire. I trust you'll make him happy?"

Carlota's mouth dropped open. "Of course."

Alex stepped away. He would do his best to accept Carlota for his friend's sake, but that didn't mean he had to like it. His blue eyes swept the room and settled like stone on Angelique. She was speaking quietly with the priest. Her earlier plea for an annulment flashed through his mind and angrily he turned for the door.

Isabella stopped him. "You are leaving?"

"It will be late tomorrow night before I reach Gonzales."

Wise brown eyes narrowed in contemplation. "I have never known you to run, Alejandro."

He looked away.

Tomas stepped up. "Mind if I come along?"

"You've no plans with Anna?" he asked.

Face dark, Alex's brother shook his head. "Anna is gone. She and her father have traveled to Galveston."

"Ah, women. Just when you need them the most . . ." Alex threw one last glance toward his conversing wife. Spinning, he left the room.

# TWENTY-FOUR

"You will give my regrets to Senora Musquiz, won't you?"

"Certainly." Angelique pulled on her glove before asking Isabella, "Are you certain you aren't feeling up to the journey?"

"I fear my age is settling in on me, my dear."

Placing a kiss on Isabella's forehead, Angelique smiled regretfully. "I fear it's this dissension between Alejandro and me that is causing you such grief."

Isabella peered into Angelique's worried face. "It would please me if things could be worked out between you." Sighing, she finished. "You will take the coach?"

"I think not. It is a bright day and warmer. Pablo is taking the wagon into town, so I will ride with him." Angelique turned for the door. "I shall return by dinner."

"My best to Senora Musquiz."

Throwing a kiss to *la patrona*, Angelique left the room.

She met Bernice in the foyer; she was about to climb the stairs, a tray laden with chicken broth and brandy in her plump hands. Noble McGuire was ill, had been since the wedding two weeks ago. Her mother had hardly left his side in that time. Reluctantly, Angie had to admit that she was concerned over her stepfather's well-being, and before leaving the hacienda she went with Bernice to her mother's room, where she offered what comfort she could to both Carlota and Noble McGuire. Carlota weepily thanked her. Noble continued with his feverish dreams.

The day grew brighter as the morning clouds broke across the horizon. Angelique bounced on the wooden seat, wishing now she had chosen to ride in the coach. But she was eager to reach San Antonio, eager to visit with her friends, Senora Musquiz and Susannah Dickinson.

The roads were curiously busy on this day. Wagonloads of Mexicans were heading *out* of town, their faces somber as they departed. Even San Antonio seemed oddly still, but she didn't find that unusual. The soldiers inhabiting the mission were better known for their late-night fiestas and cantina brawls than they were for sleeping. Only the night before, February 22, they had celebrated George Washington's birthday. No doubt everyone was suffering from whiskey's aftereffects.

Pablo pulled his wagon before the open-air market. "I must see my brother," he announced. "Then I will ride you to the Plaza."

Angelique flashed the young man a wide smile. "That won't be necessary. It's a pleasant morning, and I wouldn't mind the walk."

He helped her down. "I will pick you up at six o'clock."

"*Gracias,*" she thanked him.

The streets were slightly muddy due to an earlier rainfall. Perhaps that had something to do with the lack of children who usually occupied their time with games of tag and hide and seek about the alleys between the buildings. Still, there was something about the quiet, an anticipation that clung to the air.

In that moment, the bells of San Fernando Church began pealing. Angelique stared toward the bell tower high above the flat-roofed homes, wondering why they would ring so unceasingly this hour of morning. Men and women ran from their houses. Soldiers burst from the cantinas, hesi-

tating as they too searched up and down the streets, then
began hurrying up Potrero and Soledad Streets, across the
footbridges and into the old mission.

"They're coming!" someone called. "The Mexicans are
coming! Run for your lives!"

Angelique stopped. The Musquiz home could be seen in
the far distance, and outside their gates, Susannah Dickinson stood with her babe in arms. A horse thundered by,
and suddenly Almeron Dickinson was yelling, "Quick,
Sue, the Mexicans are upon us! Give me the baby and jump
on behind me!" The woman complied, and soon both were
riding back toward the Alamo.

She stood, uncertain what to do. Then a buckskin-clad
giant of a man stopped, and in Spanish stated firmly, "You
best get in the mission, lady. That's gonna be the safest
place to hide."

Of course. The Alamo was the stronghold, with soldiers
and guns to protect the citizens until help could arrive.
Picking up her skirts, Angelique joined the group who had
just exited the Veramendi house: Juana Veramendi Alsbury
and her baby, her sister Gertrudis . . . and James Bowie.


Alejandro and Tomas rode side-by-side, thankful the long
trip from Gonzales was almost behind them. It had been a
tiresome two weeks, and less than fruitful. The Sanchez
estate was in a mess. Alex reasoned it was no wonder Julio
had been so anxious to marry his daughter off to a rich
landowner. The union might have brought some respite
from his indebtedness.

Nothing appeared out of the ordinary as the brothers
approached their grandfather's hacienda. The gates were
open. Just as they entered, the front door was jerked open
and Carlota ran down the walk, her face ravaged from
worry.

"You must help her!" she wailed. Twisting her fingers
into Alejandro's shirt, she pleaded, "They have my baby,
my Angelique. *Madre de Dios*, you must save her from
that monster!"

"What the hell are you saying, madam?"

"The Mexicans have taken San Antonio."

A coldness crept up his back. "What has that to do with Angelique?"

Her eyes never leaving his, she explained, "This morning she went into the city to visit with Senora Musquiz. The bells warned the citizens of the army's approach, and Angelique was ushered into the old mission."

"How do you know that?"

"Pablo saw her. He called out to her to return to the wagon, but she did not hear him."

"She is right."

Alejandro and Tomas looked up to find Isabella standing a short distance away. Gritting his teeth and forcing his pounding heart under control, Alex asked, "Is the Alamo under siege?"

"Yes. Though it is quiet now, the fighting was earlier heard. It is my understanding the Texas army is surrounded. Already the Mexican forces are crowing over their ultimate conquest."

Damn, but he should have been there! He should never have agreed to travel to Gonzales when the Mexicans were so close at hand. But like everyone else, he believed they would wait another two weeks before striking. Pushing Carlota away, he started toward the house.

Isabella stopped him. Fear pulling at her mouth, she demanded in a dry tone, "What will you do?"

"My wife is there."

"Carlos will never allow it."

"That is between Carlos and me." Looking back toward Carlota, he asked, "Where is your husband?"

"He is gravely ill. He took to his bed over a week ago with pneumonia."

He looked toward his brother. Tomas looked away. "Very well, I will go alone."

Sitting behind his desk, Carlos de Bastitas looked up as his grandson entered the room. He watched silently as Alejandro strode to the gun cabinet and opened its doors. "I will not allow this," he finally stated.

Alex didn't hesitate. Neither did he respond.

"You will not resist His Excellency. I am certain he would not harm a woman, and when those ignorant insurgents finally surrender she will be released and return to the ranch."

Propping several rifles against the wall, Alex turned to face his grandfather. "You don't believe that any more than I do."

"I will not allow it."

In three long strides Alex was before the old man, his fist cracking against the top of the desk. "I don't give one little damn, senor. I am taking all spare ammunition and I am returning to the Alamo, whether you 'allow' it or not!"

Carlos was shaking as Alejandro moved toward the door. "You are a traitor to this country and my name. Should you touch one of those guns . . . I will shoot you."

Alex stopped, but didn't turn. He didn't have to. The ominous clock was warning enough that his grandfather's threat could not be taken lightly. "You won't pull that trigger," he stated quietly.

"I will."

Slowly, he advanced toward the guns.

"I will shoot you."

Wrapping his fingers about the barrel of the rifle, Alex waited. Nothing. A smirk pulling one corner of his mouth, he turned, and what he saw caused his heart to stop. Carlos had raised his weapon. Their eyes clashed, and before he could move the explosion of gunpowder sent the round, black bullet into his thigh with ragged precision. He hit the floor, groaning and rolling as he clutched at his leg.

Carlos picked up the matching gun, and with quivering chin, limped toward the man twisting on the floor. When Alejandro finally controlled the fire splintering throughout his body, he looked up, face wet with sweat, his hands bloodied and his features contorted in shock and pain. "I warned you," were the old man's only words.

"So you did." Gulping for air, Alex threw a cold laugh into his grandfather's bleached face. "Now you will have to warn me again, because as long as there is breath in my body I will defy you." His hands were raised to the wall for support, leaving smeared patches of red as he attempted to stand.

Carlos closed the door and locked it just seconds before Tomas could be heard pounding and demanding entrance. He raised his pistol again. In a soft voice, he said, "I can understand your wanting to help her."

"She's my wife!"

"Yes. And she is a beautiful young woman. But there is the matter of honor we must deal with. I am a Bastitas, and am bound by oath to support the Mexican government. You, as son of my son, are honor-bound to do the same, no matter what."

"No." Alex wiped the sweat from his brow, but not before it ran into his eyes, blearing his vision. The attempt to moisten his lips was useless.

Carlos pulled the hammer back and locked it in place. "Then I warn you that I will do what I must to protect that honor."

He couldn't swallow. His head was roaring, and though he tried desperately to claw his way to a standing position, he couldn't do it. Sliding in his own blood, he slipped again to the floor.

Carlos stood over him and leveled the gun.

"Sweet Mary." Alex closed his eyes and clenched his teeth.

The gun fired again before Tomas managed to burst through the door. His first thought was to grab the gun from his grandfather's hand. Both men stumbled backward as Isabella fell across Alejandro's still form. Carlota entered the room, as did several of the servants.

"He has killed him!" Isabella wept.

Tomas fell to his brother's side, his eyes taking in the gaping holes in Alejandro's legs. "He is not dead, *Abuela*, but he needs attention. We must get him to his bed and stop this bleeding as soon as possible."

With the help of several vaqueros Tomas managed to heft his brother's limp frame from the floor. Delores ran for water, Teresa for whiskey. Isabella waited until all had left the room before turning on her husband.

"Fool! You would destroy the dearest thing in our lives for the sake of *your* honor."

Slumped in his chair, Carlos shook his head. "I warned him."

"*Ay*, you warned him! But as you would die for honor, he would die for his wife *as well* as honor and it makes him a much better man than you!" Picking up Carlos's cane, Isabella waved it before his face. "You have chosen, senor. Now get out of this house."

"What do you mean?"

"You chose Mexico over your own flesh and blood. So be it!" The stick shattered against the desktop. "Go find your beloved dictator and lick his boots. You are finished here. *Comprende?* Finished." Sending the gold grip of the cane through the glass doors of the gun case, Isabella spun and left the room.

Angelique stood in the shadow of the old church, watching as William Travis handed his hurriedly penned letters to the couriers Sutherland and Smith. "Take this to Gonzales," he said. "Tell them we will fire cannon shot three times a day; morning, noon, and at sunset, to show we are still alive at the Alamo." They shook hands, and as the massive gates swung open, the horsemen left the mission in a cloud of dust.

Her eyes were then drawn to the sentry atop the wall. His hands cupped about his mouth, he called, "Colonel Travis, them Mexicans have raised a red flag from the church tower!"

No quarter—no surrender—no mercy.

Travis faced his men. "What shall we answer, boys?"

The eighteen-pounder pointing toward the city roared in defiance, followed by the men's cheers. Groups rushed to take their places along the sprawling walls, while others began loading and stacking guns throughout the garrisons.

It took little to make Angelique realize the waiting would seem far less monotonous if she kept busy. She helped inventory the food supply. There were thirty beefs and ninety bushels of corn. Then she scavenged for anything that could be used later as ammunition: lead from the stained-glass windows, nails, even horseshoes.

The Mexicans commenced firing in early afternoon. A howitzer roared, followed by larger cannon, but the army inside the Alamo walls rarely responded. They had been ordered to hold their fire, to save their ammunition. By nightfall, the damage was still light; a horse had been killed. Nothing more.

With torchlight dancing against the walls of the old fortress and a Scotsman playing bagpipes in the darkness, the women and children hurried to dish out plates of beef and corn to the weary fighters. There was no coffee to warm them, but plenty of whiskey. Still, they drank sparingly.

The first day of siege behind them, the troops huddled about camp fires and against the stone walls for warmth. The women and children were invited to rest inside the church where they all lay, eyes open and ears straining for the unfamiliar sounds of warfare. Angelique spoke softly to herself, convincing her own heart that this nightmare would be shortly finished. After all, word had been sent to Goliad and Gonzales that the time to rally was upon the citizens of Texas. Reinforcements were certain to arrive at any time and she could return to her family.

Family. She laughed to herself, recalling her husband's face as he stormed out the door those two weeks ago. There seemed to be little family left to her these days—only her mother and the child Angelique carried inside her. Her fingers floated to her stomach. It was flat still, and she wondered when she would feel that first flutter of life . . . if indeed she lived to feel it.

Dawn was shattered by gunfire. Bullets whined over the walls and plunked harmlessly into the ground or against walls. The troops countered by hurling insults and vulgarities that the Mexicans could not understand. Then Santa Anna surprised them all by ordering his band of trumpets and tubas to serenade the captives.

The mood among the men was varied. Many guffawed at the "greasers" and danced jigs to the blasting music. More than once Angelique found herself in the arms of

some wiry fighter as he clumsily led her through one dance
after another. They actually laughed, hooted, thumbed their
noses as the enemy fired, and placed bets on who could
kill the most Mexes. For beneath the revelry was the undying hope that Fannin and his force of over four hundred
men would join them at any time. The call to arms had
been issued. Help would come.

Perhaps tomorrow.

Isabella stood at her grandson's side, helplessly watching
as he thrashed in his pain and delirium. She pressed a damp
cloth against his feverish forehead and did her best to
soothe him. It was impossible. In his mind Alejandro was
fighting his way to his wife and friends, cursing Carlos and
pleading for someone to help him to his horse.

The fighting had been going on for days now. When all
was quiet the boom of the Texans' cannons could be heard,
reminding them that all hope was not lost. But a cold dread
settled on Isabella's shoulders as she moved to the window
and stared down on Tomas as he spoke with Pablo. The
boy had just returned from town; supposedly he had spoken to one of the sentries inside the Alamo. According to
the fighter, riders had departed the mission soon after the
siege had begun in an effort to bring volunteers to their
aid.

They were meeting in Gonzales.

Tomas de Bastitas was not surprised when, entering the
house, he found Isabella waiting inside the door. Her lined
face was puckered with worry, soft brown eyes pleading.

"You are going," she stated.

"Yes." She swayed slightly and he moved to offer a
gentle hand for support.

"I forbid it, Tomas."

"I'm sorry. Something must be done to help them."

Isabella shook her head. "I did not see you grown to be
murdered by our own countrymen. No. I need you here to
help with your brother."

"My brother will live," he replied in a quiet voice.

She clutched at his shirt. "But you will not. If you leave

here you will never come home. I know this.''

Tomas's smile was sad. ''Perhaps not. Perhaps it is my destiny to die in such a way. I have turned from many problems in my lifetime, knowing afterward that cowardice was not the cause, but for a reason I could not understand at the time. I understand now.''

''You will not make a difference!'' she argued.

''I do not know that.'' He took her in his arms. ''Ah, *Abuela*, do you not see? It is in me to do this for my brother, for Angelique . . . and for the men who are waiting.'' Laughing, he pushed her to arms' length. ''Who is to say? Perhaps I will deliver Angelique to my brother's bed and be a hero. There will be fiestas in my honor and the senoritas will throw flowers at my feet.''

She touched his handsome face, so much like his father's. ''There will be a celebration like San Antonio has never known.''

Tomas raised his eyes to the closed door across the foyer. ''You will tell Carlos goodbye for me?''

''Yes.''

''Perhaps this will prove to him that I am worthy of boasting the Bastitas name.'' He pulled away. ''I will pack my things and see my brother.''

Moments later Tomas stood at Alejandro's bedside. ''Are you awake, my brother?'' he asked in a loud voice. Shaking his head, he teased, ''I told you that someday you would push him too far. Now look where your stubbornness has found you.''

Bending to one knee, he took Alex's hand. ''I do this for all that you have done for me. For the whippings you took, for the advice you gave, for the secrets you shared with me and no other. If I could be one-half the man and friend you have been, then I shall die complete.'' Closer, he whispered, ''Rest easy in knowing no harm will come to Angelique as long as I am living. I love her. You knew that yet you entrusted me to be her friend. For sharing her in that way I am, and will always be, grateful.''

Tomas stood. ''If you remember anything, remember that I love you.''

He left the room.

# TWENTY-FIVE

Angelique thought of her husband. Where was he? Why had he done nothing to save her? Had he washed his hands of her so completely?

For eight days the men behind these walls had turned back attacks, and still no help had come. Spirits were sagging. Tempers were short. James Bonham had ridden again to implore Fannin to assist the Alamo, but that had been five days ago, and he hadn't returned.

It appeared more and more these days that the entire world thought the Alamo was expendable.

The time was somewhere between midnight and three in the morning. Angelique had just dozed when gunfire broke out again. She wasn't surprised, or even alarmed. Such spurts of fighting were not unusual, but this time something *was* different. A whoop of cheers greeted her as she sleepily pushed herself from the pallet. Stumbling to her feet, she ran with the other women into the yard, and what she found there caused her heart to skip in excitement.

Help had come!

A group of thirty-two men on horses were surrounded by the battle-weary fighters. One carried a flag of white silk bearing the words "Come and Take It" sewn both above and below a cannon. Already the dwindling camp fires were being stoked and the din of conversation was growing louder as each man greeted the newcomers and helped them from their animals.

"Angelique!"

She closed her eyes. When she opened them Tomas de Bastitas was before her. His arms opened and she was in them.

His voice husky with emotion, he held her against his chest. "Dear God, you are safe."

For the first time since her ordeal had begun, she broke and wept. "I thought no help would come."

"Shhh. We are here, little one, for whatever good it will do you." Prying her arms from about his neck, Tomas searched her tear-streaked face. "Alejandro would have come, but—"

"No!" Angry because her husband had obviously not cared enough for her to come himself, she beseeched her brother-in-law, "Do not mention his name to me now. Time and distance have assured me of what I must have realized all along."

"Which is?"

She shook her head. "I don't wish to speak of it. Now tell me, how are my mother and Bernice?"

"Frantic. And on top of worrying over you, Carlota's husband has been extremely ill. He was only beginning to recover when I left."

A blast of cold wind caused Angelique to grip her blanket tighter about her shoulders. Noticing she had begun to shiver, Tomas ushered her back into the church. When he had settled her into a chair, he asked, "What has been happening here?"

"They fight. Each day the Mexican troops are closer. Our men have killed and wounded many of them, but so far no injuries have been incurred on our side. Jim Bowie is desperately ill, unable even to leave his bed."

"I understand he and Travis are holding joint command."

"No longer. Bowie turned over his command shortly

after the siege began. He knows he's dying and asked his men to support Colonel Travis the best they could.''

"Have you plenty of ammunition and food?''

"Enough for another month.'' She touched his arm. "Are there others coming?''

Their eyes met. He knew the truth. Fannin would not be joining them. Two days after the siege had begun the commander and his troops had set out from Fort Defiance with intentions of storming into San Antonio, but problems had caused him to return to Goliad. In Gonzales, the men had waited for days, hoping for more volunteers to join them, but it had become apparent there would be no others.

Hugging the shivering girl, he kissed the top of her hair. "We can always hope, Angelique. There is little left for us now.''

Still, the garrison was thirty-two men stronger, certainly cause to celebrate. Bonfires brightened the darkness. A cow was slaughtered and soon the smell of cooking meat wafted in the air. Bagpipes were brought out and dawn found the men dancing and laughing, raising toasts to the newcomers who had so gallantly offered their lives and services for the sake of independence and honor.

Their celebration behind them, the men again tackled the chore of digging trenches and fortifying walls. The Gonzales group was shown about the encampment. Suggestions were made between them as to what positions might be strengthened by their presence.

For Angelique, hope was renewed. The endless hours of loneliness were forgotten as Tomas continually found his way to her side. When shelling burst from the Mexican troops he made certain she was sheltered from harm's way. He was forever laughing off the immediate threat of danger and boasting that Santa Anna was no closer to taking the mission now than he had been nine days before.

But that changed at noon. A cheer rose outside the walls, and at the sentries' beckon the Texas fighters scurried up the ladders to the gun platforms. Trailed by Tomas, Angelique climbed to the wooden walkways and stared through the makeshift parapets. What they all saw there made the blood run cold in their veins.

It was not the people swarming the streets and chanting *"Viva Santa Anna!"* that frightened them so. It was the column of over a thousand troops that stretched into the west horizon.

To the sound of San Fernando's pealing bells, Tomas helped Angelique to the ground. The chimes appeared to be finalizing doom, for James Bonham had arrived only an hour before with the grim news. There would be no help for them from *any* source. It was up to one hundred and eighty men to compete with the swelling thousands outside these walls.

William Travis stood atop a platform and faced the many somber faces. "Men, I will beseech our countrymen one last time for help. Have you any written words to pass on . . . then take this time to pen them."

Angelique and Tomas walked back to the church. When he had located both pen and paper, he sat down to write. She silently watched him, and when he looked up, she smiled.

"What would you like to say?" he asked.

Her laughter was a trifle forced. "Tell my mother and Bernice that I am well." Pausing, she then added, "You may tell them that I too am expecting a baby in September."

Tomas's jaw dropped, and in a single movement he was out of his chair. "A baby! Are you certain?"

"I have known for some time."

"Why did you not mention it?"

Why indeed? "Perhaps I was afraid to. Now it doesn't seem to matter."

His head fell back in laughter. "God, but my brother will be pleased!"

"I care little if your brother is pleased." Stepping from his embrace, Angelique lifted her chin. "He killed my father, a good and decent man, and knowing this he married me. He married me out of spite and cruelty toward my mother and nothing more."

"But you are wrong," he stressed. Cupping her face in his hands, Tomas smiled. "I know my brother as well as I know my own heart. He loves you, Angelique, and believe me when I say he would be here if—"

"No!" She covered her ears with her hands. "Do not mention him to me again. What was between us is dead. As dead as my dear father, and I will never forgive him. Pray I should die right here than ever see him again!"

Saddened, Tomas turned again to his chair. "Then I am to pass no word to him at all?"

After a slight hesitation, she stated flatly, "None."

Scrawling his name and Angelique's, Tomas folded the note and sealed it.

Dawn brought the heaviest firing yet. The Mexicans had moved their guns closer, and now every hit against the walls was damaging. The women were kept busy. As soon as rifles were emptied they were delivered to the church, where Angelique and several of the other women worked nonstop at reloading their chambers.

Angelique had seen little of Susannah Dickinson, for most times she spent with her husband when he wasn't arming his position. Jim Bowie had routed the Veramendi sisters to the distant barracks, thinking their walls might somehow be safer. Now she wondered if those women were feeling the same resignation that burned within her breast.

The end was near.

March 5 broke clear and warmer. A south breeze alleviated the need for the scratchy woolen blankets about their shoulders, and the smell of spring could almost tease the Texans with glimpses of fresh beginnings. But the battle did not cease. Hour after hour the Mexican batteries drew closer, and though no defender was injured, fatigue was an enemy no one could combat.

The days and nights of little sleep now weighed heavily on their shoulders. Angelique herself was bone-weary. She longed for an end to this misery. The men were no different. They waited listlessly for further orders from the commander.

Dawn had brought the belch of cannon fire, informing the world outside these walls that the Alamo still stood defended against the enemy. "When the cannon is heard no more, its silence will tell that the Alamo has fallen," was the message Travis had sent out with midnight's courier. But in late afternoon, he stood tired and ragged before his troops.

"Men," he began. "I have a confession to make. . . . Help is not coming."

Angelique sank against the wall, barely hearing the commander's speech. So it was finally down to this. How cruel was reality. It made grown men hang their heads. And yet as she watched Jim Bowie struggle to sit up on his cot, his body racked with coughing, and men's faces suffused with a kind of courage few people ever know, she realized the final outcome would outweigh the bleakness of their defeat.

William Travis drew his sword. Placing its tip into the ground, he cut a long line into the dirt. "Gentlemen, you have a decision to make. You are free to go, or stay. Those who are to remain here and die with me will step now across this line."

There was no hesitation. Soon all but two men had joined Travis. Bowie spoke as loudly as possible and requested that his friends hoist him over the line. His cot was lifted across. Only one remained, an old man Angelique knew only as Rose. He was not prepared to die, and by the time night had fallen completely he had disappeared over the walls and was gone from San Antonio.

Carlota left her chair. Face damp with tears, she addressed her husband. "Angelique is alive, Noble. Can you not share in my happiness?"

"Surely I can." Skimming Tomas's hurriedly penned words, McGuire shook his head. "Just ain't right my not bein' there."

"But you've been desperately ill," she argued. "Even

now you need help to stand. You cannot fault yourself for that.''

Eyes reflecting his sadness, the man lifted the note to his wife. ''They're all my friends, Carlota. Jim Bowie, Crockett, William Travis. I knew Davy in Tennessee. I's with Jim in Natchez when he got news his whole family had died from cholera.'' Thrusting a hand through his hair, Noble gritted, ''Now your daughter is trapped inside that hellhole and experiencing God knows what kind of fear. I should have been there with 'em all.''

The thought of her beautiful Angelique brought fresh tears to Carlota's eyes. ''I pray Tomas de Bastitas takes good care of her. How I wish she had chosen to fall in love with him instead of his despicable brother.''

''Now don't you start that.'' Fortified by anger, McGuire pointed a menacing finger at his wife. ''Alex is goin' through hell right now worryin' over Angelique and Tomas. Not to mention the pain he must be feeling with both his legs laid open. A little compassion from you right now might make a helluva lot of difference to him.''

Carlota stiffened. Her eyes wide, she lifted her chin. ''Bah! Compassion for that murderer is out of the question.''

''Lord have mercy, woman, listen to yourself. You done started believin' your own tales. Alex ain't no murderer and you know it.''

She didn't want to hear that. Skirts belling as she spun, Carlota stormed to the window. ''He killed my husband.''

''So what. Weren't no great loss the way I hear it.''

''Stop it!''

''You might as well accept it, sweetheart. You got a grandbaby to think about. And if you don't tell Bastitas that he's gonna be a papa come September, I will.'' Throwing the covers to one side, he nagged, ''Get me out of this bed, woman. I'm goin' to see him right now.''

''No.'' Carlota moved to her husband and coaxed him back into bed. ''I will tell the man. But only for you.''

''That's my girl.'' Noble kissed his wife's fingers.

• • •

The window was open, allowing the warm breeze of the March afternoon to brush Alex's face as he sat in his chair and stared out across the countryside. Distant cannon fire rolled like thunder to his listening ear, each blast striking against his heart as resolutely as it did the Alamo walls.

He did not turn as Isabella lay a gentle hand on his shoulder. "You must not tax yourself, my pet. Will you let me help you to bed?"

"No."

She motioned for Carlota, who said, "A letter arrived while you were resting. It is from Tomas and Angelique."

His head jerked up and before Carlota could barely extend the paper he had grabbed it from her hand. It read, "I have found Angelique to be safe and unharmed. As always, she is brave. Her spirits are good and she sends her love to you, Grandmother, as well as to Carlota and Bernice. She has informed me that a child is to be born in September to her and Alejandro."

Alex saw little after that. Words blurred and with shaking hands he crumpled the letter in his fist. He understood now. Her illness their last night together was not revulsion, as he had believed. She was pregnant, and he had been too damn angry and bitter to realize anything beyond his own self-pity.

Teresa lowered the water and clean bandages to the table beside the bed. "It is time to clean the wounds," she said softly.

Isabella and Carlota each took an arm and were about to heft Alejandro from his chair when the sight of approaching horsemen caused them to freeze.

"Dear God, what can it mean?" Carlota choked.

Isabella moved across the room. "Remain here and stay quiet." Closing the door, she hurried downstairs.

The two dozen infantrymen did not bother to knock. Suddenly the hacienda was swarming with men in red coats and blue trousers, black helmets decorated with horsehair perched on their heads. Their chests were crisscrossed with leather holsters and sabers dangled from their belts.

Carlos jumped from his chair as the commander entered. "What is the meaning of this?" he demanded.

The Mexican bowed. "I am Colonel Francisco Duque of His Excellency's army. We are here to seize all artillery in the name of Santa Anna."

"What do you mean?"

"The guns will be needed to support our men in their final assault."

"Assault?"

"*Sí, senor*. Santa Anna has tolerated these usurpers long enough."

"But who gives you the right to enter my home in such a way?"

"I do." A cold smile curled the commander's mouth.

Carlos eased back down into his chair. "Obviously there has been some mistake. His Excellency would never allow this pillaging of Rancho de Bejar."

Duque waited as his men emptied the gun case, then asked remotely, "Do you know Santa Anna?"

"Certainly. I have entertained him in this very house."

The Mexican turned to face him. "What is your name?" He pulled a vellum pouch from inside his jacket.

"Bastitas. Carlos Echeverria de Bastitas."

Dark eyes searched the list of names. Duque shook his head. "I was given orders to acquire all I could in ammunition from the surrounding homesteads, with the exception of these families written here."

"And who the hell are they?"

His head came up. He smiled again. "Friends of His Excellency, of course."

Carlos's head fell slightly. "It must be an oversight. I am certain Santa Anna will recall my loyalty to his regime."

"I'm certain he is right," came the feminine voice from behind the commander. Francisco Duque spun to face Isabella. Squaring her frail shoulders, she met him squarely. "You see before you, Colonel, a man who would sacrifice his own family to honor Santa Anna."

He clicked his heels, and as she offered her hand,

pressed it to his mouth. "Senora. You will forgive me if some mistake has been made. When this bothersome skirmish is done perhaps some arrangement can be made to pay you for this contribution."

Isabella watched silently as the man hauled the rifles out into the hall. She then said softly, "Is this confiscation entirely for adding to your stockpile of guns, or simply to keep us from using them on you?"

Brows lifted as he replied in a velvety voice, "One can never be *too* careful, Doña Bastitas." Clasping his hands behind his back, he walked out into the foyer, to the front of the stairs. Staring toward the upper landing, he asked, "Have you a large family, dear lady?"

"No."

"And do you share your husband's enthusiasm for His Excellency?"

"No."

He paused before inquiring, "And is there anyone up those stairs who would disfavor His Excellency's cause?"

Isabella did not blink. "There is no one up those stairs who could be of any danger to Santa Anna . . . at this time."

"Should I see for myself?"

"You may."

They stared at one another for a long moment before a movement caught Duque's attention. He looked up as a beauty with waist-length sable hair appeared at the top of the stairs.

Smiling, Carlota floated down the steps. "Is there some problem, Isabella?"

"This gentleman seems to think we might harbor some traitor to Mexico behind our doors."

"Really?" turning wide brown eyes on the commander, Carlota frowned. "There is only my husband, and he is dreadfully ill, unable even to get out of bed."

"Might I speak with him?"

"Certainly. But I must warn you of the possibility of measles. It is very contagious, isn't it?"

Duque froze, then stepped away. "Perhaps I will take

your word, Senora de Bastitas, that no one with ill will for Mexico is residing here . . . other than you, of course.''

"A wise decision, Colonel."

He turned for the door. "I will warn you to keep close to your home, ladies. The next twenty-four hours in San Antonio is likely to be costly in lives.''

Her throat tight with fear, Carlota asked, "What is your meaning?''

"Our troops are now numbering close to three thousand. I assure you, by evening of tomorrow the Alamo will have fallen.''

"And what of those who surrender?''

Deep laughter filled the room as Duque spun to face the women again. "Have you not seen the red flag on Fernando's tower? It is red. No mercy. The Texans have chosen to die, senoras. They will.''

# TWENTY-SIX

The sentry, a tall dark man in his early thirties, stared out over the Alamo wall and into the darkness. Camp fires which had dotted the terrain the nights before had been blackened. The air was oddly quiet. Only occasional whispers reached his ear, but they sounded ominously close.

Angelique shifted. Opening her eyes, she looked down at Tomas. He lay stretched beside her, his head resting on her lap. But he wasn't sleeping. He was looking at her and grinning.

"It is too cold to smile," she admonished while pretending to pout.

"Would you like to trade places? I assure you it is warm here and comfortable."

"Would your lap be so soft?"

"Perhaps not. But then I don't have on two petticoats and a skirt."

One light brown eyebrow lifted in question. "How do *you* know I have on two petticoats?"

"Don't ask."

She laughed. "Have you not rested at all?"

Tomas shook his head. "I've been watching you sleep. It is something I have wanted to do for a very long time."

"Is this confession time?"

"Yes." The smile faded from Angelique's face, but before she could look away he touched his fingers to her cheek. "I once thought there was nothing worth dying for. I was a fool."

"Please. Let us not speak of dying."

Pushing to one elbow, Tomas stared into her eyes. "Promise me one thing."

"Anything."

"When you return to Rancho de Bejar, speak to Alejandro and listen to what he has to say. If you do not, then all of this has been for nothing."

"How can you say that?"

"It is true. Who will remember us here? When we are dead and buried and the children of these men are grown with children of their own, who will recall that one hundred and eighty-some men were foolish enough to hope their deaths might mean something? But if you were to return to my brother, the two of you together will mean I accomplished a small victory for love."

Angelique sighed. "Tomas de Bastitas, you are an incurable romantic."

A smile breaking across his face, he shrugged. "I have my moments. Now promise me."

"I promise."

Sitting against the wall, Tomas pulled Angelique closer, then wrapped his arms about her shoulders. She was shivering. "Are you so cold, *querida?*"

"I'm not cold at all."

"Then you are frightened. Don't be. As long as I am living no harm will come to you. I promised my brother that I would do what I could to see you safely back to the ranch. I am not a man to go back on my word."

Angelique rested her head against Tomas's chest. The thought of her husband brought tears to her eyes. "I hope my death does not bring him so much grief as Pamela's. Did he love her very much, Tomas?"

"Perhaps at first."

"Why did she kill herself?"

He thought a moment. "He found her in bed with another man. She was in love with this man, and Alejandro
killed him. The child Pamela was carrying was not my
brother's, but her lover's. She saw no other way out."

"And he found her body?"

"Pamela bled to death in his arms."

Angelique closed her eyes. How little she actually knew
of her husband. And why, suddenly, did she feel the need
to know more? Alexander de Bastitas was behind her. She
might never see him again. But the ache to understand him,
yes, even to *forgive* him had grown each day since this
ordeal had begun.

Quiet, she listened to the constant rhythm of Tomas's
heart against her ear. He stroked her head. His lips brushed
her forehead and his breath disturbed the fine hair at her
temple. The arms about her offered a comforting warmth,
a shelter against the tide of fright that occasionally surged
and pulled at her defiance. How simple it would be to fall
trembling to this cold stone floor and weep like several of
the other women. Of course there would be an undaunted
soldier to offer understanding, but did she have the right
to ask it of them? They were battling their own hell.

Had she thought to doze? A sudden noise, a movement
caused her eyes to fly open and the breath to snag in her
throat. What was it? A cannon? A bugle blast?

*"Viva Santa Anna!"*

Surely it was thunder vibrating the very walls she and
Tomas huddled against!

"Colonel Travis! The Mexicans are coming! God help
us, here they come!"

Hands closed about Angelique's arms and gently pushed
her away. Taking her shawl, Tomas wrapped it about her
head so it draped down across her shoulders. "I've been
thinking," he stated calmly. "If you keep yourself covered
and speak only in Spanish, perhaps you will pass as Mexican. Tell them you were kidnapped by that lusty Bastitas
scoundrel and held here against your will."

She touched his face. "Don't go."

"And be called a coward again?" Tomas shook his head

and grinned. "This is one time my grandfather will eat his
words."

The Texas cannons boomed again and again. Men were
running, yelling. William Travis was calling, "*No rendirse,
muchachos!*" Don't surrender, boys!

Angelique covered her ears against the deafening noise.
Wave after wave of gunfire advanced until it all merged
into a continuous roll like unending thunder.

"I have to go now," Tomas said quietly. "Stay back
here and I promise you will be safe. I will be just outside
those doors, and as long as I am living, no Mexican will
enter."

They looked around as a tall, slender Negro stumbled
into the room. Tears rolled down his face as he rasped,
"They done killed him! They done shot Colonel Travis in
de head!" Joe, Travis's own slave, then turned and ran
into the darkness.

No sooner was he gone than Almeron Dickinson entered
the chapel. Searching frantically for his wife, who waited
in the sacristy, he called, "Great God, Sue, the Mexicans
are inside our walls!"

Tomas pulled away. "I will go now," he repeated.

"Wait!" Lifting her trembling hands, Angelique pulled
the silver necklace and cross from her throat. She pressed
it into his fingers. "To remember me by."

"A kiss for luck?"

She nodded.

Long, strong arms came around her, lifting her from the
floor. His head came down and her mouth opened under
his. Like a starving man Tomas feasted on the forbidden
pleasure denied him for so long, aching with the knowledge that he was holding his brother's wife, yet sorry he
would experience nothing more.

He sat her back, drank in the beauty of her upturned
face, then stepped away. "Goodbye, Angelique."

She reached for him, but he was gone.

Odd how she had come to recognize the sound of Tomas's gun. Sinking in the shadowed corner of the chapel,
Angelique listened to each blast of its barrel, counted the

seconds it took him to reload. But during those times she listened also to the escalating cries of pain, anger, and frustration, knowing the exact moment the Mexicans had scaled the mission walls.

It was easy to fantasize that Santa Anna would suddenly take pity on these unreluctant heroes and spare them. Perhaps Fannin would appear on the horizon and chase the Mexicans away. Of course there was her husband. He had saved her once before, had ridden into that Comanche camp and spirited her away without their even knowing.

So where was he now?

The walls shook, and for a moment it seemed the entire building would crumble around her. A child screamed. A baby cried. A woman's hysterical babbling added to the confusion of activity outside the door. Her ears straining for the sound of Tomas's gun, Angelique counted the seconds ... fifteen ... twenty ... thirty. *Dear God.* One minute, then two. Oh, Tomas, Tomas!

A figure stumbled through the door and toward the room where Susannah Dickinson was hiding. The boy tried to speak, but his jaws had been shattered by a bullet. Finding it impossible, he ran back out of the chapel.

Falling to her knees, Angelique begged forgiveness for her sins. If she could be granted one more moment to be spent with her mother, with Alejandro, she would be eternally grateful. She prayed for Tomas. She prayed for the child in her belly and she prayed for her friends who were dying at this very moment.

A man barreled in. A rifle clutched in his hands, he stared at the Mexican women huddled together against a far wall before swinging again toward the door. Suddenly the room was swarming with Santa Anna's men. Bayonets flashed gold in the harbor's torchlight, and as the hapless Texan swung his rifle above his head no fewer than five soldiers lunged and skewered him on their swords, then with seemingly great pleasure hoisted him in the air until his blood fell upon their shoulders like rain.

As several Mexicans stormed toward her, Angelique fell

back against the wall, gripping her shawl tightly about her head and shoulders.

"Who are you?" one of them demanded in English.

Recalling Tomas's words, she replied, *"No hablo inglés, senor."*

"What are you doing here?" he barked then in Spanish.

Angelique didn't have time to respond before the men turned to hurry out the door. She waited. Little by little the shooting dwindled, the screams diminished until only sporadic firing and an occasional moan infiltrated through her shock.

There was total quiet.

Closing her eyes, she waited.

"Is there a Mrs. Dickinson here?"

Angelique's head snapped up.

"Is Mrs. Dickinson here? Speak out! It is a matter of life and death!"

Susannah Dickinson appeared, her baby gripped in her arms. As the soldier ushered her from the building, several more entered and motioned for the remaining women and children to follow.

Dawn was breaking over the east horizon. As opposed to the afternoon before, when a northern had emptied freezing rain on the countryside, this day promised to be clear and warmer. It was an orange and yellow sky that greeted Angelique as she stepped from the church. She stared at it for a long moment, willing her eyes away from the carnage spread out before her.

It was difficult to breathe. Gunpowder burned her nostrils and lungs, and she coughed. Her foot slipped and as she looked to steady herself, she realized she was not standing in water, but blood. It was all around her. There was a groan, and as she watched, horrified, a Mexican lowered his gun to a man's temple and pulled the trigger. Everywhere the soldiers were rummaging through the bodies and thrusting their bayonets, making certain no survivors remained.

As if pulled by some source, Angelique slowly turned about. Tomas was there, next to the door. Though there was nothing left of his face, she recognized the pale blue shirt he had worn. Gripped in his hand was her necklace. Calmly she approached him, ignoring the barked orders for her to remain where she was.

Kneeling; "Tomas." She looked up as a large hand clamped upon her shoulder.

"Is this your husband?" the Mexican soldier demanded.

"No."

"Who is he to you?"

Her hand closed about Tomas's. Without thinking, she answered, "My brother."

"What are you doing?"

Her eyes dropped to the necklace in the dead man's fingers.

"Are you going to take it?"

She had thought to. "No." It had been her only gift to Tomas. She would not take it back.

He stepped closer and in a lower voice stated, "Then you must hide it in his clothes. There are those among us who would hang it about their own necks." He stepped back quickly and urged her, "Hurry."

His compassion stunned her. One of the very men who had slaughtered these fighters was offering her consideration. Angelique slipped the cross into Tomas's shirt—against his heart.

"Remember me," she said softly.

The Mexican's hand closed about her arm and helped her up. It was after she rejoined her group that the quiet was suddenly shattered by revelry. In unison the soldiers lifted their bloodied weapons in the air and chanted, *"Viva la republica! Viva Mexico! Viva Santa Anna!"*

He appeared through the gates. Riding a great black stallion, General Antonio Lopez de Santa Anna smiled and lifted his hand in a signal of greeting and victory. He wore a coat of indigo blue, his breast flashing with medals. His broad shoulders were enhanced with gold epaulets. He sat in a saddle stamped with gold, its horn in the shape of an eagle head, its stirrup guards of silver and gold.

Santa Anna reined his horse and waited patiently as his

men roared with approval. It continued. On and on the cheers rolled like waves and spread through the entire town of San Antonio, and out into the countryside. They were frenetic with conquest, and growing drunker with it by the moment. Men danced, caring little that they slipped and fell in their own comrades' blood.

In shock, Angelique gazed up at the Mexican leader, then down at the hundreds of bodies that lay butchered on the ground. Again her eyes were drawn to Tomas, saw what had replaced the handsome, smiling man who had kissed her only an hour before, and somewhere deep in her stomach the rage and pain exploded. It surged into her breast, into her throat, and throwing her head back she began screaming until she was emptied of all strength and could no longer stand.

No one heard. Her despair was lost against the backdrop of cheers. Falling to the ground she wept until her head pounded and her body burned. She thought for certain she would die from the pain, indeed prayed that she would. For what would happen to these few women now, some whose very husbands and sons had fallen in the massacre?

Gentle hands touched her shoulders. "Senora, you must come with me now. His Excellency has requested that you ladies be taken to his quarters. Come along. There is nothing to fear."

Angelique struggled to her feet and joined the other weeping women as they were forced to step across bodies while they made their way through the Alamo gates, over the footbridge, and into town. She was well-acquainted with Santa Anna's headquarters—the Ramon Musquiz house, the very house she had been on her way to visit when this nightmare began.

Ushered into a back room, the women waited for hours, though shortly after their arrival Susannah Dickinson was removed and shown to more comfortable quarters. They were offered food and drink. Tea was poured from sterling silver pots into fine china cups, which had traveled with Santa Anna all the way from his home in Mexico. Angelique refused it, and when the servant offered the steaming drink a second time, she spat into the cup. He said nothing but returned the china to the cart and left the room.

Without speaking among themselves, the women waited. Gregorio Esparza's wife continued weeping quietly as her four children clung to her muddied skirts. They had all watched as their father was brutally murdered. Petra Gonzales stared unseeing out the window. Trinidad Saucedo left her chair numerous times and stood by the door, listening.

After a long while of eavesdropping, her eyes grew large and she spun to face the others. "His Excellency has returned," Trinidad whispered. Her face paled as she listened to the distant voices. "Santa Anna has ordered the bodies of the rebels to be burned!"

A final insult . . . the men would not be granted a Christian burial.

She continued to listen. "He is speaking with Susannah. He—he is asking to keep her baby. He wishes to take the child back to Mexico with him!"

Senora Esparza gasped and cuddled her children closer, fearing at any moment the man would come to take her children as well.

Again Trinidad pressed her ear to the door. It seemed the rumors she had often heard of Santa Anna's sentimentality for children could no longer be discredited. She waited, then added, "He promises to raise the child in splendor. She will want for nothing."

Angelique jumped to her feet. "The man is a monster. Surely she will not allow it!"

Trinidad stepped back from the door. "She has refused him."

A key scraped in the lock. Suddenly Ramon Musquiz was standing before them. "His Excellency will see you ladies now. Follow me." They did as they were told and followed *el jefe politico* into the adjoining room. An Angelique stepped by him, he stopped her. His face a mask of surprise he whispered urgently, "Senora, what in all that is holy are you doing here? Surely Alejandro was not—"

"Tomas."

He sucked in his breath. "Tomas! Isabella will be grief-stricken."

Angelique's voice cracked from emotion. "We are *all* grief-stricken, Senor Musquiz."

Santa Anna entered the room. Behind him came servants bearing tables laden with silver and heaped with food. He took a chair behind a desk and waited as a platter of beef, a loaf of steaming bread, and hot coffee were placed before him. Motioning toward the buffet, he offered, "Please help yourselves to the food. If there is anything—"

"You killed my papa!" cried out Enrique Esparza. His mother gasped. Reacting, Angelique grabbed the boy and buried his face in her own skirts.

Musquiz quickly stepped in. "Your excellency, forgive the child. He witnessed his father's death inside the Alamo."

Santa Anna dabbed at his mouth with a linen napkin. "His father was a rebel sympathizer?"

"I could not guarantee it. But I do know Gregorio Esparza's brother fought valiantly on Your Excellency's behalf."

"Is this true?" he asked Esparza's widow. When she nodded, he directed, "Bring me this woman's brother-in-law, then locate her husband's body. It will not be burned with the others and you are free to offer him a Christian burial."

He continued eating. One by one he studied the women, pausing only once to request more coffee. He did not speak again until he had finished his food, and when he stood and stepped around the table they moved away, as if his nearness was somehow threatening in itself.

"I ask myself," he began. "What do I do with you? I have no need for more servants. My men have all the *soldaderas* they desire. Therefore, what fate is left for you?" Crossing his arms over his medallioned chest, Santa Anna smiled. "You must be the bearer of my word. Go and tell these belligerents exactly what you saw. Tell them there is no way I can be defeated, and that to attempt such a defeat will surely mean an end to them as it did to those in the Alamo.''

He motioned toward a young officer who stood at attention just inside the door. "Supply each of these women with two dollars and a blanket, then set them free."

Freedom? What trick was this? Hesitantly Angelique and the others filed out the door. Inside the foyer they waited, closing their hands as the money spilled into their palms. Blankets were thrust into their arms, then the door was opened.

Angelique was the last woman out. As she paused to look up into the officer's face, he smiled and dipped his head. She turned her back. He slammed the door behind her.

No one noticed the solitary figure who ambled through the busy streets. Church bells pealed the conquest, ringing and ringing until Angelique thought for certain her head would burst. Ahead were the battle-worn and weary walls of the old mission. It was a haunting sight. Where once the proud flag of the New Orleans Greys snapped, now fluttered the red, white, and green banner boasting Mexico's fierce eagle.

It was not the sight of the flag, however, that caused her to pause. In stunned disbelief, she watched as men poured oil over the stacks of bodies, then stepped back as others ran forward and threw lit torches to the tinder. There was a gasp from the onlookers, then a roar of approval as the flames surged heavenward.

Angelique covered her face and, not bothering to hide, bent over and vomited on the ground. She began running then, running from the city, the mission, the ghost of the man she knew would frequent her dreams for the rest of her life. Tomas had been her strength these many weeks. She had faced each lonely day, bereft over her mother or her husband's anger, knowing Tomas would be there for her.

Now he was gone.

She ran until she could run no more. The blanket clutched against her breast, she stopped and rested on a stump beside the road. For the first time since Tomas had placed the shawl about her head, she removed it and flung it to the ground. It was warmer now. Much warmer. And as she stared at her feet she noticed sprigs of new growth breaking the earth.

"Senora, may I offer you a ride?"

Not having heard the rattle of the wagon, Angelique looked up in surprise. "What?"

"There is plenty of room in the back of my wagon if you would like to ride."

"Where are you going?" she asked him.

Their faces grim, the old Mexican and his wife answered. "Away from here. In case you are unaware, San Antonio has fallen again to Mexico. The Alamo was defeated."

*Yes, I know. Dear God, I know.* "Are you followers of Santa Anna?"

"No. That's why we must leave. We must warn everyone that the eagle shows no mercy." He smiled. "Where are you headed?"

"The Bastitas ranch. Rancho de Bejar."

"Ah! Then come aboard. My journey carries me right by there."

Gratefully, Angelique threw her blanket into the wagon. Climbing in herself, she lifted her eyes to the sky above San Antonio.

The smoke was black, and lifted by a breeze . . . stretched into eternity.

# TWENTY-SEVEN

Alejandro took his place before the window, as he did every day, from morning to well after dusk. Dawn had promised a clear day; noon had assured it. A crisp breeze fluttered the curtains. A mockingbird trilled in the far pecan tree. He smelled bread baking in the ovens, listened to the distant clucking of a hen over her eggs.

Life at Rancho de Bejar seemed peaceful. The household, however, had been awakened before dawn by the muffled boom of cannon fire. On and on it had continued, and as all looked out at the horizon toward San Antonio the dark sky had flashed occasionally with orange light. Daybreak had come and gone with no report from Travis's twelve-pounder, as he had promised. Which could mean only one thing.

The Alamo had fallen.

Now what? Isabella had waited until noon, then sent Pablo into the city for word on the mission's status. Perhaps His Excellency could be convinced to show leniency toward the survivors. Carlos had quietly mentioned he would have a word with Santa Anna on Tomas's and Angelique's behalf. Perhaps a reward might be offered.

Money. Land. Anything it took to see them safely home and out of prison.

Alex was tired of waiting. Pablo had been gone for hours and might never return. Possibly he had joined the other men, women, and children who had begun leaving their homes to flee Mexico's far-reaching hand. A continuous line of wagons had passed the ranch over the last several days; entire families were transporting their meager belongings to safer grounds. Several of the peons who worked for Carlos had disappeared during the night, not trusting their fate to a dictator who had pillaged churches for money on his way to San Antonio.

He turned his mescal bottle up and drank deeply. The liquor burned his throat, his chest, then his stomach. But it felt good compared to the fire in his legs. The wounds were healing nicely, thanks to Bernice's and Teresa's care, but their scars, both emotional and physical, would forever be with him. He hated Carlos de Bastitas to his very core for not killing him outright. How would he ever live with himself should his wife and brother be murdered?

"You gonna share some of that?" came Noble McGuire's soft query. He then lifted the mostly empty bottle from Alex's lap. Staring down on his friend, the Kentuckian shook his head. "I reckon it's the waitin' that's hardest to stomach."

"The not knowing."

"Yep, I suppose that too." He sighed. "I'd give my last peso to know just where the hell Houston and Fannin are." Shrugging off the thought, McGuire finished, "Everybody's waitin' downstairs. Figured it'd be easier on you if you'd join us."

Alex hadn't faced his grandfather since that moment thirteen days ago. "Is Carlos there?" he asked in a flat voice.

"Yep. Isabella's tried to get him out of the house, but there's no budgin' him. He just sits in that one room starin' out the window."

"I think I might kill him."

"Well, you're gonna have to stand in line to do it, *amigo*."

Alex grimaced as Noble helped him from the chair. Though he had attempted to walk alone several times, the pain in his legs had forbidden him from doing so.

McGuire wrapped his friend's arm around the back of his shoulders, then planted one of his around Alex's waist. It was a slow, painful journey down the long corridor. Step by step they descended the stairs, both cursing and sweating, stumbling slightly as they neared the bottom.

They had just reached the foyer when the front door burst open and Pablo rushed into the house. The young man's face was pale. His eyes were wide and he was crumpling his straw hat in his fingers. At the sound of his frantic babbling the door of the salon flew open and Isabella joined them. Carlota and Bernice were close on her heels.

Angelique's mother rushed by *la patrona* and grabbed the frantic boy by the shoulders. "What has taken you, Pablo? We sent you from here hours ago!"

"I am truly sorry, senora, but San Antonio is in upheaval."

Isabella stepped forward. "We must all remain calm. Let us return to the room and hear what Pablo has to tell us." She then moved to help a weak McGuire usher her grandson into the study.

Alex's eyes fixed on his grandfather the moment he entered the room. What he saw stunned him. Carlos de Bastitas had aged dramatically. A silver shadow covered his face; he hadn't shaved in days. Crepelike flesh sagged from his cheeks and neck, and his clothes drooped over the skeletal frame of his wasted body.

Red-rimmed blue eyes turned up to his, and the anger Alex had felt toward Carlos evaporated, replaced by pity. Carlos was a defeated wretch whose own guilt was gnawing away at his guts. It was killing him slowly but surely, and Alejandro didn't give one little damn. He would be saved the effort of doing it himself.

Dropping into a chair, Alex pushed Isabella and Noble

aside. "What is happening in San Antonio?" he asked Pablo.

"I know little, senor. Only that the Alamo has fallen. I could get no closer than the outskirts of the city, as the soldiers are capturing and holding any outsiders they find. There is great revelry. The bells of San Fernando Church are ringing and the cry of *'Viva Santa Anna'* is filling the air." The boy shuddered. "I saw him."

"Who?" Isabella asked quietly.

"His Excellency. He was smiling, and as he stood upon a platform he stretched a flag over his head. It said 'God and Liberty; Texan Volunteers.' "

Alex met Noble's intense gaze. "The New Orleans Greys."

McGuire nodded.

"What of survivors?" Carlota beseeched Pablo. "What have they done with those men and women they captured?"

Sadly, he shook his head. "I do not know. I could ask no one, and all I heard was men boasting from a distance. There was talk of few survivors. I am sorry."

Bernice could stand it no longer. Bursting into tears, she covered her face with her hands and choked, "Lawd, my precious baby. She is gone. Gone!"

Carlota turned on the sobbing woman. "Hush that talk, Bernice! I will not believe my Angelique is dead. I would know it; I would feel it here!" She pounded her breast. Turning to Alex, Carlota flew across the room and grasped his hands. "She is your wife! Will you do nothing to help her? Will you sit here while those animals are doing God knows what to her?"

Noble closed his hands onto his wife's shoulders and turned her against his chest. "Darlin', you know if Alex could do anything he would. We all would. All we can do now is wait till all the commotion dies then approach Santa Anna himself."

Bernice *humphed* and shook her head. "All's we been doin' is waitin'." Stopping before the window, she watched another family of Mexicans creep up the road, their wagon bouncing and harnesses creaking from the strain of pulling their overloaded burden. It stopped. Blowing her nose, Bernice watched the old man leave his seat, walk to the rear of the wagon, and help a small figure to the ground. Then that figure turned toward the house, and the shawl fell from her head.

Her dark skin suddenly gray, Bernice gasped and, twirling to face the startled onlookers, shrieked, "Lawd, Missus Carlota, that be Angelique!"

Angelique was through the gates by the time the front door of the hacienda was thrown open. Carlota was suddenly flying down the path. Her arms open, she was weeping, "Angelique! *Madre de Dios*, you are alive, alive!"

"Mama!" Dropping her blanket, Angelique met Carlota with an equal embrace.

They rocked and wept, neither attempting to disguise her relief. Carlota cupped her daughter's face in her hands. "Where is Tomas?"

Closing her eyes and forcing her voice steady, Angelique quietly responded, "Dead."

"Dear God."

"They all are. Every man there was murdered, Mama." She turned and met Bernice.

The huge woman cuddled Angelique close to her bosom and crooned, "Everything gonna be just fine now, honey. Bernice gonna see to her baby proper."

Isabella stood in the door. How frail she seemed to Angelique. Her brown eyes, though hopeful, were resigned. Since Santa Anna had released her, Angelique had dreaded this moment. How was she to tell one of the dearest women she had ever known that her grandson was dead?

Her heart breaking, the matriarch lifted her chin as the girl approached. Acknowledging the trembling lower lip and the large green eyes that were swimming with tears, Isabella stated, "My Tomas is dead."

"Yes."

A flicker of panic caused the woman's stoic features to crack. But only for an instant. "Were you with him at all?"

"Until the end."

"Did he suffer?"

Angelique shook her head. "I think not."

"Good. It would grieve me to think . . ." Isabella turned away, her thoughts and words wandering as she struggled to sustain her resolve. She had prayed endlessly these last days, prayed Tomas and Angelique would return home unharmed, though she had known in her heart she would never see her precious grandson again. Tomas had bravely sacrificed his life. She must accept his decision with as much courage.

To Alejandro de Bastitas it seemed an eternity before his wife stepped into the room. He grabbed her arm, and she spun to face him. "Angel," came his hoarse whisper.

Twisting from his grip, Angelique stepped away. "Senor."

"Angelique, I have been out of mind with—"

"Have you?" she interrupted coldly. Dropping her eyes over her husband's frame, Angelique commented dryly, "So worried you chose your own brother to come in your stead to save me. How very commendable."

Stung by her words, Alex sat back in his chair. "I don't know what the hell you are saying. Angel, I didn't—"

"He is dead."

"What?"

"Tomas is dead." Disbelief flooded his face, and unable to bear his pain, she spun toward the old man behind the far desk. Never had she vented such anger, but Angelique was lashing out in any manner that might help her deal with the brutality she had witnessed.

Approaching Carlos slowly, she did not speak until she stood beside him. Gripping his arm in her shaking hands, she pulled him from his chair and directed him to the window. "He is dead," she repeated quietly. "Tomas is dead, and you helped kill him. You are as guilty as that monster you call your friend."

Bastitas shook his feeble head.

"Yes!" Angelique argued. "Coward, you called him. Time and again you reminded him that he was unworthy of the great Bastitas name." Lowering her voice, she hissed into his ear, "He faced his enemy, senor. How do I know this? The bullet was between his eyes and not in his back, as *you* might have suspected. Be assured there were no cowards in the Alamo, Bastitas. They each met their deaths with dignity, something which you know nothing about."

Bernice's hands closed about Angelique's shoulders. She didn't notice. Tears streaming from her eyes and down her cheeks, the girl gently shoved Carlos closer to the window. "See the smoke against the sky. There burns your grandson's body. They placed him among rubble, doused him in oil, and set him afire!"

Falling to his knees, Carlos de Bastitas covered his face with gnarled fingers and wept.

Angelique blinked hard as she watched the old man's thin shoulders shake with grief. Regretting her cruelty, she then looked about the room. Isabella's face was white. And Alex . . .

Alex stared at his grandfather's back before turning to Noble. "Get me out of here," he grated. The knot in his gut was creeping up his chest, into his throat.

McGuire jumped to attend his friend, helping him from the room the same way they had entered it. Confused, Angelique watched them go. Was Alex injured? She turned questioning eyes on her mother.

Carlota was the last person on earth to defend Alejandro de Bastitas, but it was hard to ignore the pain he was feeling at that moment. Facing her distraught daughter, she asked, "Did Tomas not tell you?"

Angelique searched her mind, recalling that the few times Tomas had brought up the subject of her husband, she had refused to listen. She shook her head.

"When he returned from Gonzales and learned of your predicament, Alejandro tried to take one of his grandfather's guns. Carlos shot him in one leg, but when it appeared your husband would not let that stop him, Bastitas shot him in the other."

"Then Alexander *would* have come."

"Yes."

Isabella quietly stepped up behind them. "Perhaps, my dear, we should thank Carlos after all. Had he not reacted in his foolishly spiteful way, *both* of my grandsons would be dead at this moment."

The two men were halfway up the stairs when Alex suddenly shoved Noble away. "Leave me the hell alone," he snapped. "I can walk on my own two goddamn legs."

Noble recognized Alex's pain. He had seen it once before.

Alex tottered in place, then fell against the banister. The pain was crucifying, but he didn't care. He deserved it. How inconsequential his discomfort must be compared to that which Tomas had experienced. Step by step he labored up the mountain, his legs wobbling and his entire body sweating profusely. Only when he had reached the top did he allow Noble to help him again.

"To Tomas's room," Alex directed in a thick voice.

Noble did as he was told, though he didn't like it.

"Put the chair there." Alex pointed toward the window. When it was done, he dropped into it. "Bring me my bottle." Alex waited. In moments a new bottle of mescal was wedged into his clenched fingers. "Now get the hell out."

It was a plea, a husky, urgent cry for understanding.

Noble "Kaintock" McGuire backed away, but not before throwing one last glance out the window. He understood now. Alex's bedroom had not offered this view. From here the dark smudge upon the sapphire sky could have been a hint of an approaching storm, or the smoke of a distant grass fire.

It wasn't. It was Tomas de Bastitas's funeral pyre.

Angelique waited as Bernice hefted the last pail of hot water into the tub. Then accepting her hand, she stepped into the soothing comfort and sank nearly to her shoulders. "It's wonderful," she sighed. "I thought I would never bathe again."

Bernice lifted Angelique's arm and began soaping it with a cloth. "It's a shame," came her deep voice. "Don't no man deserve to die like that. Tomas was a good boy. Good and sweet.''

Resting her head back against the brass rim, Angelique stared at the ceiling. ''He was my friend, Bernice. How will I live without him?''

Dark eyes rested on Angie's face. ''Just remember him as he was before.'' Clearing her throat, she added, ''Yore husband been awful worried 'bout you. He 'bout drunk himself to death ever' night once he got over his hurtin' so bad. For a while we all thought he might jest bleed himself to death.''

A tear ran down her cheek as Angelique turned to look in Bernice's face. ''I'm certain my mother did not share in your concern.''

Bernice rinsed her arm before starting on an extended leg. ''Your mama's done a lot of changin' since that man come into her life. Mr. McGuire don't stand for her bad-mouthin' Alex.''

Her head came up as Angelique frowned. ''Has she forgiven Alexander?''

''Ain't much forgivin' to it. More like understandin' now.''

Auburn curls spilled down her neck as Angelique shook her head. ''I can hardly believe she would accept Alexander's reasons for killing my father.''

''I suppose that would depend on the reasons he done it for.''

Angelique could hardly believe her ears. Snatching the cloth from Bernice's hand, she began scrubbing her own leg. ''Civilized men don't kill over a card game. Murder is left up to monsters like Santa Anna!''

''A card game?'' Huffing, Bernice pushed to her feet.

''Yes. You knew my father. You know he would never have accused a man of cheating unless he was absolutely certain of it.''

''I knew yore father, all right. So did everybody else in New Orleans, Louisiana.'' Picking up a pail of clear water, she began pouring it over Angelique's head. ''Seems to me you and yore mama got to come to some sort of understandin' 'bout that Alexander. He be the father of that baby yore carryin', and whether you like it or not he gonna be around for a while. Won't be no more talk of annulment or divorce. He is here and here for good.''

Wincing as Bernice began lathering her head, Angelique closed her eyes and wearily stated, ''I want to go home. Since our arrival here there has been nothing but death and destruction.''

''Weren't no different back home. If men wasn't duelin' each other over honor then the city was bein' evacuated 'cause of the fever. My own mammy, God rest her soul, died of the yellow fever not long back. The Lawd is gonna get you if He want you no matter where you run.''

Turning her face up, Angelique asked in a quivering voice, ''Why have I been spared? When everyone around me has died, why have I been left to bear the burden of memory?''

Bernice's great, slippery hands cradled her cheeks. ''There always got to be someone left, hon, to carry on that memory. Nobody ever allowed to die and be completely forgotten. You gonna carry the memory of them men in yore heart for always. You gonna tell yore children, and yore children's children 'bout heroes and courage, and when someone asks how you know, yore gonna tell 'em it's 'cause you seen it happen.''

''But it hurts. Will it ever stop hurting?''

''No.''

Sniffling, she scolded, ''How very comforting you are, Bernice.''

''Once you stop hurtin', darlin', you stop bein' human.''

Her hair clean and shining once again, Angelique relaxed against the tub. ''What makes you so wise?'' she asked her friend.

''I'm old. All old people is supposed to be wise.''

''Can you never be young and wise?''

Bernice turned and gathered the heap of dirty clothes from the floor. ''Depends on how much livin' you do early on, I suppose.''

''Then I should be wise beyond my years.''

"Um hm. You done and seen a lot, but what have you learned from it all?"

"That evil can conquer good. That there are no knights in white armor and no one lives happily ever after."

The woman stopped. Peering over her shoulder, she said, "You ain't lived near long enough to come to those conclusions."

"Am I wrong?"

"You tell me."

Angelique thought a moment. "The men in the Alamo wore no armor."

"But they was heroes."

She agreed. "But Santa Anna must be conquered."

"He will be. By a different set of heroes. And as for livin' happily ever after . . . you got to fill yore heart with love to accomplish that. You got love enough in yore heart for understandin'?"

"I-I don't know."

"You'll know it when you do." Bernice swayed toward the door. "I'm gonna bring you some tea and biscuits."

Her eyes lit up. "Biscuits?"

"Um hm. I got fed up with them tortillas. Done fixed pancakes last mornin' and biscuits this. We got fried bacon and sliced ham."

"Bernice! Are you attempting to civilize these people?"

"No, ma'am. I just refused to starve to death."

"Bernice?"

The woman paused at the door and looked back.

Angelique smiled. "Thank you."

# TWENTY-EIGHT

The hacienda rang with silence. Mirrors and doors throughout the house had been covered with black veils. All mourned the death of Tomas de Bastitas, but the loss went much deeper than that. Many men had died at the Alamo, and though the heroes were strangers to most of the residents of this city, everyone recognized their sacrifice.

It had been three days since Angelique returned to Rancho de Bejar. She had not seen Isabella, Carlos, or her husband since her arrival. They had remained in their quarters, except for Alejandro. He was still in Tomas's room; he refused to leave. He had not eaten; he slept only in the chair so his first and last sight was of the city in the distance, and he refused to speak to anyone but Noble McGuire.

Angelique rolled out of bed, slipped the robe on over her nightgown, then reached for the candle she kept lit on her nightstand. The hallways were dim and quiet. All doors were closed.

She knocked on the door of Tomas's room. Nothing. The door gave with little effort and she closed it behind her. Alejandro was in his chair. His back to her, he appeared to be sleeping.

"Alexander?"

His head turned slightly, but he didn't respond.

"Am I disturbing you?"

"No."

"I couldn't sleep." Angelique quietly approached her husband. Placing the candle on the table, she turned to face him.

The glow cast his face in gold and accentuated the hollows of his cheeks. Alejandro pulled blue eyes from the black window and looked up at his wife. She was stunning. He had almost forgotten how her wavy hair fell around her shoulders. It was like bronze silk in the candlelight and beckoned to be touched.

Catching one long tendril between his fingers, he asked, "Why were you there?"

"In the mission?"

He shook his head. Thick, sable hair fell into his eyes. "In San Antonio."

"Didn't Isabella tell you?"

Alejandro turned back toward the window. "I know what she *told* me. I want the truth."

His voice was tight, the question strained. It was difficult to judge his mood. There was no drunkenness in his tone, but a weariness in its cadence. Angelique stepped away. "If I bring you some coffee—"

Closing his hand about her wrist, Alex jerked Angelique against the chair, practically into his lap, and snarled softly, "Forget the goddamn coffee. I want to know what the hell you were doing in San Antonio that morning."

The pressure upon her arm was intensifying, and Angelique gritted her teeth. Alejandro had obviously lost none of his ability to hurt her. With one slice of that lashing tongue or spark from those molten blue eyes he would wield as deadly a blow as the one that had cut down his brother.

Unable to break his grip, she snapped, "Perhaps you should tell me since you obviously do not believe Isabella."

He flung her away. "You were on your way to speak with Father de la Garza."

She rubbed her arm. "Indeed?"

"You told me yourself you were going to speak with him about an annulment."

"I see." Narrowing her green eyes, Angelique replied. "Considering I am due a child in September I can hardly believe the good padre would grant us such consideration."

"Then it was to see a lawyer for a divorce."

"Your words, not mine."

Alex looked at her again. "Do you deny it?" He waited and when she refused to respond he barked an obscenity to the ceiling that set her back on her heels. Thrusting one long straight finger in her face, he finished, "Forget it. Any chance you had of being rid of me for good was destroyed the instant you informed this family of that baby." Laughing sharply, Alex lifted a bottle of whiskey from the floor and filled his cup. "Little fool. You should have kept your mouth closed. I would have granted you a divorce. I have no desire to spend the rest of my life with a woman who cannot stand my touch."

"A divorce."

He swiveled the glass before turning it up to his mouth. "A divorce. I had made the decision while in Gonzales."

Her heart turned over. "You—you don't want me any longer?"

"Ah, *querida*, an absurd question, I assure you."

That was no answer. Angelique stared at the top of Alex's dark head before demanding, "What do you intend to do with us now?"

"Us?"

"What of the child?"

Eyes black with emotion lifted to Angelique's face. "You will both be provided for. I will ask, however, that you remain in Texas so that I might see the child on a regular basis."

She was dumbfounded. How easily he spoke of turning her out. Spinning, Angelique moved across the room. She didn't like the feelings flip-flopping in her stomach. After all, she should be thankful to be rid of him. He was a cheat, a liar, and the murderer of her father. Her mother despised him.

Her *mother* despised him!

"I feel we should discuss the matter," Angelique blurted. Good Lord, what was she saying?

Alex released a long breath. "What is there to discuss?"

"I-I promised Tomas that I would listen to whatever you had to say concerning your murder of my father."

He looked back across his shoulder. "Is that why you came here?"

"Yes," she lied.

"Then go to bed, Angel. I will not hold you to a promise made to a dead man."

Moving to his side, Angelique spread her hands. "But I am willing to listen!"

"And I am *unwilling* to discuss it. You wouldn't believe me anyway."

"Are you so certain?"

"I am."

Finished. It was that simple. Angelique stared down at her husband. What had happened? Once he had banged on her door *pleading* for understanding. Now he was casually admitting defeat, throwing their marriage to the wind with a shrug of his shoulder.

Until that moment she had not noticed the coldness of the quarters. But suddenly she was shivering and, pulling her robe tighter about her, she looked toward the empty hearth. Needing to bridge the widening distance Alexander was placing between them, she offered in a kinder voice, "You must be cold. May I light you a fire?"

"No."

Ignoring him, Angelique began stacking the wood just so onto the iron grate.

It wasn't long before the kindled flames reached to subdue the chill. The room brightened. Objects became distinct and shadows danced. She had never entered Tomas's quarters. Blue and red rugs were spread about the hard-

wood floor. A huge tester bed was balanced by heavy rose-
wood end tables. The chair her husband sat in was leather,
and here and there were stacks of books: poetry, fiction, a
Bible. Sadly, she recognized the room lacked any trace of
the man Tomas truly was.

Then she lifted her eyes to the distant shadowed corner.
What she saw there made her smile.

Alejandro was attempting to shift in his chair when the
sound of tinkling caused him to pause. He looked around
with a curiously lifted brow as Angelique stepped up beside him. From her fingers dangled a rope of large brass
bells.

Red lips parted as she smiled, "Are these the bells you
tied to the tails of your grandfather's bulls?"

He took them from her. "He told you?"

Her heart acknowledging Alex's flicker of a smile, Angelique settled on the floor beside his chair. "He told me
you tied them on the bull just before a corrida. Your grandfather must have been furious."

Alex fingered the ornate toys. "Tomas would always
laugh."

"He told me how you stoked Carlos's fiesta fires with
cow dung. He was quite proud of you for that."

Laughter was a relief to the nagging ache inside his
chest. "Tomas bet me I wouldn't do it."

"Did your father punish you?"

"No. But I was never allowed to attend a party again
without benefit of a chaperon."

"Did Tomas really hide a spider in Carlos's chamberpot?"

Alex burst out laughing, filling the room with its warm,
rich thunder. "Not just *any* spider," he pointed out. "A
tarantula. They are as big as saucers and have black bristles
all over their bodies. When Carlos removed the lid it
jumped right in his face."

They both laughed until the relief became almost painful. Then Alex dropped the bells into his lap and looked
away. "Ah, damn," he whispered in a shaky voice.

"Would you like to be alone?" Angelique reached to touch his arm, but didn't.

"Yes."

Standing, she said, "You cannot stay in here forever, Alexander. Will you come out tomorrow?"

He nodded.

Picking up her candle, Angelique watched as Alex reached for his bottle, but shoved it away. She moved soundlessly across the floor and, closing the door, returned to her room.

Carlota stared at the window. "I do not like it. Who are those men and what do they want from our husbands?"

Isabella looked up from her sewing. "They are bringing word from Sam Houston."

"Why do they bring word here?"

Placing her needlepoint to one side, *la patrona* smiled and nodded as Angelique offered her chocolate. "I suspect they are looking for volunteers."

Angelique hesitated. The china clattered as she raised it to Isabella's waiting hands. "They cannot possibly think Alejandro can help them. He can hardly walk." She then joined her mother at the window.

Within the shadow of the great pecan tree, four men sat talking. Alex was among them. There was a watchfulness in his eyes, an intenseness placed there by determination. Alejandro de Bastitas was a man driven by a need.

That need was revenge.

Angelique closed her eyes. She knew what was happening, had realized it the moment she awoke to find her husband and Noble pacing laboriously up and down the hacienda's long hallways. Back and forth they walked until Alexander's legs had given out on him completely. But little by little they were growing stronger. They supported him now, though he still relied on one of Carlos's canes when he grew weary.

He was going to leave her. Angelique was certain of that.

Alex tried to listen to the men's detailed description of

Sam Houston's current attempts to outdistance Santa Anna. He couldn't. His eyes were continually drawn to his wife. Morning sun was spilling through the trees, into the window, and there stood Angelique, looking as fresh as spring and twice as beautiful.

"I'm sayin' Gonzales and San Felipe have been burned to the ground," Jeb Taylor reiterated. Satisfied he again had Bastitas's attention, he sat back in his chair. "By the time Santa Anna reached Gonzales Sam Houston had burned ever' house, business, and bridge he could get his hands on. Damn Mexican couldn't find a round of cheese to fill his belly."

McGuire shook his head. "Don't like the sounds of Houston's retreat. I'm sure it's givin' them Mexes plenty to crow about."

"They've had little choice," the man argued. "Once word reached them that Santa Anna's General Urrea had captured Fannin's forces outside Goliad, then slaughtered 'em all one week later, men was runnin' like hell. No sooner had a thousand volunteers from the United States arrived than five hundred others left."

The urge to look back toward the house was too strong. As Alejandro lifted his eyes to Angelique's, he gritted his teeth and twisted in his chair, offering Angelique his back. "Where is Houston now?"

"They've camped on a plantation just beyond Mill Creek and on the Brazos."

"Will he continue to retreat?"

"Until he feels his men are strong enough to wager an attack or meet one."

Angelique frowned as Alexander threw a last scathing look toward her and turned his back. The brief closeness they had shared that lonely, sleepless night might never have taken place.

She turned as Isabella requested, "Please come and sit beside me."

Angelique waited until her mother left the room, then joined her friend on the settee. Black crepe hugged the woman from her neck to her ankles. A black mantilla of

Spanish lace was secured to her head by a comb of polished onyx, a drastic contrast to the white of Isabella's hair.

As always, Isabella's gaze was unwavering as she faced her grandson's wife. "Alejandro tells me you are planning to divorce."

"Did he?"

Nodding, she sat back against the damask-covered cushion. "This morning at breakfast. He was quite matter-of-fact about it, but I sensed he was distressed."

"Am I expected to simply accept what he has done? My father was very dear to me, and my mother worshipped him."

"Do you love Alejandro?"

Angelique looked away. "That is an absurd question."

"Do you love him?" Lifting one trembling hand, Isabella caught Angelique's chin in her fingers.

Their eyes met. "I-I cannot love him. To do so would be wrong."

A flash of anger caused the woman's cheeks to flush. "You promised to love him, to cherish him for better or worse."

"But that was before—"

"Bah!" Isabella stood and, pacing to the window, stared out into the garden. "There is something about this I do not trust. It is not like my grandson to obediently roll over and play dead . . . unless he is protecting a loved one. He was continually tight-lipped when it came to Tomas's childhood pranks, preferring to spare his brother the pain of Carlos's punishment. And if Alejandro believed for one moment he was causing me grief, he would do whatever was humanly possible to end it, even if it meant going against his own principles."

She spun to face Angelique. "He is protecting you."

Angelique could hardly believe her ears. "Protecting me? Whatever from?"

"I don't know. But I see it in his eyes, the way he looks at you, the times he opens his mouth to speak, but refuses."

With a spark of her old defiance, Angelique lifted her

chin. "It is guilt you see, senora. Nothing more."

"Guilt has nothing to do with it." Isabella faced the window again. The strangers were gone, as was Noble McGuire. Only Alejandro de Bastitas sat beneath the shifting limbs of the tree. His eyes were staring down the road toward San Antonio.

Clasping her hands, she prayed, "Relieve him of guilt. Keep him from harm. Spare him . . . spare him."

It was midnight, and, slipping into the chair, Alejandro de Bastitas gazed lovingly at his sleeping wife. She looked like an angel, swathed in white cotton and resting on plump white-cased pillows with sheets to match. Her hair spilled across the bed like a fiery shadow, reflecting the red and orange glow of the candle flame.

He came here every night. For hours he would watch her face as she dreamed. Occasionally the corners of her soft mouth would curl up in that minxlike way she had. Other times her chin would quiver, her lips would part. Sitting on the edge of his chair he would wait for a whisper, a word, wanting some sign that his secret tryst had been discovered.

She had never awakened.

He would be leaving at dawn. He would ride to the Brazos River, join Sam Houston's army, and there meet his fate. If his fate was death, then so be it. But he vowed he would not go down until his brother's death was avenged in some small way. He hated leaving Angelique, and there was his grandmother to deal with. Isabella would be frantic. She had little now. A lifetime of nurturing her grandchildren had benefited her with little more than grief. But there was that bright promise of a great-grandchild; a new beginning for the dwindling Bastitas lineage.

Rising, he moved easily to the bed and there stood above the tiny woman who had so adeptly stolen his heart. The ache to hold her, touch her, kiss her was like a ragged blade in his breast. But he wouldn't. Preferring not to witness the condemnation in those outrageously beautiful eyes, he chose to end it this way. The vows he made to himself had not been shallow. He would not seek her forgiveness or understanding under any circumstances. Should she choose to forgive him, should she choose to listen to reason, Angelique must come to him. Only in that way could he allow himself to believe that the dead had been buried forever.

Angelique stirred. The quiet about her ear had been disturbed by a gentle sound. A word? A breath? Struggling, she opened her eyes.

The room was empty.

Directing her sleepy gaze toward the window, she reasoned a noise outside the room had disturbed her. Possibly the breeze flirting with the curtains had brushed her cheek. Sighing, she snuggled into her covers and slept again.

The library was quiet. Alex hesitated before opening the door, but his task could no longer be delayed. Carlos looked up. Their eyes, so much alike, met for the first time in many weeks.

"You are leaving?" the old man asked.

"Yes."

Carlos pulled himself upright in his chair. His thoughts appeared to waver as he stared toward the candle on the edge of his desk. "I am a foolish old man," he finally said. "And it is not my way to ask forgiveness."

Alex wanted to turn his back on Carlos, but he was unable to find the heart to do it. He briefly recalled Tomas saying, "We want to be loved by him" and knew, had his brother been in this very spot at this very moment, he would not have run. Alex leaned back against the door and closed his eyes.

"Tomas is lost to me forever," Carlos continued. "It is too late to ask for his understanding, but . . ."

Alejandro waited.

Finally, "Is it too late for us, Alejandro?"

"If you are asking me to understand," came his deep response, "I cannot do it. I will never understand . . . and it will be difficult to forgive." Carlos's chin quivered and Alex looked away. "But I will try, Grandfather."

Without further words, Alejandro de Bastitas left the room.

Dawn was several hours old when Angelique awoke. She listened to the excited clucking of chickens. The braying of a burro seemed distant and lazy. But there was something else; someone was weeping.

Not bothering to don her robe, Angelique left the room and hurried down the corridor. She spied Teresa. The girl was crying. "What has happened?" she demanded.

The servant shook her head. "I am so sorry, senora."

"Sorry? For what reason?"

Her brown eyes grew large, then without responding Teresa hurried out of sight.

The lacy hem of her gown flapping about her ankles, Angelique virtually ran down the stairs, but as she was about to enter the salon, a vision caught her eye.

In the Room of the Blessed Virgin, Isabella de Bastitas was on her knees before the shrine. She was rocking in grief.

Angelique entered the room very slowly. Unable to keep the fear from her voice, she asked, "What has happened?"

"He is gone."

"Gone?" Her heart was pounding now. The roar in her ears was deafening. "Who is gone?"

Isabella's gray face turned up to hers. "Your husband."

"Where has he gone?"

"To fight. To die if need be."

Angelique eased to the floor. "There must be some mistake."

"No mistake. I stood with him in this very room and watched out that window as he rode away . . . just as I watched Tomas."

Her fingers clutching Isabella's shoulders, Angelique stressed, "Then we will stop him! I will speak to Mr. McGuire and—"

"You are too late. He is gone as well."

Anger igniting in her breast, she jumped to her feet. "Why was I not informed?"

"He felt you had suffered enough."

"Angelique!"

Whirling, Angelique faced her mother.

"Oh, Angelique, my husband is gone. Gone, and I might never see him again!" Falling into her daughter's arms, Carlota continued to weep. "He will be murdered like Tomas; I know it!"

"Hush, Mama. Please don't speak in such a way."

"But it is true. What chance have these few defenders against an entire Mexican army?"

She was choking. Closing her eyes, Angelique attempted to pull away from her mother's desperate clutching. Finally, when she could take no more of Carlota's hysterical babbling, she shoved the woman away and railed, "Stop it! Have you forgotten that Alexander is gone as well? Do you forget that I too have a babe growing within me? I too love my husband!"

Angelique stumbled backward. "Oh, I-I didn't mean that. I don't . . ." She tried to say it. No she *didn't* love her husband. She couldn't. "What I mean is . . ." What did she mean?

Isabella looked beyond Angelique and into Carlota's stunned face. "Have you not depended on your daughter long enough for pity? Will you not relieve her guilt for loving my grandson by telling her the truth?"

"I don't know what you mean." Wringing her hands, Carlota backed away. "Alejandro de Bastitas killed my husband."

"Over a card game."

"Yes! He—he accused my Reggie of cheating and—"

Angelique interrupted. "No. Papa accused Alexander of cheating."

"Yes. Yes, that's it. A fight ensued and he killed my husband right there in the gambling hall. Murdered him before dozens of people."

A cold fear wedged into Angelique's breast. Stepping toward her mother, she pressed, "No. You said he killed my papa in a duel."

"Did I?" Carlota laughed nervously. "What does it

matter? He killed your father, Angelique, and that is that.''

Her mother was right. Alexander had admitted it, so what did it matter? He had killed a good, loving father and husband, had destroyed her home so completely they were left with nothing.

So why was her heart breaking with the thought of his dying? Why?

Unable to tolerate the misery any longer, Angelique fled to her room. Isabella watched her go, but before Carlota could follow she stopped her by saying, ''You are a very selfish woman, Senora McGuire.''

Carlota froze. Without turning, she demanded, ''What do you mean?''

''Can you not see she is suffering no less than you? Despite your arguments of why she must hate my grandson, she does indeed love him.''

''She loathes the man.''

''Are you deaf as well as blind? She just admitted she loved him.''

''It was her emotions talking.''

''It was her heart.''

Carlota squared her shoulders and left the room. How could Isabella de Bastitas claim to know what was in her daughter's heart? Besides, Alejandro cared nothing for Angelique. . . . The hell he spent those days of the siege was due only to his grief over Tomas. . . . Contrary to Carlos's claim that Alex had ridden to Gonzales that day of the Comanche attack to again see Juanita, Noble had assured her Alejandro was coming after Angelique . . . a likely story.

Stopping at the foot of the stairs, she swished her skirts about her ankles. Alejandro de Bastitas had come to her room on his wedding night hoping to put all their unpleasantness behind them. He was willing to start over, or so he said. He cared for Angelique a great deal and swore on his life he would cause her no pain. He would cherish her, keep her, and cleave unto no other as long as she lived. ''I love your daughter,'' he had stated.

*Dear God.*

Weeping, Angelique had buried her face against Bernice's bosom and did not hear as Carlota entered the room. A comforting hand upon her shoulder caused Angelique to look up in surprise.

"Are you so miserable?" her mother asked in a hushed voice.

Gulping for air, Angelique swiped her tears. "I am so terribly sorry, Mama. I know I mustn't love him, but I do. I do!"

Easing onto the bed, Carlota met Bernice's eyes. Bernice nodded and pulled her baby closer to her breast.

"So. You love Alejandro de Bastitas, and you are going to have his child."

She sniffed, but lifted her chin with more resolution than she had felt in months. "Yes, Mama."

Nudging a bronze coil of hair behind Angelique's ear, Carlota smiled. "I was so in love with your father. He was a handsome rake with flashing green eyes and a raffish smile. Every woman in New Orleans envied me."

"I know, Mama."

Carlota looked away. "We were so very proud when you were born." Standing, she paced nervously around the room. "It took a very long time for me to realize that his love extended no further than you. His absences became prolonged and soon rumors reached me that he was seeing other women."

Bernice's grip became tighter as Angelique attempted to sit up. "What are you saying, Mama?"

"I loved him regardless, and each time he told me he would change, I believed him. I allowed him to sow his wild oats, believing someday he would settle down. So over the years I poured all of my love into you, Angie, and watched you grow to be a beautiful, vivacious young woman. But you see, I made a grave mistake during that time. I sheltered you from the truth.

"I didn't realize my mistake until suddenly one day your father sauntered in and announced he was leaving me. He was in love with another woman. That woman was pregnant with his child, and though she was wedded to another, they were making plans to marry when each had attained a divorce.''

Angelique backed away from Bernice's embrace. Clutching her pillow to her breast, she shook her head.

Carlota didn't blink. "That woman was Pamela de Bastitas.''

He heart breaking, Angelique closed her eyes. "No! My father didn't do that to Alejandro!''

"Of course there was talk about the town, but I always made certain you didn't hear it.'' Looking toward Bernice for support, she sat on the bed and caught Angelique's hands in hers. "Then the tragedy happened. Alejandro found Reggie and Pamela in bed together. Naturally he called your father out. Foolishly I followed Reggie to the dueling grounds. I was too late. When I arrived he was nearly dead.

"He even called out Pamela's name as he died. I was so bitter; I felt so betrayed. Still, I knew I had to protect you from the truth, so I made up lie after lie. And the longer I lied the easier it became to believe them myself. When Alejandro de Bastitas stepped into your life I was faced with those lies, and, afraid you would be hurt by the truth, I did everything I could to keep you apart. I beseeched Alex to say nothing of the truth, convincing him it would only hurt you more.''

Relief evident in her face, Carlota moved from the bed. "Alejandro de Bastitas was as much a victim as I, Angelique. Perhaps more, for while I was aware of your father's affairs and hardened against them, he was not. In one brief moment he plunged from heaven to hell. Reggie ruined his marriage, indeed, his entire life. I can understand his hatred toward me. He came to Texas to forget and not only was I a bitter reminder of what had happened in New Orleans, but a threat that could destroy the happiness he found with you.''

"He said nothing.''

"Of course not. He loves you very much. He was trying to protect that image of your father, knowing that should you learn of Reggie's reputation it would be like losing him all over again.''

Angelique understood now. Perhaps she had understood all along and, like her mother, hadn't wanted to face the truth. Turning jade eyes toward the door, she found Isabella. ''You heard?''

''Yes.''

''He thinks I despise him. How can a man enter battle when there is nothing left for him in this entire world?''

''He can't.''

Slipping from the bed, she walked to the open French door. ''I have to stop him.''

''It is too late for that,'' Carlota stated in a sad voice.

Angelique lifted her head. ''Perhaps not.'' Spinning toward Isabella, she asked, ''Did he not mention where he was going?''

Isabella nodded. ''Toward San Felipe.''

''Then *I* shall go to San Felipe.''

Carlota jumped to her feet. ''Certainly not. What can you be thinking, Angelique? A woman alone—''

''There are men about the hacienda. They have guns. They will accompany me.''

Bernice hefted her weight from the bed and, wiping the tears from her eyes, stated, ''You ain't goin' no place without me, girl.''

Isabella paled. Moving gracefully across the room she caught Angelique's shoulders in her frail, trembling hands. ''I cannot lose you as well, my dear. If anything happens to my grandson the child you are carrying will be all I have left.''

''Do you not see, Isabella?'' Angelique laughed. ''I am living proof Santa Anna has no war against women. He will not harm me.''

''But it is a great distance, Angelique.''

''All the more reason she will need a companion,'' Carlota joined in.

Both Isabella and Angelique looked toward Carlota as she said, ''I will see that Delores packs enough food for us all.'' Squaring her shoulders and ignoring the women's inquisitive eyes, she scolded, "My own husband is there, not to mention my son-in-law. Shall we get started, ladies?"

Her eyes tearing, Angelique reached for her mother's hand.

# TWENTY-NINE

"I forbid it!"

Angelique ignored Carlos as she and Carlota helped Bernice, Teresa, and Delores load the last baskets of food and clothing into the back of the wagon. Facing her husband's grandfather, she said, "I would think you to be happy to be rid of me, Don Carlos."

His face paled slightly. Far less angrily, he persisted, "You are carrying my great-grandson, the last of the de Bastitas lineage."

"I fully intend to return . . . with my husband."

Isabella stepped forward. "Angelique, I wish you would reconsider."

"The men provided for our protection will keep us from harm."

The woman threw her pensive glance about the surrounding vaqueros. They were heavily armed and appeared eager to begin the journey. "I put my great-grandchild's life in your hands, gentlemen," she announced bravely. "You will be amply rewarded with my family's safe return—one hundred acres each for your own."

There was a quick inhalation of breath from each of the men. "Senora, you are most generous!" Raoul exclaimed.

"It was my husband's idea." Isabella's eyes shifted to Angelique's. The girl appeared stunned, then turned for the wagon.

Carlos limped determinedly after Angelique. "You are fools! All of you! These roads are strewn with Santa Anna's men."

Settling beside Bernice, Angelique smiled. "Then we will simply inform them of His Excellency's great respect for you, don."

His jaw snapped shut.

Raoul settled on the wagon seat, wove the leather reins through his fingers, and called out, "Are we ready, senoras?"

"Yes!" came the anxious response.

Carlos jumped back as the whip snapped over the horses' rumps. The wagon lurched. "I forbid this! Do you hear me? I forbid it!"

Angelique looked back over her shoulder as the animals broke into a trot. The clatter of their hooves and the jangle of harnesses drowned out the old man's furious rantings, but there he stood, regardless, waving his cane in the air as he cursed them all for their folly. Isabella stood at his side, her frail hands clasped as if in prayer. Angelique blew her a kiss, then with tears in her eyes turned her back. She would not look back again!

The end of their first day found them at the halfway point to Gonzales. The roadside station had long since been deserted, but it offered them a harbor for the night. Almost too tired to eat, they picked and chewed at their food and before sun had fallen completely, they had spread their blankets upon the floor and were sleeping.

Dawn found them sore and aching, but anxious to be on with their journey. While Bernice made certain everyone was supplied with leftover biscuits stuffed with ham, Delores worked eagerly over her flat grill and rolled out tortilla after tortilla. Manuel Menchaca hefted in a bucket of water and each lady took a turn sponging her face and arms. Then they climbed on board the wagon and, surrounded by men on horseback, struck out again.

Gonzales was gone. Plodding through the charred remains of the town, they could hardly believe it had once been a thriving place of happy families and prosperous businesses. They swung by Julio Sanchez's home. It had been deserted long ago.

Since it was already dusk, they decided to stay there for the evening, thinking it might offer some respite from the uncomfortable conditions of their previous night. They were wrong. Looters had ransacked and taken everything of value that had been left in the house. Still, they spread their blankets on the floor and rested again. They didn't bother to bathe the next morning, but were traveling again before dawn.

It was not difficult to follow the army's progress. The few families that had not fled pointed the way east and kindly informed them that they were fools to follow a bunch of cowards.

"Cowards?" Angelique demanded angrily.

A crone of a woman barked, "Yes, cowards! Sam Houston and that lot of spineless men have tucked their tails between their legs and run from Santa Anna. What chance have the rest of us if they refuse to stand and fight?"

The sentiments of the stragglers were all the same. The Texas army was retreating. And while volunteers from the States were beginning to lag, the Mexican forces were growing. Word was General Cos had stormed through the area only days before with a force of over four hundred. He would be joining his brother-in-law any day.

It became ever more difficult to make their way, as time and again they were forced to hide as they came upon Mexican scouts. Finally deciding they would be much safer traveling at night, the group slept through their sixth day. It was just as well. From dawn until well after dusk a miserable rain fell on the countryside.

Angelique lay on her back inside the old barn, listening to the deluge and thinking that somewhere beyond these hills her husband was huddled against the onslaught along with nine hundred other men. That was the only thought that kept them going. There had been no fighting yet. Perhaps they *would* arrive at Sam Houston's camp before the army's conflict with Santa Anna.

On their eighth day they reached the Brazos River, where they bathed as best they could and allowed themselves a little extra to eat. By dawn they had settled into a thick copse of trees to sleep.

But sleep wouldn't come, and as Angelique huddled in her bed beneath the wagon, listening to Bernice's snores and the quiet whispers of the guards, she experienced her first pangs of doubt. She thought of waking her mother, of suggesting they return to San Antonio, but before she had the chance a sudden flurry of activity from the guards caused her to roll from her bed and grab the rifle she kept close at her side.

A stranger stepped into the clearing. Finding himself surrounded by men with ready rifles, he cautiously lifted his hands into the air. Centering his eyes on the woman in the center of the group, he stated, "Mornin', ma'am."

"Good morning."

Hearing the conversation, the others scrambled from their beds.

Removing the hat from his head, he asked, "Where you folks headed?"

Satisfied the man was not Mexican, Angelique responded, "To meet Sam Houston's army."

Confusion furrowing his brow, the stranger stated, "That don't seem right smart. What you want to go and do somethin' like that for?"

"We are searching for our husbands."

"Well, you'd best keep low. Mexican troops is spread all up and down these banks."

Seeing the man meant no harm, Angelique lowered her gun. The vaqueros, however, did not. "Have you seen the Texas army?" she asked.

"Yep. North of here."

Carlota stepped forward. "How long will it take us to reach them?"

"Quickest way's by boat."

"Where would we find a boat?"

"Can't. Houston or Santa Anna's took every boat and ferry in these parts. Only thing left is the *Yellow Stone*."

"Which is?" Angelique prompted.

"Steamboat."

Eagerly, Carlota asked, "Is the *Yellow Stone* your boat?"

"Nope." His eyes shifted about the attentive men.

Angelique looked first to her mother, to Delores, Teresa, and finally to Bernice, who stood wide-eyed—as she had been the entire trip. Finally addressing the stranger, Angelique offered in a quiet voice, "We have money. There isn't much, but enough for passage on the boat if you could arrange it."

"Don't know much about that."

Carlota offered the man a sad smile. "Please, it is very important that we reach our husbands. For the sake of this young woman who was in the Alamo when it fell . . ."

Fire flooded his face. "Well, why the devil didn't you say that in the first place? Course I'll help and it won't cost you one dang peso for the effort. You just be ready after dark. I'll see to the rest." He turned to go, then pausing, finished, "By the way, my name's Red." Tipping his hat, he disappeared into the thicket.

Darkness was forever coming, but finally Red showed up and ushered the men and women with their wagon several miles down the river, then onto the boat. Standing at the railings and looking out over the water, Angelique hoped, indeed prayed, that upon landing she would find her husband. Red had informed them that the Texas army had camped for two weeks just north of San Felipe, but when word arrived that Santa Anna had reached the river they had retreated farther east.

Of course there was the possibility that Alejandro had washed his hands of her completely. And could she blame him? She was a reminder of his past. Each time he looked into her eyes he would be reminded of her father, of Pamela, of the horrible blame she had placed on him.

The paddleboat crawled up the river and docked before sunrise. Red pointed toward the rising orange ball of fire and suggested they might check with the Donohoe farm, where Houston had planned to spend his first night.

So they were off again. Weary from lack of sleep, they bounced unceasingly over the rutted road, on and on until fatigue caused them again to pull into a copse of trees and rest. Too tired even to eat, they crawled under the wagon and into their blankets . . . little knowing that beyond the next rise Alejandro de Bastitas and Noble "Kaintock" McGuire were preparing to march again with Sam Houston's army.

"Runnin' again. I'm fed up of runnin'. Jest when are we gonna take a stand and fight?"

Noble McGuire shouldered his rifle and threw the belligerent young soldier a stern look. Pointing back the way they had come, he said, "Sesma's at Thompson's Ferry with nearly two thousand men and soon to be joined by Filisola who has another two thousand. Urrea's at Matagorda with over a thousand, and who the hell knows how many Santa Anna has. Close to a thousand, I reckon. Now if *you* would like to make camp and smile real big as seven thousand of them sons of bitches surround our measly nine hundred men, then be my guest. Just don't expect me to bury your bones when they pick 'em clean."

The boy shut up.

Fleeing again? Alejandro didn't think so. Although Sam Houston had talked little of his plans, Alex was given the distinct impression the last few days that the leader had changed courses in midstream. They were now headed toward Harrisburg, which a Mexican garrison controlled.

They camped that night at Buffalo Bayou. Alejandro and McGuire were just settling down to another meal of hard biscuits and jerky when a rider burst into camp. There were Mexicans ahead, he informed them, and most importantly they were led by His Excellency—Santa Anna himself.

There was little sleep that night. When reveille sounded at dawn the men were on their feet and, for the first time in a very long time, ready and eager to march. They would take only what they needed. Any man sick or wounded who could not fight was left to guard the supplies.

Again they moved east. All day they marched and into nightfall, midnight and beyond. Just after dawn they were spied by Mexican scouts. Settling down, they waited for an attack that was sure to come.

It was a brief skirmish, but it whetted the men's appetites for battle. They continued forward and at dusk they camped inside a line of trees. No camp fires were lit. There was little talk. Their minds were on the following day, and the dawn that morning nearly two months before.

"Remember the Alamo. Remember Goliad." The whisper spread through the weary ranks. That thought was the only thing that had kept them going.

They could hardly forget it now.

Dawn broke. Then noon. Tempers were strained to their endurance as each man waited for the orders to march. Why was Houston taking so long?

"Let's get on with it!" someone rallied.

A discourse of like murmurs filled the air, but it was after three before Sam Houston stood before them. "Prepare to march!"

Cheers shattered the air.

"Well, I reckon this is it," McGuire said quietly to his friend.

A lopsided grin curled Alex's mouth. "Suppose so."

"Wonder if I'll ever get to see that kid of mine?"

Alex looked away. He needed no reminders of children. He had his own to think about, as well as a wife . . . for what good it did him. He had a wife who didn't love him, never wanted to see him again, yet all he could think about was getting home to her as soon as possible. He would inform her that he had *again* changed his mind. There would be no divorce.

Houston turned his white stallion, Saracen, toward the horizon. He lifted his sword. "Victory is ours, gentlemen! Remember the Alamo!"

Angelique slapped the reins over the horses' backs. "I cannot believe it!" she muttered for the hundredth time. Their discovery those three days before had been a grim one. Imagine their sleeping while over the hill Alexander and Noble were preparing to fight.

Carlota winced and made a grab for her seat as they bounced in and out of a hole. Her eyes searched the clear sky. It didn't look like rain, but the thunder . . . Grabbing her daughter's arm, Carlota yelled, "Stop the wagon!"

"What do you mean? Mama, we must—"

"I said stop this wagon!"

Angelique leaned back on the reins. The men immediately surrounded the wagon, their rifles loaded and ready across their saddles. They all heard it then. The intermittent roar of cannons had become quite recognizable by now.

Teresa covered her face with her hands. "*Madre de Dios*, we are too late!" She burst out sobbing.

Frozen, they could do nothing but listen.

Bernice shook her head. "Best get on back to San Antonio. Nothin' we can do now."

"We haven't come this far to turn back!" Angelique argued hotly.

Manuel moved his horse closer to the wagon. "Senoras, I fear it would not be wise to continue. Let my men ride ahead—"

"Nonsense!" she snapped, then looked to her mother. Their eyes met.

"Continue," Carlota stated calmly.

With a snap of the whip the horses lunged, driven in the direction of the roiling gunfire. They had traveled only a short distance when Carlota again beseeched her daughter, "Stop the wagon, Angelique, quickly!"

She did. Nothing. The guns were silent. Whatever battle had been fought, it had ended. Delores made the sign of the cross over her ample bosom. Carlota's hands clenched into fists.

"What shall we do?" she asked in a small voice.

Angelique thought a moment, then lifted her reins. "We continue."

They did, slowly this time, their ears tuned for any sound of warfare. Finally, she stopped again. There was something now. Voices? Music? Was there a celebration beyond that hill?

The men jumped from their horses, and with rifles prepared they hurried to the top of the hill. Fear growing in her heart, Angelique recalled the Mexicans' penchant for music during and after a siege. Wrapping the reins about the brake of the wagon, she stepped to the ground.

"What are you doing?" her mother demanded.

When Angelique refused to respond, instead following the vaqueros up the closest rise, Carlota hurried to follow. Next came Bernice, huffing and puffing her heavy weight through the tall, waving grass, then Teresa and Delores.

Angelique knew nothing beyond the far revelry of voices. Because of the distance she could not ascertain if they roared in Spanish or English, and with each step she took, her terror increased. The hill seemed insurmountable and her breathing became ragged. Her chest burned. Blood pounded in her head and anticipation rang like shrill bells in her ears.

She blinked hard as she topped the crest. As far as Angelique could see the land was strewn with bodies. Oh, God, they were too late!

A sharp gasp announced Carlota's arrival.

Bernice stumbled up beside them. "Lawd, have mercy!"

Teresa and Delores wavered as they studied the bloody battlefield.

By some unspoken understanding the women moved to join the men as they searched the soldiers. Slowly, carefully, they entered the grounds, holding one another for support. Reaching the first body, Angelique rolled the soldier over. Mexican. Separating, they moved about the fallen men. Mexican. All Mexican! Hundreds of them were strewn about the river valley, dying and wounded.

God, what did it mean? Angelique shielded her eyes against the late afternoon sun, attempting to see the men in the distance. A groan caught her attention, and stooping beside a wounded soldier, she listened as he moaned:

*"Diablos! Me no Alamo! No Bahia!"*

Carlota moved up behind her, as did the others. No one spoke, but sharing the same thoughts they began moving toward the men in the camp. A rider approached them. Suspicious of the vaqueros, as they were not wearing army uniforms, he aimed his gun and demanded, "Drop your rifles and get into camp. The battle is over!"

Manuel's gun slipped from his fingers. "But, senor, you do not understand—"

"I said git!" The stranger then motioned toward the women, "Get your sweet little skirts into camp, ladies. You'll be cooking for Texas soldiers now!"

"What do you mean, sir," Angelique demanded with a proud lift of her chin.

Thinking the women had been some of Santa Anna's *soldaderas,* he frowned, "We whipped them sonofaguns to the ground. Caught 'em when they was nappin'. Ha! Look at 'em; six hundred put down!" His horse reared on two legs, and with a jubilant cry the soldier lifted his rifle and yelled, "*Viva* Texas! Remember the Alamo!"

Speechless, they watched as he spurred his animal and rode back toward the camp. They were moving again, working their way over and around the bodies, never taking their eyes from the men in the distance. More riders approached, and pointing toward the group of men and women surrounded by gun bearing Texas soldiers, he barked, "Fall in with the others!"

Angelique stopped in her tracks. "Sir, I am thoroughly aware that we present no likeness to the ladies we claim to be, but I assure you, we are here for one reason and one reason only. It is to locate our—"

"Carlota!" All heads turned and suddenly Carlota was running to meet her husband. Opening his arms he swooped her from the ground. "Lord have mercy, woman, what on God's green earth are you doin' here?"

Tears streaming from her eyes Carlota covered his whiskered face with kisses. "My husband!" she repeated again and again.

Bernice's hand in hers, Angelique waited patiently, smiling past her own tears as she watched her mother and stepfather's joyous reunion. Still, the suffocating constriction in her breast could not be ignored. Where was Alejandro? Was he dead, injured? Unable to tolerate the anticipation a moment longer, she asked, "Mr. McGuire, please . . ."

Hugging Carlota one last time, Noble turned toward the tiny disheveled girl at his side. "Now I can't imagine what you'd be askin' of me." He was teasing, of course, and smiled.

Angelique didn't recognize his obvious lack of concern as she was too engrossed in her own worry. Clearing her throat, she stressed, "My husband, sir."

"Your husband. The one you don't want no more?"

Jade eyes wide and her jaw set, Angelique stated boldly, "There will be no divorce, Mr. McGuire. Whether my husband likes it or not, he is saddled with me for the rest of—" She swallowed hard. "Where *is* my husband, Mr. McGuire?"

He nodded toward the tent in the distance. "Over there bein' seen to."

"He's been injured?" Angelique held her breath.

"Weren't much more than a scratch."

A squeal of excitement broke out among her companions as Angelique twirled to hug Bernice. "Best you go find yore husband, Angelique." She whispered, "He be needin' you awful bad right now."

"Yes," Carlota joined in. Turning her daughter to face her, she stated forcefully, "Go to him with my blessing."

Backing away and lifting her skirts, Angelique hurried toward the makeshift hospital, and her husband.

Alex rested on his cot, waiting with his eyes closed as the doctor slowly made his way from one wounded soldier to the next. He had received nothing more than a graze, but all precautions must be taken to assure against infection. There was a certain peace within him. The anger that had been mounting since his brother's murder had been assuaged to some extent. Each time a man tumbled from his bullet he had yelled, "Remember the Alamo, remember

Goliad, remember Tomas de Bastitas, and remember my wife!''

Wife. Through the vision of bloodied men emerged a visage of ivory skin, auburn clouds of hair, and emerald eyes. He saw her painted in gold that night before the fire. Unashamed and beautiful she had gifted him with her very body and soul. He wanted that moment back. He had carried it in his heart these months like a cherished treasure, and now he wanted nothing more than to hold Angelique de Bastitas in his arms.

''I have come to clean your wound, senor.''

Hearing the soft voice, Alex opened his eyes.

Angelique smiled upon her husband as he blinked once, then twice in disbelief. As he struggled to sit upright, she placed a gentle hand on his chest and pushed him back down. ''You are injured, sir, and mustn't tax your strength.''

''Angelique!'' Alex closed his eyes, then opened them again. ''What in the name of all that is holy are—''

''I am looking for my husband. He is a wayward sort and apt to stray with the slightest provocation.''

''And what do you want of him?'' He searched her face.

Biting her lower lip, Angelique tenderly pulled the bloodied shirt sleeve from Alejandro's arm. Dabbing at the graze with a damp cloth, she shrugged. ''He left me without a word of goodbye. One might think he cared nothing for me at all any longer.''

''One would be a fool to believe that.''

His blue eyes were caressing her, warming her to the very core of her being. Rinsing the rag in a basin of clear water, she continued, ''I could hardly blame him. It seems I've been a thorn in his side since the moment he met me.''

''Roses have thorns but they take nothing from the sweetness of the flower.'' Placing a gentle hand on her wrist, Alex refused to let her go. ''Angel. Look at me.'' In a husky voice he entreated, ''Forgive me.''

The ragged edge of his voice pulled at her heartstrings, and Angelique longed to cry. ''There is nothing to forgive. You did what any man might have done, given those horrible circumstances.'' She lowered her eyes. ''I am ashamed that my own flesh and blood caused you such unbearable grief.''

Stroking her flushed cheeks with his thumbs, Alex placed a light kiss on the corner of her mouth. ''It is forgotten,'' he offered quietly. ''Pamela is but a vague dream that haunts a different land, a different time, and a different man. I am in love with you, Angelique.''

''You are certain?''

A slow smile stretched across his face. ''I've never been more certain of anything in my life.'' Reaching for the damp cloth Angelique still clutched in her hand, he dropped it to the side of the cot. ''Come here.''

Her arms came up around his neck as Angelique lifted her face to his. Whistles and shouts of approval erupted about them from the onlooking wounded, but they didn't notice, or even care.

The night air was alive with sound. Drum and fife music added to the gaiety of the celebration. The victory had been swift and sweet, but there was also disappointment. Though the Mexicans here had been defeated, Santa Anna had escaped.

Angelique laughed and clapped her hands as Carlota and Noble McGuire danced in circles about the camp fire. A long arm encircled her waist, and as she twisted to face her husband, he twirled a yellow flower beneath her nose. Her eyes brightened with excitement. ''Are you asking me to dance, senor?''

''Um hm. But not here.''

''Where did you have in mind?''

Slipping out of the fire's halo, Alex coaxed his wife beyond the tents and into the trees. A pallet had been spread in a clearing. Surrounded by overgrowth and canopied by stars, it was a perfect place for lovers.

Alejandro dropped to the blanket. ''Champagne, sweetheart?'' He lifted a bottle and two crystal glasses into the air.

Angelique covered a giggle with the tips of her fingers.
"I cannot believe it!"

"Believe it. Santa Anna never traveled without it." As
she fell to her knees and reached for the glass, he pulled
it away. "Nope. Not yet."

"No?"

"No." The glasses tinkled as he pushed them away. "I
believe we have a wedding night to make up for."

"Here?" she asked nervously.

"There is music, champagne. We will have the stars for
a blanket and a moon to catch fire in your eyes."

Smiling, Angelique looked beyond his shoulder. A moon
was suspended upon the treetops. "Someone might find
us," she said quietly, without conviction. Already her fingers were plucking at her shoestrings. "Do these men realize that I'm your wife?"

"I doubt it."

"Will you tell them?"

He shook his head. "Let them think I am with the best-
looking *soldadera* in all of Mexico."

Angelique stood and her skirt slipped to the ground. Her
blouse followed it. But as Alex reached for his belt buckle
she stopped him, then did it herself.

He smiled. "A nice beginning."

Naked, beautiful, and unashamed, Angelique lay down
against her husband. It was the moment they had dreamed
of, the coming together of spirit and body. Her entire being
vibrated with the love she longed to give him. He was
marvelous, this man—animal—so dark and long in limb
that with one graceful move he could envelope her completely, as he was doing now. All reason was slipping; she
was losing herself to the heat of his mouth against her
breasts, the warm wetness of his tongue upon her nipples,
the languorous caresses that caused them to ache with fullness. And when his dark head came up, his eyes were
shimmering pools of moonlight and desire as he looked
down into her face.

"I love you," he confessed softly. "Oh, God, I love
you."

She cried. Not sadly but with relief, happiness, and shame. She would make up for all the grief and pain her father had caused him. In time he would forget.

He kissed the salty trail of her tears to the corner of her mouth, then claimed her lips with his. She wove her trembling fingers into his dark hair and accepted the thrust of his tongue completely until she heard the groan deep in his throat and knew from experience that he was aching for her.

Alex rolled, his weight resting heavily on her for a brief moment, then easing as he shifted to one side, bracing himself on one elbow. His dark eyes moved slowly, following the teasing path of his hands across each straining breast and down to her stomach, his fingers pausing, flexing to encompass the blessed rounding above the fleecy softness between her thighs.

"My child," he said softly, in awe, to the tiny flourishing form beneath his palm. Arching then, he kissed her there, a gentle brushing of his mouth over the tight skin, and beyond.

Angelique quivered, shaken by the rush of longing that enveloped her. It was beautiful, this white hot fire that flooded every nerve ending and made her blood boil to the point of madness. Blissful agony, this desire. Even sweeter, the surrender. Oh, god, but she loved him, too.

He was over her then, silhouetted against the moon like a shadow, neither touching nor being touched, but there, a part of her that was somehow separate.

"Come to me," she whispered and lifted her arms around his shoulders. "Please . . ."

The joining shook them both, and for a long moment Alex was still, absorbing her heat, flourishing in the love he could feel against him, around him . . . inside him. And as their bodies entwined, so did their souls, melding into one, each breath a blending of life, a consummation of spirit, fulfillment of love.

He could stay here forever.

But the need was there, and as Angelique began moving,

he responded. "Ah, Angel. Angel," he groaned, "come with me quickly, my love."

"To heaven." Her mouth curved in a smile.

He rocked her, soared with her to that Eden, that pinnacle of completion that splintered all realities and left them suspended, then floating in contentment's arms back to earth. They each knew that this was how it would be . . . forever. There were no longer any secrets between them. And their future stretched before them, bright and hopeful, promising riches that, until now, they could only imagine.

A nice beginning.

Angelique smiled and nestled her cheek against her husband's shoulder. "This is only the beginning," she whispered.

Only the beginning.

# EPILOGUE

The September sun was hot, but the shade of the old pecan tree provided a cooling respite to the families gathered about the hacienda's grounds. Manuel Menchaca carried in his hands the gift of a silver goblet, intricately carved by his father. Raoul Perez and his wife cradled a tiny saddle between them, its short stirrups embossed with silver. Pablo fidgeted in impatience and fingered the cottonwood cross he had whittled the day before.

There was peace in the valley now. The whirring of insects, the rustle and whisper of the wind as it shifted through the sun-bleached grass had replaced the discord of war. Texas had come far since that morning after San Jacinto. Santa Anna had been captured. He had surrendered in writing and returned to Mexico in defeat. Families had returned to their homes and life had begun again.

Now they each awaited the news that the future don of Rancho de Bejar had been born.

Carlota McGuire took a deep breath and gripped her husband's hand. Isabella poured Carlos a cup of chocolate, but her hand was far less steady then her smile. As the sudden cry of pain erupted again through the house, all eyes turned to Alejandro.

He paled further and sank into a chair.

Kaintock cleared his throat, feeling none too certain himself. The thought that Carlota would be experiencing the same agony within days humbled the jesting remarks he might have afforded his friend in hopes of easing the tension. "Reckon you win this one," he grinned toward the distressed father-to-be. When Carlota lifted one brow he explained, "Me and Alex made a little wager. I bet him five hundred pesos you'd have a baby before Angelique."

"Someone get my grandson another drink," was Isabella's request.

McGuire did so, handing Alejandro the entire bottle. As another cry drifted into the room, he turned it up to his lips.

Carlos chuckled. "Alejandro, she is not the first woman to whelp and she won't be the last."

Bracing elbows on his knees, Alex buried his head in one hand and focused on the floor. "She is my wife and the *only* woman to have my children."

"And *my* only daughter!" exclaimed Carlota. Laboring to her feet, she waddled to the window. "*Por Dios,* I should shoot you for doing this to her," she said to Alex. A contraction gripped her belly. She bit her lip. "Someone get Bernice. I demand to know this moment—"

Isabella came out of her chair, as did Noble and Alejandro. The scream seemed to vibrate the very walls.

Alejandro was across the room and nearly out the door before Noble caught him. "Get your hands off of me, McGuire, or I swear to God you won't ever live to see that kid of yours born!"

"Now calm down, Spaniard. Angelique is gonna be just fine."

Teresa appeared at the door. All heads swiveled to face her. "Don Alejandro." She smiled.

Alex stared, then bellowed, "What!"

"It is done, senor."

There was quiet, then, as the excited babbling of the

group filled the room, the robust wail of the infant filled the house. In a run, Alex took the stairs two at a time. Distantly he heard Carlota cry, "Noble!"

The door was open. Angelique rested on her pillows, smiling tiredly toward the bundle in Bernice's arms. They each looked around as Alejandro barreled into the room.

With one sight of the squirming little form, Alex froze. Bernice, in her slow, seesawing gait, ambled toward him. "Well now," she said smiling, "what we got here is one fine little boy." She pulled back the blanket. "Ain't he grand?" she asked his father.

His eyes on his wife, Alex nodded. "Beautiful."

Bernice chuckled and turned away. He approached the bed.

Angelique frowned. "Alexander, you look as if you haven't slept in a week."

"It seems you've been having this baby for that long."

"Are you all right?" She smiled and touched his unshaven cheek.

"I think I'm drunk. I can't be sure."

"Kiss me and I will tell you."

He stared with sapphire-blue eyes into her face. Her hair was damp and curling. Her skin was moist. Alex cradled her cheek with his palm and wondered on its softness, wondered how anything so belovedly fragile could withstand the pain she had experienced the last eighteen hours.

He did kiss her, far more gently than he wanted.

Angelique tasted brandy and giggled. "You will have to sober up before you hold our son."

Son. He started smiling and couldn't stop.

She took his hand. "We have not discussed names. I had thought . . . Tomas?"

A flicker of pain crossed Alex's features, and Angelique held her breath. Finally, "Yes." He kissed her again.

"Ooowee," Bernice interrupted. "This boy—"

"His name is Tomas," Alex stated.

"Well Tomas got himself one hardy appetite. Yes, sir." She tucked the grunting infant against Angelique's breast.

Her eyes widened as the girl's face flushed with discomfort. She then looked toward Alexander.

He didn't move. "My son is hungry, Angel."

Long curling lashes fluttered over Angelique's green eyes. Odd that she should feel so timid about her husband witnessing this intimate moment between herself and her son. "But—"

"But nothing." He unbuttoned her gown, exposing her ripe breast. Tomas's head turned and found her.

Bernice backed away and smiled. "Now ain't that nice?"

"Beautiful," Alejandro said huskily. "I think I'm envious."

Angelique met her husband's eyes.

Turning for the door, Bernice *humphed* and said, "You keep eyeballin' one another like that I'll be doin' this again in nine months. Um um. No, sir, I'm too old for this birthin' business. You gots to give this old woman a rest."

Kaintock appeared at the door. "God Almighty," he croaked. "It's Carlota!"

Bernice never faltered, but swayed out the door.

Alejandro ran the tip of one long finger across the swell of his wife's breast. His mouth curled in that infuriating way that made Angelique's heart quicken. "Perhaps in a year," he said thoughtfully.

She closed her eyes, exalting in the tender tug on her body. The sweet joy she was feeling brought tears through her lashes. The love she felt for the man, the child, her home caused her to ache with happiness.

A year?

A knowing smile lifted the corners of her mouth. That wouldn't be soon enough, not nearly soon enough.